MW01035539

DE LUNA

FOUNDER OF NORTH AMERICA'S FIRST COLONY

AN HISTORICAL NOVEL

JOHN APPLEYARD

De Luna
Founder of North America's First Colony

John Appleyard

First Printing 1977

ISBN 10: 1-886104-37-9
ISBN 13: 978-1-886104-37-2

The Florida Historical Society Press
435 Brevard Avenue
Cocoa, FL 32922
www.myfloridahistory.org/fhspress

DE LUNA

Founder of North America's First Colony
forgotten in the pages of history.

A true story . . . based upon the letters,
journals and accounts of the Spanish colonial
expedition of 1559-61 at Ochuse, La Florida.

Publication of this book by
the Florida Historical Society Press
was made possible by
Richard Prescott

To My Wife, Eleanor . . .

for her continuous encouragement and countless hours of copy and proof reading, suggestions and commitment to an idea.

Publisher's Preface

As this new edition of John Appleyard's historical novel *De Luna: Founder of North America's First Colony* goes to print, twenty students from the University of West Florida are conducting an archaeological excavation in Pensacola Bay, carefully exploring the underwater wreckage of the Emanuel Point II. The small ship, about 42 feet long, was part of the fleet led by Don Tristan de Luna as he attempted to establish a colony at present-day Pensacola exactly 450 years ago. The ship and its contents are preserved under 12 feet of water, protected from deterioration by a blanket of sand. The artifacts and objects that the students are discovering will add to our understanding of the intrepid men, women, and children who joined de Luna on his ambitious quest.

In his undergraduate program John Appleyard was a student of history, but he later entered the business world. While technically a "non-professional" historian, exploring and documenting history is clearly Appleyard's first love as demonstrated by his multiple publications on various aspects of Pensacola history. As anyone who attended Appleyard's presentation at the Florida Historical Society Annual Meeting in May 2009 can attest, he is also a dynamic and engaging storyteller. The theme of that event, held in Pensacola, was "From Tristan de Luna to the Twenty First Century: 450 Years of Florida History." Presenting the Jillian Prescott Memorial Lecture, Appleyard kept his audience enthralled and entertained while providing exciting information about "The Story of Don Tristan de Luna Arellano, Governor of the First Attempted Colony of Florida."

To write the historical novel *De Luna: Founder of North America's First Colony*, Appleyard combined the skills of an accomplished historian with the passion of a great storyteller to create a fact-based book that is as compelling as it is informative. Appleyard carefully studied all of the available documentation of de Luna's expedition and integrated it into this work, logically filling any gaps in demonstrable fact with reasonable supposition and a slight bit of artistic license. Of course, no one can know the exact content of private conversations or be privy to the subtle nuances of the interpersonal relationships of people who lived 450 years ago. The best historical novelists incorporate as much fact as possible into their work to help them present believable "characters" in real-life situations, as Appleyard successfully does here.

St. Augustine, established by Pedro Menendez de Aviles in 1565, is recognized as the oldest continuous settlement in North America. Had de Luna been able to create a permanent colony at Pensacola six years earlier, the history of North America may have been quite different. The important story of the de Luna expedition, largely ignored until now, deserves to be told. Thankfully, John Appleyard has accomplished this task in an entertaining way that brings the people and places involved to life in a great historical novel.

Benjamin D. Brotemarkle
Executive Director
Florida Historical Society
July 1, 2009

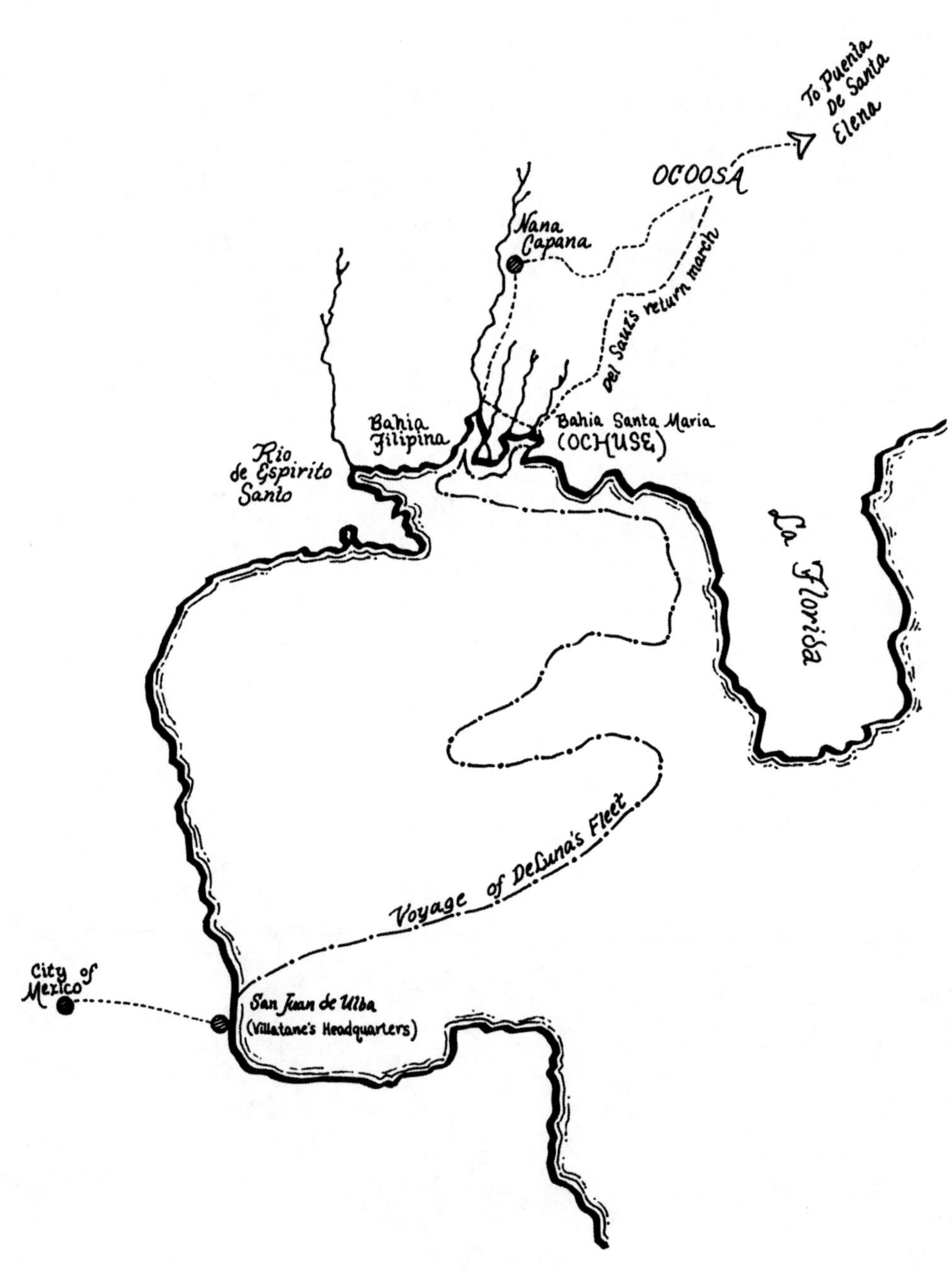

To Puenta
De Santa
Elena
OCOOSA
Nana
Capana
del Sauz's return march
Bahia
Filipina
Bahia Santa Maria
(OCHUSE)
Rio
de Espirito
Santo
La Florida
Voyage of DeLuna's Fleet
City of
Mexico
San Juan de Ulba
(Villatane's Headquarters)

MADRID
February 15, 1592

Greetings!

I speak to all who seek truth and who are concerned for the glories of Spain!

My name is Cristobal Ramirez y Arellano, by the grace of God in my 67th year and now a gentleman of leisure in this most exciting of cities.

I have lived in retirement these last ten years (excepting for special assistance to his majesty as he prepared for the recent invasion of Britain); before that I was colonel of horse serving in the new world. There I was contemporary to those whose names now are legend: Cortes, Pizarro, Menedez de Aviles, Velasco . . . the great and near great . . . including my noble uncle Don Tristan de Luna y Arellano. It is of his adventures that I would speak with you.

Don Tristan de Luna, you ask? Who was he? What place does he hold in history?

Appropriate questions, of course, for already one must dig deeply in our archives to find mention of him, though he is dead just twenty short years.

What did he do? Perhaps it is better asked, "What did he NOT do?" for therein lies his story and his tragedy.

Since those fateful days at Ochuse, many have slandered his name and corrupted his motives. But I was there, living each day with him and the 1500 who shared his sorrows. Had he succeeded, there is little doubt that all of what is called North America would by now be controlled by the legions of his Most Christian Majesty Philip II. That he did not succeed . . . ah . . . therein lies a trail of events so complex as to be almost unbelievable. But they are as I have written here, as best as an old man's memory can recall. It all began in the year of our Lord 1557; at the time, I was a mere youth, a junior officer fresh from his first smell of powder and blood in the armies of Spain, at war with France. Don Tristan was there, too, riding close behind his king. It began, however, not in our contest for the Low Countries but in the high place that is Mexico City.

Naturally, I was completely unaware of the events as they began to unfold, but soon they would involve me . . . and Don Tristan.

It comes back to me easily now, for the incidents were told and retold countless times when hours hung heavy at Ochuse. Of course, no one of us was privy to the thoughts of all the men involved in these events; particularly we had no direct contact with King Philip and his advisors. But from the actions of these men, we often contemplated their thoughts and motives and drew the obvious conclusions. Therefore, I've tried to include their viewpoints as I write this chronicle.

Why do I write at all?

Because someone must, or the story of what might have been will be lost forever. I am the last of the noble company who might defend my uncle, not with prejudice, but with a fair account of what occurred at that place which some now call Pensacola.

But, I ramble!

It began, as I said, in the City of Mexico . . . in the palace of Mexico's second viceroy, Don Luis de Velasco . . .

Mexico City
March 28, 1557

The viceroy reached for his wine cup, then thought better of it.

"Great God," he murmured, "how can a man work in this heat? And wine only makes it worse."

Sluggishly, his eyes roamed the wrinkled report that lay, its ink splotched, before him. Three galleons with plate, one with ornamentation, the latter also with 35 slaves; all had sailed from Vera Cruz, on schedule, before the season of calms.

The new king would be pleased!

Or would he?

It was hard to know. Prince Philip had always been a moody youth. Now, after hideous years in that fogbound island, who could tell what his temperament would be? Thank God he was 3000 miles away with a war to keep him busy!

Don Luis de Velasco was what Machiavelli would have called the perfect civil servant: intelligent, ambitious, loyal (to a reasonable degree) and with a stomach strong enough to do his job.

And it was a good job! Being viceroy of all Mexico was tantamount to being a king. Almost, not quite. Yet there were great possibilities.

Velasco slumped deeper into the heavy chair; its wide leather strapping felt hot to the touch, but the room was perhaps the coolest in Mexico City.

"Have to hand it to the Indian; he knew how to build; he's taught us a lesson or two," the viceroy thought.

Velasco picked up the cup and sipped the sweet Spanish blend, his thoughts straying from the piles of papers.

He'd come a long way in six years! Luck? Perhaps. But the old king had recognized talent; he knew too what Mexico required. Strong men, men of the Faith . . . but practical men. Charles V had enjoyed little luxury in selection. Sometimes Velasco pitied the man. The world asked too much of him. Ruling Spain and the Netherlands would have been enough, but then came the New World Empire and the Holy Roman crown at the same time. Too much. When Luther's heresy came thundering upon the world, it was more than one man could endure.

Charles the Pious? Some called him that. Now that he had given the crowns of Spain and the Low Countries to his son, some said he would enter a monastary. Sad.

Very sad. The world had been his, but he'd never enjoyed it . . . except, of course, for his relations with the ladies. Prodigious! No other word would suffice.

But he had chosen Velasco for Mexico. Be grateful for that! And Velasco had been grateful, bringing efficiencies to the mines, urging on the Dominican friars in their conversions. At every season now, treasure-laden galleys plied their way back to Cadiz with the riches that kept Spain solvent in her wars. So long as precious metals flowed and the wars continued, no one bothered Velasco. Hopefully, it would continue that way.

Footsteps in the corridor aroused him from his reverie; a fist slammed against the heavy door, and it creaked open.

"Can you spare a moment, Excellency?"

The intruder was Ceron, Velasco's guard captain, a short, tough, crusty veteran who had ridden with the viceroy when they fought for their King in France. Now a combination aide and personal secretary, Juan Ceron still wore his uniform and retained his old titles. He was a man of habit, a good soldier.

"Come in, Juan. Sit down, have a cup, relax a minute."

"Thank you, Excellency . . . God, it's hot!"

No matter how long the sons of Aragon remained in Mexico, they would never quite get used to its weather.

Ceron took a long sip, smacked his lips and rumbled ". . . Aaahhh! Whoever first perfected good wine was man's best friend."

Velasco nodded. "Anything happening? No trouble, I hope. Every time you knock I suspect the worst."

Ceron settled back, his legs twisted over a long bench beside the huge oak slab that served as desk and table for the viceroy. His hand searched inside his jacket.

"Well, yes . . . I'd say this may be of some interest."

"Report? From whom? Not another revolt!"

Ceron scanned the short sheet again, refreshing his memory.

"No, not a revolt; something even more interesting. Shall I read it?"

"I thought you'd never ask!"

Ceron looked back to the paper, reconstructed its phrases in his mind again, then told this story:

"On February 14th, our galleon the SANTA MARIA DE CORDOVA left San Juan de Ulua for Havana. Four days later, contrary winds blew her to the north, and on the fifth day she sighted sail. This was surprising, for at this season we expect no inbound vessels. Accordingly, our captain, Don Rodrigo de Alba, ordered chase. By mid-afternoon they had come within search of the glass and determined that the vessel was not our own, but French!"

"French," whispered Velasco. "Here? Incredible!"

Ceron continued: "By nightfall the two were but cable lengths apart, and Captain de Alba fired a shot across the intruder's bow. The Frenchman did not reply, but tacked once more, then attempted to use his stern chasers. However, something misfired. The cannon exploded, and fire quickly broke out.

"Aha!" Velasco rasped.

"The SANTA MARIA DE CORDOVA quickly closed, but the captain wisely did not grapple. Instead, he lowered a boat with marines and boarded the Frenchman with no difficulty."

"They were occupied with the fire, no doubt?"

"The marines took the captain, three officers and 23 men as prisoners, then fired the magazine. The vessel quickly exploded and foundered."

"Good riddance," muttered the viceroy.

"For the next two days Captain de Alba questioned his prisoners (I might add that the captain is very able in such matters) and eventually obtained a confession."

"Confession? They were pirates!" Velasco assumed.

"The French vessel was enroute back to Calais after spending four months of exploration in La Florida," Ceron replied.

"My God!" the viceroy muttered.

"Her instructions from King Henry had been to seek sites for colonization. Other than this, the ship's officers had no specifics. They were to report directly to Queen Catherine and King Henry."

"That's all, then?"

Ceron folded the paper. "Isn't it enough?"

Velasco nodded. It was to be expected, of course. Ever since de Leon's visits, men had brought back tales of the new golden empire! De Soto had urged colonization; and the rogue Cabeza de Vaca had staggered back from de Narvaez's fiasco filled with tales. If one could believe but half of them!

The problem was time!

In six years Velasco had spread Spain's forces throughout Mexico, built mission churches, improved the mines. But North America and Florida were far away, and time and men were short.

Ceron's message was not the first of its kind. The King's dispatches had mentioned French exploration far to the north; and the pesky English were forever darting along the upper coast. Their fishermen were there every year, some said.

"What do you think?" Ceron queried.

"I'm not sure," Velasco murmured. "The war with France may go on forever . . . probably this is just a feint. Or . . . perhaps Henry's planning a diversion. . . ."

"An attack on us? Impossible!"

"Perhaps a colony."

Ceron nodded. "A fort located where French ships could play games with our treasure fleet. . . "

". . . OR lay claim to a whole continent."

Ceron knitted his brows. "But the Pope's line gave all of the land to Spain."

Velasco nodded. "Of course, but when men like Henry of Navarre and Charles have battled for three years, will they let a line on a map stand in their way?"

The captain stood, wiped his lips with the back of his hand, replaced the paper in his tunic.

"Any action?" he asked.

"Yes . . . get me the names of the French officers and write a draft to the King. Give details in full and summarize this way; Say that we suspect some kind of colonial search and that we recommend that the best men in Spain be put on the trail."

"You think Philip will act?"

"Don't know. Who knows Philip yet? But think on it! We've been TALKING new colonies for years: now perhaps there's going to be some action and even some money to work with. How'd you like to be captain-general of something like that, my friend?"

Ceron replied. Yes . . . he would like that very much.

On her knees in prayer, Queen Mary of England, with her husband, King Phillip II of Spain.

IN A MEADOW NEAR CALAIS
March 28, 1558

"Holy Mary, mother of our Savior, we thank thee for our many blessings, and beg your intercession for our failings. . . ."

The soft voice pattered on, the phrases short, the objects of the prayer crisp and clear. Spain's Philip II was a man accustomed to prayer; five times each day (sometimes even more) he knelt and bowed his head, asking divine guidance. Now, as the bustle and sounds of the tournament began to grow, he initiated this day as he did every other.

It was cool in the tent, and Philip, in battle dress with plumes and the red and gold of family colors in his jacket, was trying to set his mind for what would be one of the great days of his life. Philip, tall, gaunt, stern, diffident, difficult to approach, was pleased with the prospect.

The war was over! And today, at the invitation of his adversary, knights of the two battle-weary countries would stage a grand tournament as a fitting end to it all.

"Your majesty, may I have leave to enter?"

From outside, Ximinez was suggesting in his tactful way that it was time to move out.

Ximinez! God, what would I have done without him, thought Philip. The man's a tower of strength, as his grandfather before him. If only we had others as able.

"Come in Ximinez," Philip called, rising from his knees and rearranging the pillow where his knees had rested.

"A beautiful morning, absolutely gorgeous," the graying diplomat ventured. "Did your majesty rest well?"

"As well as man might in these foul contraptions. Man was not made to live in a tent, at least this one wasn't. Won't it be wonderful to be home again?"

Ximinez nodded.

It HAD been a long time, for him as well as the young monarch. How long had it been? For Philip . . . four years now. For him, nearly three.

"You have signed the final drafts?" the king asked.

"We have, sire. Would you like to see them now?"

"No, I'm sure you've done nobly . . . after all, what did we gain . . . or lose?"

Ximinez shrugged. "How can 80,000 men on each side kill each other for four years and not gain something? Experience, perhaps?"

"You're becoming a cynic in your golden years, my friend," the king replied. "I can't blame Henry, really. After all, father had ringed him in very neatly. He could see the handwriting on the wall, and he had more enemies at home than the law allows."

"So he did what any good general does when all looks hopeless; he attacks! Is that it?"

Philip shrugged. "Something like that," he replied.

Ximinez smiled. "Have to hand it to your father, though. Marrying you off to England was a stroke of genius."

The king wrinkled his long nose and frowned.

"Diplomatically it encircled France from Austria to the poles, but I hope I never have to repeat my part of the bargain."

Ximinez cleared his throat: "Perhaps some day your majesty will be good enough to tell us about Queen Mary . . .?"

Philip snorted.

"Tell? What is there to tell? The poor creature is a cow . . . an absolute cow of a woman, so anxious to please she positively slobbers."

"I gathered, however, that you did your duty nobly, sire!" Ximinez replied, his lowered eyes laughing.

Philip shook his head sadly. The English adventure had not been of his choosing. But it HAD been a stroke of genius! His marriage to the eldest daughter of Henry VIII might have sealed off the troublesome French for good, and made all of the New World Spanish in the bargain, despite agreements he'd signed concerning the English throne. The prospect had been so great! Charles' fertile mind had dared suggest it, and Mary, with no prospects for a husband elsewhere, had leaped at the chance. Even her father, wily Henry VIII, had few misgivings. The fact that the marriage had been a farce was not her fault. Or Philip's either, for that matter.

"It's difficult to mate May and September, Ximinez," he said at length, "and she wanted a child even more than I. After all, she has little love for her sister, and Mary is loyal to the Holy Church, if nothing else."

Ximinez nodded.

"Twice we thought you had succeeded," he said.

The king shrugged. "Two false alarms, two seizures of dropsy, not pregnancies. Never was a woman more mortified!"

"What is it the peasants say? Something about being sure before calling the wolf's alarm?" Ximinez suggested.

Philip shook his head again, IF only . . .! IF! An heir would have meant that the church's struggle in Britain would have been won, France would have been quelled, the New World his oyster . . . IF . . .!

Ximinez broke in: "She did assist us in the war . . . at the crucial moment."

"To her credit, but even that proved a disaster for her. Calais is in French hands again, and the English lords blame her, and me. I'm glad I don't have to go back there!" the king said.

"She's finished then?"

"Dead within the month. That's one reason Henry made his peace offer."

Philip fastened the sword belt around his narrow waist, nodded, and the two men left the tent, moving into the bright sunlight onto a field now alive with color. Horsemen were everywhere, and the flags and full pageantry of the Spanish camp made Ximinez's eyes glitter.

The diplomat scanned the field. Even common soldiers were smiling this morning. After four years of tramping back and forth, seeing fellows brutalized by the new long cannon and the charges of horsemen, the war was ended. Ximinez's own signature had written the finish. Two days before at Cateau-Cambrasis the treaty had been signed. What had Spain gained? Peace, and little more.

It had to come. Both countries were bankrupt. Despite the flow of precious metals from the New World, Spain's treasury had been bled white. And French peasants were close to revolt over taxes. France, of course, had Calais once more, after how many years? England's 'pearl' was gone now. No wonder her lords were bitter.

The two men strode to horses held by grooms, and mounted. Ximinez was a poor horseman. Philip was . . . well, improved. His skill with a mount had grown, as had his ability to lead an army. When he took to the field, few felt he could whip troops into a passion, or plot strategy. The king's manner had deceived them! He had at least produced a stalemate. His meetings with France's Henry IV had produced even more . . . a settlement.

Now the treaty was to be celebrated by a tournament, and shortly (as soon as word came across the channel that Mary was dead) Henry Valois would announce betrothal of his daughter, Elizabeth, to the Spanish sovereign.

Times change quickly, Ximinez thought.

Soon there would be two Elizabeths in his king's life, one a wife, the other an antagonist. The King had hoped that the red haired English princess might become an ally, even a friend. The diplomat doubted it! His spies at the English court painted a different picture of Elizabeth: headstrong . . . her father's daughter . . . close to the people . . . eager to protect the new religion . . . ambitious. She would be no friend to Spain!

The pair galloped slowly to the head of the long line of Spanish horsemen who would parade into the arena. The arrangements were complex, colorful. Philip would join Henry in a royal box, accompanied by Henry's sons, his queen Catherine dė Medici and young Elizabeth. There would be preliminaries, horsemanship, jousting; then as a climax Henry would demonstrate his own skill against one of France's most famed knights in a rebirth of the ancient rites.

As the procession entered the arena, Philip's practiced eye slowly swept the huge crowd.

"Henry's outdone himself, wouldn't you say?" he murmured.

"100,000 if there's a man," Ximinez agreed, "and each one with something to celebrate."

Philip nodded. "Nero said 'give them circuses.' Henry reads his history."

As the Spanish King entered the gate, a slow, rumbling cheer arose, and slowly applause mounted as thousands of throats signaled their pleasure at the end of the war.

From beside the royal box, three horsemen broke away and thundered toward the column.

"Here comes Henry," Philip muttered, "always the showman."

"He looks the part," Ximinez agreed.

His horse's hoofs breaking waves of dust as it came, Henry Valois thundered towards the long string of Spanish officers. Philip raised his arm to halt his column. Henry reined to a stop, his spirited mount half rising on its hind legs.

"Welcome, my friend, welcome!" Henry shouted. "May this be a day we will all cherish! Come, join me. Have your men assume positions to the left. My family is eager to see you. Ah . . . and Senor Ximinez! So good to see you again! You'll join us, of course."

Ximinez nodded gravely, and at Philip's signal the long troop of Spanish knights rode to their positions, their heads and spirits high. The long war was over!

As they stepped into the box, bright with the flowing Valois colors, matched by the banner of Castile and Aragon, Ximinez stared ahead. Seated in the second row were the French king's sons . . . young, slender, timid, sickly looking boys, with little of their father's color. The girl was there, too. Pretty thing, Ximinez thought. An improvement over Mary, God knows!

In the front row, in a gilded chair between those saved for her husband and Philip, sat Catherine. Her dark Italian beauty was fading now, and even the flowing gown could not hide the added pounds! But it was her eyes that Ximinez studied. "Cold," he thought. "If ever she had power, she'd be a witch!"

Now Henry was making appropriate introductions.

Philip responded with the usual cool, crisp phrases, and to Ximinez's relief, the party was seated without incident. It was a day to be thankful for, but he'd be most grateful when it was over and done with. After all, most of the spectators had good reason to hate the Spanish sovereign. A quick stroke of a knife, a sudden movement. . . .

Ximinez shivered. What would life in Spain be like THEN?

Across the arena a trio of trumpets blared a signal in a weird harmony. The festivities were about to begin.

The graying diplomat scanned the seats nearby a final time. It looked all right. He was probably too protective. After all, what could happen to the most powerful king in Christendom?

MEXICO CITY
April 1, 1558

Fray Domingo de Santa Maria swung the censer gently, side to side. The incense boiled up, its pungent aroma drifting back over the rows of pews, filled now by Spanish worshippers; towards the back of the huge cathedral, numbers of Indians also knelt, their heads bowed, paying rote heed to the friar's Latin they did not understand.

"Dominus Vobiscum," he chanted, his fine, true tenor singing out the phrases. Behind him, acolytes and subordinate priests executed the offices of the mass. Fray Domingo turned his back to the worshippers, bent knee to the altar, and began his final prayer. The hundreds of men and women lowered heads further, drinking in the heady sounds, relaxed in the splendor of the huge church.

The last Amen rang through to the vaulted ceiling; worshippers arose, genuflected as they left their pews, and slowly moved out through the massive doors. Fray Domingo, followed by his associates, passed serenely from the sanctuary, his magnificant trappings, inlaid with gold threads painstakingly sewn by Indian women, making a great show.

As he exited, the towering, muscular friar felt a grip on his arm.

"Your grace," the voice whispered, "his Excellency Don Luis asks an audience with you." Almost as an afterthought, the voice added, "at once. . . ."

Fray Domingo nodded, and walked quickly into his study. An Indian acolyte helped him remove the robes and cap and hung them carefully in the ornately carved clothes press that covered almost the entire wall.

The friar donned the sweeping black cape and flat black hat of his order. "My stick, Juan," he said, and the youth handed him a gnarled length of oak with a shaped handle.

"I may not be back for dinner. His Excellency has summoned me," he said. The boy nodded.

Once in the quiet back street, Fray Domingo de Santa Maria began to collect his thoughts. What was on Velasco's mind today? Another push for a mission to the north-east? Couldn't the man realize his limits in manpower? No, it wouldn't be that; they'd discussed it last Monday. Perhaps it was construction on the church at Vera Cruz. The viceroy was growing sensitive over that, too. Yes . . . that was probably it . . . !

Fray Domingo de Santa Maria had headed the Dominican Order in Mexico since 1555. He was a determined man, deeply alert to his calling. He had come to the New

World because here there were limitless opportunities to bring the heathen to Christ, and because, well, here one might avoid the tensions of Madrid and Seville. The aftermath of Martin Luther and John Calvin had made life in Spain less than pleasant, and the continuing threat of Inquisition made him uneasy. Mexico, he had bargained, would be more like "the good old days."

He had been only half right. With Charles V growing old and the French war bleeding Spain's people white, life had grown austere at home. But there were demands here, too. And trying to maintain discipline in the Order while meeting the requests of an ambitious viceroy tried a man's temper.

"Ah well," he murmured, "at least we are freed from politics!"

Once inside the viceroy's palace, the black robed friar masked his face in a pious frown, and was quickly admitted to Velasco's study. Velasco, his jacket open for comfort's sake, was pacing back and forth; at the table, scratching his back comfortably against the edge, was Juan Ceron.

"Good evening, your Excellency!" rumbled Domingo.

"Good friar, welcome!" echoed Velasco. Ceron nodded and waved amicably.

"Some wine, your grace? It's warm walking, even at this season," said Velasco.

"Gladly, I'm parched!"

The priest helped himself to three fingers of the deep red Spanish brew that seemed to flow from a spring in the table of the viceroy. Fray Domingo sipped, then belched appreciatively. His eyes slowly scanned the table. Ah . . . there it was! The clue to his summons! A long scroll stamped with the king's seal lay across the desk. There was news . . . or trouble.

"You have some problems of the soul, Excellency?" he asked innocently.

"Happily, no," Velasco replied. "No . . . instead, I need your memory . . . and your knowledge of geography."

"My knowledge of geo. . . ."

"Yes . . . as I recall you have spent considerable time studying the maps and reports from La Florida."

"Well . . . yes."

"Then perhaps you can provide some guidance. Here . . . read this. It provides background. . . ."

Velasco pushed the grayish-yellow paper with its neat lines of script to the grizzled cleric, who picked it up, then slumped carelessly into one of the room's heavy chairs.

Carefully, he read:

"Liege, November: 1557

"HONORED SENOR:

"The fates have delayed your dispatch concerning French explorers and the able action of Captain de Alba. I have been on the move representing His Majesty for months, and couriers from Spain have frequently been delayed. I applaud the actions of Captain de Alba, and I urge you to reward him appropriately.

"As yet I have not had the opportunity to discuss the meaning of the French actions with His Majesty or our other advisors, but it is my opinion that the action by the French vessel was intended, as you suspected, as a preliminary to markings for a settlement. Even now, as our King has recouped our fortunes in the field, I believe the war on land will draw to a close. Our relationship with the French crown should become less strained, perhaps even cordial. However, dispatches from agents in Paris suggest that Queen Catherine may be most directly responsible for the explorations; she is attempting to find means to reduce pressures raised by Protestant reactions within France. Those reports say that perhaps one fourth of the people have fallen prey to the heresy and that even leaders of King Henry's forces, including Adm. Coligny and Prince Louis de Conde, are in their camp. Therefore, we may assume that the Queen has proposed settlements in the New World to be peopled by these Huguenots as a means of removing them, and that the exploration in question was part of this plan.

"I am concerned also that, with the impending death of England's queen, there will ascend to that throne the Princess Elizabeth, whom we must suspect will overturn the religious restoration undertaken by Queen Mary. Our ambassador, who is Mary's confidant, warns that already there are those about the young princess who press their schemes to establish settlements on the new continent.

"Therefore, although His Majesty has yet to discuss the matter with me, and the political scene is much in flux, I propose that you make such studies as are prudent in determining what point or points on the continent might best succor suitable fortified settlements from which our forces may defend the honor and rights of Spain against either or both of the powers. I further encourage you to begin gathering of suitable supplies and materials, and the identification of such men of war and of God who might direct such accomplishments. Further instructions shall be prepared once the pending settlements with France are concluded, and His Majesty has had suitable opportunity to review these recommendations."

Signed/XIMINEZ"

Fray Domingo reread the final portions of the document, then laid it back on the table, pushing it back toward the viceroy.

"Well?" Velasco said.

"Your excellency wishes my assistance in determining . . . ?"

". . . in selecting the place, the starting point, the harbor. Where shall we begin?"

Ceron leaned forward. "We have given this great thought. . . ."

(I imagine you have! thought the friar.)

" . . . and we believe the mission may require at least TWO settlements, one on the southern coast of La Florida, to command that area and the great river, Santa Maria de Espiritu, of de Soto, and a second midway on the coast of the Atlantic, perhaps on what was called Puento de Santa Elena."

Fray Domingo nodded. For all his other duties, he had enjoyed his hobby in his new land. Maps were a passion with him, and he had encouraged his scribes in the copying of every scrap brought back by marines who had ventured into the northern hemisphere.

He leaned forward, and grasped quill and ink pot. Hastily scratching the outline of the Florida shore, he imprinted several dots.

"Here is where de Soto began," he said, pointing at the southwestern coast. "The harbor is excellent, but there are savages here, and the location is not right."

Ceron concurred. "It is too far from the great river, and the currents and winds may be wrong to help defend our treasure fleets," he pointed out.

Fray Domingo agreed. "This is where we believe de Narvaez landed," he noted, pointing to a second dot. "The land lies better, but the harbor is poor. You will remember his fate?"

Both men nodded. Storms had disabled the explorer's tiny fleet in 1528, and rafts carrying survivors had foundered there.

"Now, THIS, I think, is more like it," the friar continued, indicating his third dot.

"This is Bahia de Santa Maria?" Velasco asked.

"That is what some have called it on the sketches. However, it has other names . . . Ochuse . . . and Polonza."

Ceron clarified his impression: "This is where Maldonado anchored awaiting rendezvous with de Soto?"

"The same. You will recall his description? A harbor sufficient for all of the world's navies, friendly people, clear water, rivers to the upland, fertile ground."

Velasco nodded. "And as I recall, it is within two days' sail of the great river's mouth."

Fray Domingo assented. "That is my belief. Of course, we will do well to examine the maps with care."

Velasco and Ceron exchanged glances. The viceroy continued: "Good friar, I would consider it a great favor if you would assemble your best charts and materials and be prepared to assist Captain Ceron and me with these determinations. We have lost much valuable time."

(The friar calculated hastily: A YEAR already! Unbelievable!)

"Will tomorrow evening, say after vespers, be agreeable?"

"That will be fine. Meanwhile, we're trying to assemble men who have sailed to this area, those few who remain that returned from de Soto's march, and others who may have visited your Santa Maria. I would like to finish my report by Saturday."

"I will be here tomorrow, excellency," the friar concluded. "Now, if you have nothing else, I must get back. Should an expedition be ordered, it will require a substantial number of Men of God. I must think about them also."

"Of course," Velasco added, "but I dare say we have a few days yet."

His chuckle brought smiles to the other men. To the Dominican there was irony in the tortoise-like speed with which the greatest power in the world moved. To Ceron, the mirth was of another kind. He could see fortune beginning her radiant smile upon him.

April 2, 1558

Fray Domingo de Santa Maria's historiography and mapping included hundreds of pages of sketches and reports which began with an account of the voyage in 1516 of Fiego de Miruelo who had skirted the entire coast of La Florida bartering with the Indians. However, he made no charts, and later, as a pilot for Lucas Vasquez de Ayllon, could not even find the areas he had described with greatest interest (some said he had died from the mortification of it all)!

Three years later Alonso Alvarez de Pineda also sailed the length of La Florida's gulf coastline, and nine years after, the ill-fated Panfilo de Narvaez had reached St. Marks before his fleet foundered and its survivors were left to stumble home on foot.

The better known expedition of Hernando de Soto had begun in Tampa Bay and had marched back and forth over much of the mid-south; the plans had been well conceived, and the fleet had been ordered to rendezvous with de Soto in the great bay which some man in an unknown era had called Ochuse, at the base of the Rio de Ochuse in the west of La Florida. The fleet commander, Francisco Maldonado, arrived there in the spring of 1540 and spent two months in a combination of waiting and exploring, waiting for an army that never returned in that direction because its leader had redirected its efforts westward.

Maldonado returned to Mexico with tales of the harbor's excellence, of the few gentle Indians who visited there, and of the desirability of the site for future colonization.

Later Luis de Moscoso, who ultimately led a remnant of the de Soto troop back to Mexico, devoted many pages to his party's encounter with the great Indian nation of Coosa, where the expedition had spent numerous days in recouping its health, and where several of the ill were left for a hoped-for recovery. Coosa was a great empire, he said, though the countryside had many undesirable qualities. He spoke also of a second settlement where the Spaniards encountered a well disciplined, domesticated tribe. This he called Nanicapana. In his account, Moscoso said that he believed that Nanicapana was but 50 leagues from Ochuse, to the north and west, and that Coosa was perhaps 350. From reports given by Indians in this locale and elsewhere, the great Puenta de Santa Elena was estimated at some 300 leagues to the east of Coosa.

There were other explorations, but these summarized the major points of interest, except that there was disagreement among the various chroniclers as to just where Ochuse was located! Which was best suited to colonization, and what was its exact location?

In weeks that followed, the viceroy, Ceron and the Dominican pored repeatedly over the maps and accounts. Still the question plagued them; an error of this type could prove critical with a major fleet and expedition involved.

At length, the viceroy settled the matter. He summoned Capt. Juan Bazares, provided him with a caravelle and crew, and ordered him to sail 'as rapidly as possible' to the area in the west of La Florida, and to deal specifically with the question of just where the best landing could be effected.

In May, 1558, he departed from the port of San Juan de Ulua, and during the next seven weeks probed the coastline as ordered. He reported to the trio that, indeed, there WERE several large bays, two of which were entered by sizeable rivers. By his recommendation, the one farthest to the east was selected, for it had '. . . the finest landlocked bay I have ever seen,' and was protected from the high winds by a narrow island, a long peninsula, and steep bluffs to the inland side.

This site was thus officially labeled as OCHUSE on Fray Santo Domingo's charts, and the bay again given its name of Santa Maria.

"It was an expense well worth the effort," the viceroy reasoned. "Bazares has done his work well."

"I trust so," Ceron added, "but it's a large ocean."

Calais
March 28, 1558

It is one of history's undeniable truisms that people enjoy diversions to steer their minds from misery. The French, a volatile, exuberant nationality, are especially susceptible, Ximinez thought.

How long had they been here? Three hours? Perhaps even four. Delightful refreshments and the bubbling wine from a huge hamper had made the noon hour a delight. The royal box supped, and as far as the eye could see other spectators were lunching on the familiar twisted loaves and heaven knew what else!

Before them, the action never stopped.

Fencers displayed their skills with the long, slender blades the French love so well. Time after time they parried and thrust, their form perfected by years of action; as each event ended, the winner was led to the honors circle before the royal family, where Henry bestowed some medal or trinket, and the crowd roared its approval.

Ximinez yawned.

All this is a buildup to let Henry mount his own horse and do battle against three knights who had better mind their manners and fall properly if they know what's good for them, he thought.

The trio of trumpets let forth another blast (the musicians were growing tongue weary now, and their harmonies were increasingly discordant).

Admiral Coligny, the quiet, stately mariner, leaned over and whispered, "The jousts will begin now. We're coming to the finale!"

Ximinez smiled.

"Is your bottom as tired as mine," he asked.

"I'd give 1000 francs to be anywhere else," the admiral replied.

Two stubby knights, one with bright blue colors, the other in gold and white, were helped to their horses. Each was surrounded by retainers who checked cinches, tightened the fittings, then handed each combatant his lance, shield and helmet.

Ximinez wondered how long it had been since they'd played at such games. These men had been busy with the real thing for an age. This must seem like play indeed.

Each knight spurred his horse and guided it into position. Each was led to one side of a long sturdy rail, a meter in height. Its length was perhaps 100 meters; the ground was level, the grass green and even, as though it had been freshly clipped.

Ximinez wondered who in his insanity had developed such games for men to play.

From his box, the French king raised his arm as a signal for readiness. Each knight dropped his visor. Across the field, trumpets sounded again . . . a long, unison blast. The king's arm fell, and both riders kicked sharpened spurs into horses' flanks.

Both mounts streaked forward, their hooves pounding the fresh earth, faster, faster . . . closer . . . closer! The three meter lances were down now, flashing parallel with the earth, and each man's shield was held high and at an angle, to ward off the thrust of his opponent. On and on they came, meter by meter, and as they thundered on, 100,000 voices roared approval. On . . . on . . . on . . . then . . . with a wrenching, crumpling, rendering crash like the sound of two colliding men-of-war, lances smashed against shields! The Blue Knight lurched to his left, gripped hard with his legs, his horse staggered, his lance wrenched from his hand . . . but he remained erect.

His opponent in white and gold raised a foot in the air, his shield pierced by the blunted point of the lance. His left flailed, the shield, torn from his grasp, flying to earth and bouncing wildly there. One leg wrenched free from the stirrup. The lance, now deflected outward, fell free, and with both hands White and Gold tried vainly to maintain his balance.

It was a futile effort! Arms flailing, legs kicking, the knight, burdened with nearly 100 pounds of armor and helmet, wavered and bounced backward, his shoulder striking the horse's flank, his rump thudding into the turf like a dropped meal sack.

White and Gold lay still, his breath coming in gasps, his eyes smarting from the dust, his head swimming from the dazing blows.

Aides ran to him, snapped open the visor, then lifted off the dented helmet. Slowly he was lifted to his feet. His eyes, still dazed, watched as his successful Blue opponent trotted in triumph to the royal box. The King was standing, extending the traditional scarf in the royal colors. As one knight basked in glory, the other, helped by downcast kinsmen, limped from the field, grateful that he bore no obvious scars.

Ximinez, who had stood with the throng to watch the ten seconds of combat, now sank back into his chair. How many more of these must he endure? Three . . . four?

Actually, it was even more. Three more pairs of knights were raised to horse, two were dismounted, the third pair coming off a draw.

And then it was Henry's turn.

Bronzed, toughened from months in the field, his pointed beard turned up in a natural curl, Henry was a truly athletic figure, far more so than Philip, who stood to shake his hand. Henry nodded, bent down, kissed his wife on the cheek, waved gaily to his children, then stepped from the box to where attendants held his mail.

The dressing of a knight for combat is no small task, Ximinez thought. God, the poor horse! The diplomat watched with his usual sarcasm as layer after layer of cloth and steel were spread over the French monarch. Finally . . . with all but his helmet in place, the king climbed two small wooden steps beside his horse, and with great difficulty hoisted an armored leg over the saddle. An aide helped guide the steel-shod foot into the stirrup.

A second aide handed the king his long, slender lance. The monarch tested it, raising it, dropping it, thrusting it forward. Its balance must have felt good, for he nodded, then reached down for his visored helmet with its plume of the French Blue and Gold. Carefully, he slipped it onto his head, the visor still open.

"All right, Marcel, my shield, if you please," he said, the soft words somehow audible above the now hushed murmur of the crowd.

Once more, Henry II of France turned to his family and saluted. Philip rose and bowed formally; Ximinez followed suit. The mounted monarch of all the Frenchmen turned and rode slowly to his place.

Henry's climax to the tournament was to be three encounters for himself, two against members of his royal household, the third with the Duke of Montgomery, the most famous of France's men in the field in the recent wars. Why three, Ximinez wondered? Perhaps to prove to Philip who was the better man.

Now both knights were in position, and the queen raised her arm as the signal. The trumpets sounded once more, and Catherine's white clad arm came down. Away pounded the horses, faster, faster down the run, each rubbing close to the guide rail. On and on they came, their canter climaxed by the now familiar din of collision.

This time both riders held their mounts, but the king's opponent had lost his lance, and his shield clattered to the ground also.

The king had bested his first man!

The second enounter was a perfect copy. Henry, obviously savoring the fervor of combat, spurred his horse to a fast pace, and again sent his opponent's weapons flying.

Score two for Henry!

Ximinez snorted to himself! Will anyone bet that the third bout will go otherwise? Montgomery knows who is sovereign here!

One hundred meters apart the two mounted men eyed each other. Montgomery, calm looking in gray armor and gray colors, lifted his lance in the traditional sign that he was ready. Once again the queen's arm was raised . . . the horns blared . . . the signal was made and the horses were spurred forward. Philip tensed, his own back bent as he watched Henry spur his mount and grip his knees against the flying brown mare. This time even Catherine looked uncertain. On and on they came . . . and then crashed together, the full impact of the weight of animals and men felt in the maximum strike. Metal scraped metal, and the crack of splintering wood could be heard by all within fifty meters. The king lurched, raised in his stirrups, clutched wildly with his knees, then settled back, Montgomery, his lance snapped nearly in half, swung wildly seeking balance, his shield arm clutching for support against the horse's back. With a wild effort to keep from falling, his right arm came forward a second time, its shortened lance now little more than sword's length. For a split second the men hung almost together, then the horses braced and passed on. As they did so the king's scream broke through his visor. He rose again on his mount, dropped shield and lance and clutched at his helmeted face.

"My God, my God, I am done! I am done," he screamed. His horse still laboring, lurched once more, and the king, his grasp on the rein now gone, crumpled into an armored heap in the dust.

Montgomery, his broken lance still in his hand, came quickly to a halt.

A low moan swept across the arena. One hundred thousand shouting, cheering throats suddenly stilled; from the sides, aides and nobles rushed forward to their stricken king.

Philip rose with the rest and made one stride toward the field. Quickly, he felt Ximinez's grip on his elbow. The diplomat, transformed from bored observer to professional guardian of the monarch, simply shook his head. Philip responded. Turning, he gripped the hand of the queen and urged her to sit down.

On the field, aides had reached the fallen Henry and carefully opened the visor. Even hardened battle veterans were shaken by what they saw. A splinter from the lance perhaps 200 millimeters long, had pierced the king's eye. Blood gushed forth, cascading down his mouth and chin, soaking into the tight collar below his armor. Bright red blended with the royal blue and gold.

Henry II had received his death wound.

The knight Montgomery, his eyes filled with tears, was on his knees, his lips moving in prayer.

In that one instant, the future of the Christian world took a wild turn.

April 12, 1558

The road from Calais to Madrid is long, and even in spring it can be hot and dry.

The ten days of slow plodding by a weary army had deeply fatigued Philip. Riding surrounded by his guard, the tall, thin, usually taciturn monarch was more withdrawn than usual. Ximinez, his own thoughts brightened by the prospects of home, held his mount a stride to the rear of Philip's charger.

For days now they had barely spoken. The aftermath of the tragedy at Calais hung over them. Prospects for a proper peace now seemed remote. With Henry Valois dead there already was intrigue on a grand scale throughout France.

A thought struck the diplomat. Spurring ahead, he addressed his king:

"Your majesty, I hestitate to ask, but have you read my notes on the report of Velasco and the French explorers?"

Philip nodded.

Ximinez continued:

"In the pleasures of the peace, I had hoped my alarm might be . . . ah . . . premature? But now, I wonder. . . ."

Philip turned in the saddle and wearily adjusted the soft pad that now was always part of his britches. Boils were a curse!

"You were with Coligny at the tournament . . . what do you make of him?"

"He's a Calvinist and a heathen! Other than that, I'd say he's an honest man and a fine sailor."

Philip nodded.

"And where do you feel he'll end up in all of this? Protestants got along well under Henry. . . ."

"What choice did he have?" Ximinez interjected. "After all, a fourth of the people have accepted the heresy. . . ."

"A rather expected result of taxes and war . . .," Philip responded.

"The point is . . . what will Catherine do? She must protect the throne for her son. . . ."

Ximinez shook his head.

"That boy is not long for this world, and neither are his brothers."

"Exactly," the king replied. "The dissidents are at work already. If we were in her place, what would we do?"

Ximinez, the wisdom of a generation in the courts of Europe in his mind, replied cautiously:

"I'd get rid of at least some of the Huguenots . . . perhaps with the help of the Holy Father."

"With the help . . . or the blessing. . . . ," the king agreed.

"What better way than to offer the leader an opportunity in the New World, especially if the people might finance the venture themselves," Ximinez concluded.

Philip lapsed into silence, his horse's feet spewing up wavelets of dust from the rut-filled mountain trail.

How quickly life changes, he mused. A month ago there was peace, and after battling Henry's armies, he had found the French monarch a delightful man. What might they have accomplished, with their two houses united in marriage?

Now? Ximinez was right. The queen was a Medici, slippery as a snake, willing to use her wiles in any way. . . .

The marriage to the young Elizabeth would take place, of course.

By agreement, there would be a delay of one year out of respect for the dead king, and for Mary.

Poor Mary!

Her death had been mourned by almost no one, save those English who clung to the true faith. She had been their hope.

Now she was dead, and the red haired bitch was queen.

Philip had not even considered going to the burial. After Calais' loss, he was less than popular in London. Instead, he had penned an appropriate tribute to be delivered by the ambassador. Few missed him.

In a year . . . what sort of bride would Elizabeth be? She had youth and Henry's charm . . . and Catherine's figure as a girl. She was shy yet natural enough.

The wedding would take place in Paris with the Duke of Alva as proxy for Philip.

The king shrugged.

After playing husband to Mary and spending his youth in the field, it would be good to return to the warm beds of Madrid!

Ximinez's thoughts followed a similar course. How many years it had been since he traveled with the old king to the Low Countries! His blood had thickened now and he could make brave stands against the cold in the army camp, but . . . great God . . . it would be good to sleep warm again and to taste the heady buds of garlic!

The pair rode in silence for a time, the diplomat's thoughts turning again and again to the French operations.

For 25 years Valois explorers had sailed far to the north, concentrating on the great river that flowed east. Why now the interest in La Florida?

"Probably they want to be sure Coligny's heresy doesn't poison any people they settle near in the far country," he mused. "And of course they would always enjoy embarrassing us!"

To the rear, a horse moved away from the mass of the guard and pulled even with Ximinez. The rider, of medium height and with field rank, raised a gloved hand in salute.

"Your pardon, Excellency, but how much longer will his majesty wish to continue tonight. I believe there's a village about an hour ahead . . . Savignon. With your permission we'll ride ahead and obtain lodging for the king."

Ximinez glanced to his right. The sun, now partly hidden by light haze, was moving through its last quarter.

He nodded.

"Go ahead, Senor de Luna, Oh . . . and tonight see if we can't find a place with something besides straw husks for a mattress. The king has some, ah, discomfort . . ." Ximinez winked wisely.

"I understand, Excellency," de Luna replied. "If there's a manor house, we'll seek it out, otherwise . . . the best available."

He saluted, spurred his animal about, and rejoined his troopers. Choosing half a dozen, he skirted the long, marching columns and began the slight assent that carried the road over a gentle ridge and into Savignon.

The horses, anxious to run after a long day of plodding at the infantry's pace, sped along. Then, as the village came in sight from the hilltop, de Luna slowed them. "No sense to alarm sleepy peasants," he muttered.

Don Tristan de Luna y Arellano looked the part of a soldier of Spain. He was of average size, swarthy of complexion, with his jet black straight hair flowing nearly to his shoulders.

Powerful hands expertly gripped the reins, and his frame, kept lean by months in the saddle and short rations, made him look what he was . . . a professional soldier of Spain.

His father, Marshall Don Carlos de Luna, was lord of Barobia and Seria in Aragon, and would one day be governor of Tucutan also.

The son had been raised in the role of a nobleman's offspring, educated in the classics, with a deep, abiding faith in God and God's Holy Church, and a servant of the King.

De Luna had fought in France and Italy, then had seized the opportunity to go to the New World.There he had been assigned to the staff of the viceroy and had helped reduce several of the northern prairies.

A true conquistador, de Luna had acquitted himself well and then had served as Master of the Camp for Coronado's famed search for the Seven Cities of Cibola, returning to Spain to accept command of a troop when war resumed in the Low Countries.

At year's end, with the death of the venerable Dominguez, he had been named captain of the king's guard.

It was a good record.

De Luna smiled; his father and older brother would be proud!

And his wife!

Holy Mary, it would be good to feel her again! How long had it been? Two years . . . no . . . more than that!

His marriage to Valencia had been carefully planned by both houses. Painstakingly arranged by his father, a marriage calculated to strengthen the family's positions both at court and as lorded gentry. The bride's father, a shrewd landowner, was distantly related to the late, great Queen Isabella. Her grandfather's hatred of the Moors had been proven through much of his life, spent in perpetual wars that ultimately had driven the Muslims from the land in 1492. King Ferdinand's gratitude had been considerable. The Don had been given lands of size and beauty, and Valencia would inherit a substantial share.

But she was more than a lady of wealth and family. Valencia de Cordova had been groomed to be a lady of charm and many talents, and as her husband had quickly learned, she possessed all of the passion that Spanish men dreamed of in their women.

It was a second marriage for de Luna, his first having been to twice-widowed Dona Isabel de Rosas, whose husbands Juan Velazquez and Francisco Maldonado had left her a lady of New World properties. She and Don Tristan had bred two children, Carlos and Joana. Her death three years before had hurried Don Tristan's return to Spain.

His marriage to Valencia had been carefully planned by both houses. He had been 41, she 22. Now, four years later, they were favorites in the countryside, loved by the peasants, approved by their peers.

With his new military role, de Luna would be a part of the King's court also. The court had enjoyed little function in recent years. The wars, the continuing absence of first one king and then the other, had provided little opportunity for pageantry and pleasures.

De Luna had been there in prior days, of course, in a trivial role. Now, however, exploits in the King's service had elevated his position if not his title. He would be part of the new court. And Valencia would be there to meet him when he arrived, God willing!

The troop entered the town and horses hooves began their steady clap-clap against the worn stone-paved street. Dusk was coming on rapidly now, and it would be wise to complete the arrangements quickly. The king was weary, in no mood for dallying.

The young knight's eye sighted the one building one could always expect in such a hamlet . . . a combination inn and tavern, usually headquarters for news and guidance, where one might get direction to the best houses. The building was two stories high, its name emblazened in red on a smooth planed sign. In front, three horses were tied, and a groom absentmindedly held a bucket of grain for one.

Spanish! De Luna noted. From the army? Unlikely. Well . . . perhaps there would be news! The young knight swung from his saddle and tramped stiffly into the common room. A fire glowed brightly on a ramshackle hearth, and there were perhaps a dozen men, in twos and threes, sipping wine and chatting idly. The landlord, his long apron clean and crisp, was bustling over a table, serving the three Spanish travelers, easily recognizable from the local citizen.

"Good landlord," de Luna called out, "I am the messenger of His Most Catholic Majesty, King Philip, and I would talk with you."

The man put down the final glass, glared at de Luna and nodded.

"One moment, your grace. Your countrymen have ridden far and have a great thirst!"

The trio turned to de Luna, and one rose.

"Is the king close by?"

"A league away, no more," de Luna answered.

The horseman smiled.

"Then our journey's ended. Is Ximinez with him?"

"Of course."

"Our message is for him."

"He should be here in an hour. Wait here. Nothing's so urgent as to hurry a man from good wine after a long ride."

The three men murmured assent, and de Luna turned to the innkeeper.

"Who is lord of this place, and what sort of house does he keep! I seek lodging for the king!"

April 12 . . . in the evening

Philip of Spain always ate sparingly. He took most things in moderation and after a long day's march, he was content with a thick slice of lamb roasted over his host's spit, some good French bread and a cup of wine.

Now refreshed, he gazed into the fire, deep in thought. Ximinez, his own appetite still unsatisfied, gnawed at a tasty crust dipped in the natural sauce of the meat.

The king broke the silence.

"Our English friends have lost no time."

Ximinez wiped his mouth across his greasy sleeve.

"No more than we expected."

"Elizabeth's hawks have not been idle. Read the text again."

Ximinez unfolded the disptach. It was from his office, and had been forwarded from the ambassador in London. It read:

"On February 15th last the English vessel SPIRIT left the Thames with orders to explore the middle coast line of the northern hemisphere. It has been determined that certain counselors of the new Queen are to be given patents for colonization and trade, and that a stock company is being formed to bear the cost. Officially, the Crown will have no involvement. However, leadership of the venture includes men of both naval and military experience and it is my opinion that they propose creation of a citadel which would oppose our rights there. The entire project has been executed with maximum security and I have just learned of it today.

Your obedient servant. . . ."

J"

Ximinez stopped, deliberately folded the parchment and glanced at his monarch.

Philip sat silently for several minutes, then rose, walked to the fire and stood with his back to the crackling embers.

"So now there are two! If we don't hurry, the New World will be as crowded as Madrid at mid-day even before we arrive."

The diplomat nodded.

"We're at a disadvantage, working so far from our base," he said, "and while our energies have been dedicated to pacifying our French neighbors, others have been at work."

Philip flexed his long legs, then rose and began to pace the comfortable room. He paused, then continued the conversation.

"In your dispatches to Velasco, you've spoken of preparedness?"

"I have."

"How far would you say they have advanced?"

"Difficult to say! His replies may be waiting when we reach Madrid."

"How do you envision all this? I mean . . . shall we simply patrol against these pirates . . . or is the time right to raise our flag there? Have we the manpower? Have we the men of the church we'll need?"

Ximinez shrugged.

"Velasco's an able man and ambitious. He's not one of those looking for gold in every stream!"

The King nodded affirmatively.

"Then perhaps the time is right to do as my father had hoped. . . ."

"A total effort . . . full control from the great river to the fishing grounds . . . ?"

Something like that. Let's see . . . we will be in Madrid . . . in . . . ah . . . six days . . . perhaps seven . . .?"

"About that."

"Then suppose we return the messengers after they've rested, with orders to convene the full council for planning purposes."

Ximinez agreed, "Shall we give our reasons?"

"No . . . ." the King paused, "No . . . I'll do it. I have a few things I'd like to add myself. Send for the scribe. . . ."

The diplomat left the room and dispatched his waiting aide with two messages. To the three troopers he sent instructions to rest until midnight, then be ready to return to Madrid.

Then, he sent for Juan Menendez, his clerk.

Minutes later the young clerical aide reported, somewhat out of breath, his pen, ink, parchment and sand vial in a cloth pouch.

Ximinez nodded greeting.

"The king has a project," he announced, ushering the young man into the monarch's presence.

Menendez bowed low; Philip motioned him toward the low table where a gigantic candle burned fitfully.

"How quickly can you write tonight?" Philip demanded.

"Quite well, I think, your majesty," Menendez responded.

"Let us begin then," Philip commanded . . . and dictated the following statement to his council, the ten senior nobles who by birth, privilege and custom acted as advisors to the Spanish throne.

"For many years, we have encouraged our leaders in the New World . . . civic, military and religious . . . to pursue their tasks with such dispatch as to spread the Faith, fortify our position in the land, and organize a body politick in our name. This they have done well, including explorations of the sea north and east of Mexico, and of the coast of the great ocean northward."

Philip paused, considering his next phrases deliberately, choosing each for effect.

"Now I believe that events in Europe, and particularly in France and England, have been such as to encourage even greater haste in securing our position. With peace restored, facilities and resources which might have been otherwise occupied now are free for roles in exploration, colonization and the spreading of the Faith.

"Therefore, I request that each council member marshall his thoughts for creation of such a force as may be required to meet these objectives, and that all be prepared for appropriate deliberation when we arrive some six days hence. Hopefully, we may send preliminary accounts to the viceroy in Mexico, Don Luis de Velasco, within the month.

"Ximinez joins me in hearty best wishes.

"Signed Philip Rex"

The dictation had required perhaps 15 minutes, the scribe writing effortlessly, with an occasional pause, but with obvious urgency. It was not often that the King prepared his own letters!

Young Menendez looked up to see if there might be more; the King's head moved slightly, side to side.

Menendez nodded, his eyes still on the King's face, the gravity of the message sinking into his own brain. His hand reached for the pot of sand to dry the ink. Almost absentmindedly his fingers gripped a vessel, turned and shook it in the familiar motion.

Instantly Menendez realized his error as the thick red ink flowed over his fingers and onto the paper, passing in blood colored rivers over the neatly styled lines.

Philip's gaze met the eyes of the young writer. For a moment, neither spoke.

Ximinez coughed uncomfortably.

"Menendez," the King said icily, "ink is for writing, sand is for drying!"

He turned abruptly and left the room.

The diplomat, who had been in similar straits, patted the youth's shoulder.

"Sit down, sit down," he said calmly. "Come . . . be careful! I think that between us we can reconstruct what he's said."

The young scribe gave the older man a grateful glance, nodded, dried his fingers, drew out a new sheet and began again.

Minutes later Philip returned. He glanced carefully over the rewritten document, nodded coldly and scribbled his initials in place. Menendez added the seal.

Philip retired without another word.

Next morning the three still-weary horsemen hurried south from the hamlet, and began their trek to Spain's capital.

In his bed, Philip of Spain, his eyes wide open in the dimly lighted bedroom, reflected on what he had done and what he knew of his "new world."

Down the hall, Ximinez wondered how quickly an expedition might be launched.

Bedded down with his command, Don Tristan de Luna stretched his saddle-weary body and wondered what had brought the royal messengers so far only to turn about so quickly.

"Oh well," he mused, "it's not my worry. It doesn't concern me!"

In seconds he was asleep, dreaming of the warm curves of a loving wife now just a week's ride away.

April 19, 1558

Philip's triumphant return to Madrid is still recalled as an epoch. How many lined the streets to cheer the armies, now bone-tired from having pounded across mountain and plain from the English channel? How many grains of sand are washed by the seas?

For Spain, the peace won at Cateau-Cambresis meant that a new golden age must begin, an age in which the precious metals of the New World would bring a rebirth of the Holy Church, and new enterprises for a war-weary people.

Philip rode with the rear guard of his troops, more than 60,000 strong, their uniforms shabby from combat and travel but their spirits high.

From balconies lovely ladies eagerly waved or threw flowers, flags and banners brightened house fronts, and old men and young boys cheered.

Philip, his face an impassive mask behind its well-styled beard, occasionally waved. Otherwise, he steadied his horse and stared straight ahead.

The diplomat rode a horse-length behind, straight in the saddle, dignified yet bending regularly with courtly bows, first right, then left.

Don Tristan de Luna rode modestly at the head of his guard, his beard freshly trimmed, his tunic brushed as clean as an army steward could make it.

Block after block they rode, towards designated dismissal points. The sun was high overhead now, and the dust kicked up by the horses and thousands of marching feet raised a cloud over the ranks.

Ximinez, every muscle aching, judged that they might dismount before noon. "Great God, won't a bath feel marvelous! A bath . . . perhaps with some Moorish oil . . . and a cup of cold red wine." He'd have time for that before the council convened.

Philip was pacing himself, giving the cheering thousands ample time to enjoy the circus, to eat tasties hawked by vendors, to savor the return of marching husbands and sons and lovers.

Ximinez had planned the day well . . . a morning entry and parade, a respite for refreshment, the council meeting, then a grand ball to re-establish the court! As the climax, Philip would announce the new colonial enterprise. It would be a fitting end to a memorable day.

The great plaza was just ahead now. The King spurred his horse into a slow trot, pulled into the square and began a paced walk around its perimeter. On the opposite side stood the Cardinal of Madrid, his scarlet robes bright against the contrasting gray and black clerical garb and the gray and brown homespun of the townsmen.

The long line of soldiers approached the churchmen, Philip raised his gloved hand, and through the army officers and subordinates repeated sharp commands to halt.

Philip dismounted, handed his reins to an aide who had leaped forward, strode the four steps to the Cardinal, and fell to his knee.

A hush fell over the square; thousands of heads instinctively bowed as a ringing blessing was delivered in faultless Latin. For long minutes the prayer of thanksgiving continued, not in a church where few could see, but here before thousands who shared this triumph with their sovereign and his army.

The Amen rang loud and clear, and cheers broke forth. The King rose, embraced the Cardinal, then turned to de Luna, standing close by.

"Give the order for dismissal," he said.

Don Tristan turned, and in a high, piercing tone issued the command.

In seconds neat ranks dissolved and war-weary veterans turned to rush toward waiting loved ones.

The war was over.

Ximinez walked to the King's side, ready for the brief final march to the palace.

De Luna remounted his men for the same duty.

Philip, again on his horse, gave the signal and the detachment moved out.

"Fabulous!" murmured the diplomat.

Even with the army at large dismissed, thousands of onlookers remained in place to watch the movements of their king.

It seemed as though the saints were watching over Philip. Surely, now a great era must begin.

Minutes later king and guard were inside the palace; Ximinez was in his bath, and de Luna was walking arm in arm with the lovely Valencia towards the house she had taken.

April 19th . . . that afternoon

The meeting of the Council of Madrid was the first full gathering of the nobles in five years. Some, of course, had joined Charles, and then Philip, in the field; but the traditional meetings of this cabinet had been omitted, each man caring for his own area of responsibility.

Now, each noble was present early, his aides nearby, armed with ledgers and accounts to report recent activities if these were required, and prepared to answer the King's request for data on the New World project.

Precisely at two o'clock the door from the King's anteroom opened, and a page called out:

"Your Excellencies, His Most Catholic Majesty, Philip II of Spain!"

The King strode into the chamber, his eyes straight ahead, his body clad in pure black velvet except for a simple gold cross at his throat, his thin legs outlined in close fitting trousers and boots.

The Councilmen rose as one man from their heavy oak chairs. Philip, like his father, was not a man to mix pleasantries at business sessions. The King reached his seat, glanced at the full table, then turned his head slightly to his right, nodded, and the Chaplain intoned a lengthy prayer.

The Amen sounded, the King took his seat, and the Council members followed, their aides grouped in a second row of chairs and benches.

"Gentlemen," the King began, "I'm grateful for your presence and for the loyal and thorough method in which each has conducted his office."

The Councilmen nodded gravely.

The monarch continued:

"And I appreciate your prompt response to my call for assembly. I assume that the content of my message was clear."

Again there were grave nods of assent.

"To put matters in perspective, I have asked Senor Ximinez to review the reports he has received and our initial thinking."

Ximinez arose, and after acknowledging the King's introduction, began.

"In March 1557, the Viceroy of Mexico, the Honorable Don Luis de Velasco, prepared a report which rekindled our thinking on La Florida," he began. "All of you have received the information from our previous explorations there, of course. . . ."

There was murmuring assent from the council members.

"The reports from the de Soto, Alyon and de Narvaez parties suggested that Indians there are of different confederacies, are alternately friendly and hostile, and have no civilization comparable to Mexico or Peru.

"And," the diplomat paused for effect, "you will recall also the reports of a city of gold thought to lie in the region travelled by de Soto before his death."

Again, the grave men around the table nodded assent.

"In 1535, reports came to us of attempts made to effect a settlement for France along the great river which drains to the east in what they describe as the land of furs. Again, you will recall our discussion and the protest registered with the Pope."

Don Jose de Sanchez, Admiral of the Navies, interrupted, "The Pope's line is now considered null and void following our own activities of liberation in Italy, is this not true?" he asked.

Ximinez nodded affirmatively.

"At that point, of course, we had no way of controlling further French action other than by military force in Europe, and you all are familiar with what has occurred here."

They were! The succession of wars had halted the French. It also had required every peso drawn from the wealth of the New World. It was a standoff at best.

Ximinez continued.

"We had hoped that with peace and our accord with Henry Valois we would be able to begin our mission to the north of Mexico. Now, however, we have intelligence that both France and England are about to effect landings there . . . or close by!"

For the next hour Philip and Ximinez shared the bits of information they had acquired and the suspected reasons behind the new aggressions.

At length, the King spoke:

"Sr. Ximinez and I believe that we enjoy several alternatives. You may anticipate others. Suppose we begin with the choices as we see them."

Philip spoke in flat, even tones, striding slowly back and forth at the head of the long table, his hands clasped behind his back.

"First, of course, we could do nothing, at least for the present. It will take our enemies years to establish meaningful resources there. Their supply lines are long, their naval forces limited, their treasuries poor. By restricting our expenditures we may build our army and navy, and be prepared then to attack and destroy whatever efforts they establish. However," he added, "such a posture must ultimately provoke a new European war, perhaps against both countries."

The King paused to let the effect of his logic drive home. Then he continued.

"Second, we can protest the actions which we understand are proposed. This is Sr. Ximinez's department, of course, and quite frankly, we dismissed the wisdom of such a move."

Again he paused. This time he returned to his chair and reseated himself. Speaking even more softly, he said:

"Our third option is to move immediately to build our own position north of Mexico, to create a combined colonial and military effort which will make it impossible for others to intrude. With our existing base in Mexico, this appears to be a relatively simple step, one which I am sure will have the full backing of the Holy Church as well."

Thus began the discussion. Each of the twelve counselors had reviewed the status of the Mexican venture, knew its strength and weaknesses and the allure of further adventures in the New World. Each had studied their limitations also.

At length, Ximinez rose to summarize the discussion.

"Our most recent report from Velasco suggests that he can assemble a fleet of six vessels and equip them with 850 persons, including the Dominican contingent. He feels that with arrival of suitable food, military personnel and supplies from Spain, including horse and small cannons, the venture can proceed within a year.

"His recommendation is that the colony be established in the harbor of Santa Maria, the sanctuary where Maldonado wintered to rendezvous with de Soto's forces. You have his text with its description, I believe.

"With our approval, he suggests that the fleet can be readied and provisioned by mid-July of next year from San Juan de Ulua."

An expedition of 850 men! This was twice the number who accompanied Cortes!

One by one the counselors rose to speak.Each became more excited in his turn! Each was anxious to prove how much his own service might contribute to the expedition's success. At each response, the King nodded approvingly, then turned to the next man for input.

Finally, when all had spoken, the King rose and resumed his pacing. A minute passed, then two. Finally, he halted and pointed at Sanchez.

"Do you have the charts of the New World areas?"

Sanchez leaped up and with the help of his aide produced a brightly colored map which cartographers had recently made.

"This is the most recent we have, Your Highness," he explained.

With the two men holding the map aloft, Philip began anew.

"Senors," Philip began, "my father attempted to teach me many lessons. Some, from his own bitter experiences, we must view with some skepticism, but others I hold to strongly. One of these is his single statement: MAKE NO SMALL PLANS. . . ."

For a moment he paused to permit his words to sink in. Then he continued:

"What has been said today and written in your papers and Velasco's is all noble and true. But I fear we are thinking too small, and this could be our undoing. For example. . . ." And he pointed to the Florida Gulf coast line. "Suppose we accept Don Luis' proposal and build a base here. What will we have accomplished? We will have moved our perimeter several hundred miles further to the north, but our control of shipping and of the land area will be incomplete."

The assembled dons furrowed brows and leaned forward.

"I say," the monarch continued, "that Velasco has proposed but half a solution. I concur that a superior harbor such as Santa Maria should be our first objective. But then, we should use that same base and same force to push across," and here he pointed carefully to Puenta de Santa Elena. ". . . to HERE, placing a second Spanish stronghold where it will dominate the entire Atlantic seaboard."

Murmurs of surprise and assent were heard. All eyes were now focused on the Cape of Storms which Allyon had described so vividly.

"With our position firmly fixed in both bodies of water and commanding both land areas, I am confident that our land and naval forces would easily discourage attempts by others. . . ."

In an instant, the room was abuzz with comment. Council members clustered about the King, poking inquiring fingers at the map, spanning distances, talking numbers, projecting requirements. For an hour the informal inquiry continued. Then Philip called for order, and the Councilmen resumed their places about the table.

"Well, gentlemen, what do you think? Is our plan too large? Can this be done?"

What followed must rank as one of the most far reaching planning conferences in the history of Western Man. In the end, their agreement included these points:

The expedition would begin by deployment of a major force from Mexico City to Santa Maria (or Ochuse as it was listed on some maps). Manpower would include between twelve hundred and fifteen hundred men, women and children, and would include at least five hundred professional men at arms, a contingent of ten men of God of the Dominican order, with the remainder to include farmers, artisans, their wives, children, and two hundred and fifty Indian and Negro slaves to assist in ways that would become obvious.

Once the initial colony was established at Ochuse, manpower would be divided. A portion would be established in the Coosa nation, some three hundred leagues from Ochuse. The remainder would march overland to Puenta de Santa Elena, where a third colony would be created. This distance, too, was estimated at three hundred leagues.

Each city would be fortified to protect its people against attack, and its buildings would include a church and such other structures as might be required to bring the message of Christ to local inhabitants.

Above all, each colony was to bring with it the skills to become quickly self-sufficient, and to make possible reasonable economic returns to the mother country.

Gentlemen entering into this company would be sent forth in search of the natural wealth of the land and opportunities for additional colonization.

And, as rapidly as possible, explorations would be sent forth to gain knowledge of the land and its endowments.

It would be days before each council member completed the logistics of his specific discipline, but before the festivities of the court convened that night, Ximinez's report to Velasco was written. Included in the concise view were these items and instructions:

"Hopefully, the project may be launched before the end of next summer. This, of course, will require substantial provisioning, both from Spain and Mexico but this should prove no barrier.

"Second, the increase in manpower beyond our original considerations will require additional vessels. I believe Adm. Sanchez will be able to provide six galleons of 150 tons or greater. You will still be responsible for the lesser craft.

"In selecting artisans and men of farm experience, I urge that you choose younger men with wives and families who will profit from the personal opportunities of colonization.

"And in preparation for work within the Indian nations or guiding our efforts inland, recruit all available men who have previously been present in La Florida. (I frankly suspect the truth of many of their tales of riches and wealthy savages; however, their experience may prove valuable.)

"Please communicate to His Excellency the Cardinal our desires that the contingent of his friars be of diligent and earnest mien prepared by temperament for difficult tasks ahead.

"Finally, give us your nominations for leadership. Because of the urgency and shortness of time, His Majesty thus far has made no suggestions."

Less than a week later this memorandum and other papers were in route to Mexico City.

His initial task complete, Ximinez smiled. Ordinarily he detested the pageantry of court function. But tonight, after so many years, it just might be enjoyable.

He called for his valet and began preparations.

At the same hour the newly assembled men of the King's bedchamber were preparing Philip for the glittering function.

In their own chambers, Don Tristan de Luna and wife reluctantly began to dress also.

Both would have preferred to spend the evening where they were.

April 19, 1558. . . . in the evening

There is something very special about a Spanish celebration. Latin people know how to play and when the ingredient of royal pageantry is injected, the result is unrivaled anywhere.

The announced return of the prince-turned-king had given the nobility of Madrid ample opportunity to prepare a suitable fiesta, and as the clock neared ten, thousands of tapers made the palace glow. Musicians and singers vied for attention among a thousand guests.

Choice food served on pure silver trays, washed down with goblets of Spain's finest wine, added a touch of gaiety. Titled ladies proudly displayed handsome figures in gowns of shimmering cloth, graced with Venetian lace; jewelry fashioned in patterns backed with heavy silver or gold hung at every bosom; the most fashionable even wore the latest popular innovation, a timepiece which hung from the neck by a tiny chain.

The men, many of whom had removed military garb just hours before, were even more brilliant than their ladies. Bright scarlet and violet tunics topped with braided lace at neck and wrists were popular. Athletic legs looked thinner in white hose, and many wore medals won as honors of combat in the wars.

Conversation in the small groups that flowed together centered upon sights and sounds to the north.

Were French women beautiful? How did they wear their hair? And what of their famed perfumes, the ladies asked.

Were you there when the French king was stricken? Was there much blood?

As the night wore on and the room grew rank with smoke of candles and the press of warm bodies, guests began to ask: where is the King?

Tristan de Luna and Valencia were pressed in the middle of the gaiety, each handsome, each tastefully dressed, each contributing pleasantly to the buzz of conversation. Both had been to the court before, of course, but as youthful functionaries with little standing. Now, as captain of the King's guard, de Luna was a tested veteran of battle as well as the New World.

For a moment they drew apart.

"How long must we stay?" Valencia whispered behind her fan.

"A decent time only after he arrives," her husband returned. "He'll be here shortly. I'd wager he'll arrive on the stroke of midnight, just for effect. Philip's an actor, among other things. . . ."

He was so right!

As the great clock in the cathedral began its stroke, three trumpeters sounded their harmony, and Philip of Spain entered the great hall, his trim figure again garbed entirely in black save for touches at the throat and wrists. He advanced twenty paces to the dais, halted, and a page sounded:

"Loyal subjects, His Most Catholic Majesty, Philip II of Spain, by the grace of God."

Throughout the hall, men dropped to one knee with heads bowed, and ladies curtsied low.

Philip, tall, spare, serene, spoke out clearly:

"Thank you, loyal friends. It is good to be home, to drink in the good air of Spain once again, to see her lovely ladies and enjoy her heady wine.

"Yes . . . it is good to be home, and to bring peace to our world, and new hope for the extension of our Lord's kingdom.

"Many here have earned your gratitude for their valor in the field. I urge that you honor them as they are justified.

"Soon there will be news of additional challenges for our beloved country, and to those who serve it. But for tonight . . . let joy and pleasure reign! Let us have music and dancing and joy. May God bless you and Spain!"

Cheers and applause swelled through the hall, and Philip, his lips parted in a rare smile, took his position to receive his subjects personally.

As the line formed, an orchestra began to play rhythmic melodies for dancing, and slowly the huge throng broke into three groups, one forming a line to greet the king, one to step lightly to the music, the third returning to the tables heavily laden with food and drink.

The receiving line moved quickly. Philip was not a wordy man at any time, and tonight his greetings were brief but cordial.

De Luna and his wife turned first to the dancers, stepping and clapping lightly to the finger-snapping rhythms. After three rounds they returned, breathless and smiling, for a tasty tidbit.

"Isn't it wonderful?" Valencia smiled. "After all these months without our men and no court . . . it's like being reborn!"

Her husband smiled. "It's good to be home, but I'd far rather spend my first night alone with you! Come on . . . the line's moving faster . . . now's our chance."

Ahead of them in the line knights and nobles introduced their ladies, exchanged a quick pleasantry with the king, then moved on. Each was pleased, for the new monarch, even with his brevity, gave promise of more warmth than his taciturn father.

Then it was the de Lunas' turn.

"Your Highness, it is my pleasure to present my lady, Senora Valencia de Luna, the light of my life."

The king bowed slightly from the waist, took her hand and pressed it to his cold lips. Looking up, he gazed into her hazel eyes with a penetrating look and smiled slightly.

"Ah, Senora, now I understand why your husband fought so valiantly! He was wise to try to shorten the war and return to you. He is indeed a fortunate man!"

Valencia blushed, bowed her head and replied softly, "Your majesty is too kind."

"Will you do me a great honor, senora?"

"If I can, your highness. . . ."

"Soon we will have greeted all our subjects. Then, will you honor me with my first dance in many months?"

"Of course, your majesty."

Taking her husband's arm, Valencia moved away, her face flushed, her hand trembling just a bit.

"He noticed ME! He asked ME for his first dance. Can you believe it?"

Her husband smiled wryly. "All of which means it may be light before we get home! I hope his feet hurt."

His hope was vain.

When the King had shaken the last hand and greeted the last subject, his eyes rose and spied out the de Lunas. Signaling with his head, the King stepped forward, and extended his hand to the lady's shapely arm. "You will excuse us, Don Tristan?" he asked.

"Of course, your Grace."

The orchestra began anew, and Philip, exhibiting surprising skill, led his partner through the intricate steps.

Back and forth they moved, slipping between the other dancers, hands and hips and heels moving in a harmony of motion. Faster and faster the music, faster moved arms and feet and legs. A glow of perspiration ringed Valencia's crown of curls; beads of sweat snaked through the channel between the king's eyes; a smile set his lips.

The music reached its climax, and with a crack of castanets came to an end. The King bowed, his partner curtsied, and he took a step forward seizing her hands. "May we repeat that rare pleasure?" he asked.

Her eyes cast down modestly, Valencia nodded slightly.

The music began again, and the dancers began a repeat of the dance. On and on they maneuvered, two thousand eyes now viewing their monarch.

The aging Admiral Sanchez sidled close to de Luna.

"Your wife is fortunate, senor; she has captivated the King. A wonderful diversion for him, of course."

"Of course!"

The rhythms of the guitars and other strings sped faster, their counterpoint adding to the excitement of the dancers. Faster! Faster they moved, until at length, as the music crescendoed and suddenly ended on an upbeat, the dancers halted, throwing heads back, faces moist with glistening sweat, breath coming in short, uneven gasps.

The audience, eyes riveted on the scene, burst into spontaneous applause, which the King, a trace of a smile showing, ultimately acknowledged with a slight bow. Two thousand hands clapped all the louder.

"Senora, this has been a moment to remember," he said, reaching for her hand and bringing it to his lips.

The applause began again.

Valencia de Luna, her poise unshattered by a sudden appearance in the spotlight of her world, dipped low in acknowledgement, and behind her fan, whispered, "Thank you, thank you so much!"

No one in the great hall applauded louder or longer than Don Tristan.

Murmured a friend, "You are a lucky man, indeed, Senor!"

"And I know it!" de Luna replied.

Hours later, lying naked beneath the sheets of their canopied, high poster bed, the anticipation of two years absence momentarily satisfied, the de Lunas lay locked in each other's arms, her long black hair trailing over his cheek and tickling his nose.

"Sometimes . . . sometimes I told myself that I was wrong . . . loving you could not have been so perfect," he murmured.

"I think you missed me, at least a little," she teased.

"A little? I'll show you again!"

And he did.

Later, as the first rosy rays of the Spanish dawn crept into their room, Valencia lay awake, half watching the deep, even breathing of her slumbering husband, admiring him, loving him . . . still aglow from the events of the past night. Imagine! She . . . the dancing partner of the King! Not once . . . but several times. And the people . . . how they enjoyed it . . . and the compliments they paid her. It was good having a husband in the King's favor!

Her husband, sleeping the sleep of the totally exhausted, had no dreams. For him, everything good was coming true.

Or so he thought.

Ximinez . . . counselor to Spain's Phillip II.

Mexico City July 2, 1558

Juan Ceron had always been considered an energetic man. His whole career had been built upon accomplishment, as a soldier, an administrator, a builder of cities.

But he had never worked so hard or so long as during these past weeks.

Great God, HERE was the chance he had dreamed of all his life! With luck his would become a name greater than Cortes, than Pizarro! If only half . . . or, only one quarter . . . of the legends of La Florida were true, his name would be linked with the greatest glories of Spain!

The planning was moving at full speed now, after months of endless waiting.

But at first? Holy Mother, it had seemed at first that the viceroy's message must have been swallowed by the sea! Both had agreed that Ximinez must have ignored them.

But then it had come, the signal to prepare, to organize for an expedition to defend against the intrusion of the heretics!

The small, wiry soldier put down his quill and casually wiped the sweat from his forehead. His candle flickered idly, casting its weak, wavering light across the supply list he was checking.

Manning the expedition was proving no problem. Ever since that rogue Cabeza de Vaca had staggered back, more dead than alive, his tales of streams studded with golden stones and red men as rich as Croesus had excited the blood of those who now found Mexico and its problems routine.

The man who has little finds little glory even in the midst of plenty if he sees no share for himself.

La Florida and the world to the north were another matter. Scores of soldiers and armorers heard the news of the new colony and stepped forward at once. Others—the small farmers, the untitled, men with Indian wives and growing families—saw this as a chance to carve out fortunes in land.

The clergy . . . ah . . . the clergy became more excited by the day for the more the plans were discussed in home, tavern or churchyard, the more the prospects ballooned! The men of God could already hear the choirs singing sweetly in cathedrals that existed only in their minds . . . and a keen Spanish nose could even detect the aroma of incense rising on the salt Gulf breeze.

Ceron smiled . . . then returned to his lists. There was much to do! Of course, no specific dates had been confirmed yet. But this was certain; the voyage to the northern continent would begin the next summer. And with a fleet involved, no one wished to tempt fate by sailing into the season of hurricanes.

The veteran soldier halted once more and rested his chin in his hands. JUAN CERON, CONQUISTADORE! The man who preserved all of the northern continent for king and country! It had a good ring. Fate was treating him well.

Ceron, the professional soldier, the man of action, the confidant of the viceroy! From the first, it had been taken for granted that he would lead the expedition. There was no one else to be even considered.

MADRID
April 20, 1558

Philip of Spain, unlike his father, was never a man who indulged himself to excess. When there was wine to be drunk, he sipped it. When fine food was served (as it was during every meal in his household), he nibbled at it unemotionally. His appetites with women, sport, even work, were well controlled.

Thus, when he dropped his long legs to the floor from his bed the morning after the triumphal ball marking his victorious return, the king was clear of head and steady of hand.

The servants of his bedchamber, most of whom did not share their king's composure that morning, leaped to assist him. After a spartan breakfast of the juice of oranges and Spanish bread, he hurried to his desk to begin the Herculean task of trying to make heads or tails of a backlog of work that had been building for half a decade.

Painstaking secretaries had made lists, and advisors prepared to carry out his assignments. The problems were huge! The treasury was nearly bare, despite regular arrival of treasure ships from the New World. Taxes were too high, local revenues too low. And petitioners were everywhere! For years now, appointments of every kind had awaited his royal approval; only the most exceptional items had been forwarded to him in the field. Now he must put youth, England and the recent wars behind him. Now he must begin building the future empire of Spain.

Philip worked deliberately for an hour, assigning this noble to a council, approving that loyal follower's use of royal lands. It was all routine. Then, promptly at ten, as though he operated by clockwork, Ximinez arrived and took his place at the King's right hand.

"Your majesty rested well?" he inquired.

"Very well, thank you. And yourself?"

"I slept like a boy!" the diplomat replied. "Well, I see that you have an early start. Where have you begun?"

"Oh, on routine items, mostly things I could do without you. But now that you're here, first things first."

"Which means?"

"Where do things stand on the expedition?"

"After yesterday's meeting, you mean? Well, I've begun the follow-up with the admiral. He will have six vessels available by the end of August."

"Excellent!"

"The armorers are collecting weapons surplus from the men who returned yesterday and will restore them."

"You have been busy!"

"Food is a problem, of course, at this season."

"Can we make do?"

"I think so. Don Bernardo has begun a survey. We'll have more on that tomorrow."

"You say that Velasco had been planning in terms of six or seven vessels?"

"Approximately."

"Will he have enough manpower, then?"

"That's questionable. Besides, we don't want to rob ourselves in Mexico. We're a long way from being out of the woods there yet."

"Of course. Then . . . we'll need men for all assignments . . . soldiers, farmers, artisans. . . ?"

"Men and women; I think we should make provision for full families of gentry to assure lasting leadership."

"And the church?"

"I don't know . . . we're checking that. We may want to ask the Pope to nominate a few people, too. It won't hurt to give him some feeling of participation."

The king nodded.

"Good thought, I'll dictate a letter shortly."

A pad at his elbow, the King had been making brief notes as his secretary of state rattled off answers to the flow of questions. What a jewel Ximinez was! His mind was everywhere, his ideas a step ahead, always well organized.

Philip looked up, his eyes staring absently across the room.

"Ximinez, there's one key question we haven't even discussed, even in the council meeting, though I'd have thought there would have been a hundred suggestions."

"What point is that, your majesty?"

"Who is to lead this expedition? After all, if we enjoy the success I foresee, someone is going to become very rich and rather famous, don't you agree?"

"Velasco has nominated his associate, Juan Ceron, you know."

"Yes, I remember his recommendation. I don't know Ceron, do you?"

"Not personally."

"His record is good?"

"It appears to be . . . courageous, loyal, a true son of the church. He's a good man, the kind of adventurous soul that gave us Mexico and Peru."

"And his family?"

"No noble ranking, I'm relatively sure of that."

"In other words, he went to Mexico . . .?"

"Like so many others, he went either to make his fortune or to escape his past."

Again Philip lapsed into silence. As he leaned beard and pointed chin onto tightly clasped hands, his eyes partly closed and his stare through slit lids focused far in the distance. Behind him, several quills scratched noisily as clerks transcribed earlier decisions.

"Ximinez," he began again, "I believe as my father did that men should be rewarded for loyal service. Do you agree?"

"Certainly, sire."

"Then, would you not say that a man who served his country and king with distinction in the recent wars . . . and who understands life in the New World . . . might well be rewarded with the leadership of this expedition?"

"Well, yes, I should say so," the diplomat answered cautiously. "Of course, the latter point is most important. Building two or three cities, pacifying Indians and perhaps being involved with the armed forces of two unfriendly powers is going to require no little expertise."

"Precisely!" Philip replied. "That's why I cannot believe this Ceron is our man. He has the abilities of a street fighter, not a strategist or diplomat. No . . . I can't see him. What we need is a man proven in battle . . . a man with family background . . . a churchman . . . yet a man with experience in America."

"Is there such a man who can be prepared so quickly?" Ximinez querried.

"I think so," the King answered.

"May I ask . . .?"

"I believe that almost everyone would be pleased if we nominated Don Tristan de Luna."

Ximinez sucked in his breath. De Luna? De Luna? Well . . . why not? Checking off the requirements, he met them all . . . fine family, good military record, devoted to the church, years in Mexico and North America, loyal to his king.

"I think the choice would be brilliant, your Majesty!" he answered. "But what about Ceron? After all, we can be sure Velasco's already given him assurance that the job will be his."

"I've thought of that," the monarch responded. "We'll name him Master of the Camp, and leave him as governor at Santa Maria when the second phase moves to Santa Elena. This way he will have his command, his promotion, and his chance to retire a rich man."

"Your Majesty thinks of everything!"

"You will prepare the papers, then, suggesting de Luna's nomination to the Council?"

"Of course."

"I suggest that you do so this morning, before others begin flooding me with suggestions that might prove . . . ah . . . embarrassing."

"I'll prepare the document at once."

"Come back when you've finished. There's a lot to do here."

Ximinez walked out of the King's workroom and into his own where three clerks awaited his pleasures. Soon, quills were scratching, and within the hour de Luna's nomination was enroute to the councilmen.

De Luna, his energies robbed by war and long hours of love, lay peacefully in his bed. Innocent of intrigue, unaware of the King's thoughts or motives, the young nobleman slept on.

April 25, 1558

The announcement that Don Tristan de Luna would head the expedition to La Florida met with mixed emotions from the Council. As might be expected, several members had quietly planned their own nominations, including Don Angel Villafane, the journeyman among the current explorers. Villafane had served in Peru and Mexico, had met with favor at the Court of Charles V, and was well respected by the church fathers.

But Villafane was not in high favor with the viceroy. Past correspondence had illustrated that and so his name was mentioned, then relegated to the list of "possible selections."

Adm. Sanchez had his favorite, of course: a son-in-law, ready to make his mark.

And there were others, although no Council member had time to develop a campaign for a favorite before the King made his announcement. After that, there were moments of pause for reflection, then a gradual nodding of heads in agreement.

Ximinez had misgivings about the young Don's diplomatic acumen, but he could not argue with the soldier's other abilities.

"And he has a delightful wife who will remain at home and at court for several years," he mused. "Why not?"

The grizzled diplomat quietly ignored the glowing reports from Velasco about Ceron. "Everything in good time," he thought. "We will find a suitable reward for Sr. Ceron."

The conference between the King, Ximinez and de Luna was brief, and for the young officer, a moment of highest excitement. The King called for the meeting and wasted no time in coming to the point.

"You have heard of the plans for new colonies in the northern continent?" he asked.

"I have, your Majesty."

"You understand our objectives?"

"I believe so, sire."

"You have ridden with me this past year and served well. You are a man I know I can trust."

"Your majesty is most kind."

"Therefore, I am nominating you to serve as captain-general of the expedition. Will you serve Spain and me?"

De Luna hesitated only a moment.

"Your majesty does me great honor. If I am worthy, I accept with gratitude and humility."

"Each man in our time seeks to build a great estate for his family, and to serve God and country. Hopefully, this will afford you such an opportunity. I have watched you perform as a soldier and a King's man. What you have done will make your father proud. This is why I nominate you."

(This and the fact that you have an alluring wife, Ximinez thought to himself.)

"I pledge my best effort and my honor, Majesty," de Luna said.

"Go with God," the King replied. "I will have your appointment confirmed tomorrow. Then, I suggest you begin at once the planning of men and provisions. I would like to have your fleet leave Spain in mid-summer. This will allow eight months of preparation in Mexico before you depart."

"I understand," the young knight replied.

After de Luna's departure, the King glanced at his diplomat. "Well?" he asked.

"He will do as well as many, and better than most," he shrugged.

"So be it," the King added.

De Luna, wearing a smile that stretched beard and mustache, swept through the door and confronted his wife, whose hands played with needlework.

"You will never believe our good fortune!" he began, and then with a torrent of words he overwhelmed his young wife with a glowing account of his interview with the King. "It will take a year, of course, perhaps more, but in that time our fortune will be assured and our fame honestly earned. We are lucky indeed, you and I. . . ."

The young wife listened to her husband's tale without replying, her gaze upon the stitching in her lap. She had been without a husband for two years . . . and now, after a matter of hours, he was planning still another crusade, this time on a foreign shore for God knew how long! Was this what marriage meant? Tears coursed down her cheeks, and soft sobs shook her delicate shoulders.

Slowly, the tear-filled eyes rose, and looked into his face. "Of course, you know what is best, my darling, and what each of us must do for the glory of God. We are young, and the days will pass quickly. Then, perhaps, when your name is linked with Cortes, you'll be with me always. . . ."

She took his battle-hardened hand and pressed it to her cheek. Softly, salty tears streamed onto his fingers. Slowly, he drew her to him. In the excitement of his appointment he had scarcely thought of his wife. And what a woman she was!

But then . . . perhaps such an opportunity would never come again.

Tristan de Luna was a product of Spain's golden age, a man born at the right time to perform courageous acts, to fight the heresy of Luther, to extend his country's flag on the shores claimed by Columbus a half century before.

He had been born in 1517, the youngest son of a family dedicated to the ideals which had surfaced so strongly under Ferdinand and Isabella. His mother had been his early tutor, teaching him letters, reading the legends of old Spain and initiating his studies in religion.

At seven he had entered the school operated by Dominican Friars in the hamlet included in the recently gained family lands. At twelve, he enjoyed the first two years of fragmented studies, first in Seville, then in Madrid.

From the time he was able to walk young Tristan followed his father and older brother Pedro about the estates, mimicking their antics in supervising the tenants, and worshiping the father's actions in the study of arms.

At six he was given his own small bow, and at nine he was studying fencing and swordsmanship under the skilled tutelage of a dueling master.

Almost before he could walk, the young scion of the de Luna estates would ride out behind his father, gripping him about the waist astride the spirited horse the elder de Luna had won in the field. By the time he entered his teens young Tristan was skilled in horsemanship and had been given long, grueling training in the rigors of military life.

At 16 he was commissioned in the king's horse and saw brief action for Charles V in the religious wars against the German princes.

At 24 he enlisted for service in America, spending four years in the endless campaigns to subdue those few redmen who fought withdrawing actions against the forces of Spain in northern Mexico. Then came his service in the arm of Coronado, wandering in the wilderness, seeking fabled cities of gold. At one time he was in command of a contingent and served ably. His rank, Master of the Camp, indicated his success in the field.

In Mexico and then with Coronado he learned the local languages, the customs, the problems of loneliness and command. As a soldier he was respected by his men, and learned to honor certain abilities of the Indians employed as guides and in a few instances where tribal enmities permitted, as combat troops.

Naturally curious, the young officer had spent many evening hours with the friars at Mexico City's cathedral, studying their works and the charts and records they supervised for the viceroy. In there, he worked quietly, unobtrusively, without apparent objectives; he made numerous friends and no enemies. It was during this time also that he married the widowed Isabel, sired two children, then became a widower (and a rich one in the bargain).

When he returned to Spain, his arrival came at the opportune moment to further his military career. War with France had begun, and the Emperor Charles sought enlistment of able and experienced knights. Philip was in England as the husband of Mary, and the opportunity for service on foreign soil in the mounted corps held great promise.

It was during one brief furlough from the service in the Low Countries that his marriage to Valencia was consummated.

The courtship and marriage to Valencia had followed a due process. The two families were deeply entwined in the affairs of Borobia, and the marriage of the rising Don and the 22-year-old maiden had been arranged with amazing ease. Despite their few short weeks together between campaigns, they were a well adjusted, happy pair and soon were deliriously in love, and secure in their belief in the future.

The family holdings, skillfully assembled by the senior de Luna and now administered by his first son, Pedro, were neither large nor wealthy, but the estate was well organized. It soon would provide the ideal retreat for a successful knight-adventurer.

Tristan de Luna was a student of his times. He had read and re-read the accounts of de Soto, de Narvaez and de Leon; he had cast aside literal belief in golden cities or fabled empires waiting for conquest. But he was realist enough to recognize what discovery and conquering of another Peru or Mexico would mean to King and country.

Time away from a beautiful young wife was not a pleasant prospect. But he was a worthy citizen of Spain in 1558. He saw duty and opportunity, and he was prepared to accept them both.

Mexico City
July 23, 1558

Ximinez's first letter, dispatched to the viceroy following the meeting of the Council at which agreement had been reached to proceed with an enlarged expedition, reached Velasco after a record crossing by the galleon Santa Maria. Recognizing the urgency of the diplomat's seal, the commandant at Vera Cruz dispatched a post rider immediately, hurrying the message to Mexico City.

The rider arrived late in the afternoon; the hot rays of the sun had kept most men indoors, and Velasco, his volume of paper work mounting, was bent over his huge table, a pitcher at arm's length and his cup glistening with a dew-like gloss at his elbow.

Arrival of the special pouch, sealed with the ornate wax closure of Ximinez's office, raised the viceroy from his chair; with brief thanks to the courier, he carefully undid the wrappings and withdrew the contents. The message was surprisingly brief, authored before the beginning of work on the gathering of stores and nomination of people.

His eyes quickly scanned the page; as he read, his eyes widened. The response was incredible! As the impact began to be felt, he returned to the beginning. THREE colonies! Unbelievable! Thirteen ships, a strong deterrent in Gulf and Atlantic! Approval to begin organization at once . . . Velasco could hardly believe his good fortune! Great God! There was so much to do.

He seized the hand bell on his desk and rang for his clerk.

"I must get word at once to Fray Domingo and Captain Ceron. Tell them the word has come from the King, and that I hope that they can do me the honor of dining with me this evening, say . . . nine o'clock. Oh . . . and tell each one that the news is good . . . very good."

"Yes, Excellency," the man replied and scurried away.

Velasco, his eyes focused on some far away scene, sank deep into his chair to reassemble his thoughts. Several times since his arrival he had assembled expeditions to secure areas to the north and southeast. None, however, had resembled the dynamics this venture would demand. Item by item, he began to fix the specifics in his mind. Back of it all lay the thought of what success might bring . . . to Spain . . . and to the house of Velasco.

The supper that night was delightful, even broader in scope than the food-loving viceroy usually enjoyed. But the three men scarcely noticed the tastefully prepared fish and fowl.

The friar, bustling over his prized charts and lists of his worthy men of God, was as seized with the project as the viceroy.

And Ceron, seeing himself as the leader of the greatest expedition of modern times, became more enthusiastic with each item they discussed.

When they adjourned at midnight, many more primary decisions had been made, and responsibilities had been assigned. By tomorrow word would be broadcast throughout Mexico City of the great plan, and men tentatively selected would be contacted. Meanwhile, notices would be posted for peasant families, artisans and private soldiers; and stores gathering would begin. No date had been formalized for departure, but Ximinez left little doubt that the King wished the first stages of the venture underway at once.

As they departed, Ceron commented:

"This is a dream! I can hardly believe my good fortune."

"Go with God, my friend, and thank Him for His blessings," the friar replied. "He gives each the assignment which His divine plan has devised. Never forget that!"

Velasco nodded assent.

The plan, now much broadened at the King's initiative, posed great promise for them all. Each strode to his bed grateful for this turn of events.

PARIS
July 24, 1558

The months following Henry Valois' death had been filled with near panic for his widow. The monarchy, so stable and strong under the dead king, now seemed unable to make decisions, or to cope with growing internal divisions. Now plots were rumored almost daily, and growing tensions between Catholic and Protestant threatened civil war.

Catherine, an able daughter of the Medicis, was beseiged by advisors as she acted as regent for her son. Advice flowed like water, much of it tainted by the obvious self-serving objectives of even her own dead husband's family.

Thus on July 24, her head swimming with reports of plots and counter-plots, the queen mother sent a brief note to the Paris residence of Gaspard de Coligny, the able admiral who was to her the most trustworthy of the Protestant heretics.

His response was prompt and gracious.

The two were seated in an ante-room of her personal chamber; the Queen provided brief refreshments, then came quickly to the point.

"Dear admiral, we . . . you and I . . . must act responsibly for two points of view that threaten all of France. . . ."

"Your majesty refers to . . .?"

"To the religious problem, of course."

"Of course."

"You are as aware as I of what is happening."

"I believe so."

"Do you not agree that to continue as we are threatens violence . . . perhaps anarchy?"

"Not of my choosing, your grace!"

"I do not suggest this. But between your clergy and the priests of the Holy Church the people are being stirred violently."

"What relief does your Majesty suggest?"

"A diversion."

"A . . . diversion?"

"At least that is what it would be as a beginning. Later, I believe it would become a point of national pride and accomplishment."

"And the proposal is . . .?"

"I propose that my government help to underwrite a series of colonies in the New World . . . and that the leadership and manpower (and some of the financing) be supplied by your people."

Coligny was caught up short!

"You mean . . . Canada . . . a frozen wilderness . . .?"

"No, no! Far to the south, below what is called the Cape of Storms. . . ."

"The Spanish claim this!"

"A fragile claim at best. Two years ago my husband sent three expeditions to those waters. Two returned, with glowing reports. The climate is temperate, the land fair, the savages few and peaceful. There are rivers teeming with fish, and fruits the like of which do not exist in all of France."

"And you are proposing . . .?"

"I suggest that you and I jointly announce this effort. The cost will be shared by the crown."

"Including the vessels and armament for defense?" Coligny interjected.

"Including food, articles for homes, all that will be required for 200 souls in a first sailing, followed by 200 more one year later. After this, you and I with our advisors will reassess the needs."

Coligny hesitated. The offer was so unexpected, the opportunity so exciting that it might at least ease the enmity between the rival religious groups.

"May I discuss this with my associates?" he began, "I am charmed by the prospect . . . but they must confer upon it, of course."

"Certainly," the Queen responded. "There is much to decide if we are to proceed. Suppose we meet again . . . say . . . in one week?"

Coligny nodded, rose, and took his leave.

Catherine, alone, smiled to herself. "The old fox has taken the bait! Now, if only the others will agree." At one stroke she might be rid of this thorn in her flesh and provide also a concern for Philip. How could she lose?

MADRID
August 1, 1558

The Spanish people have a reputation for procrastination, sometimes deserved. But pursuit of preparations for departure of the de Luna expedition from Cadiz would have done credit to the most energetic citizenry.

Despite its efforts to fight a major war and supply its American colonies, the nation's bureaucracy was remarkably able. Each council member wielded substantial power, especially in the king's absence, and with hostilities now ended and the provender for a 60,000 man army returned to stores, it was not difficult to find the vessels and generate the military force which the mother country was to provide.

Finding six suitable ships proved easy. Adm. Sanchez chose to equip a fleet for the transport of large numbers including horses and supplies, reasoning that the expedition would encounter no naval opposition. The vessels included two galleons, with their high platformed sterncastles and 52 guns, and five wide, roomy East India type merchantmen, of the type designed and preferred by the Portuguese. These broad vessels, which rode deep in the water, were armed to ward off Barbary pirates and corsairs; hence while they could not rival the fire power of the heavy, higher galleons, they were formidable in a line fight, and more maneuverable. Counting use of the several decks, each had a capacity of up to 150 men, including normal gear. Horses would be carried in the deep hold.

To lead the naval force Sanchez chose Adm. Gomez Arias. Arias had held a command 18 years before in the fleet of Diego Maldonado which had anchored in the harbor of Santa Maria to rendezvous with the forces of de Soto, a meeting which never took place.

Arias, a seasoned sailor, was a wise choice, an able seaman used to command and well acquainted with the waters of La Florida.

The armory, under Don Juan de Fernandez, issued arms recently returned by troops who had marched home with Philip. Here the experience of de Luna came quickly into play, for he knew the value of light armor in America as opposed to the heavier plate employed on the field in Europe.

For his officers, the captain-general chose peaked helmets, with a light breast plate which fitted from navel to shoulder and gave adequate protection from weapons used at long distance by the Indians. Other uniform items were the responsibility of the officers and men themselves, except that a large supply of cowhide boots was requisitioned for foot soldiers, and extra pairs of long boots were drawn for horsemen.

Discussions on the actual complement of the army lasted for weeks. From Muscoso's report of de Soto expedition survivors and the much quoted tales of Alvar Nunar Cabeza de Vaca, who had literally walked back to Mexico from the de Narvaez failure, Ximinez was convinced that the land at Santa Maria must be very fertile. He reasoned that in the first stages the expedition might obtain extra foodstuffs from the Indians at Coosa, who de Soto's captain described as hospitable and 'most civilized.' This point was critical, for if the need for farmers and other artisans was reduced in the original sailing, the military strength of the two proposed colonies would be all the greater.

De Luna was not so confident as Ximinez. He had viewed the impressive works of the Aztecs and read the reports of journeys into La Florida. He had also seen the less able civilizations of the Southwest. No one had returned with actual evidence of a superior inland civilization in La Florida, and without a proven food supply a summer landing could leave the force in difficulty and perhaps delay the second colony by a year, waiting for crops to mature. Counting on supply traded from Indians was risky, he said. Better to carry extra farmers and slaves to aid them than risk the danger of food shortages, he argued.

The Councilmen finally compromised on a plan to man the expedition with 550 soldiers (including 300 foot and 250 to horse), plus 200 men experienced in farming and crafts. The latter would include families and would be enrolled by Don Luis de Velasco's lieutenant in Mexico.

Once the decisions were made, the act of composing the force was pushed forward with surprising speed. De Luna and Valencia remained in Madrid during the recruiting and enlistment of officers and men, and the first assembly of stores. Then they moved to Cadiz where he, together with Arias, supervised the loading.

In all, slightly over 200 men were drawn from Spain herself, the balance of the force to be enlisted in Mexico. Considering the speed with which decisions were made and manpower selected, preparations were little short of miraculous.

Two days before his departure for the seaport, de Luna had a final interview with the King. The two met in the monarch's workrooms, surrounded by charts and lists which Philip had prepared in duplicate.

The conversation dealt mostly with a final view of logistics, the King much concerned for the safety and comfort of his people. Repeatedly, he made known his view that these would become 'cities of substance, extending the glory of God and Spain into the New World. . . .'

Then he came to a final item in intelligence.

"Ximinez is a master at obtaining information from among our . . . ah . . . our neighboring kingdoms."

De Luna nodded. The King continued:

"We've learned that Queen Catherine has proposed to Coligny that his Huguenots become the thrust for settlement in the New World. We lack full details, of course, but we believe that their plan would have the admiral's people attempt a settlement on the coast of the South Atlantic. . . ."

De Luna gasped. . . .

". . . in somewhat the same longitude as our own proposed second city . . . probably south of Puenta de Santa Elena."

Don Tristan interrupted, "Have we any advice on the timing? How rapidly can they move?"

"Unfortunately, we lack this intelligence. So far as we know, this is still just a proposal from the Queen."

"How does this affect our plans?"

"Not at all, save to emphasize the speed with which your force must meet its schedule. You can see that we must build the eastern stronghold as quickly as possible."

Conversation continued on this subject, but there was little of value either could add. The knowledge that Catherine was urging a solution to her religious problems through outward settlement reaffirmed the thinking of the court for years back. The answer to the threat was speed and force. The King concluded:

"And remember always that you act for the Holy Church. Catherine insults us by offering heretics as our opponents. In any encounter, offer no quarter, accept no compromise. Do you understand?"

"I do, your Majesty."

With that, Philip reached into the depths of his table and withdrew a heavy leather pouch, boldly emblazened with the King's arms. From it, he took a heavy, rolled scroll, and handed it to Don Tristan.

"Please read this. It is your commission. Read it, then I'll have it sealed for your delivery of it to Don Luis. In it, you'll find confirmation of our plans, and most of all, your authority as captain-general. Also set forth are the obligations we have established for the viceroy."

Don Tristan read the closely written script, then read it a second time, pausing to grasp the full meaning of his own commission. Everything the king had promised was in order: full leadership authority, grants of land, a percentage of the earnings of the colonies and of riches gleaned from native sources. He returned the document to the king.

"You agree with the content?" the King questioned.

"I do, your majesty."

"Then go with God! May the blessings of our Lord travel with you. And go without fear. Your house and family will be under my protection while you are absent."

"Your majesty is good to me!"

"I expect great things from you."

The King replaced the scroll in its pouch, personally affixed his royal seal, handed the document to his agent.

De Luna rose, bowed deeply, and backed from the chamber. Once outside the ornate rooms, he paused, drawing a great breath, and a broad smile spread across his face. He hurried to his house, quickly completed his affairs, and with his wife began preparations for the hasty, dusty trip to Cadiz.

The great adventure was beginning.

A LIEUTENANT IS CHOSEN

My uncle and I had not been what one would call close. How could we have been? Our homes were separated by 50 leagues, and he had served in the New World and in the field with King Charles.

But these past months we had drawn close together in the wars, and through his good offices my career had prospered. Not that he treated others unfairly to my advantage! He wasn't like that. But my introduction to general officers and even to Philip himself as the nephew of Don Tristan de Luna did not hurt me, and I can say without boast that I served well if not with distinction.

When we returned to Madrid I strutted about in my colorful tunic as other officers did, a subject of adoration by the ladies, a man of leisure with long-due pay and allowances finally remitted by His Majesty's paymaster.

The days rolled one upon the other without pattern or purpose, and I was about to quit the pleasures of the capital for resumption of family affairs in Barobia when I received an invitation to wait upon my uncle in his apartments. Naturally, I responded.

After customary amenities, he came directly to the point.

"You have heard of my new assignment?" he asked.

"Who has not? You must be very proud."

"Honored, nephew, honored. It is a great obligation, and an opportunity without equal. When we've completed our assignments those who have served will be well rewarded. Many will become nobles in a great new land."

Then he outlined in full the grand strategy which he would execute.

"You have a great opportunity, uncle!"

"I believe in it . . . as I believe in Spain's destiny to rule the world. That's why I have pledged my fortune to its success!"

"You have pledged . . .?"

"Yes . . . you know that my brother Pedro is getting old. In fact, he will be seventy next year. With his health failing the family inheritance will shortly be mine. Besides, my holdings in Mexico from my last expedition are considerable."

"Not to mention the money your wife left you, eh? But what have you pledged for the expedition . . . I know enough of the King to know he lets no one ride free."

"How right you are! Philip has offered to provide 300,000 pesos from the treasury if I provide 100,000. I'll mortgage my Mexican properties to him, and he will pay me 8,000 pesos per year for my services."

"But what about uniforms and weapons?" I asked.

"Officers raising troops will provide this, and the church will pay for its servants," he replied. "On the whole not a bad arrangement when you consider what is to be gained."

"And exactly what is that?" I asked.

"I've been promised one-fourth of the returns from the colony and the appointment as Governor of La Florida. The King's appointment as governor of La Florida is perhaps the greatest chance for riches any man could dream of. Have you read the accounts?"

"I have seen what was written by Cabeza de Vaca and some tales of . . . what was his name . . . de Soto, Hernando de Soto? But that's all."

For the next hour my uncle regaled me with details of the fabulous continent on which Spanish rule and the message of the Holy Church was to be established. The lands were rich and fertile, and the Indians numerous and amenable to the teachings of the Faith. Above all, there would be opportunities to exploit great mines of gold controlled by the savages at Coosa, where de Soto had wintered, and to build estates whose size would dwarf even the holdings of the Emperor!

As he spoke, Don Tristan's eyes glowed, and his face took on the appearance of a man whose entire spirit had been inspired. Then he came quickly to the point. "Come with me, Cristobal! Join me in America. I have the opportunity to enroll many of my own officers; old del Sauz will be our sergeant-major, and you know him! Nieto is coming, and Pedro de Acuna, of the King's Horse. I have a captain's billet for you . . . and the promise of both service and adventure. It is a chance to become rich as Croesus. Will you come?"

To young men of my generation, adventure was life's paramount motivation. To serve Philip and Spain would have been enough. They could not have held me back! To serve God also! Ah . . . and perhaps to build the fortune of my house . . . that was too great a dream! I accepted on the spot.

"Uncle, how can I thank you? What an opportunity for me! What an adventure! To tell you the truth, uncle," I confided, "I haven't quite known what to do since we returned from the wars. I mean I enjoy the women and good drink as much as anyone I know, but even I was growing a bit weary of such constant pleasure. And now this! I can hardly wait. I have no strings to tie me here . . . and think of the riches that can be mine . . . ours . . . oh, you know. . . ."

Immediately Don Tristan thrust upon me lists and assignments which occupied my hours day and night. Quickly I got in touch with the other officers whom I knew, and we began to plan what items must be carried by an officer and gentleman.

There was scarcely time enough for a visit to my family; they too were delighted that Don Tristan would offer me his commission. By now talk filled all of Spain about the expedition. And I was to part of it!

How well I can remember the excitement I felt as plans for the expedition grew and were put into action. Here, of course, I became directly involved in the events of which I write. Looking back from this distance in time, I hope I can speak without bias of the actions of my uncle and myself, as well as those who influenced us both near and far. I have tried to fit the pieces of information together as they happened, though some things I did not learn until much later as I searched for answers to many unsolved puzzles. But let the reader judge for himself how successful I have been, for now I am an old man.

Then . . . oh, then I was a young man filled with excitement as the day for our departure approached.

CADIZ
August 22, 1558

The dockside at Cadiz was alive with activity, lined with carts and wagons whose mounds of barrels and chests were quickly swallowed into the deep holds of the six ships. Longshoremen sweated mightily as they strained over blocks and tackle, hoisting cargo high into the air, then down below decks where waiting comrades carefully stowed it according to the plans mapped by Arias and his subordinates.

In campsites nearby, men at arms lounged lazily awaiting orders to embark. We officers spent much of our time in the local wineshops or in conversation with ladies who vied with one another to entertain the exciting conquistadores bound for adventure in the New World.

Don Tristan and Valencia enjoyed a pleasant apartment close to the sea; his schedule was torturous, but he returned each evening to savor a few precious hours with his wife. Together, they shared dreams of what must come in their future, of the life of tomorrow in Seria and Barobia on estates much expanded by wealth earned by his adventures.

By day he labored among his captains, six of whom now were assembled, four of horse and two of foot, all seasoned veterans, but none with experience in America.

Included were Alonsode Castilla who had served both in Italy and the Low Countries, an able horseman and respected commander; Balthazar de Sotelo, a tall, thin, morose man with a livid scar meandering across his left cheek who had also served the King in the north; Juan Xaramillo, like Don Tristan a native of Aragon, and a nobleman, one whose house had fallen on bad times and who had turned to the sword to recoup his fortunes; and Gonzalo Sanchez de Aguilar, short, stocky, a happy-go-lucky sort of man with a great sense of humor, a man who looked strangely out of place on his great mount but who owned a deserved reputation for valor.

The foot captains were both Castillians, younger men of good family who had volunteered for the King's service in 1556 and had acquitted themselves well. They were Antonio Artiz de Matienzo and Rodrigo Vazquez, each quiet, resourceful, able in the camp, each a proven leader of men in the field.

De Luna had known them all during these past few years. His own solid reputation had earned him their good will, and his selection as captain-general had encouraged the two foot captains to volunteer for the mission.

Now, in the waning hours before departure they became a team, assigning troops to transports, carefully inventorying stores for use en route, and checking the huge quantities which would accompany them onward from Vera Cruz or San Juan de Ulua to Santa Maria.

Target day for sailing was September 4th. Four days before, the council of captains met, as they did daily, compared notes with the progress of Adm. Arias, and agreed that we would depart with the appropriate tide on September 3rd. Word swept through the town, for the departure of such a fleet was the signal for celebration.

The church announced a solemn high mass for 6:00 A.M.

September 3rd dawned fair. As the first rays of golden sunlight added their sparkle to the swell of the bay, more than 1000 worshipers were on their knees in the ancient church, offering up prayers for safe deliverance of the men.

In a front pew the de Lunas, dressed in somber finery, knelt together, hands clasped on the back of the rail, their bodies touching in a final intimacy. In front of them priests intoned the ritual of the mass, the soft spicy aroma of incense wafting through the musty air of the high vaulted house of worship.

A final sound of the tinkling bell signaled the end of the service, and as a youthful choir sang a sweet postlude, we all rose and silently began our exit, each one of us closeted with his own thoughts . . . of fame and fortune, glory and honor . . . and in a few cases, perhaps, death.

Outside, we milled among a crowd of well wishers, townsmen, friends, family, the curious . . . each present to enjoy the holiday atmosphere. Vendors shouted their wares . . . food morsels and drink, even religious charms. Women clung to men, and throngs of children alternately cheered and cried.

As we reached the dockside we could perceive shouting and swearing as sweating longshoremen completed the task of loading 120 horses aboard vessels which swayed gently in the soft sea.

Then, suddenly, what had been a disorganized pageant became a military operation. A trumpet sounded, and each captain called his command to assemble. Noncommissioned officers shouted smartly, urging troopers into rows, as corporals began checks of the roll. Drummers beat a cadence, and one by one seasoned soldiers trooped aboard the waiting vessels. De Luna, as captain-general, stood back, carefully noting the precision of movement.

He stepped to his wife's side, took her shoulders and held her at arm's length, then crushed her against him.

"Be patient, my love, the months will pass swiftly and when I return, the world will be ours. . . ."

Valencia, tears streaming freely from her deep, dark eyes, smiled wanly and clung to him. She nodded.

"I know my darling, I know. Do what you must do. Go with God!"

He kissed her, long and hard, then, with no further words, ran with long strides to his ship and up the swaying gangway. We were on our way.

THE VOYAGE

The voyage from Cadiz to Vera Cruz was one of the truly relaxing moments of my young life. The weather was warm and relatively calm, and our quarters, though restricted, were reasonably comfortable. During the trip I had my first real opportunity to know my uncle. Each morning Don Tristan followed a precise ritual which emphasized his methodical nature. Mass was said after sunup, followed by a frugal meal. Then he closeted himself for two to three hours, studying and rereading every scrap of writing he had been able to find dealing with La Florida. Maps drawn by scholars were screened repeatedly, as were the writings of Cabeza de Vaca and Capt. Maldonado, who had anchored his fleet in the harbor where we were to begin our efforts. There were accounts also transcribed from those who returned as survivors of the de Soto expedition and writings from the captains of other vessels which had sailed the Gulf.

He studied temperatures and rainfall statements, learning all he could about prospects for agriculture. Don Tristan was a man who took seriously every aspect of his responsibility and made personal knowledge his first weapon.

But on lazy afternoons I learned to know my uncle and his temperament. He was an intense man, with piercing dark eyes that sparkled when he became excited, a state he enjoyed almost constantly as his interest grew.

I must be honest, of course. Don Tristan was a man of great energy and enthusiasm, but he was of only average intellect. I recognize this now, after a life that has permitted ready intercourse with men of genius; not that he was dull or unlettered, but his mind was plodding rather than bright, his methods those of the parish priest rather than the scholarly monk.

Woven through his fabric, however, were fierce loyalties to God and to his King. These loyalties, I think, more than any personal quest for glory, motivated Don Tristan de Luna. As a child he had been schooled as a son of the true faith; as a man he had lent his skills to the service of the evolving empire. He was cut from cloth unlike that from which Cortes and Pizarro were trimmed. For while de Luna was a soldier, he was a man of warmth and kindness, and lacked the streaks of harshness which characterized the conquerors of Mexico and Peru.

Above all of these traits, however, was the captain-general's stern sense of determination (some would call it stubbornness). Once committed to a course of action, he was reluctant to change. Indeed, there were times when less insistence might have served him well. However, the combination of his upbringing and military experiences had taught him to plan with care and to make no decision lightly; but once made, plans were rigidly followed. That was his method.

To me, he became both friend and teacher, an advisor anxious for my success, eager for me to enter the adventure prepared for responsibility.

We talked by the hour, he pouring out his knowledge of the new land, and social concepts which he believed would inspire the settlers to their greatest efforts. In Mexico he had observed the force with which the natives were used, and he vowed to promote far different designs. He felt, too, that the common soldiers' lot could be better and he planned for their employment in ways which would provide greater personal gain and participation in the social community.

Day after day, as our ship broke the gentle swells, he would stand at the rail and gaze into the northwest, his eyes trying to focus on the vision his mind had created of a great new land where thousands of the people of Spain might reside, engaging in a new, better life, amid a civilization of savages brought to Christ. That was his dream, and I am convinced that he believed in it firmly.

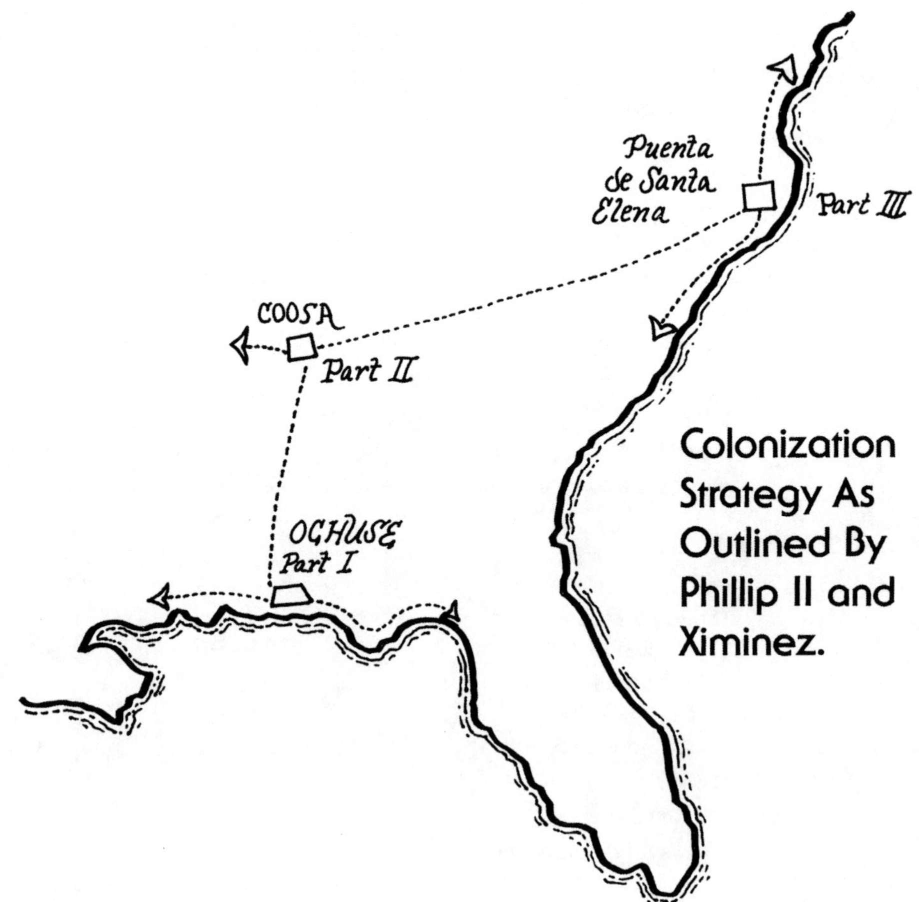

MADRID
September 11, 1558

Ximinez collapsed weakly into his chair, his eyes weary from constant writing. The arrival of messengers from Cadiz announcing the successful departure of the six vessels cheered him. The other intelligence he labored with did not.

That morning the post rider had hurried a dispatch from Gueron de Spes, Spain's veteran ambassador at London, with two disquieting reports. From inside the court of Elizabeth was talk (and the ambassador carefully underscored this) that the newly-crowned Queen had approved efforts to disrupt the fall shipments of silver to Spain.

And second, de Spes quoted 'a lady of the Queen's bedchamber as discussing the pursuit of several gallants to actively promote a company to found a trading colony on the shores of the New World.'

"Miserable intelligence this is!" Ximinez muttered disparagingly. "Gossip from the bedchamber!"

The third item in this lengthy dispatch contained more meat. Here de Spes claimed to have become privy to portions of a report to Elizabeth from her ambassador at Paris, Sir Nicholas Throckmorton. In it, Throckmorton declared that '. . . Catherine seeks to sooth the feelings of her Protestant subjects by proposing that they be outfitted as colonists along the south Atlantic shores of the New World. Adm. Coligny appears favorably disposed. . . .'

The diplomat wrote a final sentence in his report to the King, sanded the whole, and called for his runner. Moments later the article was en route.

Ximinez closed his eyes, stretched noisily, and leaned back, his mind focusing on the complex web that was to be spun 3000 miles away.

One thing was certain: his action after receipt of Velasco's original report had given Spain a fast start. With any luck, royal forces should give Spain a firm foothold on both coastlines long before smaller, weaker competition might be attempted.

The remaining question was, should Spain officially protest the anticipated competition? After all, the only basis for diplomatic action now lay in rumors. And less credibility was given to Pope Alexander's line of demarcation with each passing year. That line, drawn when the Vatican was literally under Spanish guns, had dissolved when Luther and Calvin's religion redrew the power lines of Europe and when the new nationalism began to force a hard look at the values to be found across the Atlantic.

Now the struggle was taking the form of a religious clash as well as a national one.

No . . . a protest would in all likelihood be parried with diplomatic denials.

The other alternative? Ximinez saw several. Spain could accept the rivals, but this plan he considered unthinkable. A second choice was to await word of the foreign settlements and to demand their withdrawal with general war as a consequence of refusal.

Or . . . (and here he smiled to himself) . . . a third choice was to simply overwhelm any efforts to found foreign settlements. "We will have the power on land and sea. We'll simply crush them! I doubt that Catherine would risk war over a few hundred heretics whom she is trying to remove anyway! And Elizabeth has no forces worthy of the name. That is our method. . . ."

Thus the strategy which Spain would follow in the next forty years was framed. It would not affect Don Tristan, now happily sailing westward. But this background provided the urgency for his action and set the scene for what would be the largest colonial effort by any western power in the New World.

MEXICO CITY
September 20, 1558

Never had the great Spanish capital in the New World seen such frantic activity! The report of the viceroy that over 1000 men and women would sail 'hopefully within nine months' had spurred the staff to action on all fronts. To date there had been only one major dispatch from the King and prime minister; other lesser statements had followed, however, concerning procurement of horses, arms, tools, implements and stores. All of this was taking form without difficulty.

Juan Ceron, confident that he would head the force, was faithfully exercising his considerable talents in recruiting. Already, he had named the two captains of horse and four of foot who would match the leadership to come from Spain.

It had not been difficult, despite Velasco's ruling that as many as possible of the company must have been of de Soto's company and thus have seen Coosa, or otherwise have experience found in the land to the north.

The identifiable survivors of the de Soto saga had remained soldiers of fortune in Mexico; now, hardened veterans who had been little more than boys in 1540 were willing to return as part of a force where their personal fortunes might prosper. In their minds, memories of Coosa and La Florida had grown great in the ensuing years. The dangers and the starving time were less vivid.

Ceron had chosen with deliberation, selecting officers known to him, men who had served under his command and would respect a personal loyalty to him.

As officer of horse he chose Pedro de Acuna, 44, a tall, well-built officer who had carved an estate of some size for himself forty leagues from Mexico City. Acuna's wife had died a year earlier, and now, childless, he was restive and anxious for action again.

Alva Nieto, 41, had spent the intervening years on the frontiers, leading troops in the gradual suppression of tribes which refused to accept Spain's leadership. He was a quiet, sometimes moody man, with few friends, and occasionally given to fits of cruelty to captives. Because of this Nieto was viewed with suspicion by the churchmen, but he was an able soldier, and a good choice for arduous duty such as the long trek to the Atlantic was likely to involve.

None of the four foot captains selected had made de Soto's long march of 1540, but the chosen ones were tough veterans nonetheless.

Their names: Ladron de Guevara, Juan de Porras, Alonso Valezquez and Gonzolo Sanchez.

Enrolled also were non-commissioned officers in the appropriate rank and specialties, and private soldiers who would serve as pikemen, bowmen, and men at arms with the harquebus of smaller firearms. Cannon for the fortification at Ochuse and Puenta de Santa Elena would be removed from the supporting men of war. Additional heavy armament for the second city would be sent later by sea; no attempt would be made to propel guns over the estimated 300 leagues of inland travel.

Ceron met regularly with the viceroy and Fray Domingo, each reporting on the progress of his own roles.

The churchman had completed his roster first, selecting six Dominicans who belonged to the Sainted Order of Preachers, men who by earnest devotion to God and the furtherance of Christ's Kingdom had illustrated fitness for this massive effort among the Indians.

Selected were Fray Pedro de Feria, Fray Domingo and Fray Bartolome Matheos, the latter having begun as a lay brother after service as a soldier.

In the viceroy's chambers, church and lay leaders debated assignments for the Florida expedition.

On September 20, as they dined regally on fish, fruit and wine, the three concluded that, barring setbacks or delay of the fleet from Spain, the expedition might expect to depart the following June.

Wiping lips with his silken sleeve, the viceroy waxed eloquent:

"My friends, you have done well, I'm confident his majesty will be pleased . . . very pleased!"

"Thank you, sir," Ceron returned.

The friar nodded, adding:

"I think you'll find charts and all that my people will require are ready. Frankly, I've never seen people more cooperative."

Velasco assented. "Everyone is interested. And I believe we were wise also to give an opportunity for freedmen to enlist. They are good soldiers and they understand the land."

Ceron said nothing. He made few public statements about his feeling for the red man. He distrusted them, feared them, felt that in situations where loyalty was required they would not stand up well. The viceroy's recent decision to make some of them Spanish citizens had not met with the captain's approval. Neither did he wish to include large numbers in his party. He had therefore kept that contingent as small as possible . . . just over 100.

Fray Domingo spoke once more.

"I hope his highness has asked the Pope for a special blessing . . . for use in the Cathedral Service before you leave."

Velasco nodded enthusiastically.

"That is one part of the ceremony which must be letter-perfect," he said. "I want every subject of King Philip to feel the urgency with which his majesty is sending God's word into the wilderness."

Cristobal Ramirez y Arellano, nephew to Don Tristan de Luna, his scribe and defender.

Ceron lowered his eyes and mumbled agreement.

The friar beamed. "Each of the members of the Order will have a place in the Mass," he promised, "and I will participate also. I've already selected my text. . . ."

"And we must be certain every subject is urged to attend," the viceroy interrupted. "The cathedral must be packed to overflowing! At the beginning of such an adventure, nothing is more important than the understanding that our soldiers carry the message of Christ's kingdom!"

"The cross will lead the way," the friar affirmed.

The three men pored again over their lists. Kegs for water on board ship were being seasoned; corn and beans were being harvested now and dried. Beef was being slaughtered, salted or cured. Fish were being caught and dried in the villages near Vera Cruz. Salt was being prepared, and for fruit sweet grapes were being dried as raisins. It would be a simple diet, but a staple and abundant one.

"I am still concerned about the housing of the soldiers from Spain," Ceron said at length. "It seems foolish to march them all the way to Mexico City, then turn them around again a few weeks later."

"It's a lot of walking," the friar answered, "but remember, they'll have been on board ship for weeks; a good march, some warm sun, with good food and a chance to see the country will restore them before they sail again."

"Not to mention the opportunity to participate in the mass," the viceroy added. "I don't know who these men will be; I want them prepared for their service to God."

The friar and Ceron agreed.

"Besides," the viceroy noted as an afterthought, "where in God's name would we put over 200 men in San Juan de Ulua? They'll have time enough in La Florida to sleep under the stars. Here, at least, we can offer them beds and good wine. . . ."

"And perhaps the friendship of a woman?" Ceron interjected. "Begging the friar's pardon. . . ."

"Perhaps even that," Velasco agreed. "By whatever measure we use, it makes good sense to have them come here. We'll leave their stores aboard ship, exercise the horses, and have our own supply trains begin to move from here as soon as the armada has landed. Do you agree, Ceron?"

"I only want to get things moving."

Days passed quickly. Item by item, supplies were accumulated, arms were polished, gear checked. It was late afternoon of October 5th when a brown stallion came racing into the city, foam spitting from its mouth, dust caking its sweat-stained flanks. Pounding through the streets, the rider lashed at his mount, hurrying expertly along the cobbled surface, dashing by familiar landmarks until finally he drew up in the courtyard of the viceroy's palace.

Before he was out of the saddle he began to shout, "The fleet has landed, the fleet has landed!" Then he leaped stiffly to earth and hurried into the passageway to the viceroy's waiting rooms.

In moments, his message was in the governor's hands, a brief statement that Velasco read through quickly, then more slowly a second time. The smile with which he had greeted the post rider remained for some seconds, then began to fade as he read. The message read simply:

"By the grace of God and His Most Catholic Majesty Philip of Spain, greeting! It is my pleasure to report to your Excellency safe arrival of six ships of transport and war, together with 300 soldiers and men at arms and all necessary supplies as promised by the King and his ministers. I have received your invitation to bring members of my command to the City of Mexico and will march at sunup tomorrow. It is with great anticipation that I approach this renewed meeting with you and the fine people of your government.

Signed: Don Tristan de Luna y Arellano
Captain-General and Governor of His Majesty's Forces
for La Florida"

Velasco fanned himself quickly with the paper, then slowly slumped into his leather chair.

"De Luna, captain-general . . . oh my God!" he mumbled. "Why didn't they tell me? What in God's name shall I do now? This will kill Ceron!"

For half an hour, the aging viceroy sat quietly, mulling over the news and its unexpected complications. Finally, with an air of resignation, he rang for his servant.

"Go summon Friar Domingo at the Cathedral," he ordered. Perhaps the old priest would have some idea on how to approach the problem.

This was going to be sticky.

The discussion between friar and viceroy did little to solve Velasco's problem. The priest's suggestion was that Velasco make all the facts known to Ceron ". . . as quickly as possible, before rumor does it for you. . . " and that the three then resolve the matter of conscience in prayer.

Velasco, well acquainted with the soldier's temperament, suspected that prayer might provide a convenient shawl for the latter's feelings, but that in the long run, Ceron would harbor feelings that could hardly benefit the venture.

Should he remove Ceron altogether . . . and disappoint his loyal follower and friend?

Or should he make him second in command, with the title of Master of the Camp?

Certainly, in the viceroy's mind, Ceron deserved the opportunity to lead this exciting mission. But . . . apparently the King had made a decision, backed by the Council. The fact that the information had not come earlier suggested the politics of the matter.

"Ah, well," he muttered, "let's call him and get it over with. De Luna'll be here in a week, we can't wait for that!"

Both the viceroy and the friar knew de Luna well. The latter's sojourn in Mexico had found him frequently at the palace and of course in the Cathedral. He had been a pleasant, artful, gracious young man of good family. He had done his duty, married well within the Spanish hierarchy, been a credit to social gatherings. His own family connections suggested that he might rise in rank. But nothing then had suggested his return in THIS role.

The meeting between Ceron and the viceroy was not a happy one. Called to an evening conference, the soldier had arrived weary and dripping with mid-summer sweat after a long day at his labors. He was in high spirits when he walked in, for news had already spread through the city that the fleet had come.

Velasco used his years of experience and all of his tact in breaking the news. Even that was not enough.

"By the Holy Christ, how can you do this to me?" the soldier exploded. "YOU, my friend . . . you who offered me the position, you who know that I've earned it! What will my associates say . . . and my friends? I'll be the laughing stock of New Spain!"

"I know, I know," Velasco replied softly, "and I'm sorry. But what can I say? How could I know? You examined every scrap of correspondence with Ximinez. Did he say anything other than that I should plan the proceedings? Did he suggest an appointee from Spain? Did he, now?"

"No," replied the seething soldier.

"I know how you feel, and I apologize. But I am the King's servant, as you are. If Don Tristan bears the royal commission, I have no alternative. He will be the captain-general."

"And what of me?" appealed Ceron.

"I'll name you Master of the Camp, second in command. You'll still have rank and the opportunity for anything else you can make of the expedition. This I promise you."

"Promises, promises," muttered the now cooling soldier. "I've a good notion to throw it all up. Why should I go . . . and be laughed at by half the company? Why, eh?"

"Because you are a soldier of Spain and you know the expedition needs you. And because you'd like to make a peso or two. After all, if you don't go, what'll you do here . . . become a garrison captain again? After your role in planning the adventure, that will seem small pie indeed!"

"I suppose you're right!" Ceron sighed. "Christ, what'll I say to people? What a fool they'll think me!"

"Nothing of the kind. I'll make a proclamation as soon as I've seen de Luna's papers. I'll make it perfectly clear that the act was a belated one by the King. That'll cover you. And in the noise of departure people'll be too busy to notice you're upset. Try to see this my way, eh? What choice do I have? You're my friend, and I'll help all I can. But be reasonable, for God's sake."

Ceron nodded, wondering at the same time what miracle might occur to restore his stature.

October 17th, 1558

The arrival of the nearly 300 men from Spain created a fiesta atmosphere throughout Mexico City. The soldiers would not be there long, only long enough to be greeted like conquerors by homesick friends and countrymen, to drink great quantities of the deep, purple native wine, and to enjoy the pleasures of native women who turned out in great numbers to add sport to the occasion.

The confrontation between de Luna and Ceron was handled with great tact by Velasco, who invited Fray Domingo to be present. De Luna, unsuspecting, welcomed the appointment of the veteran frontier fighter as his master of camp and quickly set about conferences to perfect the assignments of men, officers and transports.

The public announcement by Don Luis that the King had nominated the young knight de Luna as captain-general and governor was met with surprising enthusiasm by a populace already growing happily drunk as the celebration progressed.

By the end of the third evening, Velasco felt that the problem had been smoothed over. He had promised Ceron that upon return there would be an appropriate post in relation to his rank and standing in the expedition; this action had further softened the blow. De Luna, who spent as much time as possible with the new lieutenant, quickly understood the problems raised by his arrival and privately expressed his regrets and his hope that the two might work in harmony, promising his full backing and support to his subordinate. Ceron, for his part, swung into step with the captain-general.

My own arrival in Mexico City must rank as one of the brightest moments of my life. The trek from the sea to the mountain city, over a route once traced by Hernando Cortes, was breathtaking. The country was raw and new, yet strikingly beautiful; after nearly six weeks at sea it was a joy to be on foot again, climbing to the heady heights of the gorgeous mountains.

Our arrival was like a march into paradise.

I found Mexico City more beautiful than anything I'd ever seen; and the reaction of the people to our presence reminded me of the day of our return from the wars to Madrid. Only here the welcome was less reserved.

On the first evening I accompanied my uncle and the other officers to a briefing by the viceroy; then, after quartering our men, we were swept up in a round of revelry that even now makes my face smile and my head ache!

The ladies? Ah . . . they were noble indeed, lovely of form, yet hardly so restrained as those of station at home. In a matter of hours I felt that this was indeed the land of great opportunity . . . and I, like the others, indulged fully.

The weeks that followed saw all of us slip into a new routine. My uncle employed me as a sort of secretary, keeping his correspondence as he assumed his role of drawing together the many pieces of his expedition.

Don Tristan was an energetic man, as I've said before, and a precise one. His experiences with Coronado showed him the need to have every essential spelled out precisely; so he worked carefully, enrolling men, inventorying supplies, drilling the men to keep them fit.

With Ceron and the viceroy he poured over plans for the first city, outlining the complex of streets and plazas, the plots for homes and the sites for the church and government building. There was to be no lost motion in setting up the first settlement with its more than 200 souls.

In only one area was there disagreement. The viceroy, using the license provided by the Council's action, had estimated total needs at about 1200 men, women and children, including the military contingent. My uncle, who was a man of the land, believed that more settlers were needed to till the soil and perform the work of menials.

"They will only burden you and eat your food unnecessarily!" the viceroy avowed.

Nevertheless, in the long run Don Tristan's view prevailed, and the total company swelled to just over 1500, including the children and the fifty negro slaves.

One night, late in December, as this debate continued, Don Tristan confided to me.

"Once we reach the point where real work is required, our troopers will prove of little value. They have few domestic skills and they resent labor. Then we will be happy to have willing hands. The viceroy lives in a city that was complete when he arrived. He has not seen the reaction of men in the wilderness."

In the end, the two men never had an opportunity to resolve this difference of philosophy.

From this point forward time raced ahead. Had the food reserves been great enough we might have departed earlier; but again Don Luis' estimates were correct, and the expedition was forced to wait until the early harvests of corn and beans were complete.

During these busy weeks carts and pack horses moved in steady procession down the mountains toward San Juan de Ulua, where Angel Villafane continued his combined role of port master and custodian.

Week by week my uncle, Ceron and I compiled our records. By March 30th, all were satisfied that the requisite stores had either reached port or were en route.

As they had since Don Tristan's arrival, the planners met weekly with the viceroy to report and otherwise project plans for departure. On April 2nd, agreement was reached. The army would depart on April 24th for the sea.

In chambers, the King's Council pored over plans for the mission to La Florida.

THE NEW YEAR 1559

The celebration of the Mass and the welcoming of the new year were festive occasions. Most of our company were scarcely sober for the better part of two days. For myself, I could hardly hold my quill steady, despite the need to pursue the mountain of papers my uncle had given me to check.

I was acting as his secretary now, penning instructions to subordinates, and especially his reports to the King and prime minister. It was an interesting assignment; my uncle was forcing himself to become methodical, although it went against his grain.

He was enjoying his reunion with the viceroy, whose house had been an asylum during his earlier years here. And he was making a great effort to win the friendship of Ceron; the gulf which might have grown between them did not materialize due to efforts by them both. Don Tristan also made a practice of carefully rotating his luncheon and dinner hours with his new officers, meeting with small groups to identify their characters and trying to instill in them his own spirit of the adventure, which was far different from that of the men who had earlier carved out an empire for Spain.

The more I got to know Don Tristan, the more I was impressed with his modesty and his compassion.

For example, I recall the day when he met a husband and wife who were to accompany us. They were peasant people, a simple Spanish farmer who had come out here as a soldier 20 years ago and taken an Indian wife. They were lean, flat-muscled people, obviously at home to hard work in their fields. The introduction came by accident, Don Tristan almost falling over the pair as they stopped suddenly to recover some fruit which had dropped from the bag the woman carried.

The farmer began to apologize for interrupting the grandee, but Don Tristan stopped him and began a conversation; in a moment the pair realized that here was the captain-general they were to follow, and they were struck almost dumb. Yet, in minutes the captain-general had engaged them in conversation, learned of their family, spoken to them of the great adventure that lay ahead for them all.

As the pair walked away moments later, I complimented my uncle. "You have a way with the common people, uncle, a good way. They were impressed."

"Impressed? Huh! Hardly that. But that's one thing that's hard about my task. I remember the King commenting once that his role was the loneliest in the world. He warned me to beware of fraternizing with my command. But that philosophy makes no sense. If we're to share a new life together, we must share it . . . if not as equals . . . at least as men who respect one another. Now . . . don't you agree?"

I had to admit he had a point. And that ended the conversation, but each day he made it his goal to cement relations with several more of those to whom he would look for service.

Meanwhile, I was getting to know my new associates, also. The friars were magnificent! Salazar, in particular, struck my fancy, for he had both the serious mien of the man of God and sense of humor that would have been at home in an inn or brothel. To him no man was a stranger, and he had a marvelous gift with tongues, so that soon the various Indian dialects were being enjoyed by him as men brought together from far corners of Mexico required a bridge for their conversation.

Del Sauz at first was a mystery. He was older, of course, a hard, spare man who had lived a life of grubbing discipline and seemed never to court another's friendship. One had to learn to understand him by observation rather than communication. It took doing, but after a month I found myself growing to admire him greatly. He knew his trade, that was certain! An expert with horses, he also commanded his soldiers with a sternness that made the force seem battle-ready, even though they'd scarcely met.

Several of the companies, those of Guevara de Porras, had been recruited in Mexico City itself; Nieto's men had come from near Puebla, while several hundred, of course, were Spanish veterans. All told there were six men present who had marched with de Soto and returned with his survivors. These my uncle drew into conversations around our table, quickly asking questions that might pry loose added details.

Later, when the veterans had departed, he would slyly give me his impressions. Generally, he was not enthusiastic about the expertise of these men.

"Do you believe that?" he would ask. "If their stories were true, would they have continued west? And can you imagine de Soto having told NO ONE of the presence of Maldonado's fleet . . . 350 leagues away?"

Another day he spoke of the geography through which we would pass.

"They have all repeated the same thing . . . that it is less than three hundred leagues from Coosa to Puento de Santa Elena. I am no mapmaker, but from the time it takes one to sail from east to west, I can't believe they're right . . . or even half right."

"We'll have a longer walk, you think?"

"I plan to pack extra shoes and encourage you to do so."

"Thanks for the tip. I will."

The viceroy himself was splendid. No man in his position could have been more interested or more helpful. The expedition had been his child, and even though all details might not be of his choosing, he was making every effort to assure its success. Each day he held conferences, checked lists, encouraged more supplies, worked for more zeal among the leadership to insure success of the friars' efforts. Only once . . . when he disagreed with my uncle's taking of added farmers and slaves . . . did he take serious issue with Don Tristan. Otherwise, the two worked as though they had shared a common harness for years.

As for me, I worked long hours by day and frequented the parlors of the delightful ladies by night. When I went into the confessional each week, I perjured myself regularly. But then, one is only young once. . . .

April 24, 1559

Together, Ceron and de Luna marched side by side to the great religious fete Fray Domingo had planned; together they sat with the viceroy, flanked him in the front pew of the giant cathedral which Spanish engineering and Indian toil had created.

The high vaulted sanctuary, with its row upon row of close packed pews, was filled to overflowing. To the front, the great names of the New World empire were seated, dons in sombre blacks and browns, their ladies in brighter hues, heads covered by shawls of finest lace, their heads bowed in pious reflection.

To the rear, in rank upon rank, were the officers, then the men of the great army, followed by the simple farmers, their wives and children, strong faced, simply dressed men and women of the land who fell upon their knees and prayed fervently for their safety and success.

High in the rear, in a balcony invisible to most of the congregation, was a choir of 100 youths, their fresh young voices pealing high, blending with the great organ, recently imported from Germany.

As the half dozen priests commenced their offices, music carried the responses high and clear, with occasional chants added by the faithful, first on their knees, then seated upright, every eye upon the ritual unfolding before them, a ritual born in the Church of Rome hundreds of years before and now firmly rooted in the lives of transplanted Spaniards and Indian converts alike.

Fray Domingo de Santa Maria had determined that this be a Mass never to be forgotten in the new land! He was intensely dedicated to the extension of his faith and the empire and was convinced that in this great expedition rested the security of those goals. His own voice, a rich, mellow baritone, projected the Latin words and prayers to the farthest corner of the cathedral, and as his assistants carried the ceremonies forward, the emotion-charged celebration captivated noble and peasant alike.

When the call for communion came, the congregation came to the rail in a slow, steady snake-like ribbon, down the long aisles to the altarplace, where the wafer and cup were delivered by the stern Dominicans.

When each had been served and had returned to his place, the final earnest prayer implored God's guiding goodness upon the great adventure conceived in His name.

Then it was over, and the slow-moving wave of men and women drifted silently from the doors of the great house of worship. There were no words; only the soft shuffling of feet upon the sandy stone floors kept the mood, backed by an Amen sung harmoniously by the choir boys.

Last to depart were Velasco, Ceron and de Luna, walking slowly in cadence, heads bowed, their hands clasped together in the traditional attitude of prayer. Not until they had walked a full square did the viceroy raise his head and declare: "Amen . . . and Amen!"

"A marvelous Mass, a beautiful service!" declared Don Tristan.

"Beautiful," Ceron agreed.

"The friar's a worthy priest, a holy man," Velasco added. "He will join us for our meal. Your men will have one final feeding before we march?"

Ceron confirmed the viceroy's statement.

"The captains have orders to be ready to march at four. We'll take advantage of the cool hours."

"Good. I'll be ready. If you don't mind, I'd like to march with you, in the vanguard."

"Of course," Don Tristan answered. "I thought you'd go by coach and join us there."

"No, this is my expedition, too. I'd like to play one final role before you embark, have the last word, as it were."

"Splendid! Splendid!" Don Tristan said.

"Can't we walk a little faster?" Ceron asked. "It's hot out here! A cool one'll help. We'll have time enough in the heat."

And so the final day in Mexico City was spent. The trio was joined by the friar and others of the Order of Preachers. An excellent meal was set out for us all by Velasco's staff: cold fowl, broiled fish, crisp native greens, cool red wine.

A siesta then was in order, after which each man repaired to his quarters to supervise final preparation of his gear. Promptly at three the bell in the Cathedral tolled the signal for assembly. An hour later long lines of soldiers and horse, farmers and artisans, carts and packmen were drawn up, each section led by its captain. At a command from the viceroy, calls to march were repeated up and down the line, and the great expeditionary force began its slow, steady trek down from the heights to the sea.

The march was the greatest pageant the people of Mexico had ever seen! Like a giant snake, the line of march wound down the narrow track that served as a highway between the capital and San Juan de Ulua.

Ceron had assembled hundreds of wheeled vehicles for the final movement of stores; horses and porters carried the rest, except that each soldier and husbandman was required to carry a second set of clothing in a pack. Women too carried field sacks slung over their shoulders, and even children carried small items.

"It's good for everyone to do his share!" the master of the camp declared and set an example, his own horse heavily burdened while he walked ahead, leading it with a rein.

At each hamlet the population turned out to wave and cheer; women threw blooming flowers and offered marchers refreshments.

The cool water and weak wine were welcome. The April sun, equivalent to midsummer in Spain, beat mercilessly on the marchers, and the road surface, churned by hundreds of marching feet, boiled with choking dust which caught in dry throats. Tiny gnats floated in the air, provoking a great flailing of arms and hands, and an occasional smack on cheek. But despite the discomforts, marchers maintained their good humor.

The viceroy, recalling earlier campaigns, wisely made provision for food kitchens at regular intervals; every three hours, usually under comfortable shade, the line broke for a light meal; for some, the food was far better than usual. At each stop, commanders were instructed to speak briefly to their forces, regaling them with the glories of their mission. The friars, swathed in traditional robes, sweated from every pore but maintained the steady pace, moving from group to group, keeping up a flow of encouraging words. Twice daily, at daybreak and dusk, the line was broken and in separate unions prayers were said.

De Luna, his light armor bright and his face set in a proud smile, rode at the head of the column, flanked by Velasco and Fray Domingo de Santa Maria. The flush of excitement was on each face, and as the fourth day of march was completed, the trio spoke more and more of their optimism.

"I'm confident that we will serve our Lord effectively in this new land," murmured the friar. "We have committed grave errors before, errors we will not repeat again. Feria is experienced, knowledgeable. His wisdom will be a pillar of strength."

De Luna, staring straight ahead, nodded. "Of course! You chose the men of God with skill. There will be much for them to do. I only ask that in their work they maintain communication with me. In the past, such failures were costly, Excellency."

"Agreed!" the friar replied. "On board ship, for example, we have but six men for thirteen vessels. I've asked Friar Feria to sail with you, and have assigned the other five to larger vessels, where they will be more with the people than the soldiers. Is that agreeable?"

De Luna and Velasco concurred. Maintaining discipline and enthusiasm was a key to success of the venture. Glancing behind him, de Luna was pleased with the spirit on the march. Here was a troop with a mission, and it was beginning well! These were no tired, burned out, dispirited old line troops. Most were dedicated to a permanent new life in a new land; a small minority only had made short-term plans. He turned to Velasco.

"Your excellency is planning to make final remarks before we embark?" he asked.

"I would like to," he replied. "I think it would be appropriate to have one last inspirational assembly, to have Fray Domingo here perform the Mass . . . and to ask you to give the order of march. I will deliver the King's charge. Agreed?"

June 24, 1559

And so it was on May 4th that the expedition of 1500 assembled. San Juan de Ulua, a bustling yet primitive port, offered plenty of level ground, and longshoremen and the local garrison had executed the loading plan well. Stores brought from Spain were restowed, and the total of 240 Spanish and local horses had been carefully exercised and fed. As the caravan from Mexico City arrived, vans and pack animals had been herded into position. Juan Ceron was everywhere; as master of the camp his duties included those of loading supervisor. His long lists of stowage and assignment were well prepared, and with assistance from selected troopers, slings and ropes moved up and down, in and out, hauling skins and barrels, sacks and hogsheads from lighters to below decks.

Ceron was no sailor, but he appreciated the quality of the vessels, and the work which Gomez Arias and his naval officers had done to make them dry and seaworthy.

These stores were critical, for a landing in August would leave little opportunity for new crops before the late spring; the only supplement would be later stores from Mexico, and there was no real plan for this. Keeping food dry was critical. Ceron's lieutenants inspected every barrel as it left the shore, noting the seasoning of the staves, the fit of lids, the sewing of seams. Filling of water casks from a giant spring required thirty horses and 100 men, working steadily, hour after hour, back and forth, to be certain the army would not want for drink.

The remainder of the force lazed about, seeking shade, washing and mending clothes, cooking in small lots, bathing . . . doing those scores of little things that men and women do when anticipation is great and each is anxious to be off.

On the morning of June 24th, as they concluded prayers, the officers passed the word that the company would assemble at the quayside at three o'clock, for a final blessing, and that they would then board ship. Tides were right for an early evening departure. This was the day!

3:00 P.M. . . . June 24th, 1559

Fray Domingo de Santa Maria stood on the hastily erected platform and gazed out across the sea of bronzed faces . . . young, eager faces, older, craggy-lined faces rimmed with graying hair . . . red faces, white faces, faces with handsome beards, hopeful faces of young wives and children.

Children were restless, for already the heat made beads of sweat trickle between shoulder blades and down into the waistband of dusty trousers.

A low murmur of conversation buzzed . . . complementing the hum of flies and gnats that never completely subsided.

On the whole, the 1500 souls were remarkably quiet, surprisingly alert, the friar thought. It was a great adventure! He envied them. Or did he?

Flanked by other Dominicans the aging Santa Maria began the Mass. Performed out-of-doors, there was something especially holy about the ceremony, and on that afternoon every eye could see the depths of emotion of the priest as he ministered to his flock.

In his rich baritone Fray Domingo de Santa Maria rolled the Latin phrases of the liturgy over the heads of his listeners, and when time came for the colonists to take communion, each knelt in the sand and accepted the wine and wafer.

Nearly three hours were required to perform the Mass . . . and now the captain-general, Don Tristan de Luna, stood before the waiting throng.

De Luna, a soldier who appreciated the comfort of his army, began his remarks on a chord calculated to earn the approval of his followers.

Standing tall in full uniform, his helmet and breastplate reflecting the sun which now had begun its descent, the conquistadore was the very model of his station . . . handsome, forbidding, stern. He also was very hot!

His voice, a soft tenor, neither carried so far nor sounded so melodiously as the priest's chant. But his first words drew a cheer.

"My friends," he shouted. "It's very warm, and you have been in the sun a long time. His excellency and I shall have a few words for you . . . but first, sit down, be comfortable. Try to keep cool."

Like a field of grain moving before a breeze, the throng swayed and moved to a sitting position. Their smiles and cheers told the general he had acted wisely.

Removing his pointed headpiece and cradling it in his left arm, de Luna continued, "This evening, as the breeze freshens and the tide flows out, we will begin our great adventure. I know that each of you has been counseled well by his captain, and that each knows his station aboard ship.

"For some, a voyage will be a new adventure. In this season it should be a pleasant experience. I ask only these things of you. Remember that we will be confined in close quarters. Privacy will be at a minimum. Be considerate. Follow the orders of your ship's captain, for he is entrusted with your safety.

"Our admiral, Gomez Arias, says that we shall arrive at our destination in fourteen days. I hope this is so. But there is always the possibility of misadventure, so I urge you all to use food with care and fresh water sparingly. Those with children must teach them the lessons of forbearance.

"Finally, I thank you all for being part of this great mission. We have two charges: to secure the brilliant lands of La Florida for our gracious sovereign and to bring the message of Christ to many savages whose souls will burn in hell if we fail. It is a challenge the like of which comes to few men, and we share it equally. Each of you will have the opportunity to secure land, to bring the glorious name of Spain to a new shore, to carry Christ's banner.

"Now, we commend ourselves to God's loving care as we bear His witness.

"God bless you all!"

A slow, rolling cheer came from the listeners. Old soldiers, men who had often been urged to deeds of valor before battle, were impressed.

Women crossed themselves and wiped tears from their eyes.

The Dominican friars smiled.

Now it was Velasco's turn, and the aging governor, perhaps with an eye to history, stood beside de Luna, one arm over the captain-general's shoulder, a broad smile on his sweat-stained face.

"Fellow citizens of Spain," he began . . . and a cheer broke from the massed soldiers, perhaps on signal from their captains.

"Fellow citizens of Spain," he resumed, "I salute you!

"As Sr. de Luna has said so well, today you embark upon an adventure unparalleled in this continent, an opportunity which I firmly believe will make wealthy men of you all, and which will earn the eternal gratitude of our noble King, Philip II."

Again cheers rolled forth, this time spreading to peasant and child.

"This is no small undertaking," the viceroy continued. "As you know, this whole hemisphere, which extends we know not how far, was discovered in the name of Spain by the great navigator, Don Christoforo Colombo.

"Since then, Spain's legions have occupied great parts of the land, bringing the word of the true God to countless heathen, and returning wealth and support to our country in its righteous wars against the unscrupulous French.

"Today, we know of French plans . . . and perhaps English, too . . . to ignore our rightful claims and the very rulings of His Holiness the Pope. They would, we believe, dare to occupy lands which are rightfully Spain's . . . yours . . . and threaten our plans to bring the glory of our heritage to these shores."

A low muttering rumble swept through the 1500.

"Even worse . . . they would do this by peopling these shores with heretics . . . men who have denied the succession of holy St. Peter . . . and accepted the teaching of the anti-Christ himself, Martin Luther!"

The rumbling pitched louder now . . . .

"Think if you will of the immortal souls of the red men who people this land!

"Think of the judgment to which we must answer if we fail to wall off this land from the heretics.

"My comrades, as you sail today you bear the charge of Christendom's most noble monarch. You are to build a great city on the harbor at Santa Maria, a city to defend the sea against all comers, a city to build your fortunes, a city in which you will erect a noble cathedral wherein the word of God may be preached, and from which we may teach Christ crucified to the heathen.

"Then, a part of you will march across the land to the Cape of Storms, to Puenta de Santa Elena, to create a second great city, there to bar the heretic and pretender from the land by the oceans.

"You go in good season. Your company includes leaders and gallant men of God; and you go well supplied.

"You have among you farmers and artisans, women and children, the things of which a new country is built.

"Our prayers go with you, as do those of your good King, Philip. You carry in your hands an opportunity the like of which few might see even in Spain itself. So I say go with God . . . and may His face smile upon you!"

As Velasco hurled his last words to the crowd, de Luna began a furious cheer, picked up spontaneously throughout the listening 1500.

Many were stunned by his words. The enormity of their good fortune seemed hard to believe!

Moments later we were dismissed to go about the final acts of preparation.

THE LONG VOYAGE

At seven o'clock the last meal was served. At nine embarkation began. Two hours later lines were loosed, anchors raised and the thirteen ships, large and small, slipped into the warm waters of the Caribbean.

De Luna, standing on the bridge of the galleon ESTRAMADURA, watched the proceedings with Arias and Fray Domingo de La Anunciacon, the Dominican assigned to the flagship. Slowly the breeze filled the sails, and one by one the vessels drew into a sort of formation, its speed determined by the slower vessels, the two ponderous, high sterned galleons.

"An unforgettable sight," murmured the priest.

"Indeed," concurred de Luna, his eyes scanning first one ship, then another, alert for any sign of trouble. "All goes well, admiral?" he asked.

"Of course," Arias concurred. "We have fine vessels and finer men. If the winds favor us, I'll set you down dry and happy in La Florida in fourteen days. Trust me!"

"I do, I do!" de Luna replied. "It's only that there is so much to do . . . so much depends upon. . . ."

"Upon God's will, my son," Anunciacon interrupted. "It is He whom we serve. He will guide us on His way."

MADRID
August 1, 1559

In Madrid, Philip II summoned the young secretary whom he trusted with his most confidential and personal message.

"Michael . . . I want you to go to the Casa de Luna . . . the one occupied by Don Tristan de Luna . . . you remember . . . who served with us in the Low Countries?"

"Of course, Highness."

"You are to take this ring with my seal and present it to Senora de Luna. You must see her alone . . . I repeat . . . alone, do you understand?"

"I do, your majesty."

"Give her the ring with my compliments, and say that I would appreciate the pleasure of her company this evening . . . for dinner . . . and, oh . . . for talk of her husband and his mission. You have that?"

"Yes, sire."

"And add that I won't take no for an answer . . . you understand?"

"I do."

The youth departed.

Philip's narrow face broke into an unusual smile.

"After all," he mused, "her knight has been gone months now. She must be lonely. And since I dispatched him 4000 miles . . . I have an obligation. . . ."

In her chambers, Valencia de Luna dressed with care. She had seen Philip only once since the great ball, and then at a distance. To think that he was concerned for her entertainment! Life was exciting indeed. Tomorrow she would write a long letter to her husband and tell him all about it.

AT SEA
August 1, 1559

The lantern in de Luna's cabin swung in wide arcs, side to side, the candle's flame throwing weird and changing patterns against the rough planking of the hull. An able sailor, the captain-general was not disturbed physically by the long rolls of the ship, but as day after day of the pitching and rolling continued, his concern rose.

"Great God!" he said to me. "Had the wind been normal we should have entered the harbor at Santa Maria today, or at least tomorrow. As it is . . . even Arias, that calm and deliberate seamaster, is at a loss to explain it. Almost from the moment we rendezvoused off land from Vera Cruz the adverse westerly has pushed us at right angles to our course. When will it cease? Arias only shrugs his shoulders and counsels patience. How can I be patient?"

He was right. Hundreds of the colonists fared badly, their bellies twitching with nausea induced by ship's motion, and their desire for food, even if good meals had been possible, was small. The hardy lounged on deck or peered ahead over the rails; the less fortunate, including most of the women and children, remained belowdecks in the stifling heat and stench. With close quarters already enforced by the ship's loading, life had become a stinking succession of days filled with retching, puking humanity which could curse the wind and sea and pray that the winds might shift, or that at least a stomach-quieting calm might develop.

A knock at the door of the cabin roused the captain-general from his ramblings. He was dining (if one could dignify a meal under such circumstances by such a name) with Arias, Anunciacon and myself.

Arias and the friar entered. All but the churchman had adopted informal dress aboard ship, and now, served by an Indian steward, relaxed in the small but comfortable leather chairs the cabin afforded.

The cold meal passed quickly . . . dried beef, figs and biscuits, with plenty of sweet red wine. While we ate, conversation centered about the adverse winds and their position. As always, the admiral explained as best he could a phenomenon he did not understand, climaxing with his favorite philosophy, "this too shall pass."

With the comfort of food and the settling effect of the wine, the talk gradually turned to other things . . . of home . . . to the King . . . to the future of the colonists. It was Arias who asked:

"Good father, I must confess . . . I envy your zeal. How do you do it? I'm afraid

I'd be lost if my lot was to convince red savages of the kingdom of Christ."

"Why so?" Anunciacon responded. "You believe in it yourself."

"Of course, but believing and convincing are different matters."

"Ah, good admiral, these things are a matter of discipline. Now . . . tell me (and his gaze swept all three of his listeners) . . . tell me . . . how often in your lives have you actively worked to bring a soul to Christ? Once per day . . . once per year . . . how often?"

"That's just the point," Arias said. "I believe in the message of Christ and in the work of His church with all of my heart, but somehow I would shy away from actually seizing some unbeliever by the arm and trying to convert him."

"And you, de Luna, what of you?" asked the friar.

The captain-general stared at the deck below his feet and thought for several seconds before replying.

"When I was a child, I was taught that the message of Christ was love . . . and the God had sent His son to us because he loved us. . . ."

"Which is very true!" the Dominican announced.

"Yet as I grew to manhood and became an intimate of holy men such as you, I saw a second message . . . that a man's soul is condemned forever if he does not accept Christ as his Savior . . . and if he does not live by the ordinances of the church."

Anunciacon nodded. "This I firmly believe."

De Luna continued:

"Yet there is still another precept that we must be judged by our works. . . ."

I interrupted, "Which is why some build great cathedrals, collect holy relics and serve the poor. . . ."

"Or go into the wilderness to extend an empire that truly loves Christ and His Church," interrupted the captain-general.

"Precisely!" the priest almost shouted. "It is as St. Paul has told us. . . ."

"But Father," I cut in, "if this is true, how do we justify our acts upon the Indians? How can bondage and slavery in the mines be called love? I can't understand what seems to be a conflict in policy."

The friar nodded sadly.

'I agree . . . and that is why Fray Domingo has tried for years to end such contradictions. How sad it is that thousands died before such acts ended."

"Were their souls saved, father?" the captain continued.

"If they truly accepted Christ!" the priest declared. "Otherwise? Otherwise . . . I fear their souls are in torment."

De Luna had been carefully capturing every syllable of the dialogue. Now he interrupted.

"Fray Anunciacon, it is my hope that in this new land love will be our credo, and that as we bring Christ's message we'll do so by making the natives our friends."

"Even if they refuse to accept our faith?"

"Even if they seem at first to do so. . . ."

"You are aware of what the king has said . . .?"

"I am. But I believe that we must bring these people the message as it comes to little children. We must come to them with brotherhood and live together in harmony. If we are to fulfill our total mission, these people must become our allies. We cannot afford to alienate them."

"I know, my son," added Anunciacon, "we must carry the cross on high and act as brother and teacher. . . ."

Again I interrupted, "There is no predicting tomorrow. We come as conquerors, yet these people have a free spirit. How do we capture a spirit?"

"By good works we will show them what the Christian spirit is!" de Luna almost shouted. "And by love we will convert them."

"Amen and amen," the priest added gravely. "We may have erred in the past, may God forgive us. Our objectives were noble, our means were not. Fortunately, we have the opportunity to begin anew."

Arias, no philosopher and rocked by the motion of the sea, belched noisily and stretched.

"Very well, good friends, I'm convinced. When we land, I'll leap onto the sand and throw my arms about the first savage maid I see, tell her how much I love her, then carry her into the privacy of the shrub to explain all of this to her. Perhaps with such practice I too can become a missionary!"

Anunciacon smiled and shook his head.

"Arias, you concentrate on the good work of getting us to La Florida. I shall give you dispensation from conversions lest you prejudice our whole effort."

We all laughed as we rose to leave. Then, suddenly our chuckles ceased.

"Listen!" commanded Arias.

"The wind . . . it is dying . . . look . . . the candle is almost upright," de Luna added.

"Aye . . . perhaps now we can go about the business of reaching our harbor," Arias added.

"I pray this is so!" the priest said.

On deck, the watch noted the change of wind velocity. On the other vessels similar checks were made.

Hours later, when the rising sun enabled the fleet to reorganize, the gale had ended. Signal pennants rose on the flagship, and slowly the 13 vessels came about.

The ordeal was over. We were finally on course for La Florida.

In retrospect, it's easy now to reconstruct what happened to us; at the time, it wasn't that simple. The voyage had in fact taken us to the west, approaching the latitude of Rio de Espiritu Santu. The winds, however, had forced us backward, to what present day mariners call the Alacran Reef, off the coast of the Peninsula of Yucatan. When the untimely breezes finally subsided, we came about and ultimately made a landfall on the shores of La Florida, near the bay which earlier voyagers (including Bazares) had recorded as the Bay of Miruelo.

Here Arias elected to go ashore, to take on fresh water and to replenish the vessels' small supply of wood for cook fires. Most remained on board, for the vessels did not venture too close to the shore. I had an opportunity to accompany one work party and splashed knee deep into the water and then onto the fresh white sands.

It was a lovely sight and the bay a delightful place, though the waters were not deep in all quarters and thus not suitable for our purposes as a colony.

We remained at anchor for two days, then set sail again on August 8th, moving west this time for Ochuse.

A frigate was dispatched, the DON PEDRO SANCHEZ, commanded by Lt. Hernando Rivera. However, unseasonal fogs plagued the vessel and the remainder of the fleet as we sailed slowly several leagues behind it.

In the night (or perhaps it was due to the fog, I can't be certain) we failed to see the narrow opening to the Bay at Ochuse. At about 10 o'clock in the morning of August 11th, signals were raised from the frigate that a bay had been sighted and the fleet closed with her.

Soon we were all at the rails, staring to the north. The people were in a great state of excitement, as we all were; but before long it was obvious to those who had studied the maps that this was not Ochuse. The bay mouth was far too broad, and the entry looked nothing like the description given by Maldonado and Bazares.

Arias and his captain took added sightings and soon agreed. We were perhaps 20 leagues too far to the west. We were entering Bahia Filipina, as named by Bazares, and not the bay of the Rio de Ochuse.

A brief conference was conducted on the bridge, and my uncle, noting that both harbors were described as worthy, suggested that the fleet push forward and investigate the place.

This we did, and on the late afternoon we dropped anchor. From our position we could see the entry to still another river.

Boats were put over the side, and officers from each ship, along with the expedition's military leaders and the Dominicans, hurried ashore.

The place appeared very low, and as dusk came on mosquitoes in great numbers swarmed over us, causing great discomfort to Fray Mateos, whose fair skin was very tender.

We hurried back to the vessels, ultimately answering my uncle's summons to meet as a body on board his ship to discuss the landing further.

We did not meet for the evening meal, but were rowed across later, there not being a suitable space to seat so many in one common area. The moon was bright, I recall, and the evening's breeze soft and cool, though the temperature was quite high. The long row across from one vessel to another was a delight, for we could distinguish the outlines of the tall pines silhouetted against the moonlit sky.

The conference lasted a short time only, for Ceron and my uncle had already reached a decision, seconded by the admiral.

Bahia Filipina was too open an area to be considered safe anchorage, especially for smaller ships. And the lowness of land close to the water discouraged the leaders considering the prospect of building a settlement.

Don Tristan's comments, directed to us all, summarized his beliefs.

"From all that we can determine, Ochuse appears to be a more favorable site. However, we have not yet inspected it. Therefore, we shall remain at anchor here tomorrow and dispatch Lt. Rivera and his vessel for an examination of Bahia Santa Maria, or Ochuse. Hopefully, he will return tomorrow or the next day; then we shall make our final decision."

Rivera sailed as ordered, made his examination, and returned to us late on the evening of August 12th. His account of the harbor at Ochuse was glowing, though he expressed concern over the narrow entrance to the bay.

"Now I understand well why we failed to see it the first time," he added.

Thus it was decided.

The admiral ordered the vessels prepared for sail the morning of August 14th, the day of the Assumption of the Virgin.

On the morning of the 13th, however, action was directed towards disembarkation of the horses, it being felt that they were badly in need of exercise.

I was assigned to this duty: the movement of the valuable mounts across country to Ochuse.

One would think this might be a delight for a cavalryman, after being cooped up for weeks aboard a hot, stuffy sailingship. However, it was a difficult assignment.

During the weeks at sea the people had fared well. Some had been seasick, but there had been no serious illnesses and no deaths.

The horses, on the other hand, kept below deck in the hot, stinking air and without exercise, sickened rapidly. Of 240 mounts taken aboard at San Juan de Ulua, only 130 survived. Considering the travel envisioned for the colonists, and that horses were our only overland mobility other than our legs, seeing to their health was no small matter.

It required nearly five hours to move the beasts from shipside to shore, after which we turned them loose on halters to regain their land legs.

Acuna, Aguilar and Xaramillo joined me, along with 100 cavalrymen, for the walk overland. Our instruction (wisely put, I assure you) was to travel slowly, to give the beasts ample time to graze and regain strength. Thus it was that we did not arrive at Ochuse until August 16th, two days after the fleet dropped anchor and the people went ashore.

The cavalry needs satisfied, Adm. Arias dispatched Rivera's frigate as guide, then drew his ships into a formation to make the brief journey to Ochuse. We saw them draw away just before noon. The date was August 14th.

I will say little of our first long walk across the sands of La Florida. Compared with those that followed, it was like a summer's promenade, a simple stroll beneath tall trees and across sandy beach, splashing occasionally across streams and rivers that wound their way into the Gulf. We hurried no one. Xaramillo, who had a great sense of humor, regaled us with stories of what he would do once his fortune was made. And at night, with the horses carefully hobbled against straying, we lolled about small fires to cook our meals. Once, we even fished in a stream and surprised ourselves with our catches.

It was a grand beginning! And after the first day, we speeded our pace; we were anxious now to reach 'home.'

While we were enjoying our walk to Ochuse, the fleet was working its way there by water. As the sun began to slip down, the lookout of the frigate, fastest of the vessels, suddenly sang out loud and clear in words that rang across the water and which no one cound misunderstand.

"LAND HO!"

Quickly the signal was snapped to the remainder of the fleet; at once, a stampede of eager, ship-weary travelers hurried on deck to try to gain a first peek at the new homeland.

In his cabin, Arias gave orders to signal the frigate to proceed, seeking out the narrow inlet which led to the great bay of Santa Maria.

De Luna joined him. "What do you propose? Is there any hope. . . ."

"Of landing tonight? Oh no. We may be lucky and sight the inlet, but I suspect we'll wait until morning to send the frigate in. Then we'll follow."

"Tomorrow, then?"

"Perhaps, I hope so."

An hour later land was visible to all, a low, sandy beach that seemed to stretch endlessly to east and west. It hardly seemed the land of milk and honey.

Then, with the light just strong enought for a signal to be seen, the frigate came back in view, her pennants flapping a new and welcome sign.

"PASSAGE SIGHTED. WILL ENTER AT DAWN."

With thanksgiving, 1500 souls, eager to end their weeks at sea, looked forward to one final night aboard ship.

August 15, 1559

Next morning, the frigate was underway as soon as it was light enough for a crewman to read his line. She slipped through the narrow inlet . . . made a rapid passage down the northern shore, then quickly came about and hurried back, drawing close by where the ESTRAMADURA lay hove to. A tiny boat was put over the side, and the ship's young captain Rivera was rowed to the flagship. Aboard the galleon every eye watched his approach. Moments later he reported to Arias and de Luna.

"The bay is absolutely magnificent . . . everything that has been claimed for it. The channel is deep and swift; no signs of inhabitants. It must be the most peaceful spot in the world!"

Arias' entry plan had long been memorized by his captains. Now, each in turn raised sail, and in the proper place each vessel fell behind the pinnace which acted as guide. The smaller, swifter vessels went first, followed by the lumbering galleon and heavily laden transports. In an arching line that stretched a league or more the armada swung north, then northeast, through the passage between the mainland and the long, narrow sandy island that creates the harbor.

The reports of earlier explorers and the recommendation of Bazares had suggested that the fleet make its landfall below the steep cliff which runs along one sector of the northern ridge of the bay. Water sloped deeply here and provided a fair anchorage, and there were springs nearby. Selection of the actual site for the colony would come after further study. Meanwhile, a campsite above the cliffs would give security against man and the elements.

One by one the vessels reached the designated area, anchor chains gave off their clattering rattles which echoed against the eroded reddish clay of the bluffs. It was almost noon, now, and in each mind there was one thought, "How soon can we be off the ships? Let me feel this good earth under my feet!"

De Luna sensed their feelings.

"Can we disembark the people now?" he asked Arias. "I'd like to put them ashore and let them eat and sleep there tonight. Let's unwind a bit before we begin the work!"

Arias agreed.

"I suspect my men would enjoy a bit of rowing about now," he said.

Fray Anunciacon touched the captain-general's arm.

I should like to conduct a Mass of thanksgiving for all . . . tonight as the sun descends," he said. "I think it would be most fitting. Oh," and he turned to Arias, "can we carry the cross ashore?"

"Certainly!"

And so, as the hot August sun beat down, thirteen vessels put boats over side, and with skilled strokes crew members carried eager soldiers, farmers, artisans, wives and children across the gently lapping waves to the white sandy beach.

As they stepped ashore, almost all responded like children at play. The water was soup-warm, and clear as crystal. Thousands of tiny fingerlings scurried about, darting between the legs of the dripping, frolicking Spaniards who at first refused to leave the pleasure of the refreshing waters.

Back and forth the ships' boats plied, depositing a growing ant-like hoard that dug and scooped the sands, gingerly felt of foliage, and trotted back and forth along the hard-packed snow-white sand trying to regain the feel of solid ground.

De Luna, high on the bridge of the ESTRAMADURA, watched, amused, delighted to see the flood of pleasure which the bright, white sand brought to his colonists. On the main deck of the SANTA CRUZ, Juan Ceron paced back and forth, anxiously checking the booms and slings which soon would begin the long task of discharging animals and supplies. For now, the need was an evening meal cooked ashore. Already the efficient master of the camp had given orders to cooks and helpers, and planned a menu.

As he barked orders, Ceron was joined by Capt. Juan Porras, the short, swarthy, infantry veteran who had served in Mexico for two decades and was one of Ceron's personal selections for the army.

"Well, amigo, we're here . . . better late than never!" he quipped.

Ceron momentarily ceased his labors, nodding brusquely, "Looks good, very good, eh?"

Ceron nodded. "No Indians. That surprises me. From Maldonado's account and the things Bazares said, I expected the place to be alive with them."

"But didn't they say they really didn't live here, only came at odd seasons?"

"Something like that. Still . . . you'd think there'd be one around . . . to say hello . . . or fire an arrow . . . or something."

"Just as well. Gives us a chance to unwind and scout around. We surely won't want to unload here. We'd all have backaches packing everything up there," Porras added, pointing towards the steep bluff.

"Agreed. You going ashore now?"

"If it's all right with you. When will you go?"

"Not for a bit. Want to be set for tomorrow. I suspect the captain-general will want to send out parties in the morning. Then, we'll have to keep the troops occupied."

"Have you watched de Luna? He seems to be enjoying this thoroughly."

"He should! A man doesn't have the opportunity to run a show like this often."

"It should have been you on that quarterdeck!"

"Maybe. But I'm not bitching. Velasco did all he could. I was his man, de Luna, the King's. You can't fight the crown."

Porras shrugged and walked forward, moving to the rail where the overside loading ladders of rope hung to the water line. Moments later he leaped into the bow of a returning boat which quickly reloaded and pushed off towards shore.

As it moved out of the SANTA CRUZ'S shadow, Porras glanced up, waving gaily to Ceron who still bent over his papers.

Seconds later Porras vaulted over the gunwhale and splashed into the warm shallows. "God, that feels good!" he muttered. For a moment he cast aside the dignity of command and leaped about like a child. La Florida was real!

5:30 P.M. . . . August 15, 1559

The sun was low when the hard ringing of the priest's bells called the wet, tired, but happy 1500 together.

The six Dominicans were gathered on a slight rise of sand scooped from the beach. In the distance at the foot of the bluffs, smoke streamed up from cook fires, and the smell of spicy dishes wafted through the air.

The children, many of whom had begun to shape the wet sand into forts and castles, were reluctant to respond, but anxious parents urged them on, and within minutes all were assembled save the marines and cargo handlers still aboard ship.

De Luna and his officers ringed the hillside; just behind them stood four sturdy pikemen chosen for special duty. On a sign from Fray Anunciacon, the service began.

It was a simple ceremony, with no attempt at a high Mass. Prayer was offered, and the pikemen knelt and slowly lifted the large wooden cross which had been carried on the flag ship. As they slipped it into a hole, Fray Bartolome Matheos stepped forward. He was a short, heavy man, with a booming bass voice that carried loud and clear across the beach.

"Let us pray.

"In the name of the Father, the Son and the Holy Ghost . . . Amen.

"Heavenly Father, we are your humble servants, now grateful for a safe journey to this land of promise. In Thy name we erect this cross as the symbol of our mission. We are here to bring the message of Christ to a heathen people of a new continent. Give us, we pray, the strength and wisdom to do what must be done as You would have us act as Thy servants. We bow our heads in humble thanks for safe deliverance . . . and may our acts and works be always acceptable in Thy sight . . . Amen."

As the prayer ended, all eyes moved soberly to the newly raised cross. Most silently, almost absently crossed themselves. This was a symbolic moment. To the committed it meant that the first phase of their work had begun. Christ had come to this new world . . . and they were His messengers.

EVENING
August 15, 1559

For those who had landed, that evening on the beach must have been unforgettable! It was not one event but many. The cooks had outdone themselves, ladling plates of steaming spicy food, laced with wine. And de Luna had ordered extra wine rations in celebration.

As the 1500 ate, the captain-general strolled from place to place, talking with his men, patting children, encouraging all for the great events that would follow. After they had eaten, the people collected in small groups around campfires of sputtering driftwood. Some sang, some danced, many lay back staring up at stars that seemed close enough to grasp by the handful.

De Luna at length said good night and was rowed back to the flagship. Before retiring he wanted a last chance to discuss the next day's activities with Arias.

He found the admiral in his cabin, poring over discharge plans with Ceron. Both were anxious to follow the camp master's program to the letter, to avoid needless searching out of items once supplies were ashore.

The captain-general watched for a moment, nodding approval. De Luna was not a clerically oriented man. He could manage people and accounts, but lists and orders bored him. He drifted aimlessly away, poking his nose into the shelf of instruments that were Arias' pride. He picked up the astrolabe.

"You perform great tricks with these," de Luna commented.

Arias nodded. "Thank old Prince Henry; his people authored most of them," he replied.

"If only you could do as well predicting the wind and the weather," the captain-general added.

"Wouldn't that be nice, now!" Arias agreed.

De Luna retreated to the deck, breathed deeply and walked to the rail. The fires were burning down now; only a few flickered, and across the water an occasional voice could be heard. Most of the settlers had huddled into little groups and were asleep on the sand, grateful that tonight their beds did not sway.

He looked up. Clouds had begun to obscure the stars, and the air had a little chill. De Luna shivered and folded his arms about his chest. Looking out across the bay he could see lights aboard the other vessels, nothing more.

Ah well, he thought, tomorrow will be a full day. Time to turn in. This has been a great day! If only Valencia could have been here! I wonder what she's doing tonight?. . .

Admiral Arias . . . commander of the thirteen vessel fleet. With hundreds of others, he perished in the storm.

MADRID
October 15, 1559

In Madrid, Valencia de Luna lay naked in a bed so large that she seemed to float on its pure pink sheets. Nearby, his royal nakedness covered by the second sheet, lay Philip II, King of Spain. His Most Catholic Majesty! His soft snores were the only sound in the ornate royal bedchamber.

Valencia lay on her back, her arms behind her head, eyes gazing into the darkness.

"Holy Mary . . . what have I done!" she asked herself over and over.

Three times the King had invited her to be his guest. The first evening had been delightful, with exotic food and wine and talk of Don Tristan and the New World.

The second evening they had enjoyed the company of Ximinez and Don Hernando Segura and his wife and had been entertained by court musicians. When she returned home, Dona de Luna had been giddy and excited as a child. Dining twice with the king! It was unbelievable.

This evening had begun much the same, with the same superb food and small talk of where the expedition might be now, and what her husband must be doing.

But then, with the settings cleared and the ladies and gentlemen in waiting absent, Philip turned suddenly to her, grasped her shoulders in a steel grip and pressed his lips to hers in a long, twisting kiss, the moist hair of his mustache rubbing roughly across her upper lip as she struggled to pull free.

He said nothing . . . but after a moment suddenly shifted his grip to hold her firmly against him with his left arm. The practiced fingers of his right hand slowly slipped along her neck, inching downward, under the cloth of her gown and over her generous breast.

Valencia swung her head back and forth, pushing, scratching, clawing at the king's back.

Suddenly he released her, and she stood back, her hair torn down from its elaborate bands, her gown twisted slightly at the shoulder, her eyes flashing fire.

"How could you . . . how could you do this when my husband is. . . ."

She got no further.

Philip's head snapped back and his laughter rolled forth. His hand slapped his thigh, and his head rolled back and forth! Philip seldom laughed; indeed, he hardly even smiled. For him this was a startling performance.

Valencia stared, now speechless, her arms folded across her chest, not knowing whether to flee or continue her protest.

Then Philip snapped back to the moment.

"Dear Valencia . . . you are delightful! In fact, you are precious! How you looked when you mentioned your husband . . . " and he broke into waves of laughter.

Valencia summoned her strength and broke in.

"What kind of man are you, to make pious speeches as God's messenger . . . and then to assault the wife of your most loyal subject. . . ."

Philip became serious again, walked two paces and slipped onto the huge wood and leather couch. His eyes never left her face.

"My dear, you are as naive as you are lovely. Surely, you must have known . . . or at least had some idea. . . ."

She shook her head.

"Valencia, my army is filled with men of great skill and loyalty. In fact, experience has proven that often such expeditions fare best when led by men of less background but more daring than Don Tristan."

"But then . . . why . . . I don't understand," she stammered.

"The night we returned, the night of the ball, you enchanted me. You were lovely, gracious, alive . . . and after all, I have been wedded to a pious cow these past five years."

"Do you mean . . . ." she began.

"And so, I felt I must have you. The only question was how to remove Don Tristan. After all, he was such an eager bridegroom . . . and with such a bride!"

Valencia's head dropped, tears began to fill her eyes.

"What better way than to give him the greatest opportunity for fame and fortune within my power. After all . . . that is what he has, you know."

The tears came easily now, and her body was racked by deep, bitter sobs.

Philip rose and approached her, this time with the gentleness of a man much practiced in the art of comforting conquests.

Slowly he slipped the graceful gown from her shoulders, then the layers of soft undergarments. In seconds, she stood naked before him, making no effort to protest.

With a single motion he lifted her into his arms and carried her into the antechamber, a room dominated by the largest bed she had ever seen, its coverlet already neatly drawn back.

Gently, he lay her on the thick mattress with its silken sheets; his hands ran tenderly down her body, coming to rest on her ornate shoes, which he subtly removed.

Then, in a moment, he was beside her, stroking her breasts, pressing and rubbing her in an effort to arouse her passion. Seconds later, he pushed her thighs apart and entered her.

Valencia de Luna stared at the ceiling, her mind whirling, her soul in torment. Possessed by the King, violated by the man who had seemed to do so much for them! Yet, what could she do? To whom could she turn? What could she say, even to her husband?

Her head turned slightly, and her eyes fastened on Philip's sleeping figure.

Slowly the tears began to flow again . . . and continued, far into the night.

OCHUSE
August 16, 1559

De Luna was up with the sun. On the beach, wisps of smoke already identified preparations for the morning meal; a few souls stirred, and the more adventurous had scrambled up the cliffs and were wandering to the east, shouting to one another at each new discovery.

The captain-general grinned. The enthusiasm was marvelous, he mused! Never had a people been so anxious to begin their labors. Well, this morning he must begin his.

In his cabin he hastily wrote three copies of a brief report, summarizing the sea journey, detailing the unfavorable winds, then praising Arias for the seamanship which had brought the fleet to Bahia Filipina, and then to Santa Maria.

"This morning we begin the duties of exploration, to choose a permanent site for our settlement," he wrote. "One squad of soldiers and horses shall be dispatched to the east, to examine the river which Bazares' report says is pure and sweet but with a low tideland. Another shall move to the west along the upland, to examine the land there, and to seek out the sweet spring which Maldonado claims to have used during his stay here. We shall permit today as a day of relaxation for the people, and tomorrow shall make preparations for temporary shelter and the unloading of the vessels.

"The pinnace carries this message to His Excellency, Don Luis de Velasco; as quickly as they are free of cargoes, two dispatch vessels shall carry identical copies to Spain to advise His Majesty of our safe arrival. Other vessels will be maintained for the journey to Puenta de Santa Elena and then the smaller vessels shall remain here for such purposes as our efforts may require.

"God has blessed our venture; and we have honored Him by divine services on the beach; the weather is fine, the beaches are flawless, the anchorage beautiful, the people happy. I am confident that God has blessed our mission and that we shall succeed in bringing His message to the Indians, and in the safeguarding of this land for our empire. Thus far we have seen no inhabitants, but today we shall begin actively seeking them.

"May God add His continuing blessing to our efforts."

Seal: Don Tristan de Luna y Arellano

Captain-General, Governor of La Florida

De Luna, Arias, Fray Anunciacon and del Sauz breakfasted together. The captain-general read the text of his report and asked for additions. There were none. Arias suggested that those selected for explorations up the broad bay be put aboard the pinnace, and that the small vessel carry them to an appropriate landing, where she then might check her bottom, take on water and be prepared to sail with next evening's tide. De Luna agreed, and Arias left to send orders to Manuel Ortiz, who commanded the small vessel.

In any army men learn not to volunteer as part of an unwritten orientation, but now came an exception. Among the officers, everyone wished to head one of the two exploratory land missions. To choose the site of the new city, to perhaps be the first to converse with the Indians here, to see at length the horizons of their new homeland . . . all were desirable after a month at sea.

De Luna closeted himself with Ceron after breakfast, and the two agreed that Porras should lead the march up river. A man of some education, his observations would be clear, and he had the ability to communicate well what he experienced. To accompany him as captain of horse would be Capt. Pedro de Acuna; twenty troopers were selected at random from the companies of the two men, and they were given orders to go aboard the pinnace with their gear by noon next day, providing the horses had arrived. Balthazar Sotello and Rodrigo Vazquez were chosen to lead the quick tour to the west.

Later that morning we did in fact arrive with the horses. Delighted with the new land and refreshed by our leisurely journey, we were eager now to rejoin our comrades and find out the next step to be taken.

Next afternoon, with the horses now in camp, the two squads departed while the rest of us concentrated on camp preparation. By sundown, Porras and Acuna had pushed north and east along the river almost ten kilometers. The march along the river which someone long ago had called Ochuse had been delightful and surprisingly cool, for much of their path wound between and under huge oaks and towering pines, whose fallen straw made the ground a soft downy brown. The undergrowth was moderate; two troopers walked ahead with broad-bladed knives to knock down vines and climbers that might bar the way, but the march was surprisingly easy.

On the right the river's waters shimmered in the light of the August sun, and overhead birds flitted and called, unused to the blundering woodsmanship of the heavyfooted Spaniards. Occasionally large game was seen, and there were signs everywhere that deer were present.

From time to time they would come into a cleared area where the cover was a fine bladed grass that ran in long trailing shoots across the ground, sometimes matting into a handsome turf. Where the ground was bare, it was a porous, yellowish-white sand that scuffed easily under the soldiers' boots.

The scent of the piney woods was sweet and fresh, and as they trudged forward the troopers quietly discussed its potential. "It will be good for cattle," they agreed, "but for beans, who knows?"

At nightfall they made camp, Acuna posting a rotating guard. Their campfire was carefully ringed with sand, and they soon discovered that the pine pitch in the fallen limbs made a fire that blazed up handsomely.

As they sat sipping a second cup of wine, Acuna and Porras agreed on the virtues of their new homeland.

"It's a beautiful place," the infantryman said.

"The good life at our fingertips," the other replied. "It's almost too easy. If only something doesn't spoil it all."

After the long weeks at sea, the weary soldiers slept like children; the guards paced easily about. Only the hoot of an occasional nightbird broke the peace. They might have been alone on the planet.

To the west, the second patrol was enjoying a similar experience.

Late in the afternoon they had come to the spring, a small stream perhaps six meters wide that broke easily down the slight grade that approached the bay.

The bluffs under which the ships were anchored had extended only a kilometer or so to the west from the anchorage. Thereafter the land gave way to a gentle slope, and the troopers had encountered a narrow inlet from which brackish waters flowed out of a bayou which they at first mistook for a river. However, examination of Bazares' sketchy map showed that this was the extension of a creek which began several kilometers upland; fresh water from this source would be too far from an anchorage.

And so the troopers sought a shallow and splashed across, then ventured further westward.

About four o'clock they found the spring; immediately all fell on their bellies to test the waters, drinking deep of the first truly fresh water their lips had tasted in weeks.

Vazquez and Sotello stood back watching, allowing their men a welcome break. Shading his eyes, Vazquez looked upland, where the waters dropped easily across the sandy bottom of their bed. The stream was not deep, perhaps a meter at the center; and at the widest it appeared less than six meters. But there was a good flow of the sweet, cool water, and it appeared to come for a goodly distance.

"I suggest we move upland, and see how far this comes," Sotello said.

"Agreed," his fellow captain countered. "Then I propose that we divide the company. You take half and move out to the west; I'll take the remainder and try to map what's near the water, and near the bay. That way the commanders will have an idea of what can be done here, if this is our permanent site."

Sotello nodded in agreement.

"All right, you hollow-legged bastards, on your feet!" he shouted. "You'll all drown poor men if we don't get underway. Come on, up, up!"

Moments later, the company divided, the two captains moved out, the one trudging through the sands bordering the stream to the north, the other to the west. It was agreed that they would rejoin at dusk at the mouth of the stream.

That night, with the twenty troopers lolling about the fire, Vazquez and Sotello compared notes and prepared their report.

The stream, which Sotello termed a spring, ran but a few hundred meters from the shoreline, surfacing from some deep, hidden source. The brief survey, however, revealed level land, much of it free from heavy trees, and with a pleasant, gentle slope towards the bay. With the spring at its center, it would be a perfect location for the settlement. To the north the soil became slightly richer and more dense. There were many trees, and clearing land for farming would not be easy, but it was not impossible.

To the west the second squad had walked the beach until members came to the mouth of a second brackish bayou, which they had scouted, thinking that it too might be a river. However, it had quickly narrowed, with only two tiny creeks as the arms of its source. These streams too might be considered as a water source, but the land about was densely forested, and the mouth of the bayou was too shallow for any but the smallest vessel, so this would hardly be considered a primary site for the city.

The officers agreed: the land was lovely, the breezes sweet, the air pure, the water fresh and cool.

"It's a good land the Lord has given us," Sotello commented.

"Indeed, I'm anxious to bring these reports to the captain-general. The sooner we begin clearing the land, the sooner you and I become landowners."

Sotello smiled. "Dream on, old friend. So far this has been too easy."

Next morning they continued their mappings; then, after noon, started the return march.

At dusk, both eastern and western squads returned at almost the same moment. As the men began to disperse among the colonists to tell their tales, the four captains were rowed to the ESTRAMADURA, where de Luna, Ceron, Arias and Fray Anunciacon waited. I was present, too, though in no official capacity. My uncle had simply invited me.

A light supper had been prepared in the master cabin, and together the nine of us took our ease, the four explorers reporting in turn, closely questioned by the others. Ceron, in particular, posed item after item to the captains.

As each point was made about terrain and cover, water and sand, the possibilities for quickly plowed fields and the raw materials for shelters, de Luna made notes as he usually did. His questions were fewer, yet his eyes probed each speaker's face as he related details of what had been seen.

At length, the captain-general from Aragon cleared his throat and made his point: "Gentlemen, you've done well. Decisions now, of course, must deal with all the factors we must consider. If tillable fields are close by, much the better. I assume from what you have said that the area near the spring is superior."

Vazquez and Sotello nodded, the others simply shrugged their shoulders.

"Second, we must have a defensible position. Today, we face no hostilities, either Indian or white men, but tomorrow, who can tell? Therefore, can the area near the spring be defended?"

Here the captains were less positive.

"The area's very flat, your excellency, and has natural protection from only the one side. It could be charged by cavalry, and it is vulnerable from artillery. However . . ."

"Yes?"

"I'd say that in this region it will be possible for us to erect walls of sand and logs that can withstand heavy ball, and I see little danger of massive attacks by sea. It's only the hostile native we need fear for now, and if we do our work well. . . ."

He left unsaid the assumption that soon the red men would be citizens of Spain, and members of the holy Church and brotherhood.

De Luna turned to Ceron. "Your views?"

"I'm certain our captains have done their work well. However, I think it would be well to make a more thorough survey, since this appears to be the best primary location. . . ."

"And," broke in Arias, "may I propose that we take the longboats and survey the bottom. We'll want sufficient depths for at least modest cargo vessels, and a good anchorage. It would be unwise, either for shipping or defense, to select a location fronted by a shallows."

Ceron nodded vigorously.

De Luna concurred.

"Very well," the captain-general continued. "I'll ask Arias here to assign sailors to half of the small boats, and to row a contingent of officers and men to the mouth of the spring. There, with Sotello's help, we'll begin a survey and actually measure the land, determine where to locate the preliminary and essential buildings, and decide where farmlands might best begin. Then, we'll reconvene in council and allocate plots to the citizens according to the viceroy's plan."

There was a murmur of assent.

"Then," de Luna continued, "we'll have the men in the longboats sound the sea approach; let's determine if we can discharge vessels there, or will have to use our present anchorage as Ceron has prepared for."

"This should only take half a day," Arias interrupted. "We'll use lines and weights that can provide a reasonably accurate charting."

"Very well," said de Luna. "Now, Ceron, suppose you and I spend the morning directing erection of some temporary shelters at the head of the bluffs here. Whichever way our discoveries take us, portions of our work must continue here; it's too much to ask God to provide weather unbroken by rains . . . especially at this time of the year."

Ceron swallowed quickly. Drawing duty of the most elementary type was not what he'd hoped for. If there was a city to be built, he wanted to be there at the beginnings, to give counsel, to make his voice heard.

He answered softly, "Of course, excellency; as you will."

August 18-19, 1559

The following two days passed so swiftly that later we had difficulty recalling simplest details. The further mapping of the spring site proceeded smoothly, and later in the evening of the 18th Fray Pedro de Feria, who had much skill as a map maker and surveyor, bent over chart paper to begin applying the viceroy's plan for the new city to the practical realities they had found. In the Spanish style, there were locations for a great church, a governor's palace, the military commandant's house, a fort and other defenses, a plaza for public affairs, and suitable precautions in the use of the spring.

Similar plottings were made for the uplands where farming and grazing would take place.

At noon on the 19th the pinnace, slightly delayed in her reloading, departed for Mexico.

Soundings had shown that the water before the proposed townsite was sufficient for lesser vessels to stand in almost to the shoreline; the larger galleons and heavily laden transports would not . . . under present load . . . be able to move within 100 meters of the land.

"All things considered, it will be safer to discharge them below the bluffs, where lighters can move quickly. We can assemble carts and use the horses to draw the supplies overland. It will be safe," Arias suggested. Ceron concurred. De Luna, no expert in such matters, accepted their proposals.

By now, the remainder of the 1500 were occupied each moment also. Some women combed the edge of nearby woods for berries and nuts to supplement the diet of dried foods, while others searched the shallows for shell fish.

Sailors and soldiers, moving at Ceron's orders, began unloading the second smaller vessel, which was to depart as quickly as possible with reports for King Philip. Fray Bartolome Matheos, the small, swarthy priest who had been a gunner with Pizarro and then accepted the call to the cloth, had been chosen to go as spokesman and was both excited and disappointed. In the cabin of the ESTRAMADURA he worked feverishly over his papers, with Anunciacon at his elbow.

On the townsite, crews with knives and axes went about the business of clearing land that would be needed first, while on the upland near the cliff, away from where temporary quarters might interfere with the discharge operation, Ceron's crews were throwing up simple lean-to shelters of sticks and pine needles to protect the colonists should rains come.

Following a brief religious service at dusk, de Luna hurried to his cabin to pen a final supplement to his report to Philip, to be carried next day by Fray Matheos. Shortly, he was joined by Anunciacon; both men were ecstatic.

"Who would have believed that things would move so well!" the priest exclaimed.

"You've said it many times, father, if God be with us, how can we fail?" de Luna added.

Ashore, in hundreds of tiny gatherings, husbands and wives, comrades in arms, all agreed: the promised land had been joined!

Before he retired that night, the captain-general had cleared a long list of things to be done for the next day. The small shallop had been unloaded and reprovisioned. The reports were written, and the courier vessel would be prepared to sail with the high tide, in early afternoon next day.

Most other activities were ahead of schedule. If all went as well for the next 48 hours, shelter would be ready for the discharge of much of the general supplies; that was the goal. Within a week construction of the first permanent dwellings would begin.

De Luna's ears could almost hear the sounds of saw and axe! His first city was almost a fact.

The thought acted like a drug and sent him into a slumber filled with pleasant dreams.

As he slept, his body began to rock gently in the berth; slowly, at first, then with gradually increasing violence, the ship felt the rising roll of waves, even under the cliffs in the sheltered bay.

Then, at about four in the morning, rain began to fall gently against the timbers of the ship.

Ashore, the more exposed colonists huddled under their shelters, and drew collars and capes about them.

Sotello, who had remained ashore, drew his garment closer, looked up and took several drops in his mouth.

"Damn," he muttered. "Oh well, we can't expect it to be perfect. Hell, what's a little rain?"

August 19, 1559—A.M.

Gomez Arias had gone to sea at 14. It was his life, that and ships. As a professional, he believed that ships respond to weather almost like the human body. They breathe, they labor, they react by some instinct to changes in barometric pressure and temperature.

He awoke in a cabin that seemed very dark, different from the week's previous mornings. No sun rays streamed across the floor; instead, rain beat heavily against the planking, and above this throaty, creaking rigging straining in the wind was clearly audible.

The admiral slowly drew his legs out of his bunk and half-dragged himself to his feet. Strange, he thought! We're showing motion, almost as though we were at sea!

He dressed quickly, throwing a canvas over his shoulders as foul weather gear, and climbed to the quarterdeck. The morning watch was on duty, carefully making rounds, checking lines and stowage.

Arias gazed towards shore, then turned and gave a veteran's studied appraisal of the weather.

Rain was falling in a steady drizzle, driven in squall-like gusts against the ship. Across the 50 meters that separated ESTRAMADURA from CADIZ, waves were washing, not high, ferocious sea waves, of course, but churning water driven by a rising wind that already sang its song in the rigging.

Arias walked aft and cupped hand over eyes as protection as he gazed at the sky. Overhead, the cloud cover seemed very low, clouds with a sickly yellow tinge that from time to time was broken by lightning occasionally followed by thunder. As he scanned the sky and the bay, Arias sensed the rising pitch of the wind; minute by minute, the rain seemed to beat upon his face with greater force, a stinging, pelting rain now with force that made the veteran seaman begin to summon his knowledge of weather in these latitudes.

He had been on deck perhaps five minutes when Tristan de Luna joined him, hunched over against the wind, his tunic covered by a cape which gave some protection.

"I knew it was too good to last, Gomez," he cried, shouting to be heard, "but then, we've been too lucky. And I guess we must have a little rain to keep the grass green, eh?"

Arias nodded, then motioned for de Luna to follow. Together, they re-entered the great cabin, shaking the water from their garments like two soaked shaggy dogs.

Gomez Arias threw off his raingear and slumped into his bunk, the water streaming off his full head of curly hair and into his eyes. Impatiently, he rubbed his forearm across his face.

"We'll lose the day, I'm afraid," he complained. "Just listen to it! Sounds as though she'll pour forever!"

De Luna nodded agreement, but added, "You know what they say about the tropics. If you don't like the weather, just wait awhile."

"Sometimes that's true . . . but I doubt it today. Just feel that wind!"

De Luna, still standing, shifted his feet to ease his position as the deck slanted.

"Almost feels as though we were at sea," he admitted. "You don't suppose this could be something more than just a squall?"

"I doubt it! In all the years our people have been in Mexico they've had few stories of anything more than heavy gales."

"Maybe so . . . but in the islands they tell other stories."

"Even so, this is the soundest harbor I've seen in this hemisphere. Come on . . . don't worry. Cheer up! You're getting jumpy because you've lost five minutes building your precious city!"

De Luna forced a smile. "Guess you're right. But . . . if you don't mind, I think I'll have your men take me ashore. The people are going to be miserable. I don't want them to think I'm dry as straw while they're being soaked. You know what I mean?"

"Always see to the horses and men first, eh? Keeps morale high. Very well, catch cold if you will. I'll have the mate take you in. When will you want to come back? Don't want to leave him on the beach if it isn't necessary."

"Oh . . . noonish, I'd say. Agreeable? Then we'll try some of that French wine we've been saving . . . something to brighten the day, eh?"

Arias laughed and nodded. "Something for everyone, eh, captain? The King chooses his diplomats well, I'll say that for him."

Moments later the captain-general was easing his way down the ropes and into the longboat where eight sturdy seamen held oars aloft, ready to pull to the shore. The boat stood in the lee of the rolling ESTRAMADURA, stout arms holding her fast to the ropes that clung to the ship's side. But once out of the protection of the looming galleon, the boat began to feel the effects of the rising storm. The waves, driven by the westerly wind, rose in sharp white caps, even though they were less than 100 meters

With undefinable force, the storm seized the vessel and whirled it skyward . . .

from the protected shoreline. Ahead, the swell was growing, and waves beat angrily on the beach, rolling up under the cliffs and licking their white froth against the yellow-orange clay. Rain drove in sheets out of the west, making it impossible for eyes to penetrate in that direction. The oarsmen, facing the rear of the craft and into the storm, squinted, keeping eyes almost closed. Water soaked their caps and poured down craggy, whiskered cheeks.

Seated in the stern, de Luna faced forward, watching the bobbing action of the boat. He could make out a few figures huddled near the base of the cliff; most others seemed to have climbed up the steep sides and accepted the meager shelter offered by the bowers of branches erected by Ceron. Fires had long since disappeared.

The boat, whipped ahead by the wind, scarcely needed the help of the sweeps. Dipping up and down, she flitted over the water, taking only seconds to span the gulf. De Luna saw the bowsman stand, bracing himself, and then time his vault over the side as the surf caught the boat and drove it high on the sand. Instantly a second wave, then a third, drove over the stern, drenching the occupants. De Luna stood and picked his way forward, then agilely leaped over the gunwale, landing thigh deep in waters swirling back down the beach. "Thank you, thank you very much . . . now hurry back!" he shouted, but his words were swirled away in the howl of the rising wind.

Wrapping his cloak double over his shoulders, the commander plunged forward to the nearest path up the cliff and started forward. The clay was as slippery as oil, the handholds slick and loose. Inching his way up, the captain-general wondered at the colonists' good fortune in having everyone up the bluffs before the hazard of such a climb. Gripping for new holds, he inched himself forward, step after step, the wind and rain lashing him constantly. The water clinging to his clothes made de Luna feel twice his weight, and time after time he halted to get his breath and relax muscles now straining from their ordeal.

"Great God," he moaned, "what's happening? I've never seen such a storm! Surely this won't happen often in our paradise!"

At length, his clothes caked with the orange mud, fingers torn from scraping against the abrasive sand-clay, Don Tristan hoisted his body over the edge of the cliff. Instantly the wind seemed to lift him forward, dumping him headlong on the ground into several centimeters of standing water which eddied with the wind.

For a moment de Luna lay still, his ears numbed by the rising wail of the storm, his body now soaked, his head reeling and his lungs sucking wildly for air.

Cautiously, he raised himself to his knees, inched forward, then peered back to the beach and the short stretch of open water where the long-boat was struggling back to ESTRAMADURA against the rising tide of the storm.

Now there was no pursuing gale to ease the rowing. At each thrust the boat plunged into the water and moved, ever so slightly, forward. Oarsmen, their backs bent to the effort, clawed oars desperately and deep into the water, yet their strength was offset by the action of the storm; the boat, its bow deep in the waves, now was raised up by wave action so that oars sometimes flailed the open air and struck at the rain.

The ESTRAMADURA, with some strain on her anchor, could hardly be seen. De Luna counted; he could see just six of the craft. The sheets of rain, backed by a deep and graying sky, obscured the rest.

The captain-general pulled himself to his feet. Quickly the wind hurled him forward, towards the groves of trees and shelters where his 1500 huddled, now a pitiful, soaked, silent and unhappy throng upon whom the elements poured tons of water.

There was no movement among them. No officers were to be seen. De Luna moved from shelter to shelter, pausing only long enough to give a brief word of encouragement, to pat a child, to reassure a frightened woman: "It will be over soon."

"Try to be calm, make yourself as comfortable as you can. I know it's bad but soon we'll have stout houses of our own."

"Perhaps by nightfall it will be over and we can light our fires again."

"Think how lucky we are that God withheld the storm until we were safely on shore and on these friendly bluffs!"

Ultimately, he blundered into a shelter where Ceron and foot captain Antonio Matienzo were trying to hold out the wind-driven rain by weaving their cloaks against small branches. It was a losing battle, and both officers knew it. They grinned as de Luna struggled in beside them.

"Welcome to our happy home," quipped Ceron.

"Gracias!" de Luna replied. "I admire your ingenuity; at least it keeps you busy for a moment."

Matienzo exposed a toothy grin, "I wish I had my paspadores . . . we'd play a hand, eh?"

Ceron shrugged. "It won't last forever; storms like this never do. We'll just ride it out. How are things aboard ship?"

"Oh, fine, fine. I'm afraid, though, that the messengers will be delayed. I shouldn't expect they'll sail into this."

"I would think not."

Suddenly Matienzo lurched to his knees, blood gushed from a cut on his forehead opened by a blow from a limb.

"Holy Mary, she's coming apart, the wind's taking the shelter apart," howled the wounded captain.

De Luna grabbed his arm, helped him to his feet and tried to stanch the blood which flowed into the injured man's left eye.

Ceron reached up, trying to repair the damage left by the falling bough. As he did so the wind's pitch rose higher to a rumbling howl, and piece by piece the entire shelter began to peel apart, one limb after another simply slipping away, the matted pine straw whipping into the air as the whole shelter disintegrated.

"Come on," shouted Ceron, "let's get out of here. Help me, Don Tristan, take his other arm!"

Half dragging the dazed Matienzo between them, the two officers put their backs to the wind and began to struggle towards the nearest shelter.

But their experience was not unique. All around them bits of wood were streaming through the air, driven at fantastic speed, making the area seem like a battleground.

"Duck down," shouted de Luna, "try to keep low, make a smaller target."

Ceron nodded. It was almost impossible to hear now. Wave after wave of rain washed over the trio, bent low and almost creeping over the ground. They had almost reached the next lean-to, backed against the side of a huge oak whose branches swept the ground, when a sound almost like the firing of a cannon momentarily drowned the shriek of the wind.

"Look out!" screamed Ceron, tugging furiously at the semi-conscious Matienzo.

De Luna never really saw the tree fall. It was more that he felt the vibrations. The high cracking, crunching sound was followed by a loud scaping as a pine, perhaps 20 meters away, tottered and fell, its towering branches interlocking for a moment with the foliage of an oak; then, the pine came sliding, crunching down.

Inhabitants of the lean-to never saw it, had no warning. Seconds later they were crushed to pulp beneath the tons of dense wood in a tree that had graced the forest for a century.

"My God!" de Luna screamed.

Quickly, they laid the injured Matienzo in the shelter of the fallen pine and began to claw their way through the maze of branches. The trunk had somehow fallen at an angle through the huge tower of the oak and had come to rest squarely on the shelter of three unfortunate Spaniards. Scrambling over limb and through cone and the long leaf straw, Ceron came upon first one body, then a second and a third. All three were soldiers, their cloaks wrapped around their shoulders front to rear, their eyes wide with fright. Each was crushed by the terrible weight of the tree, two pinned across the chest, the other with his skull smashed to jelly. As de Luna peered through the mass of tangled wood and branches, the driving rain dripped off his own head and mingled with the pool of blood swelling from the dead man.

Ceron shook his head. De Luna bowed his, made the sign of the cross and uttered a prayer. Of necessity, it was brief, the slight protection the 1500 had enjoyed was now coming apart at its weak seams. At site after site grass and straw and small wood were being blown apart, exposing men, women and children to the full force of driving rain and wind and the increasing hazard of flying and falling objects.

De Luna's reaction was to have them all retreat further into the denser woods, where trees might reduce the wind. Ceron agreed, and both turned and ran, moving from group to group, screaming, pointing, gesturing . . . pushing, urging, carrying . . . trying to make a terrified army understand what was needed.

A few grasped their meaning, and heads down, arms about comrades or loved ones, they began inching forward, buffeted by the wind, scalded by sheets of driven rain that now made it impossible to see ten meters in any direction.

Seconds later another tree fell; then a third and a fourth. As the fourth, another pine, came smashing down, screams were heard, and hardy souls fought their way to the center, to try to free the victims.

In minutes, the scene had changed from one of pitiful huts shelting a drenched 1500 to one of panic, with a terrified mob fleeing from the storm and the wind and the falling trees and flying debris.

11:00 A.M.

On board the transport CARLOS V Juan Alvarez had the watch. A lean, tough Castillian, Alvarez had spent the last decade of his life plying the Atlantic in ships of the King. His duty as second officer aboard the heavily laden transport was a good berth; one worked hard, played hard, saw the world.

But this morning was uncomfortable! Huddled in sturdy weathergear, Alvarez sat on the bridge, his back to a bulkhead, his eyes straying back and forth across the water.

"Holy Christ the son!" he muttered, "what a wind!"

The CARLOS V lay approximately 50 meters from the CADIZ, and through the gray sheets of rain the officer could make out the outline of the galleon, rolling and pitching, her anchor chain straining at 45 degrees to her side.

Alvarez looked up. The creaking, groaning, sighing of the masts were in counterpoint to the singing in the rigging. The officer stepped forward to get a better look above. As he did so the wind caught him full in the back and slammed him across the bridge and into the latticed paneling of the rail. Dazed, he shook his head and grasped the sturdy oaken frame firmly. At that moment all hell broke loose.

High above, the disaster began with a sound like a tiny pistol shot. Then, the volume increased, the pitch rising as a rift in the once sturdy oaken mast began to widen. Alvarez stood and stared . . . rooted to the spot . . . wanting to scream a warning, but with the sounds locked in his throat. He was a man watching tragedy approach yet powerless to act, powerless even to warn.

Slowly, inch by inch, the giant mainmast descended, its spars jamming into intertwining rigging and sweeping it away, its weight slamming against the superstructure that protected the high cabins. With a grinding crash it drove backward through cabin and rail and smashed into the water.

The vessel, loaded to its limits of safety, gave a lurch and listed violently to starboard. As she did so, cargo neatly stored symmetrically in the several holds suddenly snapped free of dunnage and, following gravity, fell heavily on the ship's right side.

Below decks officers and seamen off watch were thrown from their bunks, or driven against bulkheads; loose gear flew violently into the air and crashed in an unheard clatter to the deck. One by one, frightened men scrambled, crawled, clawed their way to the deck. A few made it . . . only a few.

For at that moment the indescribable full fury of the hurricane broke. Winds which had been at terrible force now almost doubled, intermixed with tornadic funnels which twisted their way through the bay, spinning and churning waterspouts which sucked up every solid object in their path.

The first blast of the new wind struck the CARLOS V on her raised port side, raising it up . . . up . . . and finally over, sending the once proud vessel reeling in a cartwheel that spun the already untrimmed ship sprawling bottom up. Juan Alvarez was perhaps the only man to see what happened, and he lived to tell no one. From what we could tell, his one frantic grab at a severed spar failed. Seconds later he was struck in the back by a flying barrel of flour. He died as he had lived . . . by the sea.

In his cabin aboard the ESTRAMADURA, Gomez Arias had held counsel with his officers. Each had been given a special assignment; cargo dunnage was being checked for security; hatches were being resecured. Crew members were on special alert, pumps were being manned, for even in this supposedly placid bay, ESTRAMADURA now was taking on water. Sheet upon sheet of rain hurled itself against the sturdy galleon, but now, as the winds increased, pieces of superstructure were being wrenched free and hurled into the gray mid-day that seemed almost dark as night. Moment by moment the velocity of the winds increased, till now the anchor was grasping frantically at the soft sandy bottom, and practiced seamen in her main cabin could feel the slow drag as the ship began to give way, inch by inch, before the storm. Arias struggled to open the way to the deck, to see again for himself how things were. Hunched forward, he staggered onto the deck, seizing handlines which had been rigged across the bridge.

Straightening, he felt the mixture of rain and salt spray that cut like a razor across his face. Above him, sturdy masts swung back and forth in widening arcs, the wind singing a siren song in the rigging which now flailed against the wood, giving off snapping sounds.

Then he saw the first one: a jet black spinning cloud shaped like an inverse pyramid, moving toward them, its tip just above the water, its funnel shape rising into the heart of the gray cloud mass above. As he watched, Arias could see tree limbs and other refuse of the storm being sucked upward and then spat out again higher up as the funnel cloud pushed forward.

Between the cloud and the ESTRAMADURA stood CADIZ, like his own flagship weaving back and forth, her body pushed by the raking wind. On and on came the funnel, its blackness silhouetted against the gray of the storm. A streaking flash of lightning brightened the scene for only a second, and as it did so the funnel struck CADIZ. Slowly, the 125-ton transport ceased to be part of the sea. Momentarily it resisted, its coppered bottom clinging to the friendly, familiar waves. Then, it broke loose, and as Arias watched in horror the vessel rose up . . . up . . . up . . . spinning faster and faster as she moved steadily closer to ESTRAMADURA, almost parallel with the shoreline.

On and on the funnel came as the admiral stood transfixed in horror; then, as tornado and transport passed to ESTRAMADURA's stern, Arias roused himself, grasped his trumpet, and shrieked an order to the watch:

"Cut the anchor, cut the anchor . . . cut us free . . . cut us free!"

The only hope for survival was to let ESTRAMADURA run free, to run with the wind and hope that the wave of tornadoes might miss them.

Somehow, two seamen made their way to the capstan and with axes glittering cut the great claw free.

Released, ESTRAMADURA bobbed up like a cork, swung about and almost raced without sails before the wind. For a moment, Arias breathed easily. Then, a voice screamed almost in his ear!

"MY GOD, sir . . . ahead . . . dead ahead . . . it's SANTA MARIA! It's SANTA MARIA!"

ESTRAMADURA, blowing almost sideways now before the wind, had no guidance, no opportunity to change direction. Second by second she raced on, accelerating before the hurricane winds that now blew as Arias had heard only in fables. On they came, closing the gap . . . twenty-five meters . . . twenty . . . fifteen . . . ten . . . five. . . .

Arias and his officers of the watch braced themselves for the crash that now was inevitable.

With a roar that momentarily overcame the storm the two great, crowded, fully loaded vessels slammed together, the starboard side of the flagship impaling itself on the wind-turned bow of SANTA MARIA. Like a knife, the one cut into the other, and then as the wind force continued, ESTRAMADURA twisted away, her starboard rent by a huge, gaping hole that left SANTA MARIA's bowsprit dangling in the rising swells and its forward section a mass of splintered wood and torn cordage. Like a bucket whose bottom has been torn out, SANTA MARIA was sucked in the heaving Gulf waves, and in seconds settled, down, down, down into the deeps until, in seven fathoms, her bottom struck the sands. The SANTA MARIA was a dead ship, her officers and crews strangling and drowning in their cabins and quarters.

ESTRAMADURA, her side split, took on water rapidly, her holds filling, the cargo suddenly overwhelmed with a tide of gray brine.

Arias, knocked to the deck by the impact, shook himself free of debris, rose to one knee and fumbled for his trumpet to call orders to abandon ship. But the small boat was long gone, and there was no time to rig rafts. Suddenly, a great gust of wind, even more powerful than the others, swept across the derelict, bringing with it a wave that carried near the masthead. Slowly, like a great stricken animal, ESTRAMADURA struggled to remain upright. But then, her belowdecks flooding, her side stove in, the pressure of wave and water upon her, the gallant sea queen resigned herself to death and slowly rolled upon her side . . . and in seconds disappeared below the surface.

Debris spilled from the shattered hull, and as lightning flashed again, it glistened upon one item . . . a bobbling bottle of rare French wine that the admiral had planned to enjoy for dinner.

On the upland, de Luna raced like a madman from cluster to cluster, urging his followers to flatten themselves, to grasp trees, shrubs, bushes, anything to withstand the force of the still-rising wind. Twice he was knocked fully to the ground; once he was stung almost senseless by a falling limb. Time after time he tripped and almost fell as he staggered blindly from place to place.

His officers followed his example. Hour after hour they somehow kept the pace, giving aid, comforting.

The priests did the same, the wind whipping at their habits, their faces caked now with salt spray and gray with fatigue.

Hour after hour the storm continued . . . and then . . . suddenly, it eased. The gray sky brightened, the wind stilled, the rain stopped.

Anunciacon, his eyes raised, fell on his knees and began to pray loudly: "Oh merciful God, we thank Thee for Thy compassion in sparing we who have sinned . . . You spared Daniel and Jonah, and like the blessed disciples, You have rescued us from the storm. . . ."

But the ordeal was not yet over.

De Luna, still dazed, joined Anunciacon in prayer; others followed suit, and soon all who were able, spread over many acres, were on their knees thanking God for deliverance. The prayer and sudden stillness seemed to revive them. There were even a few smiles to be seen . . . and then:

"Don Tristan . . . Don Tristan . . . my God, come quickly, come. . . ."

Who shouted de Luna never knew, but the man's urgency was so sincere that the fatigued commander arose and limped in the direction of the caller, in the direction of the cliffs. Viewed from the distance, screened by the trees, the waters looked almost calm now, angry and gray but less formidable than when he had staggered ashore hours before.

The captain-general saw the caller, and more limped than walked to his side:

"Easy, easy my friend, now . . . what is it you . . ." he began . . . and then he saw. Where twelve great vessels of Spain had tugged at their anchors, now there was devastation, a greasy tumble of debris. Pieces of cordage could be discerned and barrels and casks and planking but . . .?

"Where are the ships? My God in heaven, where are my ships?" screamed the commander. "Arias, Arias! Gomez Arias . . . my God, where are you? What have you done?"

His shouts brought others on the run, including Ceron and Sotello, Acuna and I. Together we stood and stared at the bay, which now seemed to regurgitate its new-found treasure; regularly new casks were coughed from the hulls of battered and sunken vessels.

De Luna sank slowly to the ground, buried his head in his arms and wept.

Ceron watched for a moment, then walked apart and stood silently gazing out over the mass of destruction.

Without speaking, the officers viewed the desolation, the absence of what a few hours before had been the greatest Spanish fleet ever assembled in the New World. Now it was gone, and with it our sustenance.

As we silently considered our fate, the drizzle began again, and over the bay gusts of wind stirred the surface. The eye of the storm had passed. There was more horror still to come.

This time there was warning.

Ceron, alert to the signs, quickly gathered the captains of foot and horse and held council; de Luna, dazed, stood on the fringes and listened; he had nothing to say.

"I've never seen one of these storms," the master of the camp began, "but I have heard stories from mariners. I believe that we have just passed through what they term 'the eye.' "

"Yes," prompted de Guevara, who had once been at the garrison in Cuba, "the winds go in a great circle, leaving a space of calm in the center. That must be what we are passing through. Now, the winds will come again. . . ."

"And the rain," confirmed Lucas Vasquez, stationed in Mexico since 1545. "I have heard of these things. We must take new precautions."

"The people are badly mixed, we can't reassemble units now," Ceron continued, "but we can get some organization. Each of you, try to group about 100, get them aside, explain what's happening."

The captains listened stoically, with little to add.

"We'll retreat into the woods; select positions near the largest trees; bed the people down. In what time we have, try to clear away loose brush and limbs, and get people to lie together, for protection and warmth."

Porras interrupted.

"Should we attempt any kind of shelter, as we had before?"

"Suit yourself. If there's wood, try it. But it did little good before."

The captains mumbled agreement.

"All right," Ceron concluded, "we have a few hours until dark, though God knows it's hardly light when the storm comes; try to maintain calm, talk to the people, encourage them. The priests are with them now; ask them to keep circulating. We'll not try to assemble until dawn. Then . . . well . . . we'll hope for the best. Agreed?"

The sodden Spaniards nodded their heads and turned toward the edge of the woods where remnants of the 1500 could be seen, many lying on the ground being ministered to by concerned friends and family.

Ceron turned to de Luna.

"Captain-general, I hope you didn't mind my. . . ."

"No . . . no . . . my friend, I appreciate your good judgment. I'm . . . I'm afraid the shock of the fleet . . . has . . . has. . . ."

He could not continue.

Ceron grasped the shaken commander by the elbow, and together they moved back, following the others.

Ceron seated his general at the base of a tree and turned inland, seeking a friar. Domingo de Salazar was there, bent low over the prostrate body of a man. "Fray Domin . . ." the camp master started to shout, but his words caught in his throat. The friar, his habit streaked with mud, his head bare, was on his knees, cross in hands, ministering to a man whose head was a mass of blood, his nose spread grotesquely across his face, his mouth a gaping scar from which his life's blood flowed.

A soldier spoke quietly. "A tree . . . it fell upon him as he lay protecting his children. He saw it, turned to scream a warning . . . and it caught him full upon the face. The friar is sure he's dying. . . ."

As the pikeman spoke, the gray, solid Dominican priest administered the last rites, the Latin words quiet and reassuring to those who watched. Suddenly, the stricken mass gasped, his body twitched in a convulsion. His head half rose, his glazed eyes open and staring, and suddenly fell back, a vacant stare on what remained of his face.

"May God have mercy on his soul . . ." intoned Fray Salazar, "and commit him to the army of angels. . . ."

Heads bowed, and strong men crossed themselves.

Ceron joined them, staring at his boots. He waited a respectful moment, then touched Salazar's arm.

"Father, I need you," he said softly.

Moments later, the priest was seated beside Tristan de Luna, talking quietly, trying to help him unfold the mental cobwebs which fogged his sense of duty and action.

Ceron walked quickly into the woods and rejoined his fellow officers in the futile task of organization, trying to get nearly 1500 miserable, terrified human beings into some form of safety for the night of horror which must come.

"God have mercy on us all," he muttered.

The effect of the storm on my uncle has been a subject of controversy for many years. Some have said that he fell into a state of shock and lost the power to reason and command for several critical days. Others commended him for attempting to restore optimism and a sense of purpose almost at once.

From my point of view neither is wholly correct.

After the officers had viewed the devastation on the beach, Don Tristan appeared dazed and confused. Fray Domingo de Salazar and I escorted him to a sheltered spot and made him comfortable. For a time we both remained with him, for we feared to leave. Ceron joined us and encouraged Salazar to assist my uncle. He could not seem to grasp what was taking place and could not command his speech, even to answer simple questions. His face, like mine, was a mask of dried salt, mixed with specks of debris which had collected in his clefts and beard. Even his eyelids were weighted by the dried sea spray.

But otherwise he appeared unharmed. Ceron departed and Fray Salazar sighted the Indian woman Maria Oslero and led her to de Luna, ordering her to get fresh water and sponge his face, and then to remain nearby and attend to the captain-general's needs. She nodded dumbly, but went about the task, rubbing a cool cloth with fresh water across his face, and sponging the matted hair and beard.

I remained nearby until I was certain the woman's ministrations would continue, then hurried to where the bulk of the company lay, stunned, drenched, cold and hungry. Ceron was there, and del Sauz, giving a sense of direction to the futile acts of recovery. They reasoned that there were certain things that must be done, and that for the others it was best to keep minds and hands busy. Thus we passed the first day and night after the storm.

Every hour or so I returned to my uncle, who as darkness fell dropped into a fitful sleep. So he remained until daybreak, the Indian woman nearby, a sort of mute and comforting sentinel.

When he awoke, de Luna was seemingly a new man.

Leaping into action, he was alert, filled with new vigor. He hurried about with a frenzied sense of purpose, encouraging people, promising that despite its ravages the storm would leave no serious permanent mark upon us. Joining his officers he assumed the proper role of captain-general, giving guidance and inspiring all to superior efforts.

So he remained during that grave and tragic time.

As I look back, I see him still, hurrying to and fro, making certain that each man received fair treatment in our sad condition, taking every reasonable step toward our salvation.

Ceron fell quickly into step and filled his proper role well. Most other officers did also, and the friars were magnificent.

That their combined roles could not produce miracles was sad . . . but inevitable. For that one night, Don Tristan was disabled, and later the drenching and anguish led to nagging, continuing fever. But, from my view, he never faltered or neglected his duty. This he fulfilled as he understood it.

August 20th

It was 4:00 A.M. when the winds began to diminish.

Normally the sun begins to rise shortly thereafter in this latitude during August, but this morning, the heavy cloud cover battled the warming sunlight for hours. For the soaked, mud plagued, hungry and dispirited colonists, it seemed as though it might never come. None of us had ever spent such a night, the wind smashing through the trees, showering us with rain, moss, leaves, branches, cones and straw. As the first gray shadows appeared, the landscape seemed like a battlefield, bodies sprawled everywhere, many covered with debris.

An hour later the officers convened.

De Luna, his spirits renewed, called the council to order.

"My friends, this is a fateful day in our lives. I need not tell you the consequences we have suffered. We don't know the fate of our comrades aboard ship; nor do we know the state of our stores, or how many losses we have suffered.

"Therefore, we must first determine what damage we have sustained.

"Each captain is to organize his command, take muster, inventory casualties and their seriousness.

"Father Anunciacon, I will appreciate your help in preparing a Mass as soon as we can organize the people, a Mass of thanksgiving. Can you do this?"

"It shall be so, Don Tristan," the friar replied.

"Also, I delegate to you responsibility for establishing a hospital, though at this moment I can't give counsel on where you'll find medicines or supplies. But, do your best."

"I'll begin at once," Anunciacon added.

"Ceron," de Luna continued, "please find five good men who are able to move. I want your help and theirs in patrolling the beach; I want to do this first."

Ceron nodded, turned and walked away.

"Any questions?" the commander asked.

"What of food, excellency?" Castilla posed.

"Hopefully, we'll find remnants of what was brought ashore. Other than that, we'll have to count on salvage on the beach. After we've done that, we'll know, won't we?" de Luna added, somewhat patronizingly.

Castilla dropped his eyes and shook his head.

"All right, then," the captain-general said. "Let's do what we can. And at all costs, encourage the people. God knows that is the least we can do!"

The seven men stood at the crest of the bluffs, looking down on a scene which defied description. Destruction was everywhere. It was almost as though the heavens had opened, pouring forth a rain of barrels and casks, food and clothing, and miscellaneous gear. Here and there a body lay on the beach, or floated face down on the gray, oily swell that was almost calm.

Not a perfect vessel remained.

One-hundred meters out, tips of two masts broke the surface. Within sight, waves breaking over her planking, lay the corpse of what must have been a transport; it was impossible to tell, for the remains were visible only in the troughs.

De Luna turned to Ceron. "Where shall we begin?" he asked. "Is an inventory practical, or should we begin with respect for the dead?"

"Let the dead bury the dead," replied the camp master. "Our first duty is to salvage what we can and put the people to work. Give them a chance to put their hands to use, and their spirits will mend."

De Luna raised his eyes and slowly scanned the horizon, from left to right, then back again. No sign of life showed itself below the bluffs. The twelve vessels were gone, except for wreckage and what protruded above the water.

"Let's go down and have a look! Let's see what shape the casks are in," de Luna said.

Slowly picking their way down the still treacherous path, the men slithered and skidded to the bottom; then, at de Luna's suggestion (it would never be an order) they fanned out and began picking their way through the unbelievable piles of destruction which the storm had thrown up.

Much of what they found was unusable. The force of whatever had destroyed their vessels had had its effect on the stores as well. Clothing and cordage were scattered in distorted heaps, sodden, dirty, mixed with seaweed and other soil.

"Who knows what we'll need before we're through." Ceron commented. "When we get started, we'd better sort out anything that we think might have some value . . . sometime. . . ."

Yard by yard they moved, keeping a file across the beach, one musketeer sloshing knee deep in the surf, the others picking their way above him on what had been a clean white beach.

De Luna came to the body of a seaman, his face buried in the sand, his bare feet still awash.

He stooped and gently turned the face upward. Already the bloat of death was visible, and the skin was beginning to change color. The face was expressionless, the body still wrapped in the weathergear of a mariner on watch.

As they walked, there were others, though not many. De Luna counted twelve.

"How many would have been on board, all considered?" he asked.

"I don't know," Ceron replied. "300, perhaps more. Some troopers could have gone back on board . . . though I doubt it. Then . . . there was Fray Matheos; he was to have sailed at noon. . . ."

De Luna crossed himself and shook his head slowly.

"Why? Why . . . in God's name . . . why? What did we do to deserve this?"

There was no answer, and the seven plodded on.

For an hour they tramped, then the captain-general called a halt and they sat down to review what they'd seen.

"There is some food," Ceron began.

"Which we must get on dry land quickly, before high tide," de Luna added.

A trooper said, "we have plenty of rope; we can rig slings and haul things. . . ."

"First of all, we must find food, light fires, get something into hungry bellies. . . ."

"How long has it been since we . . .?"

The return went quickly. Walking in an irregular line, they wound among the debris, stepping over split barrels of flour fouled by sea water into a sticky paste, and countless splintered casks which once had held fresh water.

They were approaching the starting point when the musketeer looked up, and stopped short:

"Look," he shouted, "look . . . coming down the beach . . .!"

Eyes snapped up . . . and there, marching single file, picking a path through debris much as the seven had, came a line of men, men sodden and disheveled like themselves, but in the dress of seamen.

"It's Segue! My God, it's Segue . . . and his men! Look . . . nine . . . ten, twelve, fourteen . . . fourteen men. Hey . . . oh . . . Segue! Segue . . .!"

For a moment, fatigue forgotten, de Luna leaped forward, followed by the others, hurdling obstacles, stumbling in the rubble, racing towards comrades they had counted as dead.

Now the others had seen them also, and they too hurried forward, throwing their arms around the soldiers, pounding them on the back, laughing, crying, uttering words without meaning.

Finally de Luna seized the sea captain by the shoulders and held him firmly:

"Jose, where have you been? Tell us . . . tell us, man. We thought you all dead!"

"And we you, Don Tristan," replied the swarthy sea captain. "Where are the others? Where are the ships?"

De Luna stopped . . . and slowly dropped his arms. With one hand he slowly panned the sea. "There. See? There are the mast tips, the remains of who knows what vessel. They're all gone . . . except perhaps your caravelle. You tell us . . . what happened?

Segue shook his head.

"Who can be sure, senior?" he began. "We were anchored to the west, half a league from ESTRAMADURA. . . ."

"I remember."

"When the winds reached their great force, we saw great black funnel clouds approaching. I ordered all hands to tie themselves to something solid, and they did. All of us were on deck, for I feared to be trapped below should we founder."

De Luna nodded approval.

"Then," Segue continued, "The first funnel passed and struck one of the vessels, CADIZ, I think, but I can't be sure. I saw her rise like a toy top, spinning up into the air, round and round. And then . . . she was gone!"

"How can this be?" the commander gasped.

"Then, we saw another cloud, a smaller one, coming. But this one came not from the west but from the south."

"Another funnel?"

"Yes, excellency . . . and it came straight towards us. We cried out to Mary for protection, and suddenly we were struck. It sounded like all the trumpets in the earth were blowing at once, or 10,000 cattle running at stampede. . . ."

"You held fast to your ship?"

"Yes, excellency, what else could we do? For a moment we hung in the air, then the whole vessel began to spin, round and round. . . ."

"Did you rise far into the air?"

"I think so, I can't be certain. We flew like a circling gull . . . and then . . . suddenly, we descended, not hard, not violently, but almost gently."

"Then, you dipped back into the sea? Your vessel is intact?"

"Yes . . . and no, my captain. The vessel was put down, but not in the sea. It is a full cannon's shot from the beach . . . down there, to the west, past where the cliffs end."

"The caravelle will sail no more, excellency, but her stores are intact, and her crew is safe."

"Santa Maria," murmured de Luna, "it is a miracle. Let us give thanks. . . ."

And the score of weary, bedraggled men sank on their knees, giving praise to God for their deliverance. It was a sign perhaps!

Moments later they were scrambling up the cliff, anxious to bring this bit of good news to balance the tide of disaster.

It was the only good tiding they would get that day.

The return of de Luna and his party to where Fray Anunciacon and Mateo del Sauz struggled to bring order to the colonists brought cheers from the bedraggled multitude. Quickly, the captain-general ordered what remained of the 1500 assembled, and standing on the base of the cross, addressed them:

"My friends, this has been a day of trial, perhaps sent by our Lord to test us. I know each of you has suffered deeply, especially the women and children. And by now I am sure you know of the devastation that has befallen Adm. Arias and our fleet.

"We have investigated the shore for several miles; sadly, there are many known dead, and countless others whom we may never find.

"However, just as we returned we were gladdened at the sight of Capt. Jose Segue and his officers and men. By a miracle their vessel was carried high onto the shore, an arquebus shot from the sea, and its stores are dry and safe. Thus . . . by the Grace of God they . . . and we . . . are all alive, and for the moment, safe; and there is food."

At this the dirt-stained faces broke into feeble smiles and a few men cheered.

"However," de Luna continued, "there is much to do . . . and many new problems face us. First, we must bury the dead and salvage what we can from the beach. Master of the Camp Ceron will select four officers and 100 able-bodied men to begin bringing goods from the shore before a tide damages them further.

"Another four officers and 100 men will follow Capt. Segue and his mate to their vessel and begin unloading such provisions to sustain us for the next few hours. I don't know where we'll find dry wood, but we will try to make fires to dry us and to give us hot rations.

"I shall ask Captains Xaramillo and Aguilar to lead another fifty men to the shore and to bring the dead to this upper land where they may be buried along with the others whom you have already given Christian burial.

"The women with children of the dead are to remain here; give them comfort and sustain them.

"The others are to assist Fray Anunciacon in ministering to the injured. Hopefully, there will be medical supplies aboard the caravelle, and we shall have these soon.

"Others are to assist the cooks.

"Cavalry officers and their troopers are to see to the horses. We've already lost far too many mounts in the voyage. We can afford no further deprivations there."

He looked up at the sky, where a weak sun was now well past its midday zenith.

"We have several good hours in which to work," he continued. "I know you are weary and sick in spirit. But I tell you that this thing which has befallen us is only a testing. We shall overcome it! We know that Indian cities lie nearby, cities visited by de Soto, and attested to by Maldonado. There we shall find maize and beans and other food. And soon the viceroy will learn of the disaster and send other supplies to succor us.

"God is with us! Our quest is a holy one. Be not discouraged! As sons and daughters of Spain and her empire, stand fast, do what is good, and each turn to his duty.

"Now . . . I shall ask Fray Domingo to dismiss us with prayer. . . ."

The afternoon passed swiftly, the various details working like armies of ants, salvaging goods, carrying, burying the dead from the beach and the upland storm, marching to and from the caravelle, cooking, tending to the sick and injured.

The weak sun was setting and the blessed aroma of cooking food filled the air when I came riding swiftly into view, aglow with excitement.

"Don Tristan, Don Tristan . . . a miracle!" I shouted as I reined in beside the waiting captain-general.

Leaping from my horse, I continued to shout: "There's another ship, a pinnace, washed on the beach, but I believe it is all but undamaged. We CAN send word!"

Grasping me by the shoulders, de Luna shook me vigorously. "Where, Cristobal, where? Why didn't we see it?"

"We were giving the horses their exercise and had ridden to the west, down below the cliffs. You had walked east, the direction of the winds. We were almost upon it and did not see the vessel, hidden by trees, but it's there, half in, half out of the water. And I believe it will sail again."

That evening, as bone-tired colonists relaxed before small fires, savoring their modest rations, de Luna, Ceron, del Sauz and Capt. Segue held council; three of the friars sat nearby, listening, but not participating while I took notes.

"The first question is how we'll get her afloat again, assuming she's seaworthy," Segue observed.

"Can we pull her in, with ropes?" de Luna querried.

"Even a pinnace weighs many tons, senor," the captain replied. "But that is one remedy we may attempt. Perhaps also we can undermine the sands beneath her . . . with a sort of cofferdam. . . ."

"Tomorrow, you shall take charge of this task; Maj. Sauz is an engineer and will assist with as many men as possible. I want that vessel afloat and on her way to Vera Cruz as quickly as possible. Understand?"

"Ceron," the captain-general continued, "once we've made provision for the comfort of the injured and sick and some sort of shelter for the women, I think we'd best inventory our stores, estimate what we can do with what we have, then seek the nearest settlements. At best, it will be months before help arrives."

"My fear is that even when he gets the word, the viceroy will have a difficult time assembling stores in quantity. He raped the countryside to equip us in the first place," Ceron reminded de Luna.

"I'm aware of that. That's why we've got to move quickly. It's harvest time. The Indians should have their supplies in good order. Now's the time to meet them."

Fray Juan Mazuelos interrupted from the edge of the darkness.

"As we proceed, captain-general, may I suggest that we go in the full spirit of our mission? Be certain that whoever goes to the villages is equipped with proper gifts, and that the spirit of Christ is uppermost in his work. . . ."

"Ah, Father, I never forgot that," de Luna replied. "Our store of gifts is rather sadly depleted, I'm afraid, but you're right. This must be done."

Ceron, lying on his side, his chin propped upon his palm, asked:

"What sort of force do you propose? And who's to lead it?"

"Major del Sauz has had experience in these matters, in the west as in Mexico. He is a diplomat. I propose to make him leader of the group, with my nephew and his troop, plus Capt. Nieto as leader of infantry. Altogether, that would be . . . let's see . . . thirty cavalry, ten pack horses, and 130 men of foot, lightly armed. Do you agree?"

For an hour the officers debated the needs and dispositions. The expedition could not be too large or unwieldy, nor too small to make a suitable show of force. It must have mobility, yet could not take all of the usual equippage. At length they confirmed de Luna's sketchy plan, with the addition of Fray Domingo de Santo Domingo and Fray Juan Mazuelos, men of unusual vigor.

As the fire died to glowing ashes, the men continued their talk, reviewing what must be done to preserve what was left to them and to provide comforts for the settlers until action might be made on settlement.

Should they begin to fell trees and build houses? Some thought so, despite the loss of most of the expedition's tools. Others felt that this action was premature, but advised movement to the spring, where fresh water was readily available.

Finally, with the weight of almost 48 sleepless hours weighing upon them, the men dropped off, one by one. Last to do so was Fray Anunciacon, who had spoken little during the evening.

Now, quiet reigned. There were no sentries, no men of the watch. Every man and woman slept as though drugged. Those who slept had survived the ordeal, had worked hard, and had taken hot food to sustain them. And tomorrow more work awaited.

MEXICO CITY
September 7th

Don Luis de Velasco had spent a trying day. Reports from Oaxaca were unsettling, production in the mines was down, the Indians were not responding to his bestowal of citizenship, soldiers were angry over his failure to increase their earnings. All in all, it was not one of his better afternoons.

Sweating profusely in the heat and humidity of early September, he stripped off his outer tunic, and slumped into his familiar heavy chair.

"God, the paper work is unbelievable," he muttered as he surveyed his desk, heaped with reports. "Jose," he shouted, "Jose, bring me a cool towel and some wine, some sweet wine, eh?"

From the anteroom his servant shouted, "Si, excellency," and whisked into another chamber.

Seconds later he was back.

"Excellency, there is a visitor, Lieutenant Gomez. I think you will want to see him."

"Gomez? Gomez? I can't place. . . ."

"He is from Ochuse, Excellency. He is the messenger."

Velasco literally flew from his chair, nearly upset his giant desk as he brushed it, rushing past his servant and into the anteroom. The naval lieutenant, dusty from his days of travel from Vera Cruz, stood at ease, a pouch held absently in his hand.

"My friend, my friend! Come in, sit down, Jose! Bring fresh wine. Come in . . . come in. . . ."

Once seated, Gomez poured forth the saga of the voyage, the delays, the adverse winds, the landing at Bahia Filipina, and the safe anchorage at Ochuse.

Later over dinner, at which Fray Domingo de Santa Maria joined them, Velasco probed the lieutenant with further questions.

"Then, all is well, Don Tristan has REALLY begun his work? Praise the Lord! And what of the land? What did you see of it? What are the reports?"

"There I must disappoint you, excellency. We remained only long enough to discharge our supplies and take on water. Don Tristan was anxious for you to have the word. I set foot on land at Ochuse only to supervise cargo handling."

"But . . . " interrupted Fray Santa Maria, "is the land mountainous or flat, sandy or with good soil, wet or dry . . . is it as Bazares described . . . tell us that. . . ."

The conversation continued late into the evening. Then, recognizing the fatigue of his visitor, Velasco bedded him in the consulate, ordering Jose to see to his comfort.

Over a final glass, Velasco and the friar carefully drafted a joint report to their King.

"We'll forward this to the commandant in the morning," Velasco said. "The next sailing is not scheduled during this month, but perhaps we can hurry them along, eh?"

"The King will be pleased," the friar agreed.

"If only there was some word from Ceron, too," Velasco mused. "He's a good soldier, of course. But I wonder how he's reacting to Don Tristan. If anything goes wrong . . . ah, well what's done is done! I've tried to be fair to all parties.

In seconds the aging viceroy had moved to talk of his visions of a new, virgin land, filled with handsome Indians, fields of maize and ornaments of gold. He smiled, and both men retired that night happy and confident.

OCHUSE
September 10, 1559

The salvage operations following the hurricane were well organized; men and women alike worked long days, some pursuing the back-breaking labor of raising usable materials from the beach, others repacking items and lashing them to the backs of horses which moved in caravans to the site near the spring.

Ceron, with Porras, Vazquez and Sotello, directed the sorting of ships' timbers and driftwood, from which they fashioned a hospital of sorts, a crude roof to protect the scores of victims ministered to by Fray Anunciacon, Fray Domingo and twenty women.

Medicines from the stores of the beached caravelle were supplemented with familiar herbs discovered nearby; these, plus fresh water and simple hot food worked wonders, and each day numbers of those, dazed and shocked but otherwise unharmed, returned to an active part in the colony.

Major del Sauz, with Nieto and me, spent time preparing our troop for the expedition.

After four days, we were ready.

All of the officers and Dominicans attended the council which preceded the order to march.

Del Sauz, his armor polished in the fashion of his troop, had prepared a list of the provisioning to be taken, including a few items to be used as presents for Indians.

De Luna scanned it briefly, then passed it to Ceron, who carefully checked each item, then returned it. "A thorough job, major, well done!"

De Luna came directly to the point.

"First, gentlemen, as to your men. There are no married men in your company, correct?"

"None who have wives with the expedition, excellency."

"Good. There will be problems enough without separating families."

Fray Salazar interjected:

"I have held confession for each of the 200 excellency; each says he is in good condition and spirit and wishes to go."

"Very good! Now let's review our plan once more and discuss what we know of the country into which you will travel."

"The plan is still to go west, excellency?" I inquired.

De Luna nodded.

"We have two choices, based upon Maldonado's reports. You will recall that during his stay at Ochuse, awaiting de Soto's return, his people had intercourse with two bands of Indians, one from which they called Nanicapana, the other from Coosa. . . ."

There was general nodding among the officers.

"And that when survivors of the de Soto party returned, they gave generally favorable accounts of the civilization at Coosa . . . and of its treasures."

Again his listeners agreed.

"However, Coosa is estimated at least 300 leagues distant, while Nanicapana must be far less. We can't be certain of this, however, or even in which direction to travel. . . ."

"Except that Nanicapana lies on a river, excellency . . ." del Sauz broke in.

"Exactly!" de Luna added. "Now . . . we've explored the river nearby, and we know it does not meet Maldonado's description."

"And we know that a sizeable river flows into the bay at Bahia Filipina . . . we saw it . . .!" confirmed Nieto.

"Thus it would seem to be our starting place," de Luna responded. "However, you and your men will be entering an unknown area, searching for a village we think is there . . . but we don't know exactly where, or how far . . . or even if the Indians were telling Maldonado the truth. It's not a pretty picture, my friend."

Del Sauz's mouth fixed in a hard line.

"Don Tristan, you and I have marched into the unknown before. We know the risks. That's our profession. The concern I feel is not for us, but for you and the others. Your stores will last, how long . . . a month, six weeks? Then what? We MUST find help."

"You must, and the viceroy must send assistance also. But . . . God is with us, and we shall prevail."

"Amen . . . and Amen," intoned Fray Anunciacon.

"Gentlemen, I can add but little by way of advice, except to remind you of the wisdom of Coronado as we marched with him. Mark your path well, use rations sparingly, live off the land as much as possible, treat with kindness all whom you meet, remembering our objectives here as Christ's soldiers. Any other comments?"

"I propose that Mass be said for the party before it leaves," said Anunciacon, "and I entreat the fathers who travel with you to provide spiritual bread each day."

At dawn the next morning, horses harnessed, stores loaded, a hearty breakfast consumed and Mass said, 200 of us took leave of our comrades, marching to the north and west, the officers bright in breastplates and helmets, soldiers at rout step, each man carrying a weapon, a pack, and such extra clothes as he possessed. Of the total, forty carried firearms of some sort, the remainder swords, pikes, bows and axes. We traveled as lightly as possible, many being veterans of similar marches, all fully aware of the hazards we faced.

As our caravan moved into the distance, de Luna and Ceron stood by the spring, watching the slow bobbing of marching men as they disappeared.

"Well, Juan, they go with our hopes."

"Indeed. And we, your excellency? What do you propose for those who remain? Idle hands, you know. . . ."

"Of course! This morning, call a council of all officers and we'll begin mapping short-term plans. Get the women to forage for edible items. Men can prepare temporary shelter on the building sites. Single out several farmers and get them to work selecting sites for land clearing; we're short on tools, but we can do something to get ready."

"Yes, excellency . . . and one other thing."

"Yes?"

"I suggest we begin rationing food. The people have recovered now; and we can't be profligate in our use. We don't know when del Sauz will return. Or when help may arrive. We'll lack seed grain even to plant crops; and animals for breeding are pretty limited. . . ."

"It'll be unpopular . . . but you're right. We must do it. Call the officers in . . . say . . . an hour. Perhaps we'll get another miracle, eh?"

And so the trying time began for Tristan de Luna.

September 15, 1559

The sun beat mercilessly upon the column, which quickly adopted the time honored principle of marching fifty minutes out of the hour, then resting for a time in whatever shade or comfort they might discover.

The countryside was not difficult to cross, at first. Pine and oak formed stately forests, with seldom a sign that man had ever broken their mystery. There were open places, too, where grasses and brush grew sometimes chest deep, where troopers were forced to move ahead of the column, hacking at vines and briars which raked bare skin or caught and tore at even the tough outer gear worn by the men.

When such stretches were found, the movement was painfully slow, and the advance men worked in short details, their arms flailing away at the barriers.

On the afternoon of the second day we came to a small river which ran sluggishly to the south. Here del Sauz called a halt, and we bathed and refreshed ourselves, soaking and frolicking in the shallows; then, cooled and comforted, we waded the width, which came to the armpits, holding weapons and packs overhead.

Del Sauz, Nieto and I crossed on our mounts, admiring the beauty of the stream, and discussing its origins critically.

"How do we KNOW this is not THE river?" I demanded. "After all . . . no one said there would be more than one!"

"True," the sergeant-major replied, "but it's neither in the right place nor of the size described in the legends. This is little more than a stream. . . ."

"Should we not at least move up a short distance . . . just to be sure?" Nieto suggested, glancing at me.

Hour after hour, the troop led by Del Sauz plodded westward . . .

"I think not," Sauz countered. "No . . . the description was not definite, of course, but it called for more than this. We'll push on."

Early on the second day we crossed another stream, also a silent, narrow, beautiful waterway in which the men again paused briefly for refreshment.

"At least we have no difficulty keeping canteens filled," Nieto quipped.

Had our mission lacked urgency, the march would have seemed almost a lark in those early days. The country was wild looking, and completely uninhabited, but there were birds aplenty and small game, and some edible shrubs to stretch our rations. The days were hot, but the humidity of late August was gone now, and though we perspired mightly, men no longer dehydrated, and spirits remained high. Each night as we made camp we were comforted by roaring fires and occasionally crossing smaller streams the men caught small fish and roasted them. Around the campfires they pursued the soldiers' arts of mending shoes and repairing garments torn by briars and sawgrass, but on the whole the walking was soft and easy and the men pushed forward in good spirits.

But as days stretched forward, doubt began to press upon us all. Had we erred? Should we have turned north along the first river? Nieto was increasingly certain. As a sort of unofficial aide to my uncle and thus anxious always to be correct in military decisions, I carefully mapped each day's progress and tried to calculate the upcoming land features by analyzing what I saw in the forest.

At the end of the fifth day, del Sauz called all officers and friars into council. Both of the men of God were convinced by now that the party had made an error.

"Soon we shall come to Esperitu Santu, that is certain," Salazar said. "We know that this great river must be close by. How could there be another large stream so close? It's irrational. Nature doesn't do this."

Nieto agreed. "Sergeant-major, the men are beginning to grumble, you know this. They feel that we are moving farther from our objective."

Del Sauz nodded grimly. "I understand everything you say, and I agree with your logic. Yet, something still drives me onward in this direction. We can't afford to make a mistake. . . ."

"Then, for God's sake, let's turn around before it's too late!" Nieto shouted.

Del Sauz paused.

"Gentlemen, let's take a poll. Fray Salazar . . . you favor returning and following the earlier river?"

"I do."

"And father Anunciacon?"

"I'm not certain, of course, my son, but I believe we have come too far. . . ."

"You, Rameriz?"

I said that I felt we should turn back.

"Very well . . . may I offer a compromise?"

"You are in command, major," I countered.

"I still believe I am right. However, in the face of your combined counsel, I promise this alternative. We shall continue forward for two days more, adopting shorter rations as has been suggested.

"At the end of two days, if we have not come to the river which I believe is there . . . ahead of us . . . we shall turn back, marching due east, to intercept the other stream."

We all watched him, silently; none wished to disagree, but all feared another wasted two days of march.

"Let me explain my belief again," the major continued patiently, "We are an armed Spanish column; we are traveling in a strange land, making costly errors in direction, moving at the pace of our slowest man.

"The Indians whom Maldonado met were traveling lightly, in their own land; they were athletic men, unhampered by indecision. They would make the journey as we have in just a fraction of the time. Also . . . they might have used the river itself for part of their travels. I don't know what tells me this, but I am convinced. So . . . please . . . bear with me . . . two more days. Agreed?"

Reluctantly, one head, then another, nodded in agreement.

Next morning the trek continued.

Next afternoon, the terrain began to change . . . slowly, but obviously. The ground lost some of its sandy look and texture; shrubs, too, became richer in appearance, and the trees heartier and taller.

We officers noticed it and called attention to the change to the men. As they walked, spirits rose.

At ten next morning, after we had been on the march for four hours, we came upon it. The river was wide and deep, with trees and shrubs to its very shoreline and a heavy undergrowth hanging at a broad angle over the water itself. Only with considerable use of their tools did the soldiers beat a path to the edge, where quickly they pulled off sweat stained clothes and plunged into the cool pools that formed in the bows of sand dunes near the shore.

Del Sauz stood close to me as we allowed the gentle current to soothe the tired skin of our bellies.

"You won't say 'I told you so'?" I said softly.

"No need. God is with us, as Don Tristan has said so many times. I just had a feeling. Now I have another; this IS the river."

"Shall we allow the men time to wash and dry their garments?"

"While we prepare a meal. Then we'll move forward. I just wish we knew how far we must go."

"Shall we make a wager? I'll say . . . ah . . . ten days."

"I'm a pessimist. I'll say twelve . . . and we'll wager for . . . let's see . . . a tall, cold bottle of the finest red wine in all Madrid. How's that?"

"Payable in Spain . . . on the day we return! You're on!"

September 22, 1559

When we sighted the village on the seventh day, the sergeant-major became something of a prophet. We had wound our way up the banks of the meandering river, hacking through heavy growth part of the time, at other hours enjoying an almost idyllic walk through trees whose leaves almost shut out the hot rays of the early fall sun. Early that morning came the first signs of human life: a small dead campfire and a worn trail through the trees. Then, just before noon, one of the lead troopers stopped. Holding his hand high, he halted the column, made sign for the men to quietly kneel down, and walked back to where we officers rode in the line.

"We've found it, major, just ahead."

"The city?" del Sauz questioned.

"It appears so, excellency, although we're too far away to see. I ordered the column halted, remembering your orders about frightening inhabitants."

"Good man, Sanchez! You'll get the reward I promised for sighting the first real signs. Did you see any people at all . . . any sign of activity . . . or hear anything?"

"Nothing sir. As soon as the huts were sighted, we stopped and took cover."

"You've done well indeed! Rejoin the others, and keep a sharp lookout."

Moments later customary military precautions had been taken. A network of guards was thrown out to all sides, and scouts were sent forward. I accompanied the advance party.

Slowly, we approached the village on foot, shifting from tree to tree, walking on tiptoe, carefully avoiding anything which might snap and give us away. At fifty meters, we dropped to our bellies and crawled meter by meter, from tree to tree, stopping at each major point of protection to listen, to see what might be ahead.

The village was a roughly symmetrical series of huts of limbs and dried grass, set in a pattern along streets of bare ground pounded hard by countless feet. Trees grew between the huts, and occasionally there were stark poles. Signs of old campfires were visible, but there was no sign of life . . . no people, no dogs, no animals of any kind. Nothing.

Silently, we probed the edge of the clearing, then, getting to our feet, we readied weapons, and covering first one man, then another, dashed silently from hut to hut, peering inside before moving to the next. At each stop the answer was the same. The village was deserted.

After covering a dozen such stops, I halted my squad.

"Space yourselves carefully, and follow me," I ordered. "We'll hurry through. This may be a trap, with people hidden on the other side, or beyond the clearing. Cover me . . . I'll move first, then each man in turn pass by, checking one hut. Understand?"

Each man nodded, and quickly the experienced troopers sprinted across the open space, checking house after house. As we passed the center of the village, the aspect suddenly changed; here the houses were in ruins, some burned to the ground, others so badly damaged that they were unusable. From the appearance, the damage was old, perhaps many years old.

And there were no people.

I reassembled my squad.

"All right, we know one thing . . . now . . . let's check again. Rabaul, take three men and work the right side. Thomas, you and Jose follow me. Go inside each hut and see what you find. Not people this time, but food. This is harvest season. Let's see if our friends have left us something to eat, eh? And keep your ears open. We still may have company."

Hut by hut we entered, checked, then left. In each conditions were much the same. Each contained baskets of maize, beans and several grains I didn't recognize. There was dried meat, also, and fish. And in two of the larger huts there was a general store, apparently the granary for the village.

There was no need for a report. Each man's result had been the same.

"Well, this is something," I grinned. "We'll eat well tonight . . . and if there's this much here . . . there must be more, where the people are. Probably we've just scared 'em into the woods. Come on, let's get back."

My report to the officers and friars brought smiles to the weathered faces.

"Well," the sergeant-major commented, "I guess we've found it, such as it is. It's no Cibola, that's for sure. But there's food, and for the moment that's the best news we could have."

Fray Salazar suggested that a Mass be said, and that the best posture for the column was to remain quietly outside the village, so as not to frighten the red men.

"These people must be nearby," he reasoned. "If we go blundering into their village with horses and 200 hairy Spaniards we'd cause panic and perhaps undo our mission. I suggest we make camp here, but make our presence known by having a squad go back into the village to cook. Let them see us. Meanwhile, we might prospect beyond the huts. If there is grain here, there must be fields, and perhaps another village."

"Good Father, you should have worn a uniform instead of your habit," del Sauz commented, smiling. "Your advice is sound. We are here to win souls as well as find food. We'll do as you say. Nieto?"

"Yes, major!"

"Please assemble six men with our utensils, a single horse and move into the village. Prepare a meal. When you're ready, send one man back and we'll bring forward others to help bring the food back. We'll eat here, out of sight. Draw some fresh food from the first hut . . . but do so without violence to the house or its contents. After we've eaten, we'll send a second squad to see what they can find. Rameriz?"

"Yes," I responded.

"Check the guard again. Make certain we run no risk of sudden attack. I'd suggest also that we send ten men to cut through to the river and make certain there's no force gathered there to surprise us."

"Immediately, major."

And so the forces of Spain came to Nanicapana (for that was the village's name).

The meal was prepared without incident, and we relished the first reasonably fresh vegetables we had tasted in weeks. We washed down our food with cool water from the stream, then lay back on the soft mat of pine needles that covered the forest floor. We were about 200 meters from the village. All about us remained silent, save for the quiet calls of a few birds and a family of squirrels that seemed to enjoy an opportunity to perform for the visitors.

Major del Sauz gave the men an hour to rest and relax.

Then he summoned the second squad.

"Let's see what we can find OUTSIDE the city," he ordered.

CONTINUED AT NANICAPANA
September 23, 1559

Included among the 200 troopers were three Indians, tall, athletic braves, two from Oaxaca, the third a captive returned with the Coronado expedition nearly twenty years before. Ocalo, as he was called, had been a slave; but his intelligence and willingness to act as guide and interpreter had made him a favorite of the conquistadores; several times his knowledge of dialects had assisted the viceroy, and when the expedition of de Luna was organized, it was Velasco who suggested that the tall, aging Indian be made part of it.

Now, he and the other braves were called before the sergeant-major.

"We don't know what we'll find here, but obviously there are Indians here, somewhere. Capt. Nieto is going to begin a circle of the village from the outside; hopefully, we'll find the inhabitants, men who can explain what's happening here, and where others of their tribe are located. I'd like you to go with Capt. Nieto and speak for him. These people are frightened. We want them to know that we came in peace."

The three red men asked no questions. Quietly, they stripped away their Spanish uniform items, preferring to walk forward bare to the waist.

The squad chosen by Nieto included 10 men, two besides himself on horseback. They moved out in single file, quietly passing down a well marked trail that swung away from the village. Ten meters separated each man from the others; a scout led, followed by two men afoot, then Nieto, then the remaining foot soldiers, with the other cavalry men bringing up the rear. Three of the men bore firearms. The others were lightly armed.

The squad plodded forward for perhaps ten minutes; then, quickly the forest thinned; a few meters later it ended altogether. Before them lay a field of perhaps 100 acres, largely clear of trees and stumps; remnants of the year's crops lay on the ground, and at a distance a dog was sniffing at a stump on the edge of the field. In the shadows of the trees, there were signs of movement.

Ocalo walked forward, breaking his place in the line.

Walking at an even pace, he began to cross the field, moving straight for the signs of motion. When he was 20 meters into the clearing he stopped, raised his hand above his head, and shouted something the Spaniards could not understand. He waited, then repeated his cry, and began to walk forward again.

A moment later a short, stocky Indian, nearly naked except for a fringed girdle, entered the clearing and walked towards the oncoming Ocalo. The two met in the open space. Both made hand signs, clapped right hands to the others shoulders, and began a quiet, stately dialogue.

The discussion continued for perhaps ten minutes. Then, the shorter man turned and trotted back to the woods. Ocalo stood in place. When the man reappeared, accompanied by three others, together they rejoined the tall western red man, repeated the signs of introduction, then sank to their haunches, where they conversed, hands moving in animation as the exchange continued.

Finally they stood, again clasped hands to shoulders, and Ocalo turned and walked back to the edge of the clearing where Nieto and the squad waited.

"Well?" the captain began.

"Where are the others? And what about the other cities? Will these men come and talk with us in council. . .?" Nieto demanded.

"They will come. I have explained that we came in peace. They have gone to return with the others of their family and will join us here to talk soon. I have said that we shall bring gifts," Ocalo continued.

"Well done! Jorge!" he turned to the other cavalryman, "ride back to the major, tell him to join us and bring Fray Anunciacon. Understand?"

"Si!" the man replied, and galloped off.

Half an hour later as the sun began its descent, the unlikely meeting began in the midst of the cleared field. Maj. Sauz commenced the conversations by offering presents to Alwarto, identified by Ocalo as the tribal leader. The gifts included glass beads and some small knives; they were not the grand presents which de Luna had brought from Spain; these lay in the sand at the bottom of the bay at Ochuse. These lesser items had been brought by officers aboard the caravelle; they were all that remained to barter and had to suffice.

Alwarto was delighted! When shown how to handle the knife, he quickly mastered its use on a piece of wood and in cutting brush. Together they shared a small meal, hastily brought from the village, and then, as darkness descended, each told his story to the other.

With Ocalo acting as interpreter, Major del Sauz and Fray Anunciacon began their attempts to impress the red men with the magnificence of Spain and the meaning of their religious mission. Alwarto nodded soberly, presenting a respectful mien, saying little in response.

When his turn came, his tale was as follows:

"For many years my people have known these woods and this hunting and planting ground. From a great tribe to the north we learned to plant and harvest grain, and so were able to live in a permanent place, moving only in the summer season to the great waters, where we played in the white sand and basked in the sun.

"Our people were many, and there were villages as large as this in other places nearby. We have always been a people of peace; we make war on none and observe rituals to our gods in proper season, thus the gods have been kind to us.

"But many moons ago, a runner came to us from the great country of Coosa, many leagues to the north and east, to report that great gods with white skin and riding on magnificent animals swifter than any man can run, were there; they had come in peace . . . but also they brought pestilence . . . and devoured much food.

"He warned us to be prepared lest they come upon us also.

"But . . . so legend goes . . . we were a peaceful people, and did not believe that the gods would permit this to happen to us. And they did not.

"The days passed, and we almost forgot the scout's warning; and then suddenly other tribes from beyond Coosa, tribes suffering famine and seeking food and slaves came.

"Our leaders met them in peace and offered them food and friendship, which at first they accepted. But then, in the night, as we slept, they crept among us, taking our women, slaughtering our braves, and setting fire to the village.

"Some awoke to spread the alarm, and in the dark of night, pursued by fear, those who could fled into the depths of the forest. The invaders tried to give chase and succeeded in capturing some. In the morning they returned to this village and looted our stores. They looked too for other things (I know not what they were) . . . and then they rode or walked away, seeking other of our villages where they re-enacted the same crimes.

"I know not how many died. Many who survived somehow rejoined in the forest and fled. They never returned.

"A few, my father among them, were so scattered that they were left behind. They remained hidden for days, for fear the invaders might return, but they did not.

"Then, these few people came back into the village. Their descendents are those who live here now. We are few, once we were a great people, now but a handful. That is our story."

Fray Anunciacon was the first to speak.

"Ask him, Ocalo, why they did not flee when they saw that there were white men with you?"

"That's simple, Father," he replied. "I told him that these were men of Christ, men of the true God, men who came in peace. I vouched for it . . . and they believed me. Also . . . you see . . . they are few. They have no weapons . . . and no place to go."

Then the questions came in earnest.

"Do you have more food, or is the total harvest in your huts?"

"Is there any other food source nearby?"

"What of the river? Are there many fish?"

"Is the hunting good? Can you help us get meat?"

And finally. . .

"Do you have gold?"

These the Indians answered patiently, and with honesty. No, there was no food other than the harvest in the village. Yes, the river contained many fish, and there was game in the woods. No, there were not other inhabitants, though fields they once tilled lay nearby. And gold, what is that?

That night, encouraged by the Spaniards, the Indians returned to their homes, and Nieto's squad and the others returned to our camp.

In the flickering light of a cookfire, del Sauz, Nieto, Fray Anunciacon, Fray Salazar and I sat, our faces sober, our minds seeking new answers.

"Can we believe all they say? Perhaps this is a guise to get us to leave," Nieto ventured.

"I thought of that," Salazar added. "Perhaps we should begin additional scouting. . . ."

"Ocalo says they're telling the truth," del Sauz added, "and he's usually right in these things."

"What we've found will hardly make a dent in the needs of our people," the senior friar said. "Imagine . . . amost 40 days march . . . and we've discovered a handful of poor people and their pitiful harvest. . . ."

Del Sauz came to the point.

"Tomorrow, we'll do as Fray Salazar suggests. Rameriz, I want you to take ten men of horse and make a wide swing. I suggest that you try to go . . . oh . . . 20 leagues to the north. Stay two or three days if need be. Check out what they've said . . . the old fields, the burned villages, the entire narrative."

I stretched. "I was sure I'd get this duty . . . and I thank you!"

Del Sauz grinned. "My pleasure!" he beamed. "Now . . . Nieto, I think we'd better check some other possibilities. See what you can do to organize a fishing party; let's find our how good the angling is in the river."

Nieto nodded approvingly.

"I'll see if we can't lure a few deer into a snare, get some fresh meat in the pot for tomorrow night. I don't know yet which way we'll be moving . . . or if we'll move at all for awhile. But one thing's sure; we'll need more food. What's here won't last 200 men long."

"And, my son," warned Anunciacon, "never let us forget that these simple stores do not really belong to us. We must make ample provision for the true owners."

Del Sauz smiled. "Somehow, I knew you'd say something like that, Father. Now . . . by tomorrow, I hope you'll help me understand how the Lord divided the loaves and fishes. Somehow, we're going to have to repeat that miracle pretty soon."

Anunciacon smiled and shook his head.

"I appreciate your point, major, and of course you're right. However, let us not blaspheme. The Scriptures may yet point the way. Meanwhile (and he winked), I'll sleep on it."

NANICAPANA
September 25, 1559

The others had rolled into their blankets for the night, but del Sauz and I remained awake. As I've said often, he was a very quiet man, almost taciturn at times, yet to the point when conversation was demanded.

Now he obviously wanted my confidence.

"Cristobal . . . what do you make of all this?" and his arm swept an arc to indicate the pitiful village.

I shrugged. "Think? What should I think? It's a sorry spot at best, but better than nothing. At least we have a full belly tonight."

"That's not what I meant. Their story . . . the chief, I mean. What do you make of that?"

I was silent a moment. Frankly, I'd given little thought to what Alwarto and Ocalo had said. "Oh, I take it at face value, I suppose. What else do you have in mind?"

Del Sauz shifted his weight, then spat noisily into the remains of our fire. "Just a feeling, I guess. Maybe we've all expected too much."

"Cities, people, civilization?"

"Uh huh! De Luna's given this some thought too. After all, he spent two years tramping around with Coronado looking for cities that didn't exist and mines that no one had dug. I just hope we're not chasing more rainbows."

The fire hissed gently, and the embers began to turn a pale gray as the fire gradually died. "Weeelll," I replied slowly, "who's to say? De Soto never came back, only his lieutenants. For 20 years people have wanted to return and pick up where he left off. After all, they told a good story. . . ."

"That they did . . . and I'm not saying we should have paid much attention to it at all if we hadn't had the storm. But now . . . well . . . it's pretty obvious that Don Tristan's counting heavily on there being people at Coosa to help us . . . wherever it is. He's counting a lot on what we find, too."

I nodded. "Sure . . . sure. But all we can do is look. And from what I see here these people are telling the truth. Those huts weren't burned yesterday. This place has been a shell for a long time."

The major stood up and stamped his feet to get circulation going again. He looked up at the blanket of stars that seemed to hang just above the pine tops. "Tomorrow, do the job well. Take Ocalo along. He may come in handy again. Most of all, though, don't let your squad think things are worse than they are. That's why I picked you; you've got a good outlook; better'n mine, at least. I'll do the same here, and try to get the friars busy with their work. At least that'll keep 'em busy. All right?"

I nodded agreement, then slipped into my cover. It was growing very quiet now, with only the night sounds of the forest nearby. The pines rustled and swayed gently as the breeze caught them, and from time to time a far off bird called.

As sleep came over me, one thought kept sweeping through my mind. "My God," I thought, "aren't we a long way from anyone! The world might swallow us up and no one would ever know. . . ."

NANICAPANA
September 26, 1559

My mother always said that I was born with her subtle sense of humor. My selection to lead the troopers in the scanning of the countryside pleased me, while others might have preferred to rest after weeks of steady march. The events of the previous two days seemed to me a sort of grim joke, as though God was watching our every move and toying with us. First He had delayed our arrival in North America, then He had destroyed our substance, but always there was hope held out before us. The legends handed down by earlier conquistadores spurred us on, and so our 200 had plodded for days through wild and uninhabited land, land with beauty but no promise for any of the points of our mission. Ultimately we had indeed found the village which Maldonado had reported from his talks with the red man; but instead of a thriving, prospering people there was nothing but a stand of 80 simple grasshuts, part of them in ruins. Instead of broad fields with golden grain, there was a single tract, and it of mediocre quality. Even the Indians themselves promised no more.

I kicked my horse's flank, spurring him ahead of the small company.

"Next we will turn to Coosa," I thought. "Or we'll wander blindly, hoping to find some relief. Coosa? The tales are so glowing that I wonder if it exists at all. After all, conquistadores who return without spoils usually substitute tall tales of what they thought they saw. De Soto's men were starving, but they were sure Coosa sat on a mountain of gold."

I trotted ahead, moving parallel with the river. When we were a mile from the settlement, I divided the company, one flank continuing on the present course, the others, under my command, pushing further to the east. The order was to travel at walking pace for three days, recording faithfully every sign that might prove of benefit; then we were to reverse direction, each swinging in an arc to the east, then back south to regain the village.

Each group carried a small supply of presents should other Indians be found; and each was suitably armed. Ocalo marched with me.

"Use your eyes well," I instructed his men. "Observe the signs and remember that our first concern is to find people and food. Go with God . . . and try to regroup on schedule."

September 29, 1559

As the afternoon sun was beginning to dip behind the tall trees at the river's edge, a lookout sounded the alarm. Mateo del Sauz arose from his makeshift desk, where he was still inventorying the measures of grain.

"It's Rameriz, major," the lookout shouted. "They're coming in . . . all of them."

About the edge of the village, men who were not absent on details looked up and then walked to where the major awaited my incoming troopers.

"Welcome, Cristobal, you're prompt! What'd you do, hide in the bushes and then come in together?"

My body was covered with dust and my horse moved painfully. Nonetheless I conjured up a smile.

"Aye, we have indeed been in the bushes . . . large ones, small ones, green ones, brown ones . . . I've never seen so many!"

"And what else have you seen?" the major demanded.

"Not much, I'm afraid. Look . . . let me get out of the saddle and wet my throat, eh? Jorge . . . hey . . . Jorge . . . take my horse, eh? Good man. . . ."

Moments later we were seated on the ground, with small leather cups of wine before us. I began my report.

"The Indians have told the truth, my friends. We rode God knows how many leagues . . . and we found . . . in essence . . . nothing."

"Nothing . . . at all?" querried Nieto.

"Might as well say that. No . . . that's not quite true. We found evidence as our friends here said we would. There were remnants of other villages and many fields, all of them wastes now, with the brush growing wild. Some even look like deserts . . . drifting sand that blows hard when the wind whips it."

"But . . . no sign of men?" del Sauz interrupted.

"None. The villages are falling apart, the wood rotted, the fire sites barren. No one has lived there for many years."

"And in the woods themselves?" Nieto pressed hopefully, "were there no trails, no signs of hunters . . .?"

"Oh . . . perhaps once or twice we thought we'd found something, and then we'd try to track it . . . but it always petered out. We found nothing, no fresh carcasses, no bones, no campfires, no cut trees. All that we saw that had man's handiwork on it was old, very old."

The sergeant-major picked up a stick and traced an aimless line in the sand.

"Well, I guess that settles that!"

"What's happened here?" I demanded, changing the subject. "Looks like you're pretty well moved in. Any luck hunting? And how's the fishing?"

"Fair . . . just fair," Nieto answered. "We've caught a few fish, and the Indians have been giving us a few lessons in trapping. We're eating . . . not well . . . but it's better than it might have been."

"Question is," del Sauz broke in, "what shall we tell Don Tristan? He's got 1000 hungry people counting on him, and he's expecting us to bring him relief. What'll we say?"

Both officers were silent a moment.

"The best answer is a true one," I said simply. "We can tell him what we've found and let him judge the best course of action. By now they may have gotten that pinnace afloat and even had a shipment from Vera Cruz. . . ."

"Or the damn thing may still be stuck fast, waiting for a miracle," Nieto responded.

Del Sauz nodded gravely, "We've done the first part of our job. We've found the village, scouted the land. We know what's here. It isn't much . . . but it's something. We don't know what's happening at Ochuse; things may be better . . . but being honest, they're probably worse. So. . . ."

"So," Nieto said, "we should send back what information we have and let the captain-general make a decision. Meanwhile. . . ."

"Meanwhile," del Sauz added, "we'd better stay put. With a little work we can keep even with the food supply. Then, if Don Tristan should decide to come here, there'll be a start."

"But can we recommend that he come here? There's not enough food here for everyone for the winter. And where'll we find more?" I interjected. "Whatever we say, we've got to be honest. The expedition'll be no better off here, and we'll be nowhere in sight if help comes from Mexico."

"All very true . . . but that's not our decision to make," the major concluded. "Tomorrow, Nieto, you'll march back to Ochuse. We won't try to make a mass march; take . . . oh . . . fifteen men, that should be enough. And as you say, make an honest report. Tell your Don Tristan how we see things, help him make a good judgment."

"Thank you, major, I'd like that," Nieto replied.

"All right . . . let's see what we can do about getting friend Cristobal and his men a decent meal . . . and then we'll throw him in the river. Right now he stinks!"

NANICAPANA
September 30, 1559

Next morning fifteen well rested men began the journey south and east. This time they took advantage of what we had learned. They followed the river only a short distance, then cut away, swinging through territory they had not seen before. They saved more than twenty days in their return journey. It was December 9th when they drew in sight of the first of two smaller rivers; two days later they sighted the main company. When the first of their comrades came forward to greet them, Nieto was shocked. Obviously, things had gone badly at Ochuse.

Forgetting momentarily his own report, Nieto began asking de Luna what had happened, and he heard this tale which he later relayed to me.

In the clearing, the two Indians conversed as the Spanish troop remained out of sight.

OCHUSE
September 17, 1559

Forty-eight hours after the departure of del Sauz's column, Don Tristan received one of the few pleasant surprises of this period. He had just returned to his rude shelter from watching the pathetic efforts to free the beached bark. For hours men had used rude scoops to remove sand from below her bow and rudder. But as fast as they dug out a measure, wave action returned an almost equal amount. Jose Segue and his crew had rigged lines to her bow, lines which teams of men might grasp and pull from the seaside. But . . . the more they worked, the less practical the scheme appeared.

Discouraged, the captain-general slumped down, closed his eyes, and let his mind wander. "Oh, God, you tried Daniel and you tested Job; now you have confronted me with a problem of great magnitude. I beseech Ye, give me wisdom, guide my thoughts. I pray not for myself, but for the souls of these unfortunate ones who look to me. I am not a wise man, oh Lord, Thou knowest this well. Thus I need Thy help, now more than at any time, that we may do Thy will in this wilderness."

For several moments he remained so, eyes closed, lips forming his prayer, his soul thrust into an effort to communicate with God. Then, the silence was broken. Bounding towards him was his aide Jorge Fernandez, followed closely by Alonso Valazquez, the quiet Basque who served as treasurer of the expedition.

"Don Tristan, Don Tristan," Fernandez shouted, "a ship . . . a ship is coming down the bay on the tide. Come quickly . . . some say it is a vision . . . hurry, Don Tristan!"

De Luna shook himself out of his doze and leaned up. Fernandez grabbed his arm and began to pull him, almost like a child.

"Easy, man, easy," de Luna urged, "calm down, eh? What's the problem? What vision, what are you babbling about?"

"He's right, commander," Valazquez seconded, "there is a ship, a bark, easing down the bay from the east."

"Impossible!" de Luna replied. "There's nothing there but the river; we know that."

"That's right, we know that! It's a vision, sent by God . . . or the devil!" murmured the awestruck aide.

The three moved off, de Luna trotting ahead, the others pacing themselves a stride behind him. There, 100 meters ahead, a crowd was gathered on the beach, all peering out across the water. De Luna rushed up behind them, pawed his way through. "All right, let me see, let me through, damn it, come on . . . move. . . ." he bawled at them.

The startled soldiers and peasants edged aside, making way for the captain-general. Passing through the group standing half a dozen deep, de Luna followed their gaze over the water.

"Holy Mary," he muttered, "it's true. It is a ship. One of our own. It's . . . yes . . . it's SAN MIGUEL! Look . . . look everyone, they're waving . . . it's the SAN MIGUEL!"

A shout went up, a great cheer. For, from the bow of the small vessel someone was waving a red banner back and forth; along her rail others were waving what appeared to be articles of clothing. She was moving toward them slowly, under jib and topsails only, easing her way towards an anchorage.

"It's no vision, that's for sure!" thundered de Luna. "Our prayers are answered. We have a ship, we have a ship!"

Thirty minutes later the small vessel edged toward shore, then came about, her master calling through his trumpet to prepare to catch line.

"We've lost our anchor," he roared. "We've got to make fast someway. I'll throw a line, see if you can make us fast to a tree."

Anxious men splashed into the water, raising wavelets as their thighs beat the surface. Waist deep, then chest high the water came, then the master let go his line, fixed to a weight. It flew twenty meters through the air, landing close to the leadman, who lunged for the tip, fell, plunging beneath the surface. Seconds later he came up, sputtering and gasping, his mouth spitting out spouts of sea water, but the hawser was in his hands.

Others joined him, and together they drew the line towards shore, the men aboard ship playing out rope.

Minutes later, helped by scores of willing hands, Lt. Fernando Luis was ashore, surrounded by hundreds of eager countrymen, pressing for details of his ship's fate.

"Let him be, let him be!" thundered de Luna. "All right . . . now . . . give the man room. Aguilar, help make a path, get him through. Now," and he swept his arm covering the assembled mob. "I promise, we'll assemble for vespers shortly, and I'll bring you the full account. But for God's sake let this poor man alone for a moment. And you, Porras, see to the men aboard. Help them ashore, see that they are fed. Put relief aboard, eh?"

Moments later de Luna, Fray Domingo, Fray Feria and Lt. Luis were closeted in the captain-general's shelter; wine was brought for the mariner, and slowly he unwound his account of his vessel's adventures.

"I'll not tell you of the storm." he began.

"Please don't," Fray Domingo agreed, "we've relived the ordeal a thousand times."

"All of you had gone up the bluffs, and the wind had reached the greatest force I've ever seen. All of us were fearful of being piled into one another, so I had watches fore and aft and on both rails. Then it came. . . ."

"The black cyclone?"

"Aye . . . spinning like a giant top, splitting whole trees and everything in its path. We stared at it, not knowing what to do . . . and then we saw ESTRAMADURA slip her anchor and come plunging towards us. We could see well when she collided."

"What did you do? Could you not help?" Fray Feria asked anxiously.

"How, Father? No man or small boat would have lived in that sea, even in the shallows. It was a terrible, frustrating feeling of weakness, but we were helpless. And then, we saw the other twisters coming. . . ."

"Twisters? We had thought there was only one more."

"Oh no! I can't say how many. But in a moment like that, who counts? They were many, coming from several directions. To stand anchored would have been fatal. So . . . we cut the chain and ran before the wind."

"To the east?"

"Aye . . . we were pushed east, around the point of land, then into deeper water. Things were a little better there . . . and for an hour we hurtled forward. There was no control, no way to steer; we simply hung on and prayed. Then . . . we struck."

"Struck?"

"We were driven onto a mud bank seven, perhaps eight leagues from here. I can't be sure."

"And then . . .?"

"Then came the quiet in the storm. All hands came up on deck, and then we saw SAN JUAN, sitting perhaps a league from us, up on the same flat."

"SAN JUAN is still with us, then?"

"She is, and like us now afloat."

"But lieutenant, if you've been that close these many days, why . . .?"

"We had no way to come across to you, captain-general. We were fast on the mud, our small boat was gone, we had nothing but our very planking that could be used for a raft. And I felt certain that a high tide would move us off and salvage the craft and stores."

"Then what?"

"That's what happened this afternoon. Today was the first really high tide; we came off first, and SAN JUAN has moved also. She should be here soon."

"Then . . . we are saved . . . God has answered our prayers!" de Luna sighed. "Fray Feria . . . this evening, will you lead a high Mass? We must offer thanks to God in the highest. Now . . . there is much we can do!"

"Amen . . . that I will do."

"And to you, lieutenant . . . my deep gratitude. Your seamanship may be the salvation of this entire force. We owe you a great deal, and, of course, to your men and those of the SAN JUAN."

"Don Tristan, many times in these past few days I've thought about that storm. Only a few of us survived, I know. I'm confident God preserved us for other work. I'm at your command."

"So be it!" de Luna said and embraced the young officer.

The following five days were filled with action at Ochuse. Both the bark and the larger SAN JUAN had suffered storm damage, but their hulls were intact, and with minor repairs they were ready for the sea. Their stores included food, some farm implements, and military gear. These were removed and put into shelters of sailcloth, salvaged from the storm.

Using the leverage of both vessels, lines were run from the beached pinnace. With a high tide and a suitable wind the two ships raised sail and, with the help of much pushing and tugging from two hundred able bodied men, the stranded craft slipped off her beach and re-entered the water.

Now there were three seaworthy vessels!

Within forty eight hours de Luna had provisioned SAN JUAN, and, sending her officers as his emissaries, posted the following report to the viceroy and His Majesty, King Philip:

"After I had written to your Majesty at length everything concerning this expedition to the provinces of La Florida, with everything that had happened on the voyage and afterwards until that day, and I had referred you in part to Juan Rodriguez, who was pilot major of this fleet, there has since happened here an event of which I must make a report to your Majesty, in order that you may be pleased to order a suitable remedy promptly provided. It is that on Monday, during the night of the nineteenth of this month of August, there came up from the north a fierce tempest, which, blowing for twenty-four hours from all directions until the same hour as it began, without stopping but increasing continuously, did irreparable damage to the ships of the fleet. There was great loss by many seamen and passengers, both of their lives as well as of their property. All the ships which were in this port went aground (although it is one of the best ports there are in these Indies), save only one caravel and two barks, which escaped. This has reduced us to such extremity that unless I provide soon for the need in which it left us . . . for we lost, on one of the ships which went aground, a great part of the supplies which were collected in it for the maintenance of this army, and what we had on land was damaged by the heavy rains . . . I do not know how I can maintain the people, unless it is by the means of which I am herein telling your Majesty. For this purpose as soon as some four captains whom I expect shortly . . . for I ordered them to go inland . . . return and give me information of the character of the country and the towns they may find, I shall be forced lest we all perish to go into the interior with all these people to some place where there are facilities making it possible to maintain them. I shall leave the few supplies which I have at present for the people who will remain settled in the city which is left at this port, so that they may have something to eat during the interval before Don Luis de Velasco provisions them from New Spain. However, if I am able, and have anything to do it with, I shall not fail to send them help down a river which flows into the Bahia Filipina and up which I shall have to go. For I consider that it will be difficult to provision the entire camp by sea from New Spain as safely and completely as may be done if I go away from this port into the interior. All that I have written to your Majesty in that other letter I wrote shall be done, that your Majesty's purpose may be attained and that a thing which has cost your Majesty so much may not be lost, with the end and death of your vassals who are here in your royal service, and whom I have under my command. I shall also send to the viceroy of New Spain, asking him to provide for them until they can all be maintained by means of the grants which your Majesty may be please to make us in the country. As I shall, whenever there is opportunity, always give your Majesty information, through the viceroy, Don Luis de Velasco, of the events which occur in this land, I beg your Majesty that, in order that grants may be made to those whom I have in my company in your royal service, you will represent to him the many hardships they must pass through before the most Christian purpose of your Majesty is achieved. May our Lord God guard your sovereign life, with the exaltation of your royal crown for many and very happy years so that by means thereof your Majesty may see diffused in these parts the doctrine of the holy evangel as your Majesty desires and strives. Amen. From this Bahia Filipina and Puerto de Santa Maria, September 24, 1559.

"Your Sacred Catholic Majesty's humble servant and vassal, who kisses your hands and feet.

Don Tristan de Luna y Arellano"

Also enclosed was a brief and affectionate letter to Valencia, which he asked the King to deliver in person, if possible.

The bark, with Lt. Luis again in command, was provisioned and dispatched to Mexico with a similar message.

In this de Luna detailed their remaining stores, his actions, and the prospects for the weeks ahead.

"We are in dire need, for supplies in hand cannot suffice for nearly 1300 people," he said. "I know of your good will, and of the problems you will face. However, we shall maintain a force here, awaiting your assistance and counsel."

The date was September 24.

The vessel which had been floated was retained, for use as a messenger, for fishing, or, as de Luna put it, "as we shall need her, as surely we shall . . ."

AT OCHUSE (Continued)

That night, the captain-general called an officer council, inviting the three remaining Dominicans to join them also.

"My friends," he began, "this is a day filled with emotion for me. I believe that now, with reports of our hazard en route to both the King and the viceroy, we will soon be resupplied.

"However, we know the evils which can befall our messengers, both those on the sea and our 200 friends who have been gone now for, how many days? Thus while we have every hope of overcoming our problems, we cannot simply wait for relief."

There was a general murmur of assent.

"I believe, Don Tristan, that every man here is filled with praise for you and the leadership you've provided since the storm," said Juan Ceron. "It's been a difficult time, but you (and the friars) have been sources of inspiration. We have every confidence in you."

De Luna waved his hand modestly. "Thank you, Juan, but thus far we've been very lucky, and have enjoyed what I believe to be divine assistance. But from today forth . . . well . . . who knows? Therefore, I think we should begin tonight by taking stock, to see what we've got, and what we must do."

Again the officers nodded affirmatively.

"Very well. Fray Domingo, we'll begin with you. Good Anunciacon began this labor, but perhaps you can recount for us now; what totals have we suffered in dead and injured . . . and how are the injured faring?"

Fray Domingo de Santo Domingo was a methodical man, often called upon by his order to prepare reports, to keep accounts, to observe details of life which bored others. This was his nature, and he enjoyed it. Little escaped his inquisitive eye and practiced ear.

"It's not a pleasant report, excellency," he began. "Of course, we may still find other survivors. . . ."

"Possibly . . . but we'll not count on that for the moment."

"Of course. However, from our judgments, the nine vessels which perished had on board 335 souls, plus 24 men and 16 women who became ill during the voyage and had been given permission to remain on board rather than be cared for ashore."

"That is . . . 375 then?"

"In the ships, excellency. Of these we ultimately discovered 21 thrown upon the beach by the storm, or whose remains later were washed ashore."

"And . . . of the others . . .?"

"All told, we have held final rites for 126 men and women, and 11 children, not counting those whom I had already mentioned, excellency."

"The total, then is . . ."

"I make it 512, excellency . . ."

"And of these, about 150 were of our company, and the remainder the men of our ships?"

"I make it so, excellency."

De Luna shook his head sadly. "Even more than I'd feared, though my numbers decreased when SAN JUAN and the bark reappeared."

The friar nodded. "That was a blessing. Now, would you like the totals of the hospital list?"

"Pray continue."

"I must say first that the women have performed wonders, Don Tristan, especially ones like Isabella Munoz and Patriz Alvarez; both were . . . well . . . like angels."

"I know, I've watched them."

"On the day after the storm I counted 217 in need of care, 43 with broken limbs.

The remainder were treated mostly for shock, and for running bowels."

"Working with almost nothing, you performed miracles, my friend!"

"Perhaps. But we had the help of the warm sun, medicines from the caravelle and good visits by you and other officers.

"At any rate, we now have but 84 in our shelters, most making good progress. Only 12, those with injuries to head and back, are beyond our skill. If we can keep the others quiet, and provide decent food, they will rejoin us for duty soon."

"An informative report, Father," de Luna said, gripping the friar's arm. "Now . . . are there any questions?"

There were none, so he turned next to Ceron, whose notes were at hand. "Juan, what of our stores? I know you keep a good account. How do things stand, counting everything . . . including what we took from the ships and what we know of trees and shrubs?"

The master-of-the-camp stretched his limbs, then stood. "My report, excellency, is brief, and I fear not so bright as the friar's. We began with those items which had been carried ashore prior to the storm."

"Much of which was destroyed by the storm. . . ."

"Correct. We salvaged little from them, nor were we much more fortunate in pulling things from the beach or the sea afterwards. There were some supplies, of course, but on the whole, the food harvest was sparse."

"Then came the caravelle. . . ."

"The beached caravelle helped. We've counted and inventoried, and done the same with the contents of the SAN JUAN and the bark.

"Then, I've had women and men with no other skills scavanging in the woods for fruit, berries, herbs, roots, acorns, anything that might be eaten, with special cooking, grinding, boiling . . . anything."

"And your findings, Juan . . ."

"Excellency, we are almost 800 souls here, plus the 200 on the march. By maintaining half rations, we have food for 30 days. If we drop rations to 40% they will last another week. And . . . I must add . . . these estimates include a liberal diet of such unwanted delicacies as boiled ground acorns, palmetto root and flour cakes."

"What of shellfish, Juan?"

"These will help, of course, but thus far we've not been successful in catching anything else. Effects of the storm are still with us; the waters are muddy. Perhaps this situation will improve. But . . . who can be sure?"

"Then . . . the picture is . . .?"

"I would say that we must immediately further reduce our rations. This is bad, but there will be few heavy physical demands upon the people. Our job for the moment is to stay alive. This we can do and little more."

De Luna turned to the others. "Any questions of Sr. Ceron at this time?"

"Yes," said Aguilar, "what . . . I mean . . . when . . . do you think we'll hear of del Sauz? And . . . what of Coosa? Shouldn't we be sending a force in that direction?"

"I've considered that, of course. However, considering the women and children, and the fact that we now have an opportunity for assistance from two quarters, I'm more disposed to stand fast, keeping people alive, in good health, and preparing for winter here."

"I agree," Ceron seconded. "If we further divide ourselves we'll lose spirit. And . . . no matter how we proceed, it's going to take time to pull things together. After all, if we send large groups in all directions, we may never get ourselves organized; and some may perish needlessly."

"Any other comments?" de Luna demanded.

"Only this, my son," Fray Mazuelos added. "We face a time of peril. Let us communicate with one another and with God. Keep the people informed; speak with them often; they're nervous and concerned. Keep their spirits high!"

"I will try, good Father," de Luna countered. "I guess we all know now how things stand. Tomorrow morning, after Mass, we'll give the people a full report. Then, Sr. Ceron, we'll impose the short rations. May I suggest one other addition to your plan?"

"Certainly."

"Increase a guard over our stores. In my experience, short rations lead to sticky fingers. Make ample provision for the children and the sick. Otherwise all share alike . . . and I mean . . . all!"

"It shall be so."

"Very well, gentlemen. Father Mazuelos, will you dismiss us with prayer?"

MEXICO CITY
October 4

It was two weeks following arrival of the first report from Ochuse that Don Luis Velasco received the second. Lt. Luis had not entrusted the message to an officer. His fast passage to Vera Cruz accomplished, he hurried ashore, obtained an escort from the commandant, and rode as rapidly as a seaman could to Mexico City.

Within an hour he was seated with the viceroy, spilling out details of the disaster, his own vessel's adventure, and the steps being taken by de Luna to protect the welfare of his colonists.

Viceroy pressed him with questions:

"And the dead . . . again . . . how many?"

"Over 500, excellency . . . about 150 of the company and the rest from our fleet."

Velasco shook his head sadly.

"And the other ships? You're certain there were no others?"

"As certain as man can be, excellency. I saw the collisions, and we could see submerged wreckage of some. Of others . . .? Well . . . who can be certain? Perhaps another miracle . . .?"

"Of course. Now . . . the ill . . . the injured . . . "

"Here they were most fortunate, excellency. The weather was pleasant and warm. Recoveries were swift for most, except those with damaged bodies. A few of these . . ." and here he shook his head sadly.

"Now—you say the general has dispatched 200 men to the north and west?"

"Yes, excellency."

Velasco nodded. "Good . . . good."

"Excellency . . . how quickly can you send food?"

"I don't know. You were in the harbor at Vera Cruz. What did you see?"

"Very little, excellency. There were two caravelles, a pinnace, perhaps two. Nothing large, if that's what you mean."

"It is. You know what I did to prepare for the expedition. We stripped the coast. But," and he closed his eyes and sighed deeply, "we will do what we must do!"

That evening couriers went hurrying out of the city, and within a few days slow, rumbling ox-drawn carts began to wend their way eastward towards the port.

Reprovisioning nearly 1000 people in a wilderness would be no easy matter. It was, in fact, all but impossible. Yet, Velasco did what he could. Ten days from Lt. Luis' arrival two tiny ships loaded deep in the water moved out on the tide en route to Ochuse. It wasn't much . . . but it was a beginning.

From Vera Cruz Don Angel Villafane reported to the viceroy:

"We have boarded cargoes of maize, beans, flour and dried meat. There are building supplies, gun powder and other necessities. I cannot estimate their value in terms of days sustenance; however, I would urge your excellency to pursue this matter with all urgency. This can be supply for a short time only."

Velasco showed the report to Fray Domingo de Santa Maria. The latter shook his head sagely: "Soon the winter winds will be on the sea, rains will make travel difficult here. What can we spare from our own stores? It's tragic! Perhaps from Havana . . . or Cadiz . . .?"

"Perhaps. I have already prepared a report, but it will sit in that stinking Vera Cruz for days awaiting transport. No . . . the only hope there is that the SAN JUAN makes a good passage and that her captain is heard!"

"Who commanded her . . . the SAN JUAN, I mean?"

"Sanchez. I don't know him. Luis said he was a good man."

"Sanchez? No . . . I can't place him either. Well . . . tonight we'll say an added prayer for him, eh?"

"Amen!"

October 4, 1559

The SAN JUAN, her rigging creaking before the strong westerly wind, and with only light ballast and no cargo, made rapid passage to Mariel. Here, Pedro Sanchez made his anchorage, ordered re-provisioning for the Atlantic crossing, and hurried to Havana to the palace of the Governor.

His report, given orally, largely repeated Tristan de Luna's statement to Philip II. It reviewed the casualties and the plight of the expedition and asked what relief the governor might afford.

His Excellency Jose Cortez was an experienced administrator, a loyal officer of his King, but, like Velasco, he faced a crisis in both shipping and supplies. For half a decade his fields had been stripped to feed the armies first of Charles, then Philip; he had no fleet; and those ships normally assigned there had largely departed for Spain carrying the year's harvest. But . . . he assured Sanchez . . . he would do what he could. Quickly, he penned an addition to the de Luna papers to be delivered to the King.

"And may God go with you, captain," he added. "I know you have had a difficult time, but now your speed may determine the fate of some of Spain's truly dedicated citizens. Good luck!"

Sanchez saluted and left the palace.

He rode silently back towards the small port where he had anchored SAN JUAN; Mariel was smaller, but there were fewer palms to grease in getting things done. It was a move he had made before. One became wise with experience!

It was dark when his weary mount trotted into the bustling village. Hurrying to the quay, he questioned his first officer. Yes . . . things were proceeding well. No, they could not sail before dawn. Yes . . . the tides would be right.

Sanchez started to call for his longboat, to go back aboard . . . then stopped.

After all, he'd spend weeks in that solitary cabin, eating the bland fare of the sea. Tonight . . . there was time! Why not have at least one good meal . . . and perhaps see what charming companionship the town offered.

With a word of explanation to his mate, Sanchez remounted and moved back into the town.

Mariel was a sailors' city. It existed for one purpose; to aid ships and ships' people. Its dark streets were lined with grog shops and inns, and already there was noise and light aplenty bursting from some.

Sanchez scorned these, moving instead to the largest building on the square, a two story affair built within the traditional Spanish design.

Entering, the captain was quickly greeted by a bowing landlord who recognized the mariner.

"Aha! Capt. Sanchez! How good it is! How long has it been? A year . . . two perhaps? But you always remember my poor house. Ah . . . it's good to see you. You still command the SAN JUAN?"

Sanchez patted his host's back warmly and nodded affirmatively.

"Yes, Carlos, we're here for a quick stop . . . one night only I'll be with you . . . and you know . . . I've been drooling for one of your sauces for days. All goes well with you?"

"God blesses me more than I deserve! But . . . come . . . I know you're hungry. Have you been into the city?" and his head nodded in the direction of Havana.

"Briefly. I just rode back . . . and you're right. I could eat a whale. Can I have a table?"

The landlord's face fell.

"In a few moments, perhaps. As you can see . . . each is occupied . . . unless. . . ."

"Unless?"

"You wouldn't mind sharing with that Portuguese over there . . . in the corner."

"Who is he? What's he off of?"

"His name's . . . oh, damn. . . I'm bad with names. Anyway. . . he's been here before. Skippers the PRINCE HENRY, barque, out of Marsailles. Quiet fellow. Least ways I've never been able to get him to say much. But he's sober. . . and he doesn't smell."

"I don't care much for waiting, old friend. If he doesn't mind, I'll share his corner."

The landlord made brief introductions, and shortly his cooks had prepared a masterpiece . . . a giant flounder stuffed with crab and small shrimps, all to be dipped in a white wine sauce. The house's best wine and a long loaf of crisp hard bread completed the feast.

Sanchez was a gentleman born, with the manners of a great house. As he ate, his new companion watched carefully, out of partly closed eyes. Occasionally the two exchanged a pleasantry, but it could scarcely be called conversation.

Finally, Sanchez raised his glass and offered a toast:

"To your next voyage, my friend; may the winds blow fair at your back, and your water remain fresh!"

The Portuguese captain smiled and nodded and silently joined in the drink. He wiped a great, hairy hand over his mouth, then responded, "To your voyage, senor, may your King reward you for your efforts."

The good white wine slipped down their throats.

"That was a strange toast, captain. Do I have the look of a king's seaman?"

"Not really," the other replied. "But most who come here are Spanish, and the majority are in Philip's service. So . . .?"

"Good guess! Yes . . . I've served aboard the King's vessels for 17 years, with no regrets!"

"And plenty of stories to tell, eh?" the other winked.

"Stories? Hmmm . . . now that you mention it, yes . . . and none more strange than the one I've just experienced."

"Oh? Here . . . in the Caribbean?"

"Partly. If you have nothing better to do, you might find it interesting."

"Better? Ah, my friend, this is a haven for me as it is for you. After awhile any ship smells like the bowels of hell. A night in a palace like this . . ." and he closed his eyes and breathed deeply, a slow smile covering his face.

"How right you are!" Sanchez said.

"Please . . . I'd like to hear your story."

"Very well. It began about six months ago . . ."

And for the next half hour, Capt. Sanchez quietly spun the narrative of the de Luna expedition. When he came to the details of the great hurricane, he closed his eyes and leaned back, his feet raised on an empty chair, his voice rising and falling as though he could almost hear the whine of the great storm again.

"And so, today, I have carried the captain-general's report to the governor of Cuba . . . and we sail tomorrow for Spain. It's an urgent matter, and I confess I'm a weary man. But . . . I'm lucky to be alive at all, wouldn't you say?"

For the next hour the two veteran seamen talked, the one asking question after question about Ochuse, its look, its water, its bay, its temperature and of the men and women who were now trying to settle there.

"And you say that they hope to establish two cities! Perhaps God has other ideas, eh?" he querried.

Sanchez shook his head sadly.

"I don't know. They're determined people, but now . . . who can say what will happen. Well," and he pushed back his chair, "one more glass of our host's wine and I'll be fit to sail nothing larger than a longboat. Goodnight, good friend, I shall remember you! You were a good listener!"

"And I you! Thank you for good wine and good company."

The two walked together into the night, Sanchez finally coming to his rented horse. A quarter hour later he was at the quayside, where two seamen rowed him to the SAN JUAN.

The Portuguese stood in the dusty street watching the Spaniard ride away. He waited until horse and rider had disappeared into the night, then turned on his heel and walked rapidly for perhaps half a mile. Here he turned to his left, trotted down half a dozen stone filled steps cut into the water's edge. A tiny two seated boat bobbed in the water, her oars placed neatly across the length of the craft. Fitting the sweeps in place, he pulled with strong strokes towards a smallish two master at anchor 500 meters off shore.

Nearing his vessel, the captain turned, cupped his hands and hailed the watch. Moments later he had tied up, swung himself up the rope gangway, and confronted the deck officer.

"Tell the mate I want to see him in my cabin—now!" he ordered.

Moments later, a candle lit, captain and mate faced each other, the latter still rubbing sleep from his eyes.

"Rodrigo, I want to sail on the tide tomorrow."

"Impossible! We're only half loaded. . . ."

"I'm aware of that! But I have a cargo up here (and he tapped his head) that will bring us many times the value of sugar in Paris. Forget the cargo. Concentrate on provisioning. *I want to sail!* Is that clear?"

"Perfectly, captain."

"Very well, get some sleep and alert the watch that all leaves are cancelled as of now."

"Aye!"

The mate rose and departed, and the Portuguese master stretched out on his bunk.

Sometimes God loves a sinner, he thought. What else could have put the Spaniard at his table and opened his lips? Queen Catherine and the Admiral will love this, he thought.

"They may even knight me!" he murmured. "Imagine! A hurricane . . . 1500 people stranded. It's like opening the door for Coligny's efforts. Well . . . the Spanish can't always be lucky!"

There were several sailings from Mariel next day. On schedule, the SAN JUAN crept out of the broad harbor and began her long trek toward Cadiz. And an hour later, the Portuguese smaller transport slipped quietly from her anchorage and started the race to bring the same information to the crown of France.

November 23, 1559

The meeting of Captain Sanchez with Ximinez took place in the office of the latter's comfortable stone villa. The SAN JUAN had made an excellent passage, and Sanchez had hurried overland by coach, a bone shaking experience for a man accustomed to the gentle roll of the quarterdeck. Passing through channels, he had hurried to the admiralty, where his uncle held the post of Grand Admiral of the Fleet. Ushered in quickly, the captain greeted his senior warmly, then gave a brief account of his mission and asked for assistance in gaining an audience with the king.

"Ah, you've come to the wrong place, I'm afraid," the admiral said. "Philip and many of his court have gone to the coast for a holiday. We'll get you a post there after you've rested a bit. But first, let me send word to Ximinez. He's here. He'll want full details. After all, de Luna's mission was really his plan, you know!"

And so the weary captain sped across the city.

The prime minister was working alone behind his huge desk, a slab of smooth oak stretched over broad uprights. A fire leaped brightly behind him; the room had a pleasant smell, and its warmth was a welcome change after the chill ride.

"Well, my friend, your uncle's note said you're bringing important word. Come in . . . be comfortable . . . and tell me all about it."

"The admiral tells me you've had no report at all on the expedition. . . .".

"You're the first. We thought it strange that it took so long . . . but . . . now that you're here . . .".

"I'm afraid I bring bad news . . . very bad, excellency."

Ximinez stretched back in his chair, hands clasped behind his head.

"I was afraid you might. Very well . . . start from the beginning . . . and give me as many details as you can remember."

And so Sanchez, the captain whose vessel was saved by what many considered a miracle, placed his elbows on the tabletop and began a recitation of the de Luna story. He spoke evenly, without emotion, until he reached the details of the storm. Then, his hands waving in tempo to the words, he recalled the effects of wind and wave.

Finally, the tale told, he folded his arms.

"And . . . excellency . . . that is what I know. The captain-general dispatched Lt. Luis to Mexico, and me to Havana and Madrid. Here is the special dispatch for the King . . . and a separate packet for Senora de Luna. What shall I do now?"

Ximinez thought for a moment.

"You have done enough, my friend. Leave them with me. I will post a courier tonight and begin the work of organizing relief. Go rest! I can imagine how fatigued you must be!"

"But, excellency, the captain-general's orders . . ."

"I know . . . but I am sure he would agree that you have done all you could. I will act for you. Now . . . may I suggest that you rejoin your uncle. Get some rest. We'll be calling on you for guidance again shortly. Agreed?"

"As you wish it, excellency."

Later that night two horsemen left the capital, en route to the King's seaside retreat. They carried the two packets sent from Ochuse and a summary prepared by Ximinez from Sanchez's comments. The minister closed his statement this way:

"Tomorrow, I shall begin organization of what food we can find. I am confident that Velasco is acting in the same way, though as yet we have no confirmation that he shares this information. We can only hope that the wits of the captain-general will provide sustenance during the delay, and that the natives do not become hostile. In any case, our people are in deep trouble.

"Also, your majesty, may I suggest that we not further utilize the services of Captain Sanchez. His obvious personal loyalties to Don Tristan might prove embarrassing."

November 26, 1559

Three days later Philip received both communications; quickly he dispatched a reply to Ximinez, seconding the former's suggestions.

Later that night he delivered the captain-general's letter to Valencia. They read it together.

"What will happen now," she asked. "Do you think. . . ."

"Oh, they're safe enough. People have been shipwrecked and hungry before. Most have come home to tell the tale. But, this may—ah—delay them a bit. Will that trouble you, my dear?"

Valencia shrugged her shoulders.

"Why should it?"

"I was sure it wouldn't."

"Were you?"

"Of course. After all . . . could you be happy again in a musty corner of Borobia, in your husband's miserable little house? I think you and I have come to understand each other quite well."

Valencia took his hand, and they began to walk along the bricked heights overlooking the sea.

"You always get what you want, don't you Philip?"

"Not always . . . but I work at it."

"That's what I mean. It's almost—well—almost as though you even had the power to create great storms and famine. . . ."

The king uttered one of his infrequent laughs.

"God helps him who helps himself, my dear. Let's leave it at that, eh?"

Valencia nodded. Poor Don Tristan! His world had become a shambles; and when he came home now—if he came—what would he say? What could she tell him?

"I wonder what it's like now at Ochuse," she said quietly. "Is the moon so bright, or the evening so warm as this?"

"Or the food so good? Who knows? And . . . for the moment . . . who cares?"

And Philip led the willing Valencia through the huge oaken door which led to his chambers. There, a light supper had been laid, and the royal bed linen had been turned down.

"Let's not talk about it any more," Philip suggested. "Why spoil a delightful evening, eh?"

OCHUSE
December 7, 1559

On December 7th, the first of two small ships was sighted entering the bay at Ochuse. By next evening both had anchored, and their Mexican stores were being rapidly discharged.

Juan Ceron, his lean features now gaunt, and with great shadows under his eyes, supervised the proceedings. Lieutenants Antonio Ortiz de Matienzo and Baltazar de Sotello were in charge of transporting incoming materials from the beach to shelters near the spring.

De Luna, with Fray Feria and Capt. Castilla were seated with Lt. Luis and Capt. Alfonso Ferrera, master of the second vessel.

The young mariner quickly spilled out his messages from Mexico.

"Don Luis is deeply concerned, Don Tristan, and has performed a miracle to bring these items so quickly. But I had given him your report and conveyed the urgency. He is scouring all of Mexico for other stores."

"You've done well, my friend," de Luna replied, patting the younger man's arm. "But—as you can see, you've arrived none too soon."

Luis needed little elaboration to make this point. Everywhere, the effects of hunger shouted at him. Children's stomachs were beginning to swell and men and women walked with bowed shoulders, their eyes dull. There was little of the spirit he had seen following the storm.

"What rations have you had?" he asked.

The friar replied: "First we adopted half measures, but then we discovered much spoilage in what had been salvaged. Then we went to one meal per day, with a light nourishment in the evening. Last week we discontinued the nourishment, and reduced the portions of the other. It is not good . . . and the monotony grows . . . God . . . how tired I am of flour!"

"The fish?" Luis inquired.

"We catch a few, not many, not enough to help much."

"And del Sauz's troop . . . no word?"

All heads nodded negatively.

"Then . . ."

"They are dead, I had a vision," muttered Castilla. "Some were drowned, then Indians trailed the survivors and killed them, one by one."

"But you've no word . . . really?"

"None."

"What are my orders, then, captain-general?" the seaman asked.

"If you will, good Luis, give your men two days on land, then pray go back. Hopefully, his excellency may have other supplies by then at Vera Cruz . . ."

"Don Angel suggested much the same thing; he is turning the coast upside down to help you . . . but he needs our ships."

"Then . . . please . . . rest . . . bring your men ashore, as many as can be spared. Two days? Will that be enough . . .?"

"We will sail on the tenth, excellency."

Later that night, Tristan de Luna and Fray Feria sat quietly talking by their fire. The nights were cold now, with temperature and humidity biting, and the wind whipping across the trees out of the north.

"You were wise to restore rations tonight, my friend, it did much for morale," the friar commented.

De Luna shrugged. "Anyone can see what is happening. Our people are losing spirit. They are bickering, fighting. Single men are eyeing the women, married women are complaining, mothers come to me daily to plead for more food. What else could I do?"

"How long will the new stores last?"

"Ceron says three weeks, even if we drop back to half rations again after four days. Three weeks . . ." and he raised his hands in despair.

"Pray my son. Remember . . . the Lord has commissioned us to spread His word to the corners of the earth. He will not betray us."

De Luna started to retort, then dropped his head. "Yes, father, prayer. Perhaps that is the heart of our problem. I have not believed enough. My faith is to blame. This must be the cause. Why else . . .?"

"He is trying us, Don Tristan. Be worthy. Make your people worthy."

"I'll try," sighed the commander, "God knows . . . I'll try."

December 13, 1559

On December 13, Nieto's mount topped a small rise and he sighted the first of the colonists.

"Ho . . . ho there!" he shouted. "Comrade . . . hey . . . come here!"

Two men watching the grazing of a dozen horses looked up, startled . . . then waved frantically and broke into a trot towards the troopers, all of whom had now come into view.

"Hello . . . hello . . ." shouted Nieto. "Well . . . it's good to be home . . . or is that the right thing to say?"

One of the men caught his bridle, the others rushed to the infantrymen who now stood in a knot, their travel-worn garb caked with orange clay.

"Tell us, good friend, how do things go?" the captain querried. "How's Don Tristan? Has any relief come? Is everyone well? Is the city underway . . . come man . . . speak up!"

"I'm sorry, sir, I'm . . . well . . . it's so good to see you! Word was being passed that you were all dead. Indians, some said. . . ."

"Us, dead?" and Nieto threw back his head and laughed. "No, my friend . . . in fact . . . we look much more lively than you do, if I may say so. Come . . . let's start back . . . bring your horses . . . and tell me what's happened as we go."

The captain slipped from his mount . . . and the two men, after gathering their charges . . . gave their versions of the life in Ochuse.

"It is bad, senor, very bad. These past four . . . no five . . . days, we have been back to one meal each day again. Only the horses eat well. That is our job."

That evening, in a council of officers and priests, Nieto gave a full account to the captain-general. Already, he could see what had befallen the colonists. The friars spent many hours each day now tending the sick. Women who were able acted as nurses, or minded the children who were grouped in pools. Food was running out again.

"By our count this morning," Fray Domingo reported, "we have over 100 who are patients. Some have ugly sores, others are suffering from spots in their mouths, and teeth that are coming loose. Some have loose bowels, even though they eat but one meal each day. And our medicines are almost gone," he concluded.

Lt. Matienzo added his statement. He had been placed in charge of the stockade erected to contain men who were guilty of breaking the peace.

"We now have 24 prisoners, excellency. Two are accused of rape, one attacked Lt. Acuna when given an order, the rest have been accused of stealing food."

Fray Domingo interrupted. "Are we not being too severe with them, excellency? After all, when a man's child cries through the night in want of food . . . can he be blamed . . .?"

"He cannot be blamed, Father, nor can he be held blameless," de Luna replied. "We are all hungry men, women and children. We have balanced the rations to assist the weak. Crime will only weaken our discipline." With this he turned to Nieto. "You see how things are? And it grows worse daily. . . ."

As the night wore on, the council debated the fate of the colony. To remain where they were seemed unthinkable, for it was obvious that discipline and morale were being sapped, and that slowly but surely the company was starving. Hope for new relief had to be tempered with the fact that at present they could expect only small shipments, hardly enough to sustain them, not even sufficient to prepare for a spring planting.

Nieto's report gave them their only inspiration, and that was slight.

"At Nanicapana there is food, and we have found fish in the river," he said. "There are cleared fields and good water. There are trees and bushes with berries planted there many years ago by the tribes. But—we must be truthful. The food is limited. It cannot last long. But—it is more than you have here."

"All this is very well," Fray Domingo interrupted, "but how will we move the people? The weather is turning cold. Many of these women and children—and some men, too—are ill. You say yourself that it took more than thirty days to march directly back here . . . and your men are in good health, with plenty of food."

Nieto nodded grimly.

"I didn't say it would be easy, Father. But . . . isn't it better to give these people a goal . . . a motivation . . . to provide a purpose to each day? Here, they're at each other's throats. At least the struggle will keep them busy."

Castilla clapped his hands. "Well said, my friend! Idle hands are a devil's workshop . . . and our people have been idle too long. This will give them hope . . . if we present it right."

"But the little ones. . . ."

"They can go by boat."

"By boat?"

"We'll sail our pinnace to the river . . . going through Bahia Filipina. We'll put the children and some of the women on board . . . and use the longboat when the river shallows. The rest will march by land . . . and try to keep a parallel course."

"I don't know . . ."

"You have a better suggestion?"

"No . . ."

Next morning the entire colony was assembled, save those too sick to stand.

After prayers led by the three friars, the captain-general addressed them.

"My dear friends, we have been blessed by the return of Capt. Nieto and his band of fifteen good men and true. We had all feared them dead, and we thank God for His kindness in returning them to us.

"Capt. Nieto and the others led by sergeant-major del Sauz have reached an Indian settlement they call Nanicapana. It is many miles to the northwest and borders a great river which can be entered through Bahia Filipina 70 leagues to the west. They have found remnants of a civilization which once was great, and which was reported by Hernando de Soto . . . or at least this we believe. In any event, there are but few Indians there now, and they are good men, men of peace.

"Their village is not great, but has some 80 shelters, enough to assist us through the cold months ahead. And there is food . . . beans and maize and dried fruits and nuts. Capt. Nieto reports that there are fish to be caught, and that trees are loaded with other things we can eat.

"Therefore . . . after long council, we have decided to act for the betterment of all, until such time as full relief arrives from Don Luis Velasco, and from our King, noble Philip.

"As quickly as we can ready ourselves, those who are able to march will be divided into two camps; women, children and a guard of infantry soldiers shall be embarked on the pinnace and our two longboats. These shall proceed to Bahia Filipina and up the river towards Nanicapana.

"The remainder shall move overland, retracing the path traveled by Capt. Nieto and his men. We shall attempt to rendezvous with those traveling by water at a point along the river, to complete the journey together.

"I have chosen Juan Xaramillo, along with Fray Feria, to remain here at Ochuse, along with sixty men of the infantry, to care for the sick and to await stores from our countrymen.

"Thus we will rendezvous at Nanicapana, where we know food awaits us, and we shall prepare to receive other supplies as they come.

"This will not be a simple undertaking. Travel will be hard, and we must carry food, arms and what possessions we can on our backs or our horses.

"However, I believe that God has answered our prayers in providing this succor in the wilderness, and with it a chance to begin our work with the inhabitants, for the good of their souls.

"This is our mission. It will not be easy. But you are men and women commissioned by God for a great work. He is testing us now. I know we shall not fail. Let every man and woman perform his duty. Now . . . report to your military leaders; each of them has instructions for our departure. We shall plan to leave Ochuse in two days.

"May God be with us!"

There was a hushed amen . . . and the company began to disperse. There were no cheers, only dropped eyes, bowed backs and a shuffling of feet as the people moved towards the small gathering places they now called home. Silently, almost, they made their preparations. They followed instructions. What else could they do? Perhaps their commander was right. Almost anything was better than sitting here . . . waiting to starve.

NANICAPANA
January 16, 1560

The damp, dripping fog hung over the village as dawn broke. The weather was not cold—perhaps 50 degrees—but the fog was like a wet blanket and men awakening found breastplates soaked with condensate; droplets fell like a light rain from the small oak leaves and the moss. Even keen eyes could not see across the camp.

Mateo del Sauz shook himself awake, reached for his camp basin and sloshed handfuls of water over his head and through his beard. There was no harsh camp routine here. A light guard patrolled the perimeters; one man was stationed to protect the horses, another kept cook fires alive, the banked coals sending forth a pungent aroma that permeated Nanicapana's stillness.

Del Sauz dried himself and applied what little grooming a soldier permits himself. Now awake, he stepped into the clearing. At that moment the shouting began.

"It's Nieto . . . Nieto is here . . . Haalloo . . . the guard . . . Nieto is back . . . fall out . . . fall out . . .!"

The sergeant-major broke into a run, cutting between huts to hurry to the guard post where the noise was growing.

And there he was! Nieto was standing beside his mount, stroking its mane, chatting amiably with the guard.

Del Sauz seized him by the shoulders and embraced his young friend in a bear hug!

"You're back . . . you're back! And the others? Where are they? What of de Luna . . . speak man . . . don't be a mute!"

Nieto grinned. "One thing at a time, if you please . . . and the first is something hot to drink. I've been in the saddle without a break for two days."

"Of course . . . here . . . Pedro . . . take his horse . . . Jose . . . stir the fire, heat water, get rum . . . hey . . . turn out everybody . . . Nieto's back . . . Nieto is here . . .!"

Minutes later they were seated together in del Sauz's hut, the two friars, the three officers, each warming his gut with a strong flagon of boiling hot water liberally laced with spirits. Between words, Nieto also chewed lustily on Indian style cornbread.

"All right . . . now . . . tell us, who's with you . . . and where are they?" the sergeant-major demanded.

"They're all with me . . . or almost all. We left about 175 back there . . . rear guard and the sick."

"ALL!" I shouted, unbelieving. "ALL! You mean . . ."

"I mean almost 800 men, women and children are two days march from here. They're coming, they're sick, they're starving, they're . . . well . . . they're desperate. I came on to get you to hurry back with food and all the extra horses."

"But good God, man . . . how could you . . ."

"It was a case of starve there or starve here . . . perhaps with a little more hope."

"Then, there has been no . . ."

"Two ships, small ones, two months ago. But . . . they brought a pittance. When we got there and reported what we'd found Don Tristan and the others felt that they should come on . . . and after seeing how bad things were I couldn't argue."

"And . . . they *made* the trip?"

"Most of them. We lost some . . . mostly children. Things are bad, Mateo . . . very bad. Look at me? I've not eaten a full meal in a month. They've been on short rations for days, and walking, walking, walking. The poor devils are ready to drop!"

"The horses?"

"Don Tristan has not let any man touch one of the beasts—yet. But there are murmurings among the settlers and even some of the infantry."

"You know what their coming will mean?"

"Of course . . . I know how much food we have. But . . . at least it'll give them hope for a moment."

"Then we can all grow thin together, eh?"

"Something like that. At any rate . . . what choices do we have? And what we have here may help the children, for a time."

"What do you propose, then?"

"Assemble 100 men and all the horses. Send them with me. We'll carry food, and give what help we can. I tell you, they're in bad shape. Most have no shoes now, and their clothes are in threads. Things are bad, Mateo . . . believe me," he added seriously.

NANICAPANA
January 21, 1560

Five days later the vanguard staggered into Nanicapana. Del Sauz and the remaining troopers had prepared for them as best they could; even the Indians had helped. Pallets had been prepared in every shelter; a hospital of sorts had been built, and men not thus employed had spent hours fishing, trying to swell the larder.

The sergeant-major had listened carefully to Nieto's report and had repeated it in his mind, time after time. But even he was unprepared for the sights he saw as the colonists arrived.

Robust men had become walking scarecrows; women, their hair hanging in disheveled hanks, seemingly had aged a decade. Children walked with bloated midriffs stuffed out; many staggered along with the aid of staffs or crutches. Many had lost their shoes; all looked as though they had slept little in months. Among the first into camp was Fray Domingo de Santo Domingo, his usually bright eyes now red rimmed, his beard a gray tangle, his bare feet gashed by vines and stones.

Others were equally grim in their appearance.

Del Sauz and the others did what they could. Pots of water were heated to bathe the marchers, and food was cooked and served them as they sat or lay on the ground in utter exhaustion.

Tristan de Luna arrived with the second wave.

The proud captain-general was gaunt, his black hair now liberally streaked with gray, his eyes, crusted at the corners, showed signs of fever; his arms were covered with a rash from some poisonous undergrowth.

He answered del Sauz's salute, and moments later collapsed onto a bench in the sergeant-major's quarters.

"Thank God . . . thank God . . . we are here!" he muttered. "Send Anunciacon to me, please . . . we must prepare a Mass of thanksgiving. Oh . . . and Mateo . . . keep the fires high, please. It will raise spirits."

Minutes later, a warm drink in his stomach, the commander was asleep.

Fray Anunciacon, working tirelessly to aid the sick, gazed down at the collapsed leader.

"May God protect us," he thought. "They're here . . . we're all here. But what does that mean? Even a schoolboy could judge our supplies. There's not enough for a month. May He have mercy on us!"

As wave after wave of the stragglers arrived, camp activity soared. Somehow places were found for them all, each shelter bulging as an average of fifteen was crammed inside. But . . . they were out of the elements, there was fish, and for a time at least, it was possible to feed them all.

On the third day after his arrival, de Luna ordered a high Mass performed for the entire company. With all four Dominicans presiding, the full pageantry was performed; the carefully protected chalice was filled with wine, and wafers were painstakingly made from the tiny remaining supply of consecrated flour. The voices of the friars, strong despite their ordeal, sang high and true.

At the conclusion, Don Tristan rose before the colonists.

"My friends, we have traveled far. You have suffered much. I know this, and I commend you for your uncomplaining spirit. God has spared us . . . has urged us on . . . and with the help of our native friends, we now have food, at least for a time. They tell me that the native name for this place is Nanicapana. Therefore, in the name of His Most Christian Majesty, Philip II, I declare that henceforth this place shall be known as Santa Cruz de Nanicapana . . . and that it shall be so marked on all maps and charts!

"Tomorrow . . . we shall all enjoy one added day of rest. Then . . . we must make preparations; there is food . . . but not so much as we will need to survive until new crops can be harvested. Therefore, I am asking your leaders to begin intensive search of the forest for any articles which may be turned into food. I am also asking Captain Nieto and Captain Ramirez to go forth a second time in reconnaissance . . . in the hope that there may be other inhabitants and other sources of food.

"I shall assign others to fishing, and some to erecting more shelters and protection.

"I don't know how long we will remain here, or when additional supplies will reach our base at Ochuse. Meanwhile, God has given us one primary objective—to survive. That we shall do! We will enjoy full rations two more days, then unless other items are obtained, we must again curtail.

"Finally, let me offer my thanks to the sergeant major and his men. They have found this haven for us . . . have made friends with the natives . . . and have found food to sustain us. They have comforted us in our exhaustion . . . and have given us renewed hope. Go now . . . rest . . . renew your energy and your courage. God is with us, never forget that! We will succeed in our enterprise . . . that I promise you. Master-of-the Camp . . . dismiss the company!"

Two days later the new routine began.

There were fish; and in the woods the women began to harvest apron loads of acorns and leaves which appeared promising. Nieto and I departed with our squad of 20 men. And gradually an order came into the life of the camp. But it was a time of waiting. For days there were no new expressions of hope. All waited and watched . . . and prayed.

NANICAPANA
February 1, 1560

A bitter wind whistled through the stands of longleaf pine and rustled among the leaves of southern oaks, now just falling and blowing in swirls through Nanicapana.

Tristan de Luna sat huddled in his hut, his cloak, tattered and soiled, was pulled tightly about him; logs crackled in a fire in the center of the crude building, but even a hearty blaze was scant help as wind bit through the crude shelter.

The weeks in the Indian village had taken further toll of the commander. His beard was unkempt, his hair uncombed, and the bones of his bright cheeks, once concealed by a gentle curve of flesh, now stood out starkly. His eyes revealed the fever that burned inside him. In his hand de Luna held the list of the sick prepared that morning by Fray Matheos. Each day it grew longer; at first it was a twoscore, then a hundred; now half the corps was unfit for duty.

Women and children suffered most. The look of starvation was upon them all; bellies swelled, eyes lost their look of life and assumed a faraway, listless stare. Bones protruded through arms that were nearly fleshless.

The leader sighed and shook his head, then looked up as Domingo de la Anunciacon drew open the crude door closure.

"May I join you?" the friar asked.

"Of course, my friend, my misery will appreciate your solace," de Luna smiled wanly. "Or do you have some good report? I could use one."

The big friar, now much reduced in girth but still wiry, dropped onto the packed earth beside de Luna and raised his hands to the fire.

"Feels good," he muttered. "My God, who would have thought it could get this cold! This isn't Mexico!"

"Amen to that!"

"That's Matheos's list?"

De Luna nodded. "Yes . . . and longer every day. He says that Senora Marcato's son is near death, and that the Mendosa boy can't take any food at all."

The priest shook his head sadly. "I'm afraid the deaths will begin soon, my friend. The people are—well—giving up. Confessions this morning were worse than ever. Many believe that there is no hope. They are preparing their souls to meet God."

"I had hoped you'd have some good word," de Luna said.

"Hardly. No . . . but there is something I believe you can do."

"Tell me."

"Meet with some of the women. Talk with them personally, no speeches, just—well—just try to comfort them. They respect you, you know. Let me bring some of the more outspoken ones here. Tell them what you plan. Perhaps. . . ."

"Inspire them?" de Luna said slowly. "What can I say, old friend? Shall I tell them how hungry I am? Or show them my rations?"

The friar raised his hand. "Hold . . . hold. No, wait . . . no . . . just . . . well, just talk with them. I have done what I can. I have prepared them for their eternal journeys . . . but perhaps you can still inspire hope."

De Luna shrugged. "Why not? Bring them in . . . not too many, though, and bring del Sauz with you, eh? He's good with women."

The Dominican drew himself up, and quietly went out.

The minutes ticked by . . . then, de Luna heard them coming, the soft murmur of voices, the women, earnestly trying to plead for some new form of help.

He rose, opened the door cover and ushered them inside, motioning them to be seated. The women, a half dozen, some Spanish, some Indian, drew their skirts about them and moved as close as possible towards the fire.

"Dear friends," the general began, "I'm glad you've come. The good friar says you wish to speak with me?"

Senora Valdez glanced nervously at the others, then turned to face the leader.

"Yes, my general," she began, "we have spoken with our men . . . we have listened, and watched. Perhaps we are wrong, but we refuse to believe that the end is near. You must know things we do not. Tell us, what hope is there? Is food coming . . . or will we all die here among the savages?"

De Luna watched her face, the muscles twitching with emotion, her eyes brimming with tears as she screwed up courage to ask questions she would never have dared pose six months before.

The others, their bodies shrunken, their hair long and lank, the spirit of life obviously ebbing, sat silently, awaiting his reply.

"Dear ladies," he began, "I know how you feel. You have been the bravest of us all . . . you and your wonderful children. What can I say? We came to Nanicapana because Major del Sauz and his party found food. To have remained at Ochuse was—as you saw—a probably fatal thing. We had almost exhausted supplies . . . and it was impossible to predict when others might arrive. You recall this?"

Senora Valdez nodded, her eyes riveted on his face.

De Luna continued. "We had great hopes that other supplies might be found here, or that game and fish might add to our larder. But we have had bad fortune. Within three weeks our stores were gone, and the forest has given our hunters little. You yourselves have been the providers, gathering acorns and berries . . ."

"Which the children cannot eat and which make the women ill," the Valdez woman interrupted. "If I die tomorrow I cannot eat another mouthful of the bitter stuff!"

De Luna stared at the ground. "I know," he said. "They make poor fare. We have eaten some of the horses, boiled the skin for nourishment, gleaned the grains from the fields. Now . . . it is gone . . . all gone."

A second woman spoke: "Captain-general, what of the party of Captains Nieto and Ramirez? Some say that they will return shortly, that you have had a report from them and that they will bring food. Is this true?"

Sadly, de Luna shook his head. "I have had no word. It is weeks since they left. I fear for their lives. And we have had no word from Ochuse. I know the viceroy is doing all that he can, but it takes time, and this is a difficult season for ships. All I can ask you to do is sustain hope. Pray to Our Lady! Comfort the little ones; try to get them to eat even the leaves you brew . . . anything. Help will come . . . but for now . . . well . . . I will not deceive you. I have told you everything I know."

The women sat around the fire, their eyes lowered. There were no more questions, but they made no move to go. De Luna glanced at del Sauz, then at the friar. The latter raised a finger to his lips. Together they sat in silence. Minutes passed, then quietly the Dominican began to pray: " . . . Our Father, Who art in heaven. . . ." One by one the other voices joined him, climaxing the ancient prayer in strong unison. Then Senora Valdez rose, and the others followed.

"Thank you, your excellency, thank you. At least we know. Thank you, and may God answer our prayers." Suddenly she moved towards him, put her arms around his shoulders and embraced the startled leader. In a moment she broke away, darted through the hut's opening and was gone. Slowly, the others followed.

NANICAPANA

Two hours later, as the last rays of light were fading, their prayers were answered, not once but twice.

First, from the south, came the hail of an infantry captain. His horn sounded through the cold afternoon like a clarion call, and in an instant men and women poured from their shelters and raced to the path to the south. The call sounded again, then a third time. No mistake! It *was* a Spanish troop! Moments later the smiling face of a chilled, tired but very happy Lt. Juan Xaramillo appeared. The visitor dismounted and was mobbed by his friends. Behind him walked twenty troopers, guiding horses laden with casks, barrels and sacks; relief had come!

Capt. Pedro Acuna was first to reach them. He threw his arms around his old friend, pummeling his back and arms in the timehonored greeting of comrades. Quickly the troop was surrounded, and in seconds the newcomers were engulfed by well-wishers who urged them into camp.

Moments later the young lieutenant, his lips chapped and his fingers stiff with cold, was seated with del Sauz and Fray Domingo in the captain-general's hut, relating his story.

"It was twenty-six days ago, excellency, unless I have miscounted. Two small ships arrived together from Vera Cruz. We discharged their cargo and wrote them a careful report of what has happened. They departed as soon as they had watered and weather permitted. There were two messages for you, sir; here . . . here they are," and he handed de Luna two travel-worn pouches.

The first was from Velasco.

"MY DEAR DE LUNA," it began, " I HAVE RECEIVED YOUR REPORTS AND SYMPATHIZE DEEPLY. WORD HAS GONE FORTH TO THE KING FROM VERA CRUZ, AND I UNDERSTAND FROM YOU ALSO. HOPEFULLY, HE WILL AID YOU. MEANWHILE, I HAVE SCOURED THE COUNTRYSIDE FOR SUPPLIES. IN THE EAST, VILLAFANE HAS DONE THE SAME, AND HAS WROUGHT MIRACLES. MUCH OF WHAT IS CONTAINED IN THIS SHIPMENT IS DUE TO HIS GOOD WORK. HOPEFULLY, IT WILL SUSTAIN YOU UNTIL MORE CAN BE LOCATED. HOWEVER, THIS WILL TAKE TIME, FOR THE COUNTRY WAS BADLY STRIPPED FOR YOUR ORIGINAL NEEDS. MEANWHILE, MAY GOD WATCH OVER YOU. AS YOU ARE ABLE, KEEP US INFORMED."

The other was from Angel Villafane, the quiet, resourceful soldier who was Don Tristan's friend of long standing. The message read:

"I HAVE CALCULATED THE NEEDS AND APPRECIATE THE SUFFERING WHICH MUST BE UPON YOU NOW. MY HEART BLEEDS FOR THE WOMEN AND CHILDREN, AND FOR YOU, OLD FRIEND, WHOSE CHARGE IS SO VITAL TO OUR COUNTRY AND ITS FUTURE. BE CONFIDENT THAT WE SHALL CONTINUE OUR SEARCH FOR FOOD, AND THAT WE SHALL COMMUNICATE WITH OTHERS WHO MIGHT HELP. I SHALL SEND THE NEXT SINGLE SHIP AS SOON AS ITS CARGO IS COMPLETE. MAY GOD REST WITH YOU."

De Luna folded the parchment, his eyes moist with tears.

"They are good men, good men," he muttered. Then, turning to the friar, he said:

"Order a Mass to be said tonight. I know it's cold and that it will be uncomfortable, but I want people to recognize what a miracle this deliverance is. Make your pronouncements short, and order a bonfire built so that all may see.

"Del Sauz, you and Ceron put a full guard over the food; I want staples rationed as before. Give us a three-quarter serving tonight, then half orders again beginning tomorrow, except for the children. We are saved for the moment, but God knows when we'll see more. Am I understood?"

Del Sauz nodded grimly. "Yes, excellency."

That night, the colonists slept with stomachs filled with warm food, and during the dark hours the winds switched out of the north and to the south. Next morning, as dawn broke, the temperatures warmed, and by noon a bright sun made life seem good again. It was then that the second bit of news arrived.

NANICAPANA
February 2, 1560

It was just before the noon hour that Nieto and I arrived, our men streaming along behind, singing a spirited marching song and obviously well fed.

Friends raced out to meet us, and soon we were surrounded by hundreds of cheering, waving, smiling people who had said they feared us lost forever.

I quickly pointed to a single addition to our troop.

"This is Naccoset, my friends, greet him and make him welcome for he's our good, good friend. Now . . . let me through . . . I must report to my uncle."

Standing in the warm sun, Nieto and I unfolded our seven week saga to the other officers and friars, all of whom clustered about. Naccoset stood beside me, his young, tall frame curiously military in its bearing, his face impassive.

"Let me start at the beginning," I said. "As you directed, we began by marching north and east. Eleven days we traveled, seeing nothing but more of the same . . . including some fields once occupied by these same people. But there were no villagers, no game, no crops. Day after day, our food diminished; we conserved carefully, and each time we came to a stream we fished.

"On the twelfth day we turned east and after four days march began to see signs of hills . . . the beginnings of the mountains."

"That's what de Soto's men reported!" de Luna interrupted.

"So we thought," Nieto said.

"We pushed on," I continued, "and then on the 32nd day we met Naccoset."

"You met . . . but where . . . and how? Did you find his village?"

"No . . . he was alone, a scout for his people, for they had heard we were coming."

"And he then escorted you to his village?"

"Not exactly. You see, Coosa is much farther than we thought."

"Then he is from Coosa?"

"No . . . an outlying village. But he knows where Coosa is . . . and he's agreed to guide us all."

"Then . . . you haven't actually *seen* it . . . Coosa, I mean?"

"Naccoset said that it would require twenty marching days to reach the heart of Coosa. Twenty, then twenty back . . . added to what we had already gone . . . well . . . we were afraid of what might have happened here by then. So . . . we decided to come back and let him guide us all. And well . . . here we are!"

"What does he say about Coosa? Is it still a great nation? Are there supplies? Will they give us aid?"

I continued the report: "Naccoset says that Coosa *is* a great nation, but that there are other tribes nearby too, and that there's possibility of war between them this summer. He urges us to hurry ahead, to become established now, before hostilities begin."

"Anything else?" de Luna asked.

"No . . . not really . . . except a great lesson in geography. We've seen beautiful rivers and land that appears rich for crops. But we saw no other people. Naccoset showed us a great deal about hunting and trapping, though. I tell you, he's something!"

"Well," de Luna said. "Well!"

"What do you say, your excellency?" Ceron asked. "Shall we prepare to move out?"

"Can we believe this *one* Indian?" Fray Mazuelos asked. "Are we *sure* this is the right course? After all . . . this will take us much farther from Ochuse . . ."

"He says there is food, Father," Nieto ventured. "And he has been a good friend to us. I believe him!"

The discussion continued until well into the afternoon. The troopers were fed and quickly voiced their stories abroad. A new light of hope crossed the faces of the colonists. Now . . . twice in 24 hours good news had come, after weeks of the starving time.

An hour before dusk, de Luna ordered the entire colony brought together. After a prayer offered by Fray Domingo, the captain-general climbed the simple platform in the square and spoke.

"God has answered our prayers . . . not once but twice," he began. "First, he has brought us food, enough for many days if we use it wisely. Then today our dear comrades have returned bearing good tidings.

"They have been guided by our new friend, an Indian whose name is Naccoset, and whose village is in the great Coosa nation which Hernando de Soto discovered twenty years ago. They are confident that if we march there we shall find help.

"However, I have carefully examined the reports of our good friars and their hospital. The weather may remain severe for many days yet, and I am afraid that to attempt to march so great a distance with women and children would be a fatal error.

Therefore, this is the plan upon which we have agreed:

"Three days from now 200 soldiers will depart for Coosa. They will be led by Major del Sauz and six captains, and accompanied by Fray Domingo de Salazar and Fray Domingo de la Anunciacon. Hopefully, they may make this march in 40 days or less, establish a base for us there, and then send messengers to act as our guides.

"Meanwhile, Lt. Xaramillo and his party will return to Ochuse, to await more supplies from Mexico. The balance of our party will remain here at Nanicapana. We now have food for some days, and there are other supplies that can be forwarded from Ochuse. Shortly we shall plant a crop here, and I have ordered those at Ochuse to do likewise.

"Thus, God willing, we shall have a base in three places, and may recover our initiative. By this method we shall conserve the energies of the sick, the women and children. I shall order none of the married men on the mission to Coosa.

"Our prayers have been answered, my friends; we have food, we have hope, and we have a new friend. We know that our people in Mexico are hurrying to our aid. I ask you to have faith . . . and to be of good spirits. We still face a time of crisis . . . but two miracles have answered our prayers. Let us give thanks . . . and then perform what must be God's will."

During the following three days Santa Cruz de Nanicapana buzzed with activity. Preparations were made for a march by the chosen 200; Lt. Xaramillo and his party departed for Ochuse. Selected farmers worked with the natives of Nanicapana, discussing preparation of the fields; others returned to fishing and hunting with new vigor. Busy hands hid despairing thoughts.

NANICAPANA
February 5, 1560

My uncle and I sat huddled in his hut, our cloaks wrapped tightly about us as the wind roared almost unopposed through the drafty shelter.

Don Tristan remained silent much of the time now. Before the assembly he bore himself well and spoke with firmness and optimism. Alone, however, he shrank into a shell of despair, his eyes reflecting the fever that clung to him. His bowels were in an almost constant flux too, weakening him. His weight had declined, and the outline of his proud face was altered considerable by the combination of tensions, illness and lack of food.

This afternoon he had asked me to sit with him to receive his special instructions to me for the march.

"I want you to make this march, Cristobal, because you have a strong heart. Del Sauz is a good officer and will do his duty, and the priests are able men. . . ."

"They are *all* good men, uncle, each is doing his best!" I insisted.

"True, true . . . but at times like this, leadership is all important. I say this to you alone, because I would not insert a word of doubt for anything. Frankly . . . I am concerned about the distance you must travel. The maps are nothing but sketches . . . and the more we learn of de Soto's tales the less value they have for us. . . ."

"I believe the Indian will help us, uncle. . . ."

"Perhaps. But watch him well. I recall a similar case in the west that almost destroyed us . . . took us hundreds of leagues into the mountains, then left us to wander aimlessly. No . . . watch him with care."

"I promise."

"One other thing. I want to say this to you . . . just in case when you return, I am not here. . . ."

"What do you mean?"

"Look at me, boy! My body is dissolving, my guts are bleeding out, my face burns, I shake with an ague. It is altogether possible that the Lord will call me before you return. So I want you to recognize certain responsibilities, eh?"

"Of course, uncle, but what . . .?"

"I cannot predict the future or know how God will favor this expedition; there are some among us, I'm afraid, who don't agree with the way things are being managed."

"Nonsense! You're doing all any human could do."

"Perhaps; but others may not think so, especially when they see people dying and their own lives in jeopardy. No . . . one day there may be a reckoning, and I may not be present to answer for my deeds, or my crimes, as others may see them."

"I doubt this, but what difference . . .?"

"I want you to recall each day as carefully as possible; remember what is done, what I have said, and how I have tried to care for the people. Then, if it is necessary, you might testify as my spokesman, to defend my name and our family. Will you promise?"

I was stunned by Don Tristan's frankness. If he felt that death threatened, he must have been in living torment, realizing his responsibilities and the possibility that he would be called to answer for his failings, perhaps before God and King.

"Of course I will speak for you!" I replied. "But please, don't spend your time thinking of that . . . put your mind to things that will help us all!"

He nodded, his eyes cast down. "Of course. Meanwhile, all I can do is try to keep people together, pray that food comes, and hope you come upon bright days on your march." Then he looked up and seized my hand warmly. "Go with God, nephew! Much depends upon you. Go with God!"

30 DAYS FROM NANICAPANA
March 7, 1560

Trooper Manuel Ortiz sat hunched under an ancient water oak, his knees drawn up, his arms wrapped about his middle. His eyes were closed, and his head slowly moved back and forth, soft moans slipping through tightly pressed lips. About him, the rest of us sat or lay, barely noticing the soldier's agony. Our uniforms, tattered when we began, now hung in shreds; leather belting which had supported our arms was missing in some cases; it had become food, boiled with acorns and leaves in a desperate effort to ward off starvation. Thirty days of continuous marching, first north, then east, had all but destroyed the 200.

The growing warmth of the mid-March days made life less physically uncomfortable, but it was fast becoming obvious that del Sauz's troop would soon face death unless new stores were found. The major, thin, wan, his once dark thatch now heavily streaked with grey and his proud beard a ratty twist, sat in a circle of men that included the two Dominicans and his six officers. Our council was now a daily affair as each desperately sought to sustain the spirits of men who now had not eaten a full ration in a month.

"Manuelos was right, we should have listened to him," muttered Fray Salazar. 'Can we trust one Indian?' he asked . . . and no one paid him any heed. Now where is our fine friend?"

No one answered. It was oral ground plowed many times since the night three weeks earlier when the red man had silently disappeared. Why had he left? Why had he helped us in the first place? No one had an answer.

These three weeks we had blundered forward, realizing that it was equally oppressive to return to Nanicapana where food now must be almost exhausted.

"We've just got to hope that de Soto's information still has value . . . and keep marching. Otherwise . . ." del Sauz let his words trail away.

An inventory that morning had disclosed that only ten sets of full body harness remained, and now the men's stomachs had begun to reject the bitter gruel made from the boiled leather and forest bits.

"My gut never stops rumbling," grumbled Lt. Vazquez. "And look over there . . . look at that poor devil. The cramps have him again!"

Fray Domingo painfully pulled himself erect. "I'll go pray with him; at least it may take his mind off his miseries," he explained and limped slowly toward the moaning soldier Ortiz.

Del Sauz spoke again. "We'll wait an hour, then start again. I hate forcing the march, but the men are no worse off walking than sitting here. At least they'll be occupied. Pass the word, eh?"

The pace that afternoon was snail-like, perhaps a kilometer per hour. We passed over pleasant ground, hilly, occasionally cut by small streams, the soil with a loamy look. But there were no signs of men, no trees with fruit or berries, no tilled fields.

At the fourth hour we came to a small river, less than a bow shot across. The water was swift and clear, and del Sauz ordered the troop to stop and drink. Selecting three of the younger men, he directed them to move up stream two leagues, then to return to camp. The rest of us were ordered to try our fortunes fishing, a skill at which we Spaniards had displayed little cunning.

Del Sauz seated himself with pad and quill, painstakingly continuing his map and log. Occasionally an officer would stop for information or to report a small fish caught; elsewhere a few men bathed, but most took advantage of the stop to stretch out in the warm sun and sleep.

Thirty minutes passed, an hour, then from the distance del Sauz heard a shout, followed by a shot. Alarmed, he leaped to his feet and called the troop to readiness. Tired, sick men assembled as best they could, clutching weapons, forming into a haphazard battle line.

The shouts continued, coming closer; del Sauz dispatched three troopers as scouts, then began to deploy his men. But then the calls became clearer . . . and a scout burst back into the clearing.

"Food, excellency, food, they've found food. Trees, with ripe nuts!"

No orders were required. Sick, trembling men burst into a trot, the weak aided by the sturdy. Moments later one of the scouting party came into view. His hands clasped heaps of walnuts, and his small pack was jammed with chestnuts.

"Food, sir . . . food . . . huge orchard . . . standing just back from the river. It's food . . . food!"

To emphasize his words he rushed from man to man, handing each one or two of the precious nuts.

"All right . . . form up . . . form up," the major urged, "just because we have good fortune is no reason to forget we're soldiers."

Reluctantly, the men regrouped, then moved out, traveling at several times their earlier pace, following the scout who trotted proudly in the lead. His two companions were at work harvesting, he explained, for there were hoards of nuts on the ground, and the trees were loaded.

That night, for the first time in weeks, we filled our stomachs. Chestnuts were roasted, and walnuts cracked and hulled and eaten in huge quantities. Stewed leather was forgotten, and the men, cautioned by the medically-wise Dominicans, ate small but frequent snacks of the tasty nuts. I think perhaps I have never since eaten anything that tasted as good as those nuts did to me that night. After I had relieved that aching hunger, I joined the other officers around the small campfire, and we convened again.

"Where there's a planted orchard there must be a village . . . close by," Vazquez insisted. Del Sauz agreed, as did the others.

"The river's the obvious place. Perhaps we are near Coosa . . . or at least a tribal village. But . . . which way . . . and will they welcome us?" the major queried.

"I say, let's try both directions . . . send out two parties, and the remainder will remain here finishing the harvest," contributed Lt. Juan de Porras.

Del Sauz nodded. "In the morning we'll form two parties, nine men each with an officer. One will proceed downstream, the other up. Each will travel two days, then return. Then, we'll compare notes and judge which direction offers most hope. . . ."

"Assuming they do not find an actual settlement. . . ." added Fray Salazar.

"Of course. Now . . . we'll want men in the best condition, those who can march well. A rest here will help the others. Take full packs and weapons, but at all costs, avoid conflict."

Lieutenants Vazquez and Porras were chosen as group leaders, and next morning the major called us all together, outlined his plan for the following four days, and the two scouting parties departed.

Two hours later, one man returned from Porras' group.

"We've found a village, small but lived in, on this side of the river. There are no people to be seen, but they're about. The lieutenant asked for additional men, and has pressed on."

Eagerly, del Sauz chose another ten men who quickly followed the messenger upstream. By nightfall, Porras and his entire squad had returned, excitement etched in their features.

"We passed four small collections of huts," the lieutenant reported. "There are planted fields and other orchards, too. The people have been warned of our coming and have disappeared into the woods. But we saw signs. They were watching."

That night the council of officers drafted its plan. Next morning, 100 would move to within half a league of the largest village, to where they might be observed. There they would bivouac and erect shelters of branches, and send messengers with gifts to the Indians. Only a few would go forward in search of the people, for fear of creating an incident. The balance of the force would remain in the orchard until the return of Vazquez and his men; then we too would advance.

Next morning, our packs filled to bursting with the remaining harvest, the bulk of the 200 moved out, marching the roughly three leagues. There, in the shadow of a small pine forest, we used fallen limbs to piece together rough shelters, and established elements of the military camp. Nearby, a clear, tiny stream bubbled along, to join the river a few hundreds meters away.

The problem of meeting and communicating with the Indians proved easier than del Sauz had feared. Together with Fray Salazar and two veterans of the de Soto expedition, del Sauz walked slowly towards the first village, a collection of two dozen huts set back on the high ground above the river.

The friar carried a crucifix held high on a slim rod; and the others extended handfuls of the shiny glass beads and trinkets which earlier explorers had promised would please the red men.

Quickly, they were proved correct.

First to emerge from hiding was a small boy, perhaps ten years old, who shyly worked his way from tree to tree, his eyes riveted on the glistening beads. Sighted by Salazar, the boy stopped but continued to look. The party halted, and by signs offered him some of the gifts.

The child looked back towards the woods, then with the courage of youth, hurried forward. Del Sauz knelt down, patted the boy's head, and gave him three of the glass trinkets. Making use of sign language, the men tried to communicate their desire to meet others from the village. The youth smiled, admired his prizes, then suddenly broke away and ran back into the concealing darkness. Moments later he returned, joined this time by two others, a young girl and an older man.

The ritual was repeated. Soon, del Sauz was surrounded by excited, delighted Indians, each admiring one or more of the baubles.

Smiles curved across their faces, and a playfulness developed. Soon, Indian and Spaniard were conversing in a crude sort of way. By nightfall the entire village had returned from hiding and had gathered among their huts to play host to their visitors.

Acting with caution, del Sauz added no men to his party. That evening and much of the next day we feasted, and gradually understanding improved. Late next afternoon several Indian elders returned with the four to the Spanish camp, where del Sauz tried to make them understand the shortage of food.

By next afternoon Indians began arriving, carrying maize, vegetables and fruits from their fields.

Two days later, Vazquez's force, with the remainder of the Spanish party, arrived and joined the bivouac.

Even hunting improved, and during the next ten days the humor of the 200 improved greatly. The Indians were good hosts and treated us with a combination of awe and respect. All was going well . . . but del Sauz recognized that the respite was temporary.

He made his feelings known to the two friars.

"Our 200 will empty their storehouses soon, and they know it," he began, "and our mission is to supply the main force. That is impossible with what we see here. Our people must push on . . . yet we need guidance. Coosa must be nearby . . . it must be!"

Fray Salazar spoke softly,

"These people have befriended us in our time of need. We must return that love and do nothing to disturb them. Perhaps . . . perhaps now is the time to begin our service for Christ . . . to try to give them the message of forgiveness."

"What are you suggesting, Father?"

"I'm simply trying to gain perspective from what de Soto's people saw and said. They were befriended, found food, returned good for good . . . and left ultimately with a bond that has lasted these years, else we would have found no welcome here. This I believe."

"So?"

"I cannot understand their tongue any more than you can, major, but I can see their eyes. They're afraid, afraid . . . not physically, perhaps, but that we will consume their food, destroy them by bringing about starvation of the kind we ourselves faced."

"And what does that mean?"

"If there *is* a Coosa—today, I mean—they will help us find it, if only to remove us from their presence. Look at them! They're frightened. I say we must nurture their friendship . . . and this will encourage their further help. If only we could communicate . . ."

Fray Domingo de la Anunciacon interrupted.

"I think my Brother is correct, major. We've been derelict in not erecting some form of simple chapel here. Suppose we proceed with this project . . . and then invite the elders of the tribe to witness the Mass. Perhaps . . . perhaps the Lord will find some means to show us the way . . ."

"You're suggesting we may enjoy some kind of miracle," del Sauz suggested.

"Nothing so dramatic, my friend, but . . . stranger things have happened. After all, I am here as a man of God. Perhaps our work will truly begin on this remote spot."

Del Sauz shrugged. Lt. Sotello slowly turned his back to hide his smile. Vazquez folded his arms. "Good friar, I wish we all held your faith. But I agree! What have we to lose?"

That afternoon the work began. Troopers gathered limbs tipped with long leaf pine needles fresh with the scent of cone and sap; these formed the framework; others hacked loose stubby branches of scrub oak in full leaf, which formed a kind of canopy over the pine. The chapel was not large, simply a shelter beneath which they drew heavier boughs for an altar which was covered with dried pine straw. Over all of this the friars draped their precious altar cloth, and on this they placed the elements of the Mass.

The invitation to the tribe's leaders was presented by the major, two lieutenants and Fray Salazar. Using the usual mixture of pigeon Spanish and signs, they urged the half dozen older braves to join them.

The Indians, smiling but apprehensive, walked in single file with their hosts, silently observing the gathering of nearly 200 men who had taken their places before the altar.

The long shadows of the March twilight were cast upon the faces, faces relaxed now by several days of food and rest. It was St. John's Day, a day to be properly celebrated by all men of the true faith, and as Fray Domingo began the service his strong baritone rolled the Latin phrases forth, bouncing them off the sturdy trees that surrounded chapel and congregation.

Assisted by Fray Salazar, the senior Dominican moved from stage to stage of the Mass, the responses of the 200 voices sounding like a mighty male wave in the forest.

The Indians, uncomprehending, were nonetheless fascinated; they made no effort to imitate the motions of their guests, but they hung on the procedures.

Anunciacon raised the cup high in both hands, his prayer sent high in the air as he lifted his head skyward. Then, with a deep bow to the altar, he replaced the cup, faced the prayerful men, and began again.

As he did so a huge, grey-green worm dropped from above onto the fringes of the altar cloth. The lowered eyes of the Spaniards did not see it; the Indian guests observed and watched, fascinated, as the sticky creature began to crawl slowly towards the cup. Inch by inch it moved, towards the gracefully turned silver foot, then slowly up the stem, to the very lip itself.

"Amen . . . !" intoned the priest.

Eyes rose . . . and as the Dominican's hands again reached for the chalice every eye saw. Many crossed themselves, several swore softly to themselves. For by now the insect was in such a position that any attempt to remove it must inevitably result in its falling into the cup of spiritual wine.

Fray Domingo never hesitated. Raising his head to the sky, he prayed:

"Our Father, the devil is again testing your people in the wilderness. Here, in the presence of those whom we seek to bring to Thy glory, a vile serpent would profane the very cup of our Lord's blood. Come to our aid, oh Lord! Help us end this invasion, help us to bring the message of the true faith to the heathen; help us end our travail in the wilderness, which we pursue for Thine own glory . . . Amen and Amen!"

Every eye fastened on the green creature. It clung, steadily, to the very lip of the chalice. Then . . . slowly . . . leg by leg, it relaxed . . . each tentacle-like feature separating itself from the metal. One quarter . . . one half . . . then three fourths of the legs fell loose . . . and then the creature dropped to the cloth. It lay still; it was dead.

. . . Behind the friar, the worm dropped to the lip of the chalice.

Slowly, the aging priest turned to his flock, bent his knees, and assumed the classic pose of prayer.

"My Lord, my God . . . Thou again has shown your people the power of faith and prayer . . . and have helped us to renew our belief. This message is the miracle we have sought, helping us to cleanse our spirits, to renew our courage, to reconstitute our constancy in Thy purpose. It is Your will that we help bring Thy word to this noble land and these childlike people. You have given us the sign. We humbly thank Thee . . . and praise Thy holy name. Amen . . ."

Each man crossed himself, and rose silently. As the 200 Spanish Catholics and their Indian friends walked silently away, a new spell of hope and feeling hung over each of us. We *had* been given a sign! The friar had prayed for such a miracle. We had *seen* it . . . with our own eyes. Truly, with God's help, everything was possible!

THE OUTSKIRTS OF COOSA
April 10, 1560

The days following the mass of St. John's Day were a joy to Fray Anunciacon! Though he could never divine precisely what the Indian neighbors thought of the ceremony, or of the 'miracle,' it was clear that the actions were impressive and that this fellowship together erased more of the reserve.

Slowly, communications developed. Salazar, who was a master of languages, spent endless hours trying to piece together fragments of words and expressions which might promote understanding. Del Sauz, who was no scholar, was amazed when the priest told him that the stream by which they had came was called Olibahali, and that the tribesmen also used this name for themselves.

Coosa, of course, was the friar's target, and he desperately tried to ferret out information about the 'great Indian culture' which de Soto's men still described. Gradually, this too was understood. It was two weeks following the Mass when Fray Domingo de Salazar asked for a council with the major, and with his superior, Fray Anunciacon.

"I think I've learned enough now to at least make some sense of this," he began, "though I can't be sure how much is truth and how much fable."

"As I understand it, Coosa includes several villages, one large and others much smaller. They have tilled fields, are expert fishermen, and have a culture of sorts. However, the number of people is much smaller than de Soto's men described because, as I understand it, of a continuing war with another tribe."

Del Sauz listened with his eyes cast down. "How far away? How difficult a march . . . or could we go by water?" he asked.

"Not far at all, if I define their words correctly," the priest replied. "And . . . if I understand them, they soon will receive their monthly visit from a chief of the Coosans . . . a sort of ambassador who comes here to receive their tribute."

"An ambassador . . .?"

"Something like that. They give him tokens of respect . . . food, mostly, and he brings a message from the chief of the tribe."

"When's he coming?"

"Inside this moon, as they call it. Could be any day now."

Two days later, the 'Ambassador' arrived. Finely dressed in well-tanned skins and with a headdress of feathers, the man was young, well-built, athletic. He stood taller than the villagers and spoke with a booming voice. The Spaniards were fascinated, for he was different from any Indian they had seen to date. Del Sauz urged Salazar to communicate, and the newcomer quickly was introduced by his local friends. The friar's report brought smiles to the faces of the leaders.

"Again, remember that I'm getting only every third word or so . . . but I take his message to say that they have heard of us in Coosa and invite our attendance there. He's asked the local chief to fill our packs, and he says that he will act as our guide."

April 17, 1560

Two days later we moved out, amidst handshakes, smiles and waves from our hosts. The 'Ambassador', carrying a feathered spear, led the way, chatting amiably if haltingly with Salazar, who strode at his side. With food in our packs and weeks of rest and recuperation, we had assumed a whole new outlook.

Then, on the third day, the Ambassador disappeared. Or rather, on the third night. We had camped on a high place above the river, had eaten well on maize and fresh fish, and had retired early, hoping that one more day might take us into Coosa itself.

When we awoke, the Indian was gone without a trace.

"Do we never learn!" thundered del Sauz. "Twice now we have followed such men . . . and twice . . .!"

Salazar was crushed. "But all said that the city was nearby, that we would find a friendly welcome there!"

Four hours the officers debated. Should we return to Olibahali where food was certain? Or should we press on? All information suggested that Coosa indeed was close. Ultimately, we moved ahead.

"What good will it do us—and the captain-general—to remain there?" the major questioned. "Soon we'll eat them bare, and we'll be no better off. Surely there is not sufficient here to think of feeding the whole force. No . . . we must press ahead."

Three days later we came to the first outpost, another village perhaps the size of the last. It was empty, but the inhabitants were obviously closeby, for food was still in each house, and fires were still glowing. Leaving a small force behind as a rear guard, del Sauz pushed ahead. Next morning we discovered a second village, then a third and a fourth. As before, each was empty. As we marched, we could sense the presence of observers in the woods around us.

"I can almost feel their eyes," muttered Porras. "Damn, why don't they come out?"

"Would you?" I replied.

Del Sauz dispatched scouts, who moved half a mile before the main army. After two hours, two runners returned.

"There is a larger settlement ahead," they reported, "we make out thirty larger huts and many outbuildings. And people are there."

Del Sauz halted the troop and made camp. Then, taking 20 men, ten mounted, he moved carefully forward. I was among that party. In the late afternoon we approached the village. Three men rode forward, including Salazar who first made signs, then began to speak to the Indians across perhaps fifty meters.

Great excitement broke out among the tribesmen, and they were startled at hearing their own speech; after a few moments several men came forward. Half an hour later Salazar returned to the scouting party.

"This is Coosa . . . if God be willing. And they welcome us!"

Over the next day del Sauz brought his 200 men forward in small groups. They erected a camp several hundred yards removed from the village, and continued their talks. The major, careful lest he alarm the tribesmen, allowed only a few men at a time to enter the village. Each group carried a modest quantity of trading items and delighted the Indians with glass beads and other trinkets.

At intervals, Salazar reported his findings: "They remember Hernando de Soto very well; some were alive when he was here, and they say that relations with our people were very good. They tell of two who were left here who lived among them until recently, when both died."

"But . . . is *this* all of it? Is *this* the great empire de Soto's men described?"

"I can't be sure . . . and we must figure that they too may be deceiving us. But the man with whom I speak best says that there are seven smaller communities . . . several of which we've already seen. In all, there may be 1000 people, not more than that."

"What about our 'Ambassador'? Where's he?"

"Here. He came ahead to warn them. He's here. We'll see him again, I'm sure."

The land did not resemble the fabulously rich, black soil which legends had described; it seemed adequate for simple crops, and the Indians had cleared large sections. There was food, in plenty, but thus far the Indians had made few signs of parting with their crops.

Then, on the third day, del Sauz, with the military man's wisdom, probed the question of the Indian War.

"See if you can find out what's happening and who they're fighting." he asked.

The Indian leaders were eager to discuss the war. The enemy, called the Napochies, were from an area north and east of the Coosan settlement. "They are many in number, fierce and evil men," one tribal leader said. Another said that the war had developed because the Napochies, who had come to the territory from over the mountains, coveted the land of the Coosans. "We have fought many times," he added, "and often they surprise and defeat us," he lamented.

For days the Spaniards and Indians continued their conversations. The Spaniards moved freely into the tribal encampment and were treated courteously. Food was purchased using the trading trinkets, and Fray Anunciacon and Fray Salazar began their attempts to instruct the Indians in the Faith.

As they did so, del Sauz slowly demonstrated the military capabilities of his troop.

Sometimes, of a morning, he would draw the men into an open area and perform a formal parade. At other times, he would form them into squads and simulate battle conditions. At such times the men with firearms fired their harquebuses at large, fixed targets, demonstrating their power.

All of this was done with great care so as not to alarm the Coosans. Day by day del Sauz would extend invitations to tribal leaders to come and view the proceedings. Later, in the cool of the evening, he would sit with them. With Salazar acting as combination instructor and interpreter, the major would explain the meaning of the maneuvers.

The Indians were impressed!

Weeks passed, and as spring flowed into summer, a report arrived that war parties of the Napochies had been sighted. With harvest time nearing, the enemy was slipping into position to plunder the crops and perhaps to kidnap slaves who might help them develop their own lands.

Great excitement swept through the settlement! Chief Wechumka called a council, first of his sub-chiefs from the village, then with the Spanish leadership. Fray Salazar acted as primary interpreter as Wechumka attempted to converse with Major del Sauz; later he recorded the conversation this way:

"Many years ago (the chief began), when your own great leader de Soto was among us, we were a numerous and proud people with many houses and so many braves that it would require a wise man a day to count them all. Our fields were filled with grain, and our orchards bore magnificent fruit. So it was when your people came—so it was while they dwelt among us in peace—and then they departed. But then came the Napochies.

"Periodically, they have swarmed among us, abducting our sons and our women, burning our homes, despoiling our trees, destroying our fields.

"Once (the chief continued), when they had just fled here from over the mountains, the people of the Napochies Nation were subservient to us, and paid annual tribute, which was just, and all lived in peace. But then, traitors among them counseled war, and the invasions began. We are a peaceful people; we do not retaliate; we have tried to end the hostilities, but they have refused, coming again and again in the night like thieves. With each victory they became more defiant, and have so reduced our numbers that we can no longer offer the hospitality we laid before noble de Soto. Indeed, if we were able, we would long ago have urged you to send couriers to your own chief, the noble Lord de Luna, to come and share our abundance with us . . ."

All of this was carefully detailed by the friar, who painstakingly grasped each nuance of the chief's meaning.

"Today, noble friends," the chief continued, "we have received word that the Napochies march again. Indeed, they are nearby, hiding, waiting for the appropriate time to advance and slay us. That is why I asked this counsel with you. We have taken you into our homes, shared our fields with you; now, we ask that you help us. We ask that you and your men, with their sticks of thunder, stand shoulder to shoulder with us. You say that you are partisans of justice. Stand with us to chasten our enemies!"

The major listened gravely, then asked the chief for permission to retire and discuss the request with his officers. Gravely, Wechumka agreed.

Moments later, we met with del Sauz, the friars looking on, and discussed the question. Salazar reported in his memoirs: "It didn't take them long. They believed their host, whose father had befriended Spanish troops in another generation. Del Sauz returned to the chief and pledged the assistance of the 200."

For hours the chief, his sub-chiefs and the Spanish leadership conferred. It was decided that del Sauz would assign captains Porras and Aguilar along with five men of horse and fifty footmen to march with the Indians. The remainder of us would stand in reserve. Then, del Sauz offered Wechumka a horse to ride, to be guided by a Negro porter.

More than 300 Indian warriors were assembled, and with the Spanish officers they rehearsed their maneuvers. It was a simple plan, so elementary that there was little real preparation. Much stock was taken in the belief that the thunder of the guns and their quick devastation would rout the enemy, permitting braves with bows to complete the job.

The next morning, the ceremony of preparation began. Without notice, eight sub-chiefs raced screaming through the Indian and Spanish camps, rushing up to their chief whom they lifted on their shoulders and amidst great outcry, carried to a nine-foot platform some 300 paces away. Here they placed Wechumka on his stage, while they (the chiefs, the braves and the Spanish) sat on the ground and gazed up at him. Wechumka stood with much gravity. A sub-chief handed him a large fan, or fly flap, of beautiful feathers which he pointed four times with great ceremony towards the province of the Napochies, motioning like one taking a reading at sea.

Then, another handed him some small seed grains which he placed in his mouth. Once more he pointed with his fan, removed the seeds which he had ground with his teeth, and scattered them as widely as he could, saying to his audience:

"My people, be comforted, for our expedition shall be a success, our enemies shall be vanquished, and their forces shall be destroyed like these seeds in my mouth!"

The entire force stood and cheered; thereupon, Wechumka dismounted and climbed upon his new horse. With him at the head, a column of 350 Indians and Spaniards marched towards the nearby river marshes where scouts had reported the Napochies in hiding.

They traveled only a short way, making camp near the river for the night. Scouts were sent out, and a strong guard mounted. No fires were lit, and the troop settled down to await the morning.

"At about 10 o'clock (Salazar's account continued) the Spanish heard a hideous din among the nearby Indians. Thinking it was an attack by the enemy, Porras and Aguilar ordered their men into battle formation, taking advantage of the shelter of tall trees nearby.

"But there was no attack; instead, the din came from the chief, exhorting his army to great deeds in the coming day. Shouting loudly, the sub-chiefs responded, saying (Salazar translated) that they would not return to their homes and families until full satisfaction for past wrongs had been achieved. Before dawn they marched off, quietly slipping through the woodlands near the river to where scouts had reported the Napochies camp to be."

Porras and Aguilar rode side by side, their men strung out in a horizontal line perhaps 100 meters wide, following the red men, who alternately took cover behind trees and sprinted to the next point of hiding.

It was perhaps half an hour before the first red rays of dawn, and each man moved as though he feared to be the first to awaken even a sparrow.

Gradually, the troop moved forward, drawing into a wide arch as Wechumka directed his braves in an encircling movement. The goal was to draw a ring around the slumbering Napochies' camp, then to drive in with screams and whoops to cause maximum disruption and force the sleepy enemy to run into the fire of the Spaniards. It was a simple plan of which Porras approved, though Aguilar had his doubts. The two captains had left ten men at arms in reserve, 100 yards back of the main party.

Slowly they crept onward; there, in the mist of morning lay the camp, with its fires still smouldering from last night's cooking. There were no sounds, no sentries, and no one moved.

Wechumka signaled silently, and two scouts crawled forward on their bellies, slithering from bush to bush . . . across the clearing . . . towards the camp's center where sleepers might be expected to congregate. The remainder hung back, awaiting the signal to advance . . . the low hoot of a native owl.

Minutes ticked by . . . and no sound came. Then, from the center of the camp, eyes picked out a standing figure, then two. One signaled, then the other. Wechumka rose, beckoned two others to follow, and walked to where the scouts stood. Porras and Aguilar could see the rapid exchange; there were no other sounds. Finally, the old chief walked to the fire, stooped, kicked the ashes with his moccasined foot, then roughly stamped at the remains.

Quickly he turned and trotted to where the Spaniards were seated on their mounts. Beckoning to Fray Salazar to help him, he reported:

"The she-dogs have gone! They've fled. Not long ago . . . but they're gone. They must be nearby, but they've gone. We will wait until light, then follow."

Just then one of the scouts whooped loudly from the center of the camp! Wechumka turned and rejoined him, then he too let forth a scream!

Porras glanced at Aguilar, then the two spurred horses and trotted into the smoky, misty clearing where by now half a hundred Coosans were stamping the earth and shrieking horrible curses. Quickly, Porras saw the reason for the outburst. In the center of the clearing stood a pole raised by the Napochies. At the top hung scalps, perhaps a dozen, some still dripping with blood. From the hair style they were obviously Coosa scalps, and two were women, old women.

The bitter weeping and screaming of the Indians stunned the Spaniards. They had witnessed the dance of preparation, but it was nothing beside this. Driven by fury, the Indians cut the pole and gathered the grisly remains, burying them in a hastily dug trench. As the scouts had guessed, the Napochies had fled in great haste. Their stocks of food still lay where they had dropped them, and even weapons were strewn about. A moment later, another brave uttered a whoop and began dragging a form from the shadows of the clearing into the light of the fire which had now been rekindled.

The 'bag' was an old—indeed, ancient—man, his long, matted hair white with age, and his heavy features lined. It was strange that such a man should have been carried with a war party . . . but here he was . . . old . . . and obviously very ill, too sick to flee with his companions. He had been left, probably forgotten in the frantic rush to escape.

The Coosans leaped upon him, hammering his face and back and gut with savage blows. Fray Domingo attempted to intercede, but was brusquely pushed back. Time after time the frantic Coosa braves struck the man; blood coursed down his face and matted his hair; and it was obvious from their odd angles that both arms had been broken.

Then, quickly as they had begun, the Coosans stopped and dropped the beaten victim where he lay. Fray Domingo crouched over him, wiped his face, and attempted to talk to him, trying to communicate his message of salvation. It was no use; the beaten hulk was dead . . . and had died a heathen. The friar made the sign of the cross, closed the dead man's eyes and stepped away.

Meanwhile, an argument had broken out between Porras and Wechumka with Fray Salazar trying frantically to make both sides heard.

"Tell him that his men must *not* burn these supplies. We need them, our captain-general needs them, and to do so will be . . . will be considered by us an act of war," the Spanish captain shouted.

A few feet away a torch flickered in a basket of maize, and the fire began.

Two Spaniards flug themselves at the blaze, stifling it with their frayed shirts.

The Indians stared menacingly.

"Tell him . . . tell him!" Porras shrieked.

In his stumbling manner, the friar spelled out the words.

Wechumka listened, frowning. He too glared . . . but at length squared his shoulders.

"Tell your captain that we will obey, but that it is our custom always to destroy the provision of an enemy. He makes us break a sacred tradition," the priest translated.

During the balance of that day the combined Indian-Spanish force deployed scouts and carefully pursued the enemy. Two horses were cut from the troop; these were loaded with the captured food; ten Indians and two Spanish soldiers were dispatched with it to Coosa, to display as a prize to those remaining.

COOSA
June 20, 1560

Domingo Salazar was a man whom many painters have caricatured as the typical friar. He was fairly short, stocky, dark complected, with a ring of dark black hair that swept around his largely bald skull and curled with a flair at the back. His face was round, his cheeks bulged, and his eyes were small, almost closing when he smiled or laughed, which was often.

Salazar was devout as his calling demanded, yet he was unlike many of the friars and priests of his time. Like Anunciacon, he had a deep appreciation of man's frailties, and he believed that the Lord's forgiveness was intended to reach out to people; unlike many who had come early to the New World and had earned conversions with harsh means, Salazar recognized that patience was required; he also had been a teacher of young boys at a school in Toledo and recognized the importance of being able to communicate his message in terms people could understand.

As a student and friar he had mastered his native tongue and Latin; there had been little opportunity to study others. But when he had come to Mexico he had drifted naturally into study of the native dialects, and he soon found he possessed a natural aptitude for them. During our early days on the march, first at Nanicapana and now at Coosa, we had often ridden side by side, talking of the background of these primitive people, as compared with our own proud Spanish nationals and even the descendents of the proud Aztecs.

"It's fascinating," he said one day, as our horses nosed slowly along, keeping pace with the infantry. "I am still far from real comprehension, but I find that these savages have many beliefs in common with us. They worship pagan gods much like our Roman forbearers, they have rites not unlike those of ancient Greece, and their society is founded on the model of tribes in the Middle East I have read of. Very interesting . . .".

"We're just lucky we had you and Ocalo. Actually, we've gotten on very well here, all things considered."

"Oh, indeed, indeed!" he answered. "We could have been welcomed with slings and arrows and all that. Instead . . .? Well . . . at least we appear to have made a friend or two."

"Tell me frankly," I asked, risking a lecture, "how will you proceed to bring these people to Christ? How are you going to preach to them?"

Salazar rode silently for several moments, his eyes riveted on the forest ahead. "Oh . . . that's hard to say. If we were living thirty years ago I'd probably answer that they would accept Christ . . . one way or the other, perhaps ending up minus a hand or foot in the bargain. But . . . we've learned from our experiences, haven't we? No . . . I can't give you a pat answer, old friend. My colleague and I agree that first we must set an example, win their friendship and confidence, then gradually reveal the glory of Christ and His message. How? I'm not sure. Perhaps one day a single man will show us the way. That's happened before, you know?"

I said that I did, and we rode on in silence for awhile. Salazar broke the spell. "In a way, I feel like one of the great saints (though it's sacrilegious to say so, I suppose)."

I said that I wasn't sure what that meant.

"Well . . . take the story of Boniface . . . or even Patrick! There they were, sent into barbarous country, sometimes with an army, more often without. Their mission was like ours, you know: seek out the heathen and bring him to Christ. And those heathen spoke no better Spanish than these Indians, I assure you."

I agreed that there was a similarity.

"That's the challenge, you see? Here is what Christ told us to do, to go to the ends of the earth carrying His message, baptizing, preaching, healing, teaching. Where else in our lifetime would we find such an opportunity? You see what I mean?"

"So this is why you work so hard at languages . . .?"

"Of course. To some it's a way to communicate, to me it's the way to communicate *the* message, ultimately, you see? And . . . I have time, I'm patient."

The horses plodded along a few meters more, then I asked: "But . . . suppose they do not respond? *That* has happened too . . ."

"Of course it has, and to better men than I'll ever be. But, Christ tells me to try, and He has blessed me by placing me in the command of your good uncle, who sees such matters as I do. So . . . who could ask for more, eh?"

I nodded and we continued on. From time to time Salazar and I found opportunities to philosophize further. He was a man of modest learning but deep faith and enormous energy. As I think back on those events, I believe that at times he was what stood between us and complete disaster. Perhaps, after all, *that* was his great call. Who can say?

July 7, 1560

Weeks later, when I had rejoined my fellows, I recorded from memory the events of those days, and the ones that followed. Beginning with that next day's account, my journal read:

"WE SEARCHED NEXT DAY, BUT FOUND NO TRACE OF THE ENEMY. CAPT. PORRAS ASKED REPEATEDLY WHERE THEY MIGHT HAVE FLED, AND THE CHIEF ANSWERED THAT THEY MUST HAVE LEFT THE FOREST TO HIDE IN OCHECHITON, WHICH MEANS THE GREAT WATER.

"WE ALL BELIEVED THAT THIS MEANT THE SEA, AND COULD NOT THINK THAT THE OCEAN WAS NEARBY, OR THAT THE NAPOCHIES WOULD ATTEMPT TO TRAVEL SO FAR. HOWEVER, WE LATER LEARNED THAT THE WORD MEANT THE RIVER OF THE HOLY SPIRIT. MARCHING IN THE DIRECTION SET BY THE COOSA CHIEF, WE TRAVELED THREE DAYS, AND AT LENGTH CAME TO A SMALL VILLAGE, MUCH IN APPEARANCE LIKE THAT OF THE COOSANS, AND A SATELLITE OF THAT NATION. IT WAS ABANDONED, THOUGH ITS INHABITANTS HAD LEFT GREAT STORES OF MAIZE AND OTHER GRAINS; APPARANTLY ALL HAD FLED AT THE APPROACH OF THE NAPOCHIES. WE SAW ONLY TWO INDIANS, APPARENTLY NAPOCHIE SENTINELS, STANDING ON A FLAT ROOF AT THE RIVER BANK. WHEN OUR PEOPLE PURSUED THEM ON HORSEBACK, THE PAIR LET THEMSELVES DOWN AT A RAVINE AND SWAM THE RIVER. AT THE PLACE WHERE THEY HAD STOOD, WE FOUND A BOW AND ARROWS WHICH ONE HAD NOT BEEN ABLE TO TAKE WITH HIM.

"WE WATCHED THEM SWIM (AND VERY SWIFT THEY WERE). MINUTES LATER THEY CLIMBED UP ON THE OTHER SIDE . . . AND THEN, OUT OF THE TREES CAME OTHERS WHO MOCKED THE COOSANS, MAK-

ING MANY INSULTS AND MIGHTY THREATS, CERTAIN THAT OUR PARTY COULD NOT CROSS THE WIDE STREAM.

"THE COOSANS HOWEVER, KNEW OF A FORD AND REVEALED IT TO US. AT DUSK, WE APPROACHED IT AND WITH OUR HORSEMEN LEADING, WALKED SAFELY ACROSS. WE WERE ABOUT HALF WAY OVER, WALKING ABOUT CHEST DEEP, WHEN THE NAPOCHIES APPEARED, AND BEGAN A SCREAMING DEFIANCE. SEVERAL RELEASED ARROWS AT US. CAPTAIN PORRAS AND CAPTAIN AGUILAR, BOTH ON HORSEBACK, SEIZED AN HARQUEBUS FROM A MARKSMAN, AND AIMING IT BETWEEN THEM, LET FIRE. THE SOUND ECHOED LIKE THUNDER IN THE TREES, AND BY GREAT FORTUNE THE BALL STRUCK ONE OF THE NAPOCHIES, WHO FELL SCREAMING TO THE GROUND. THE BATTLE HAD BEGUN."

I further recalled the action that followed:

Porras and Aguilar spurred their horses through the shallows and scrambled ashore, followed by infantrymen who scurried into position behind trees. The Coosans followed, straining to keep low.

But the precautions were unnecessary.

The Napochies were in a panic. Quickly, they picked up the corpse and fled, racing down the narrow path that bordered the river. A Coosa sub-chief shouted to his men to go in full pursuit! "There is another branch of the river just downstream," he cried. "They'll try to cross there. Cut them off!"

Porras' horse sprang ahead. Waving his sword, he urged his troopers forward, several cutting through the edge of the trees to gain a better angle of fire.

"They're going to cross," the captain shouted. "Hurry! Here, Suarez, set your piece here. Fire high . . . no need to spill blood!"

The roar of the harquebus filled the air, and its smoke drifted downwind towards the fleeing Napochies, whose total must have neared 300 men.

The sub-chief screamed at the fleeing men: "Enter that water and you are all dead men! Our thundersticks will strike you down. Stop . . . and receive the mercy of our great chief, Wechumka."

The Napochies hesitated, then, almost as a man, they halted, some already knee deep in the swirling river waters.

One, obviously a leader, raised his hand, and the flight was halted. Turning back, he walked forward, his right hand raised in the air.

The sub-chief walked towards him; briefly the two spoke, then each clasped the other on the right shoulder.

A second sign was given, and the Napochies turned and walked, following their leader who in turn fell in behind the Coosa sub-chiefs. All eyed our firearms nervously. The narrow file of men thus retraced their steps down the riverbank to the ford, the Spaniards bringing up the rear. Half an hour later the armies stood in two files on the original bank, Wechumka standing on a raised mound of earth, with Friar Domingo de la Anunciacon beside him. Wechumka squared himself majestically, looking every inch the monarch.

Porras whispered to Fray Salazar, who stood nearby: "He looks almost like a Spanish king! Look at him strut!"

The friar nodded. "He feels that he's re-established himself in the eyes of his people."

"What's he saying?"

"Can't make it all out . . . but . . . he's making good use of us, I'll tell you."

The Napochies stood silently, heads hanging, eyes nervously flicking at the line of Spaniards with their firearms. Most feared the worst and stoically awaited what most were sure would be their death sentence. Their memories held visions of the scalps on the pole in their camp.

But after a moment, their expressions changed. Fray Salazar, at the chief's side, nodded gravely as the old man spoke.

"You have come in war, time after time, and despoiled our lands, stolen our women and our grain, and killed our people. You have broken the bonds which bound our tribes in the years of the Golden Forest. Even in this time you have come with stealth, intending to do us harm.

"But—the gods have befriended Coosa! These men (and his arm fanned a great arc indicating the Spanish troop) have come from a white father across the great sea. There are many with us. Those you see are just a few. And they have the magic to kill you all with a single blow.

"But also they come with peace in their hearts. This man (and he pointed to Fray Salazar) has told me that they will aid us so long as we deal with our enemies with compassion. This we shall do!

"We shall give you mercy. We shall not destroy the Napochies, though we might easily do so. Instead, you may have your freedom to go in peace . . . providing you promise three things."

By now every Napochie eye was riveted on the old Coosa chief.

"You must swear that you will never lift hand or bow against Coosa again, and that we shall live side by side in peace.

"Then, you must promise to bring tribute to Coosa three times each year, tribute of grain from the earth, nuts and fruits from the trees, and meat or fish, dried for the winter.

"You must now bring us all that 100 men can carry of such harvests for use by our friends of the thundersticks.

"And—you must permit our friends of the crossed sticks (so he referred to Anunciacon and Salazar) to speak with you of their God. I listen . . . so must you.

"Do these things . . . and we shall part in peace. Deny any one, and we shall smite you with the great might of the many braves of Coosa and their new friends who bring great magic of war."

There was no debate, no negotiation. The leader of the Napochies stepped forward, grasped the Coosan by the arm, then bowed before him. His braves nodded approval.

Wechumka continued.

"It is good! Let us go in peace, then, agreeing that henceforth our people shall live together without war, sharing the goods of the earth, and with Napochies recognizing as they did in early times that tribute is due to Coosa!" he thundered.

A shout went up from a Coosa sub-chief. It was taken up by another and another. Soon all of the Coosa braves went shouting and dancing, creating a din that drowned out conversation between the Spaniards.

There really was little to say.

"A short war," quipped Porras.

Fray Salazar grinned and walked to Anunciacon's side.

"You did well, brother, very well."

"The Lord continues to watch over us, even here," the older man replied.

Before dark, the two armies separated, each moving towards its homeland. Three days later the victorious army returned to Coosa's main village. The entry generated a great celebration, with fires and dancing which went far into the night. As we watched from a distance, del Sauz debated the course of action with us.

"There's food enough for us here, at least for now . . . but for the remainder . . .? I wonder!" he began.

Fray Anunciacon summarized the situation: "We've been gone nearly half a year. Our captain-general may think us dead. Indeed, he may be dead, and the others with him, if food has not come from Mexico. But . . . what good will it do any of us to go in numbers to Nanicapana? There's nothing there. I propose that we send a small party with as much in stores as they can carry. We'll remain here and help with the harvest. Give Don Tristan what information we have. Let him make the decision. Once he has our story he'll have all the facts at his disposal."

"As usual, Padre, you do the best job of summing up," the major smiled. "I have little to add . . . except to decide how we'll divide the force."

Porras added: "It's funny, really. Look at us! Our clothes are gone, but we still have plenty of glass beads."

"Who can eat them?" I interjected.

Porras ignored me. "Our horses are still fit, yet we hardly have shoes to walk. Here there is food . . . but only enough for a modest number. Yet somehow we manage to survive . . ."

"Yes, my son," Anunciacon interrupted, "but we *have* made a beginning. We are alive; lesser men would have given up. We have made good friends, and they have helped us as we aided them. We have food for the moment, and I see the signs that the men of Coosa could accept the salvation of our Lord and Savior."

The officers nodded agreement.

"Very well, then," del Sauz added. "Tomorrow we'll choose men to return to Nanicapana. Porras, I'd like you to lead them."

"Of course."

"The remainder of the men will work tomorrow gathering stores for you. We'll use ten horses for transport. This will give the main camp at least a little help; meanwhile, you can communicate our position, and assist Don Tristan with his decision. Agreed?"

An hour later the major assembled the troop and gave them his decision. "We don't know what the next days will bring, but we can be certain that we will remain here—or nearby. Therefore, remember: We must make every effort to win the lasting friendship of these people. They are our hosts. We will set rations at reasonable levels and help with whatever we can do in the gathering of food. Now . . . we will go into the chapel for Mass. Fray Anunciacon will lead our prayers for the safe journey of our comrades."

Two days later, thirteen men plus horses, and as much food as could be packed onto them, marched slowly from the Spanish camp. The Coosa chief was among the party bidding them farewell.

COOSA
July 8, 1560

Being a scribe for my uncle had its good points—and bad. The worst was finding something on which to write. Wechumka was helpful, showing me how to treat the white bark of the birch tree in these forests. He said that it would endure many moons, (like Salazar I'd begun to think a little in Indian terms).

Our adventure as a military ally to the Coosans was more like a game than a battle. Most of our men enjoyed it, I think. To those who had fought in Europe the thought of traipsing along a stream in pursuit of Indians who obviously were frightened out of their wits was hardly a military maneuver. But as Salazar put it, we did justice to both sides, and that in itself was worthy of our calling here.

Porras and his squad departed July 8th. To succeed in remembering all the messages and injunctions given to him he would have to have had the mind of a scholar! I was as guilty as the rest in this. We sat together at breakfast on the morning of the departure and chatted about my uncle. I told him how concerned I had been about Don Tristan, and how the captain-general had concealed the extent of his illness from the company, even from most of his officers.

Not a deep person, Porras was a simple soldier, a man whose family had many sons, thus for him the life of the military man was the best choice of professions. He had no hope (or little interest, really) in the church, and the family lands were too limited to accommodate him and all his brothers. And so he married his sword.

From all I had seen of him in the various councils, he was a decent man, and loyal. He did his job, whether it be scouting a plain or hunting a place to fish, and he seldom complained (at least no more than the rest of us, and after all, complaint is part of the soldier's nourishment).

As we talked he told me of his own feelings here. I had asked him in confidence how he felt now about the expedition, and whether he was sorry he had enlisted his services. Perhaps it was not a well chosen question, but it was a subject much in our conversations generally; heaven knows that every man on the march had made one statement or another during those days when we dined so royally on harness straps and acorns.

Porras had little to answer, really. He shrugged his shoulders, and then muttered that he'd as soon be here as in Mexico.

"Either way, someone tells me what to do. Here, so long as we have enough to eat, every day brings a new adventure. Back there . . . every day was the same. Barracks life is a bore. You know that. I came here . . . well . . . because there was a challenge . . . and perhaps an opportunity to build a new life."

"How much do you really count on that?" I asked.

"Oh . . . I don't know. I don't know how much I ever thought we'd really find ourselves lords of the manor. It's a dream . . . and we may still get there. Who knows what's over the next hill?"

It was then that I asked him to deliver my message to Don Tristan.

"Tell him . . . tell him that we have done what he asked," I began. "Tell him not to give up, that this country will never end its surprises. I think he will understand my meaning. You have that?"

Porras said that he did.

Del Sauz joined us at this point, squatting down with his plate, wolfing down his portion, keeping a watchful eye on the loading of the beasts which Porras' squad would lead.

"Don't take time out to explore," he urged.

"I've no desire to walk one unnecessary step," Porras responded.

And that was the bulk of it. As he departed our camp, the squad captain shook hands all 'round, received a solemn blessing from Fray Anunciacon, then moved out. He was in the best of spirits, a good soldier. There were no signs that this would prove to be anything other than another of our more routine actions.

NANICAPANA
July 28, 1560

While we enjoyed a relative life of ease at Coosa, my uncle sat in his hut, a list in one hand, a quill in the other.

"My god," he muttered, "seven dead this week, 222 on the priest's list!"

He shook his head. His hair, matted and dirty, hung dank upon his neck and shoulders. The lines etched in his face were deeper now, though much of the flesh was gone and his skin stretched tightly over protruding cheekbones.

"What shall we do . . . what shall we do?" he repeated to himself.

In the weeks since del Sauz's party had marched out of camp following their guide, two small shipments of grain had arrived from the viceroy and Villafane, packed to Nanicapana on horse and human backs from Ochuse. Two small shipments! Each had buoyed the spirits of the roughly 800 survivors, but each had lasted only a few days. A few real meals, then half rations, then one quarter . . . and then . . . as always, back to the gagging diet of acorn gruel and whatever wild flora the fumbling Spanish women and trappers could fetch. Slowly, surely, the de Luna expedition was starving to death.

Children felt the pangs worst of all. Though their number had been small, most were now dead or dying. The older women had proven tough, but the younger white ones had begun to falter weeks ago. Now he watched them drag about the camp, their shoulders humped, their once proud hair in strings, their teeth beginning to show the effects of the diet imbalance.

Footsteps approached, and a moment later Juan Ceron popped into the enclosure. The firey Master-of-the-Camp showed less wear than most. Small and wiry by nature, he had managed to discipline himself and his consumption habits; he had lost weight, but his condition remained good, and his spirits, too. His greatest concern was for his general, who in Ceron's mind was giving up.

"Come in, Juan, come in, sit down," de Luna urged.

"Thank you, thank you . . . thought I'd see how you were. This heat's terrible!"

"Almost as bad as the cold in winter."

"And to think I once complained about the weather in Mexico City."

"And . . . I suppose you groused then if the beef was too rare, or the wine too tart . . .?"

"Probably."

"Well . . .?"

"Well, what?"

"What do you think?"

"I don't think, excellency, I just try to keep body and soul together, and to encourage the others. The important thing is . . . what do YOU think?"

"You want the truth, old friend?"

"I think the time has come, excellency, when you and I must be very plain with each other. We are responsible for 800 human beings . . . and their eternal souls may rest upon what we do. They are dying, Don Tristan . . . many of them will not last another month."

The general dropped his head,

"I was so certain . . . so sure that del Sauz would save us . . . so sure."

"Del Sauz is dead, Don Tristan, I'm sure of that. He would have sent word by now if it were otherwise."

De Luna nodded. "I'm afraid you're right. Each night I pray for their safety . . . and recently I had a vision that they had fought a great battle and had been victorious. Then—as I told Fray Feria—I was certain we would hear. . . ."

"But . . . we haven't."

"What choice, then, do we have? If Coosa is no more . . . if there is no help from that quarter, the only answer is to return to the harbor and try to begin returning the people to Mexico . . . as quickly as ships are available."

"That may take a long time, excellency."

"What was it Xaramillo said on his last trip? Oh yes . . . there are two small caravelles only available, but that others are promised from Havana. Perhaps by now . . . ."

"Perhaps, excellency, there may also be food on the way to Ochuse. In my eyes, that's our only hope . . . that and our ability to take food from the sea. Otherwise (and he gestured hopelessly) otherwise . . . we'll starve here. Winter is coming."

"Can we make the march . . . I mean . . . will the people survive it?"

"Will they survive here? Which is better . . . to die waiting, or to perish trying to find relief? Let's give them hope, at least. I say, let's scrounge what we can . . . and strike out, the healthy supporting the sick."

"At least we can travel a straight line now. Xaramillo has done noble work in his mapping."

"Four trips? He should! He's no fool, and a good soldier."

And so preparations began for the retreat to the harbor.

The remaining officers and two friars moved quickly among the companies, making provision for the care of the invalids. Food substitutes of every description were gathered . . . acorns, of course, leaves, roots, a few nuts and the modest amount of maize and beans that remained from Xaramillo's last trip. Two days were spent patch-ing shoes, harness and equipment, and in building slings and litters for those who could no longer walk at all.

Fray Feria raised the ultimate question: "What message shall we leave for those in the other troop?" he asked.

"Father, they're dead, they must be . . . otherwise. . . ."

"My son, we never assume that. As a soldier, you know better! Only the devil himself would conquer Fray Anunciacon. No . . . they will come . . . and we must guide them and advise of our actions."

So it was decided. Fray Feria composed a detailed letter, telling of their hardships, the arrival of the two shipments of food, and the decision to return to the harbor. This they placed in a box and buried at the foot of a large oak. On the tree they hung a board with the words DIG HERE scored into the wood with a knife.

Satisfied, Fray Feria ordered Mass said, and the pitiful troop moved out. Of the 800, just over half could be considered fit for duty. The remainder were in varying shades of ill health. Almost 200 had to be carried or assisted.

"May God give us strength," the friar had prayed.

There were many Amens.

OCHUSE
August 6, 1560

The third shipment of food from Mexico had come in three small vessels, two of which had remained behind by order of Angel Villafane.

Cristobal Xaramillo had used them well, seeking food along the shores, fishing, and in further examination of bays and bayous.

If the schedule followed, another small flotilla might arrive in September. Meanwhile, his small cadre did what it could to strengthen the base camp should the main party elect to return there.

Xaramillo was certain it would.

In each of his transports to Nanicapana, the young officer had been the height of optimism, relaying messages of hope from the viceroy, declaring that 'surely the king will by now have fitted a fleet to come to the aid of the company.'

Only he knew what the officers of the small transports had told him. The crops were poor in Mexico that Spring; the denuding of stores for the original shipment had left insufficient seed grains. Famine threatened parts of Mexico itself. And there was no word—none—from Madrid to the viceroy concerning the fate of the expedition.

Thus Xaramillo worked from dawn to sunset trying to assemble what he could.

"They will have to come back," he said to himself. "Coosa was a dream; they'll have to come back."

MEXICO CITY
August 14, 1560

In his palace, Don Luis fanned himself langorously as beads of sweat trickled between his shoulders.

Nearby, Fray Domingo de Santa Maria fingered his beads and prayed silently. The two said nothing. They were talked out. For hours they had discussed the plight of the expedition. The report from the captain recently returned had put both men in a fit of depression.

Finally, the friar mumbled "Amen" and pocketed his beads.

"Well, my friend, any more thoughts?"

Don Luis sighed. "None."

The priest swung his bulky frame into one of the viceroy's ample chairs. "You've combed the countryside . . . and there's just not enough . . .?"

"Hardly. We made a mistake last summer, that's all. We stripped away too much. We should have known . . ."

"We can ask the people to eat less."

"They will simply hide more. They're not fools though they be peasants. They hide now every time they see my men coming. 'The Food Tax' they call it."

"And still no word from Philip?"

"Nothing. I can't understand it."

"We know the vessel arrived."

"Oh yes. The replies have come through in good time. He has acknowledged the problem and sent his regrets. Says he'll do his best to send relief. But so far . . . nothing . . .

"1500 people. And I'm responsible!"

"Six of my most devoted, dedicated men."

"Well . . . all we can do is keep trying. Villafane's worked like a madman gathering what he could. He and de Luna are close friends."

"At least they're warm for the moment," muttered the perspiring friar.

"I suspect it may be easier to die warm than cold. Hadn't really considered the point before."

Silence dropped over the pair again.

A servant refilled their wine glasses.

The viceroy continued to wave his fan.

MADRID
September 16, 1560

Ximinez munched noisily on an orange, one leg thrown over the arm of the ornate chair that flanked Philip's. He sucked one last bit of juice, then belched horribly.

Philip looked up, cleared his throat, and glared at his minister.

"Do you *have* to make those noises? Please be quiet!"

"Does the sound of eating disturb your majesty at this time?" the minister asked slyly.

Philip paused, then smiled slightly. "Perhaps."

The two had spent the last hours compiling a list of stores for the relief of the de Luna expedition. Couriers had been sent to all corners of Spain, and a memorandum had been dispatched to Velasco with details.

"It's a pity, an absolute pity!" declared Ximinez. "How in heaven's name they could have failed to discharge the vessels is beyond me. Criminal . . . nothing less."

The king arched his eyebrows. "Perhaps. But then . . . we are here, and they are there. Who looks for hurricanes? And who knows what kind of conditions he faced? The wretched ship captain came as bare of details as a new infant's bottom. I know de Luna. He's thorough. It was an act of God, though I can't explain why." Ximinez shrugged and watched the monarch's expression out of the corner of his eye.

"Do you really think we can salvage the affair . . . now? Can these supplies really get there, I mean, in time to do any good?"

The king was silent for a moment. "I don't know . . . but we've got to try," he said quietly. "We can do no less."

"What does Valencia say?" Ximinez pressed his point.

"She is . . . very disturbed. She urges me to do all I can."

"Naturally."

"She loves her husband."

"Of course she does . . . most women do."

"And she wishes him back alive."

"Don't we all?"

"We do!"

The king finished his dispatch, called the runner, and gave instructions for delivery.

Then, standing before the minister, he murmured: "I wonder what Catherine and Elizabeth are thinking. Surely they know by now. I wonder if they'll test us. . . ."

"Wouldn't surprise me at all to have them try to cut the supply line . . . the barbarians!" Ximinez countered.

"Barbarians . . .? No . . . hardly. But they are ambitious . . . oh, how ambitious those two bitches are! We must never let them gain a foothold there, you hear me, Ximinez . . . NEVER!"

Ximinez heard!

"Will you need me further tonight, your majesty?"

"No . . . you need your rest. Just be certain the messengers are on their way before dark."

The minister made his exit, then walked to the work room where clerks were completing the last of the food orders.

"A fool's errand," Ximinez thought. "There they are . . . 3000 miles away, surrounded by savages . . . with no more food than Velasco could furnish. It'll be weeks before we can sail . . . weeks! God save them."

As he made his departure, a closed sedan chair approached the building, carried by four men. At the door it halted and was placed on the ground. Aided by the bearers, Valencia de Luna climbed down and quickly disappeared into the king's chamber.

"Poor de Luna," the minister sighed. "Oh well . . . ours is not to reason. . . ."

To Adm. Gaspard de Coligny . . . the queen's suggestion seemed one way out of the Huguenot dilemma.

PARIS
September 17, 1560

Sitting in the stifling late-summer heat of Paris the aging admiral mopped his face carefully with a scented handkerchief, pulled himself erect in the tall-backed chair and waited. His audience with the Queen had been called for two o'clock; it was now three, and in the airless anteroom Coligny pondered his choices. The message from Catherine had been brief; there was news from Madrid, and she was anxious to pursue plans for 'their project.' That was all.

'The Project!'

Coligny closed his eyes and stretched his limbs. What kind of compromise was it . . . shipping a hundred or so willing churchmen to the New World, perhaps to found some place where religious differences might be ended. He was a Frenchman! So were his colleagues. But then . . . the Queen and her family held the power. Perhaps it was the only way.

An attendant approached: "Her majesty will see you now, excellency. . . ."

Coligny rose and followed the brightly costumed youth into the Queen's chamber. Catherine sat at a high desk, papers before her, a cup of cool liquid at her elbow.

"Admiral . . . so good of you to come," she purred.

Coligny bowed deeply: "Your majesty is kind," he answered.

"Be seated sir," she continued. "Some lemon juice? Fresh lemons, from the south of Spain. Excellent in this weather. I recommend them."

"Thank you, it is warm."

Catherine beckoned to the aide, who brought a cup and filled it for Coligny. Catherine waved him away, and the young man slipped from the chamber.

"Now, to business, your time is valuable, sir."

"Thank you."

"The post from Madrid has brought additional information."

"You refer to the de Luna affair?"

"What else? Yes . . . Philip has sent out an appeal to all parts of Spain to gather food. Apparently our information was correct. They are in grave trouble. Our man suggests that Philip is really only going through the motions of assistance. He has already written off the de Luna venture."

"Then, there would be no opposition . . .?"

"There will be none soon. That makes our project a very practical venture."

"Militarily, at least, we have fewer problems. There is still the very practical need to establish a garrison in a hostile land. . . ."

"True, but in the warmer climate, with no opposition save a few Indians, it can be done."

"Of course."

"You've given thought to who should lead the first effort?"

"I would propose Jean Ribault, your majesty."

"Ribault? Do I know him?"

"Excellent record, navy, merchant shipping, several sailings to Canada, your majesty. He would have my fullest confidence."

"What else?"

"I would suggest, your grace, that we begin by sending one vessel, a sort of preliminary, to select a site, to determine the attitudes of the natives, and to bring back a plan suited to climate and geography."

"You would *not* then send your colonists at once?"

"I think this would be unwise, your grace."

"I see." Catherine had not envisioned the project quite this way, but de Luna's problems lent strength to the admiral's thinking.

"One vessel . . . for how long? Six months, a year? What will it take?"

"One vessel, perhaps 75 men, for not more than a year."

"And you will help underwrite this, of course?"

"We will, your majesty."

Catherine nodded. "Very well. I suggest that you begin recruiting at once. Make certain that this Ribault understands his mission well. I have no mind to plant a king in this new land. France's role must be spelled out, and that of your church. Do you understand?"

"I believe so."

"Very well then. You have my permission to begin active planning. My secretary will draw a contract. How long would you judge your preparations may take?"

"I have not spoken with Ribault. Let me get his views, then report back. He has made such voyages; I have not. However, I should judge that we might be underway in six months or less. . . ."

Catherine nodded. "Agreed."

Coligny rose, bowed, and backed towards the door to the queen's study. Moments later, escorted to the outer door by a page, Coligny was in the dusty, steaming street once more.

"Well," he thought, "we're committed."

Then his thoughts strayed. "I wonder what it's like in America, with no food, and help 3000 leagues away. I wonder . . ."

OCHUSE
September 20, 1560

Later, in his accounts, de Luna referred to the return journey to Ochuse as The Long Hungry Walk. It required less time than the original travel from Ochuse to Nanicapana, but the toll was far greater. Along the way 37 men, women and children met death and were buried with the offices of the church in shallow graves scooped from the sandy soil. Somehow, advance parties found food, and there was game which by providence fell before them. But many of the marchers were beyond help, their bodies wasted by lack of food, and the gnawing dysentery which became a bloody flux.

Because of the slow pace of the lame and halt, the party moved only a few miles per day; de Luna used horses to carry the worst cases, but there were not enough mounts. The strong supported the weak, and each evening the officers, friars and those women still able to make such rounds helped the sick as best they could. It was a pitiful march.

On the 39th day they sighted the Gulf, and two days later the advance party was welcomed by Xaramillo and his men, who hurried out to assist the remainder.

The young officer and his party, most of whom had been strengthened by the life at Ochuse, had dried fish and had grown a modest crop of maize from seed corn taken from the earlier Mexican shipments. With these they provided meals that raised the spirits of the returning army.

For three days all attention was given to the comfort of the sick and care of the children. The friars worked from sun to sun, aided by the more robust crew of Xaramillo's troop; and on the evening of the third day, a weary group of officers and friars were called into council by the captain-general.

He began the discussion.

"My friends, I believe we should begin by making an expression of our good will to Xaramillo, to Fray Matheos and the good men who have made ready for us. They have performed admirably, better than we had reason to hope. Cristobal," and he threw an affectionate arm about the shoulders of the young officer, "may God grant you peace. You have performed well!"

The others joined in a chorus of approval, and Xaramillo, embarrassed, smiled, and carelessly waved his hand in acknowledgement.

"Each has his duty," he replied. "We did what we could."

De Luna restored order, then proceeded: "The question now, of course, is where we go from here. We are, it seems, back where we began."

No one spoke.

"We have scant hope of assistance from our friends in Mexico, if the reports are correct."

Again, heads nodded slightly, but no one commented.

"We know nothing of the fate of our brothers at Coosa; frankly, I suspect the worst. And now . . . within weeks, cold weather will come. The question is, what are our options?"

"At least, excellency," Xaramillo interrupted, "we *have* begun to master the art of fishing. And there is now an abundance in this bay."

"That's true, and it will help. But it's not enough, as we all recognize. We can put forth our best efforts at fishing and farming, but without cleared land, or adequate seed, we're in grave difficulties. . . ."

"Not to mention the absence of adequate tools, general," suggested Nicto, whose family had been farmers.

A low rumble of individual conversations began, interrupted shortly by Fray Pedro de Feria.

"Captain-general, my brothers and I spent many hours discussing the possibilities during the long return. We have a proposal."

"Please begin."

"At present there are three craft in the bay, tiny vessels hardly suitable for transportation of our entire force, but usable for many things, fishing . . . and for the carrying of messages."

De Luna concurred.

"Should we not send more forceful ambassadors to His Excellency, to make him recognize his sacred obligation to these people?"

A low murmur spread through the group. Ceron broke in: "Just what do you have in mind, Father? If the officers that have gone before have not made the point, then who . . .?"

Nieto agreed. "We have sent capable men. And surely those who have come with provision ships have seen. . . ."

De Luna raised his hand. "Let him finish."

Feria brushed his hand across his face, then continued. "Please understand, we do not negate the efforts of these good men, or their sincerity; neither do we underestimate the concern of the viceroy. But to our view, Don Luis cannot realize the hopelessness of our task here. He cannot realize that nearly 1000 other human beings may die unless succor is obtained. In short . . . *we believe that the case must be pressed more strongly!*"

"We, Father?"

"I speak for Fray Santo Domingo, Fray Mazuelos and myself. We have spoken, we have thought, we have prayed, and it's our opinion that one of us should be sent as emmissary to His Excellency, and without further delay."

"You feel that you might exert a stronger appeal than a military man carrying a report. . . ."

"And we might also appeal to Fray Santa Maria. Our order is not without resources. Perhaps he can open granary doors that even the viceroy cannot touch."

The council adjourned with no decision, to meet again that evening after the Ave Maria. This time there were more questions, more emphasis upon WHAT should be proposed.

Ceron and Nieto proposed a different method. The master of the camp urged that the message be carried first to Havana; Cuba had not had its food supplies taxed to support the expedition; perhaps here there might be a better chance of gaining immediate help.

Fray Mazuelos, who was personally acquainted with Cuba's governor, replied that he was a compassionate man and surely would help in a cause which bore the king's own seal.

Aguilar then proposed another alternative. "Why not dispatch two separate ships and send the word with equal force to Cuba *and* Mexico City," he said. "We might send a friar in each vessel, and also place on board the most seriously ill, to get them to medical care."

There was a general nodding of heads to this, but then Fray Mazuelos observed: "This is, after all, an expedition to serve God, no? Well, then, to place our full emphasis why do we not send all *three* of our men of God, first to Havana, which is closest, then, should we not gain relief there, they might go on to Vera Cruz. I believe this will have even more impact."

"But what of our spiritual needs?" demanded de Luna.

"What of the care of the sick, and those who may die?" Nieto questioned.

Ceron interrupted: "I think the plan makes sense. There *is* strength in numbers. Such an appeal will carry more weight. Perhaps we have too long sent a boy on a man's errand."

The debate went on, far into the night, the faces of the men lighted by tiny flames licking up from a small fire of pine branches. One by one, the officers conceded that three friars would have more influence than one, but many were fearful of the result upon the nearly 800 who remained. "Who will say the Mass?" they asked.

"I shall answer that!" the captain-general ultimately replied. "It is my responsibility to establish this colony, and mine to bring all home safely. I am not a priest. But Fray Pedro and Fray Domingo can ordain me—temporarily—to act in their stead. . . ."

"And I am confident that Salazar and Anunciacon will shortly walk into your camp to resume their office!" Feria murmered. The quiet monk had never lost hope for the men at Coosa.

OCHUSE
September 21, 1560

And so next morning plans were completed. Within 48 hours the two tiny vessels had taken on water, dried fish and what added supplies might be spared. Friars Domingo and Feria were placed in the caravelle, along with 22 of the sick; Fray Juan Mazuelos went in the second vessel, with 24 of those closest to death. With the tide on the second afternoon the two ships moved out to the west, to the mouth of the harbor of Ochuse, en route to Havana.

"May God have mercy on our souls!" prayed de Luna.

"May He give them strength," intoned Nieto.

Ceron shook his head. "They're gone, and we are here. We must build shelters for those who remain, and continue Xaramillo's good work at fishing," he urged. "How long will we remain? We now must hope for another shipment from Vera Cruz . . . and depend upon our own resources. Keep the people busy!"

As their first act, the officers made good their promise to Fray Feria, who had given them a small box of sacramental flour. The box, once used to pack small clothes worn in the Mass, was buried below the ceremonial cross which had been raised at the first landing. The friar's plea remained in their ears.

"You cannot serve the wafer and the cup, but I know—as God speaks to me—that both Salazar and Anunciacon will return. With this flour preserved, they can resume the Mass. Do this, please."

The box was placed in a shallow hole in the sand, well back from the high water mark.

Then the officers rewrote their duty roster, hoping to somehow feed the remainder of the people.

October 1, 1560

Eight days after weighing anchor at Ochuse, the pair of caravelles sighted the western tip of Cuba, and hours later they made an anchorage at Mariel. The three friars supped at a church near the quayside, and borrowed shoes from the priests.

The next day they spent traveling into Havana; they hurried to the Governor's Palace and appealed for an audience.

A deputy greeted them.

"I am sorry," he began, "but the governor took ship for Spain three weeks ago. It is his time for a reunion with his family, you know; the deputy governor, The Honorable Pablo Senorra, is in charge. I shall be happy to arrange an audience."

Senorra was amiable, gracious, sympathetic, understanding. He fed the trio well and made certain their personal needs were well supplied. Beyond that he had little help to offer.

"Cuba is a rich country . . . in certain things," he explained. "But we have no food surpluses. Sugar? Of course. But much of our land grows only barter crops. In foodstuffs we grow for ourselves and little more. I have no authority to confiscate private supplies, and no funds in my treasury to help. Only the King can do that, good friars."

That evening, over the first beef they had tasted in a year, the friars conferred further with the willing deputy. Medical aid and supplies were hurried to Mariel, to assist the more than 40 disabled men, women and children who lay there.

"My best thought, my friends, is to provide you with swift transport to Vera Cruz. This I can do. Perhaps when you have seen Don Luis . . .? We will return your ships to Ochuse, and put on board what food I can buy with my limited resources. And perhaps the church will assist. You, of course can make that appeal. . . ."

The trio remained in Cuba three days. During this time they arranged for contact with every parish, and for an appeal to each community for aid; from Havana itself they obtained food to fill both caravelles. Their patients, two of whom had already died, were left under the care of church physicians. Senorra, good as his word, made available a carrier vessel which had been scheduled to depart later for Mexico.

Sailing against prevailing winds, the voyage required nine days. At Vera Cruz the Dominicans were greeted by Angel Villafane, who listened eagerly to their accounts. His reply was simple:

"We are doing all that we can, believe me. I have scoured the coastline, and the viceroy has sent couriers to every part of the lands within 100 leagues of Mexico City. For this year, it will be almost impossible to do more, and still avoid unrest among the people."

His ultimate suggestion was in keeping with his belief in the expedition itself. "Go see the viceroy. Tell him what you have seen and of the suffering of the people. I don't know what else he can do, but perhaps you can encourage a miracle."

Weary, but still filled with hope, the three took to the road. There were still two possibilities: perhaps Don Luis *would* uncover some new source of help; and then there was the King. Hopefully, he was moving mountains at home.

September 8, 1560

Capt. Porras' squad of twelve infantrymen and their caravan of horses required but twelve days to make the march from Coosa to Nanicapana, a trek that had required five times as long on the outward passage.

They were well fed, and enjoyed the feeling of the expedition's first real accomplishment. But before they were halfway to their objective, it was obvious that something was wrong.

It began the fifth night out, when Pablo Sanchez, a bearded, grizzled infantryman who had been with de Soto, approached Porras as the latter finished his brief meal.

"Captain, a word with you?"

"Of course, Sanchez, sit down. Here . . . a drink?"

"Thank you, sir, don't mind if I do." The foot soldier stretched himself on the ground.

"Feet hurt?" his captain querried.

"Not really. After twenty years of pounding callouses onto my soles another day's march makes little difference."

"You march well, Sanchez. You're a good soldier."

"Thank you, captain."

"Anything troubling you?"

"Well, sir, now that you mention it, the men do have a question to ask."

"Well?"

"Sir . . . what's to become of us? Do you think the general will want to march back this way again . . . to Coosa, I mean?"

"I would judge so. There's food there, and after all, that's what the people need most."

"Yes sir, there's food, but begging your pardon, it just isn't like it was when Don Hernando was there. I've talked with them that were there, and that's what they say. What the old chief said was true. They've fallen on hard times, the Coosans have. . . ."

"So . . .?"

"What we're saying sir, is . . . well . . . does it make sense to go back THERE? Can the land support all of us? The general spoke of building a fort there, and some of us staying. For me, sir, I have little liking for the place . . . now."

"Oh?"

"Yes sir . . . and the others . . . well . . . they feel the same. They say . . . well . . . that there's little to be gained, and unless we make slaves of the Indians we'll be in for hard times. That's what they say."

"They do, do they?" Porras was surprised by Sanchez's straightforward comment . . . or was he? Similar thoughts had plagued him, but then, the promise of a grant in his own name, an opportunity to stake out life as a landowner . . . this meant much, no matter where it was.

"What do the men propose, then, Sanchez?" he probed.

"They wanted me to ask you, sir . . . is this really the plan? And would we have to go back?"

"That was your enlistment, Sanchez, to help establish the two cities, then to have land for your own if you wished to stay."

"But no one put the storm into the bargain, begging your pardon . . ."

"No, they didn't . . . but an act of God doesn't relieve a soldier of his responsibilities. . . ."

"We know that."

"What you're saying, if I understand you, is that you'd like to go back to the coast. . . ."

"And back to Mexico, sir, back to where there's civilization. We see no hope now, unless some new fleet helps us. Even then. . . ."

"Even then the days are long and the food poor, eh?"

Sanchez lowered his eyes. "Perhaps there's something of that, too, captain. But we've seen what's happened to the others, the women and children dying and all. We just question whether we can make it, that's all."

Porras nodded. "I understand . . . but, Sanchez, for the moment, we'll just forget we had this talk, eh? Some others might consider your feelings . . . well . . . a bit unusual. But, we'll think on it, the two of us. Not a word to the others now, and that's an order."

Sanchez scrambled to his feet. "Thank you, captain, and . . . yes . . . I understand."

NANICAPANA
September 20, 1560

On the afternoon of the twelfth day the troop approached the first outlying village of the chain that surrounded Nanicapana. The first hint of fall was in the air, and the grasses were beginning to turn a pale tan, blown by the still-hot winds.

"We'll be sighting someone soon, I'd guess!" one trooper said.

Porras, riding at the point, nodded in agreement. It would be good to see them all again . . . Fray Feria, the general, even the dowdy Indian women who occasionally made a night by the campfire interesting.

They trod on, camping late in the dusk about five kilometers from the main site. They rose at dawn, prepared a light meal, and approached the principal village two hours later. Porras called to Sanchez: "Take my horse, Pablo, and ride ahead. Spread the word that we're coming. I always appreciate a bit of a homecoming."

Sanchez, no horseman but a country man who loved the feel of a mount, smiled, scrambled up and soon trotted out of sight. Half an hour later they sighted him returning, at a full gallop! As soon as he saw his comrades he began to shout.

"They're gone . . . they've left. There's not a soul in Nanicapana!"

They gathered about his lathered horse, plying questions. Were there signs of violence? Had there been a battle? What of the Indians? Was the village itself intact?

Sanchez replied as best he could, urging them to come see for themselves. Porras reclaimed his horse and paced the troop, moving into the cleared area and then the village proper. As the trooper had said, the place was deserted. There were no signs of life, no fires, no food, no dogs.

Patiently, they toured the shelters, seeking some sign. There was none. The Indians, like their guests, had gone.

"Well, this is one hell of a situation!" muttered Porras. "Could they have followed us? Or have they started back?"

A usually silent soldier suggested that there *must* be some sign, somewhere. They wouldn't simply walk away.

Porras divided the village into squares, giving each man a zone to inspect. "Check the trees, the posts, anything where a sign or a message might be hidden," he ordered.

Minutes later a trooper named Ortiz called, "I've found it!"

They gathered around the tree where the sign was neatly tacked. DIG HERE, it said. They did, and soon they were poring over the general's instructions and the prayer left by the three retreating friars.

"Well, I guess that's the next step, men," Porras said, trying to sound cheerful. "With your spirit we'll cover the distance in—what—20 days? By now they must have almost worn a trail there."

Porras ordered one day of rest and sent three troopers to fish in the river. Later, they enjoyed a full, hot meal, then slept well. Next morning they were on the trail shortly after sunup.

The thirteen, hardened by time on the march and fed from the ample supplies they carried, moved at a battle pace. In just over fourteen days they were on the rise overlooking the Gulf. As before, Porras sent a scout to announce their approach. This time the welcome was present . . . and it was warm!

De Luna, greeting the captain, threw his arms about him, smiling from ear to ear, words spilling from him: "We thought you dead, old friend. After all these months, and you come bearing food! You are a gift from God!"

The returning troopers were hurried into the settlement, where they spent a few hours refreshing themselves and trying to recite what they'd seen and heard.

That evening Porras had read the dispatches sent by his sergeant-major, and also provided an eye witness account.

"You've done well, captain!" de Luna began. "You found Coosa, made friends of the people, began the work of the Lord . . . even helped bring peace among troubled nations. Extraordinary!"

"Thank you, excellency."

"Now, tell us about Coosa! Del Sauz is his usual taciturn self, even on paper. He'll not become excited even when he sees angels at the gates of heaven!"

Porras grinned. "That's him, all right. But . . . well . . . where shall I begin?"

"The journey, was it difficult?"

"We all but starved, excellency," he replied, suddenly becoming sober. "It was across difficult country, filled with swamps and rivers. There was no food, no comfort, no people. We were very fortunate to survive, I swear to you."

De Luna nodded gravely. "Then what?"

"The arrival in Coosa was a pleasure, of course. Everything went well, as the sergeant-major has said. But . . . well . . . we were all disappointed, as I'm sure you understand."

"He does not write a glowing account, but. . . ."

"Even the men who marched with de Soto acknowledge that there has been much change. Warfare has decimated the Indians; the lands lie untilled, many of the orchards are in waste. . . ."

"But you have brought us food . . .?"

"We have, excellency, taken from the Indians. Much of it was captured from the Napochies. But they have little enough for themselves; they could hardly spare even this. Frankly, I don't know how long the villages will support the people who remained. It is difficult, very difficult. . . ."

De Luna fidgeted. "What are you trying to tell me, captain?"

"I'm saying sir, that if you believed that our entire force can be moved to Coosa . . . and supplied there . . . you will have made a critical error. Any such arrangement will be temporary. We will end by destroying the natives and ourselves."

"But . . . I can't countenance this! Coosa is a fertile land, its fields grow great harvests, it has vineyards and orchards with great abundance. De Soto's reports said. . . ."

"I know what they said, excellency . . . but that was 20 years ago. I've just come from there. The Indians are what de Soto's people said they were, fine, handsome, friendly people; but the land will not support us. As things stand now, it will be a mistake to go there."

Porras' report, somewhat in contradiction to that of del Sauz, threw the council of officers into a turmoil. For hours they wrangled over the many aspects, finally retiring with little semblance of order.

That night, as he lay rolled in his blanket, Porras heard footsteps approaching. He had not been able to sleep and was not surprised when he heard the whisper of his name. "Porras . . . Porras, are you there? It's Ceron."

The two old soldiers drew up together, and for the balance of the night they talked in low tones. Ceron, shaken by the report, demanded honest answers:

"I have had my sergeants singling out your men, talking with each one . . . privately. I wanted to get their feelings."

"You got them?"

"I did . . . and most parallel yours. Apparently the sergeant-major's report was honest; he's never one to gild the lily. Only this time his words needed some interpretation. Your men say. . . ."

"They say that it will be hopeless to march 800 people to Coosa and try to survive there, eh?"

"Exactly. They parrot what you said to us tonight. De Luna is furious."

"He doesn't believe me?"

"He says the only hope of survival is to go to Coosa."

"He's a fool."

"What will happen if we do go?"

"Del Sauz, or rather Fray Salazar, for he deserves most credit, made friends with those people. We've served them. They are our friends. But there's just not enough food there. And to clear more fields, plant crops and create a surplus large enough . . . my God, Ceron, it can't be done . . . not without some grain reserves. We'll starve, and the Indians with us."

"What other choice do we have?"

"To stay where we are . . . and begin ferrying the people back to Mexico."

"You mean, give up, now?"

"It's either that or expect a miracle. I tell you if we try to march to Coosa, we'll be dead men by winter's end."

"He'll never give up."

"Why?"

"He's convinced either Velasco or the King will supply us."

"As they have thus far?"

"A good point, but . . . my friend, how can we convince him? How can we alter his thinking, make him see reason?"

"I don't know. If it were my choice, I'd recall the men at Coosa and have them bring with them what they can. Then, we could begin withdrawing forty or fifty people a month, with the vessels we have—more if the viceroy would send them. That way we'd get out alive . . . I think."

"But . . . I know him; he'll never agree."

"Perhaps . . . perhaps other measures will be needed."

Ceron raised his eyes.

"Perhaps," he replied. He rose and retreated into the gray of the dawn that was breaking.

October 10, 1560

In the days that followed, rumor swept through the camp. As de Luna made plans to dispatch the bulk of the company to Coosa, a counter-move built among his officers. Porras was at the hub; gradually, Ceron succumbed to the former's pleas. If de Luna was aware of unrest, he said nothing,

On the morning of October 10th, the captain-general called a general assembly, including the women of the company. He himself led a prayer, then addressed the assembly.

"My comrades," he began, "you have witnessed the return of Capt. Porras and his gallant men. I know that stories of their hardship and their accomplishments have been spread among you.

"Best of all, they brought us food that heartens us and mends our hunger. I regret, however, that they do not bring with them the report in terms which we had all hoped for."

Porras, near the rear of the hundreds who stood listening, muttered to Sanchez: "He is honest, that much I give him."

The captain-general continued:

"For many years we of Spain heard glowing accounts of Coosa and its people. We dreamed that when we re-discovered it and conversed with its people, we might establish an inland base there and find such food as we would need until our own city and farms were well begun.

"I regret that Capt. Porras and the reports from Major del Sauz do not paint such a picture . . . at least in its entirety."

A low murmur swept across the throng. De Luna continued:

"They have found food, it is true, but not in abundance. And it is their counsel that perhaps this country may not sustain us as we had hoped.

"However, there is still another nation to the north and east into which they ventured in behalf of the tribe of Coosa; here there was food."

The murmuring decreased . . .

"And thus I am convinced—as I have ever been—that we must resume our master plan and march as a company to this place, rejoining the 200 who are there, well and firm, making a place for us.

"Therefore, this day we will make plans to break this camp. As in our previous journey, I shall leave here a company of 75 men to meet ships due from Vera Cruz. Again, I shall ask Capt. Xaramillo to command this point. We shall leave here also those who are ill or injured. Others we shall form into companies and prepare for the march three days hence.

"I know that this threatens further hardships; we are all tired of the march; many are unwell. But—I believe that God has shown us the way. We shall be prepared to do His will."

The low murmur began again. De Luna stood, his arms behind his back, his eyes sweeping side to side across the assembly.

Suddenly, there was movement to the rear. Three men were pushing forward to the elevation where the general stood. One was Porras, the second Ceron, the third the enlisted soldier Sanchez.

Eyes turned to the trio. Ceron, his face grim, moved close to his commander. "Excellency, with your permission, we would speak with you."

"Of course."

"There is—if I may say so—strong feeling among the people that yours is not a wise decision."

"What do you mean?" As he spoke, de Luna turned his back on the crowd so that his emotions and his speech would not be seen.

Ceron shrugged, spoke quietly, "We believe Capt. Porras' report makes it imperative that you reconsider, excellency. We are starving good people; there is no hope that all can survive another march. There's not sufficient food for us here or there."

"And so you propose . . .?" de Luna demanded, his face red, the corners of his mouth twitching with emotion as he scanned the faces of his subordinates.

"That we begin to ferry the ill and the infirm back to Mexico."

"With what? Two vessels have already been used to send the priests. What would you have me do, conjure vessels by prayer?"

"No, excellency," Porras interjected, "but we do feel that we should make plans to evacuate this place as shipping *is* available. Otherwise, we will simply add to the graves," and he motioned towards the line of mounds topped with simple wooden crosses.

De Luna stood silent for a moment, the corners of his mouth working, his eyes blazing, he glanced over his shoulder at the crowd, whose members were watching the discussion among their leaders.

Abruptly, the commander turned full to the assembly and raised both his arms. "My people," he shouted, "my people, one moment, please."

Crowd noises subsided.

"I ask you now to begin gathering your belongings. Officers, we will convene for further discussion at dusk. To all, I ask that you make your prayers for our success. Plan now for our departure. That is all; the company is dismissed."

He turned to Porras and Ceron.

"We will discuss this further in my headquarters. This man (and he pointed to Sanchez who stood nearby) has no business in the discussion of officers. Dismiss him!"

He turned on his heel and walked away. Ceron and Porras exchanged glances. Ceron shrugged. "Why not now?" he said. Porras nodded agreement, adding to Sanchez: "You're dismissed, and you are to repeat nothing—I say nothing— to anyone, you understand?"

The foot soldier saluted, turned and left the pair. Slowly, they followed de Luna, who now was entering his flimsy shelter. Moments later they joined him.

"Well now," he began, "suppose you begin again. What is this nonsense you propose? You can't be serious!"

The master-of-the-camp and the infantry captain eyed one another, then Ceron spoke. "Don Tristan, we think you must take another look at what you're asking. We can't believe you've truly considered how things stand. You are asking nearly 800 people to do the impossible. . . ."

"The impractical!" Porras corrected.

De Luna waited a moment, then raised his eyes to the two officers. "For months I have been tried by adversity," he began. "I have led you through storm and famine and have been faced with every kind of incompetence—from laziness and sloth to your own dallying with the wives of our Indians and Negroes. I have been patient, recognizing your frailties, but this is too much! *Do you realize that you are questioning the military orders of your commanding officer?*"

Ceron responded: "I will not respond to each of these things, excellency. You have your opinions and your observations; we have ours. But it is obvious where things stand. We are barely surviving with our meager food supplies. The reports of Capt. Porras and del Sauz are plain; we can't support these people in Coosa. Napochies is little better. You are simply asking these tired, sick, downhearted souls to brave another 400 leagues of march for nothing. We ask that you use reason; begin to send the lame and the halt home. If relief does come, those who are fit and willing can stay and we will regroup; otherwise. . . ."

"That is *enough*!" the commander shouted. "We have been given a mission by the King and by the Holy Church. Thus far we have failed both. I will not accept failure. The report (and he picked up the thin birch sheets written by the sergeant-major) is not pessimistic. I believe that with everyone's good efforts and the help of God we will succeed."

Ceron shrugged. "The people will not follow you, excellency."

De Luna's face darkened. His voice level dropped. Looking the master-of-the-camp full in the face, he continued:

"If I return to Mexico contradicting people who have assured the viceroy that the province of Coosa is most fertile, he will demand proof of its barrenness which I must either produce . . . or lose my honor. Will I be able to uphold it if I refer merely to *these* letters which declare the land as being more uncultivated than poor? Or if I quote the soldiers who have returned and are at variance according to their individual character? I want to go personally to Coosa to disillusion myself so that I may disillusion others; I want to learn the reason either for the change or the deceit which has been practiced. Who can persuade himself that Spaniards would remain there if it were as bad as it is painted?"

Sweat beaded his forehead and his hands shook. The commander's face was ashen, and his frame, reduced many pounds by months of fevers and reduced rations, was hardly regal.

Porras, who had sat silent during the interchange, cleared his throat.

"Sir," he began, "so miserable is the province of Coosa that it could not support the 200 if the spoils of war with the Napochies had not produced a plentitude of maize, beans and bear grease. Before that, in order to live, we gathered all the maize in the territory, but it was not enough, for the Coosans as well as ourselves were threatened with hunger. Some of the barrenness can be attributed to depopulation: in fifty leagues there is no considerable settlement. Those outlying settlements we discovered are so small that they resembled temporary shelters rather than villages. We found that the province of Coosa is extolled in New Spain for no other reason than that it is distant! And I am certain that if it is decided the army must go there, everyone will perish, for it will be impossible to withstand the adversities of such a march."

"Then why is del Sauz there and not here, eh? Tell me that."

"I'm not sure I understand your question, general."

"If del Sauz and his men were not better off there, they would have returned with you. They'd be *here*, not in Coosa. I say you are distorting truth, captain! You have given up . . . you want to go home!"

"Excellency, I have been there. I have seen Coosa. I have seen the people of Napochies. They too are poor. They fight and raid the Coosans to keep alive. Del Sauz remained only until he could determine if help had come from the viceroy. He did not want to further burden you. Believe me!"

De Luna shook his head.

"Beyond Coosa is Napochies . . . beyond that, who knows what paradise? No, captain . . . we will not turn back. I owe these people fulfillment of my promises. We will go. Day after tomorrow, after the first meal. Now . . . please leave me, I have a lot to do. . . ."

The two officers retreated to Ceron's hut. Ceron called an aide, asked him to locate Lt. Sotello and Capt. Acuna. "Ask them to join us, please."

Sotello and Acuna had served with Porras and Ceron for a decade and had been recruited for the expedition by the camp master. Both were trusted friends, both had been among the first to share Porras' message of despair.

Ceron began the conference.

"The old man's set his head. He means what he said. Day after tomorrow we go."

Sotello faced Porras. "You explained it all, the food, the insects, the poverty of the villages. . . ."

"Everything, amigo, everything. He is blind to truth. He sees only his glory and (and he spat into the campfire) and his *honor.*"

"Damn him for a gentleman. He'll kill us all."

"What are the people saying," Ceron demanded. "Is the word getting out?"

Acuna rubbed bony fingers through a scraggly beard. "You saw them, my friend. They're scared! They fear authority because they live by it. But they fear death, too. They've helped bury enough of their friends. But . . . some would go, and some would stay."

"The numbers?"

"Who can say . . . there are many of each persuasion."

"If only he wasn't so damned stubborn. . . ."

Porras broke in: "One suggestion?"

"Yes?"

"Suppose my squad left camp . . . tonight . . . while the company is asleep . . . and returned to Coosa."

"What would that accomplish?"

"Well . . . for one thing, I believe that del Sauz may convince the general where I cannot. And . . . if I'm any judge . . . it will be far easier to convince the general to remain here if he has no base camp among the Indians. He'd have no objective."

"Will del Sauz back what you've said?"

"Essentially. He's tired, too, and talks a lot about the warm women and good wine of Mexico City. The Indians were pleasant . . . but . . . well . . . temporary, and very greasy."

Ceron grinned toothily.

"So you'd slip out, make the trip, bring them back . . . and meanwhile. . . ."

"Meanwhile you'd stay here, keeping things too stirred up to permit a march. You'd need only a few incidents. Simply be sure we have enough officers committed to our point of view."

"I wish we had a priest here. . . ."

"Ach . . . they'd side with him. They are weaned on authority. We're better off this way."

OCHUSE
October 11, 1560

Two hours before sunup, the thirteen-man squad slipped from camp, using the same horses they'd had on arrival. When he learned of the departure, de Luna was furious!

"Porras has taken this on himself? I'll hang him, by the eternal God I shall stretch his neck from that tree!" he shouted, pointing at a nearby water oak.

Ceron listened quietly. "Excellency, they are doing what they believe is best for all . . . including you. They want you to hear the details from the major's mouth."

"It is desertion, by any name you give it," de Luna stormed, "and I shall brook no more. Sr. Ceron, I wish a notice read to the company today, announcing that any *military* man of this company who absents himself without my leave, or who knowingly disobeys my military orders shall be subject to execution by hanging . . . without trial. Do you understand me?"

Ceron never blinked. "I do, excellency."

"Then get about it! Oh . . . and Ceron . . . the departure of Porras does NOT alter my order. We shall depart as scheduled."

OCHUSE
October 12, 1560

Twenty-four hours later it was obvious that Don Tristan's order would not be carried out. One by one he called his officers to him, questioned them, asked for the sentiments of their people. The men were direct and honest, or, at least most of them were.

Lt. Xaramillo spoke for many:

"They love you, Don Tristan, but not above life itself. What you are asking is vanity. Many cannot survive another such march. Look at the people! Make plans for survival . . . then . . . let us go home. It's hopeless!"

Next afternoon, his tally complete and his command split almost down the middle, the commander ordered the march postponed.

A week passed; then a second. Ochuse was a camp divided. De Luna ordered each command to work at fishing, gleaning of foodstuffs from the land, anything to keep them occupied. He ignored Ceron, communicating through those officers in whom he kept trust.

Otherwise, nothing happened. The 700 sat . . . and waited.

COOSA
November 12, 1560

Porras' soldiers traveled easily to Coosa and delivered a shaded picture of events at the main camp to del Sauz.

"Your report has been interpreted as one of futility, major," the captain said. "I added such detail as I felt was justified, including our sampling of the fruits of Napochies. Like you, I suggested that keeping the total company alive here through the winter would be difficult. Consequently, the general has ordered your return to Ochuse."

"How is the general?" del Sauz querried.

"He is not well, major. Neither are things at the camp. Another 100 are dead. Food from New Spain, what little has arrived, barely keeps body and soul together. The three priests have gone off to try to organize assistance. There has been no word from them. And the people are very discouraged . . . very."

"They want to go home, eh?"

"They want to go home, yes. They are tired of dreaming of becoming landed aristocrats in a new continent. They are tired of seeing children with bloated bellies and women aging before their eyes."

Del Sauz studied the ground at his feet. "We have made progress here. . . ." he began.

"But not enough to provide for another 700 mouths until the next harvest."

"Probably not."

"With your backing, de Luna will believe this. He'll start sending the sick back; by spring we'll all be safe in Mexico, away from these cursed swamps and cramped stomachs." He carefully watched the major's response.

Del Sauz remained silent for a moment, then sighed. "I suppose you're right, though I could learn to like life here. The Indians are our friends, we help one another . . .".

"And you've found a squaw to warm your bed, eh?"

"On occasion," del Sauz spat. "However . . . we have others to consider. Let's talk with the friars."

Fathers Salazar and Anunciacon accepted the news quietly. Both enjoyed the countryside, but they were discouraged over their failure to bring the Lord's message to the Coosans. Only one moribund woman had accepted baptism, and the general attitude of the tribesmen was of friendly indifference. The fact that their three associates had departed for Cuba concerned them.

"If this is so, the entire body is without spiritual comfort," Salazar moaned. "This is terrible!"

"Our first duty is to them, you're right," his superior agreed.

November 14, 1560

And so the decision was made. I was not consulted, but at that point I'm not sure that I would have urged that we stay. In any event, two days later we broke camp. The action brought a strange response from our Indian friends, who wept openly, declared their friendship, and marched three full days at our side.

"There is no dishonesty in the report that the people of Coosa are warm and fine; if only there was time to truly teach them the message of salvation!" Salazar sighed.

"We shall return!" Anunciacon added. "Give us time, and we shall be back!"

December 17, 1560

Our arrival at Ochuse turned out the entire camp. It had been ten months since we had departed the village at Nanicapana; friends rushed to greet us, embracing and slapping our shoulders, asking countless questions.

Within the hour, de Luna had summoned del Sauz and the friars. He included Ceron and Porras in the conference; most other officers were excluded. I was invited to attend.

"Well, my friends," the captain-general began, "we are delighted at your safe return. You look well, very well indeed!" and he cast a stern look at Porras who, too, appeared well fed.

"It has been a long march, excellency," del Sauz replied, "and we're happy to be among friends."

"You have had a report, I assume, from Capt. Porras."

"We have, excellency. He's told me of your interpretation of my letters, about the countryside."

"Well, major, let me then hear from *you*. You are aware, of course, that Capt. Porras slipped from this camp *without* authorization and recalled you without authority?"

"I am aware of the differences of opinion, excellency, if not all the details."

"Then may I have the benefit of your personal views?"

Del Sauz settled back, his brow creased, his eyes raised to the roof of the flimsy structure. "We found Coosa, excellency, only after greatest difficulty. The men experienced grave hardships; we were verging on starvation when we discovered the first outlying villages."

"I have read your letter, major."

"The people of Coosa were almost at once cordial and our friends. We were mutually helpful; they provided food, we helped drive off their enemies and forced a peace which I hope they can maintain now that we are absent."

"Very commendable . . . but what of the land?"

"What Capt. Porras has told you is true, excellency. Once, the population there was great, now it is much reduced. It is my opinion that many died from the pox, probably brought by de Soto's people. The Coosans have become a small and a poor people; much of the land they once cultivated lies abandoned. . . ."

"But it *could* be reclaimed?"

"I would assume so . . . though with much effort."

"Please continue."

"The question as I see it is 'could we sustain our whole company through another winter at Coosa?' I honestly don't know. There are so many things we don't know. We could not survive with what now exists there, but we might march out against other villages, perhaps invading Napochies. . . ."

De Luna swung and faced Porras. "You see," he said shrilly, "it is exactly what I said!"

Del Sauz cut in: "But that is only a guess, excellency, and to do so we would starve others to aid ourselves. The question I have asked Fray Anunciacon is: could such be the way of Christian men? He says *no*."

De Luna lapsed into silence.

Each of us watched, glancing quietly at our fellows, idly playing with caps and harness. Finally de Luna spoke.

"Fray Anunciacon, I have not asked your counsel, for this is a civil matter. However, I now ask your assistance. I am going to adjourn this meeting without further action. I don't wish to seem a dictator. We are all officers together, in a common mission for our King and for God. Therefore, I shall forget all that has happened: the disobedience, the lack of cooperation, the acts done behind my back and without my knowledge. I shall give each officer an opportunity to correct his position and to redeem himself in my eyes. I will wait until tomorrow . . . hoping that each will commune with God . . . will pray for forgiveness, and will then prepare to obey my instructions. Then, on the third day, we shall begin the march to Coosa. I have spoken."

He turned his back on us, we all rose, eyeing one another, then one by one, we moved out of the cramped shelter into the watery sunlight.

"Well father," Ceron turned to Salazar, "our general has thrown down the gauntlet."

The friar nodded. "He has . . . as he has every right to do. We have two days to heal this terrible breach."

That night Anunciacon and Salazar called all officers together. All save de Luna. There, we calmly recounted the position of the company, which now numbered close to the 900 mark. In turn, each man was permitted to speak his mind. The priests pressed for harmony, subtly urging the officers to obey their commander.

"If we revolt against authority, we revolt against God," they reasoned.

But their appeals had no affect. The council adjourned with its members almost equally divided; part favored the general, the remainder following Ceron's views.

"May God have mercy on us," intoned Anunciacon.

December 17, 1560 . . . continued

After the others had departed, I sat with my uncle for a time. His eyes had the feverish, watery appearance I had last seen at Nanicapana, and his body was even more thin and drained than it had been months before. Yet he had lost none of his zeal.

"If you are not too weary, nephew, I'd appreciate a word with you," he said. I remained, of course.

"Well, what do you make of all of this now," he began.

"I don't know, uncle, I just don't know. I gathered that things were not well here, but I hardly expected this."

"What in hell has happened to Porras? Has he lost his mind?"

"I don't know."

"He has been guilty of gross insubordination, at the least. I could have him hung tomorrow."

"He has been unwise, but I don't think hanging will solve anything."

"He has caused 200 men to march 400 leagues for nothing . . . and delayed our whole salvation, that's what he's done," Don Tristan screamed at me.

"The delay is certain, the salvation . . . well . . . that appears to be a matter of opinion, uncle."

"What do you think?"

"You heard del Sauz. He has doubts. I have some too."

"But it is not *impossible* to succeed, you would not say that."

"No uncle, I would hardly say that. I've seen several things that border on the miraculous this past year. One more won't surprise me."

Suddenly, Don Tristan's high strung, emotional outburst subsided, and he sunk back, his voice soft, his eyes gazing into mine with something of a faraway look. "Cristobal . . . you are of my family. We face this together as no others here do. Our name, our honor is at stake. If I fail—if *we* fail, rather—there will be no recovery for our family. Do you understand that?"

I answered that I had honestly given this little thought, but I assumed that the King and others would consider the total facts involved.

"You don't understand, you're too young, too . . . well . . . naive. If we fail to fulfill all, or even part, of Philip's mission, our careers are at an end. We shall be assigned to some God-forsaken spot at the end of the earth and left there until hell itself freezes over. No, my nephew . . . we have no choice; so long as there is any reasonable chance that this expedition can succeed, we must pursue it. We have no other choice."

I remained silent a moment, then returned his gaze. "Uncle, no man here seeks success for this—and for you—more than I. You honored me with my position and command, and I've done my best to fulfill your trust. But . . . as we've gone from week to week, I've learned a few things, too. I've watched old del Sauz plug ahead, push his men 'til they all but dropped, make them keep going when we had nothing but slops to eat, keep them from killing the horses only with his own will.

"And I've watched the good friars go about their work as men who are so deeply committed that . . . well . . . who can say more. . . ?"

"What are you trying to say?"

"I really don't know, uncle. It's, it's just that you are right in the pursuit of your duty, yet all of them see these people as driven to near their limit. If we go back to Coosa we *may* get a foothold, we *may* get in a crop, we *may*. . . ."

"Are you too against me, then . . . ?"

"Of course not. I only suggest that what is happening is not insurrection but rather the honest feelings of good people pouring out after they've given all that human beings might be expected to give."

"Nonsense! These are not toddling children. They're solid peasants and proven soldiers. They are in a campaign for the glory of Spain. And Spanish soldiers do not know the meaning of defeat. *That* you can appreciate, I'm sure."

"I can, uncle; and I also know how I feel when I see a child whose skin hangs on his bones or whose mother has just died of starvation because she gave her share to the babe. We have all seen this now for months. Somewhere in between there must be an answer that will suit everyone. I don't know what it is. . . ."

Don Tristan sighed. "So be it. I will do what I must do."

"I only hope that nothing precipitates actions that will force your hand, uncle. My God, let's not fight among ourselves!"

"I shall fight with no one. I am the captain-general and will do my duty as I expect others to do theirs. Nothing less, nothing more."

I rose to take my departure. "Uncle, please know that I will stand with you in whatever happens, and I understand what you're doing, believe me, I do. But . . . please be tolerant. All of these people are not made of the stuff you are. Please remember that."

"I'll try," he said dryly.

I left his hut and walked back to where I was billeted. It was a cold night, but clear, with many stars. There the air was damp, however, as we had found it frequently during the winter, hence the chill bit well into the bones. I sat down and drank a long swig of the cool, delightful water that was one of the great boons at Ochuse.

"Damn . . . he's a stubborn man," I thought to myself, "but he is a good man. He has a job to do and intends to do it. Who can blame him for that? This is the penalty of rank and command. How can I help him?"

I fell asleep with that thought flitting back and forth in my mind. The question was there, but no answers.

OCHUSE
December 18, 1560

At about two-o'clock the next morning Alvar Nunez and Juan Ortiz slipped quietly from the camp. The two foot soldiers had been with the Coosa contingent, and had returned to Ochuse with del Sauz. Now faced with the dilemma of the division, they made a decision. They would slip away by themselves and return to Coosa.

"We have found women, we have found a place where we can build a new life. De Luna is mad!" they told each other.

Taking their own gear, two horses and a small supply of grain, they rode quietly away as the camp slept.

Challenged by the perimeter guard, they explained that they had been ordered to travel up river to check a rumored beaver dam which might afford a new food source. The guard waved them on, then reconsidered. Minutes later he awakened me. As captain of the guard, he felt I should be informed. Shaking the sleep from my brain, I heard the explanation and quickly called out a squad of six cavalrymen. At dawn we picked up the trail of the two deserters. By noon the capture had been made. At dusk the captives were ridden into the main compound.

Quickly the word spread. As Nunez and Ortiz were taken before the commander, hundreds turned out to buzz in small groups. Every eye was on de Luna's shelter.

An hour later a drum sounded, calling the entire company to assembly. As the hundreds massed together, the two captives, wrists fastened behind them, were marched before their guard to the mound from which public statements were made. The two men, their eyes cast down, stood together; the drum continued its slow, plaintive beat.

De Luna stepped forward, followed by Fray Anunciacon.

The drum beat stopped at the commander's signal, and a hush fell over the company.

"I have called you together for one purpose only," de Luna began, his eyes surveying the throng. "When we first encountered the opposition of several cowardly officers, I told you that I would accept no acts of opposition which are against the soldiers' code. You will remember that I said that any man, officer or common soldier who left his post and deserted his duty to Spain would be executed.

"Today, with full understanding of my warning, two men who have had good records and who should have been loyal members of our company arose in the night and stole like thieves from this camp, intending, they say, to return to Coosa, to make a new life for themselves.

"In part, I am happy that they did this, for it supports my belief that this whole company can exist there. However, their act was without permission and with the full intent to leave us forever. Thus they have openly violated my orders.

"The perpetrators of this unpatriotic act stand before you now. Look at them! This is the last day you shall see them alive. Tomorrow at dawn, they shall hang! Each man and woman in this company is hereby ordered to be present in that spot (and here the commander pointed to a large oak nearby) where the gallows will be set. May the Lord have mercy on their souls. The company is dismissed."

With that he turned and stalked from the mound, breaking through the crowd which had pressed close to where he spoke.

Acting as captain of the small guard, I had the pair surrounded, and marched them away to a small enclosure, where security was set.

Fray Anunciacon waited for the crowd to disperse, then walked slowly to de Luna's shelter, and called softly for permission to enter.

"You have it, enter!" de Luna barked.

The commander was seated in the dark; he had not lighted the small fire by which he worked at night; instead he sat on the ground, his arms wrapped about his knees, staring into the darkness.

"I would speak with you, Don Tristan," the friar began.

"You are free to speak."

"It is about Nunez and Ortiz."

"Naturally."

"If I may say so, I fear you are committing an error, if not a mortal sin."

"A sin, good father? They are deserters. They have broken my command. If I fail to act, there will be others. I shall soon be powerless in my own command."

"You may also provoke mutiny."

"That I doubt," sneered de Luna. "These so-called soldiers have no guts for such things."

"Don't test them, Don Tristan," the priest urged. "This is a small matter, really; our goal is to bring people back together, to restore harmony. Two men dangling by their necks can hardly achieve that."

"And your suggestion, good friar?"

"Show your good will, your understanding. Give them pardon, in exchange for agreement from your opposition that they will not press their argument. It is the perfect chance to achieve your wishes."

De Luna spoke directly to the priest who huddled near him in the blackness. "Good friar, you are a man of peace; all my life I have lived among soldiers. For the most part they are sorry samples of humanity, scum raised to honesty by a uniform. They require discipline, orders, ritual. Give them an inch, they steal a mile. In times of trouble it is all the more so. You understand a man's soul, perhaps, but I know his motives. No, Father, if I stretch two necks tomorrow I'll have obedience. Otherwise . . . I shall be in command of a mob, not an army. Thank you for coming . . . now . . . if you please. . . ."

The friar bowed his head a moment, then rose and silently left the shelter.

Walking across the clearing, he approached the hut where the two condemned men sat huddled around a small fire, their hands tied, their legs stretched on the ground. "May I speak with them, captain?" he asked me.

"Of course, padre, though I doubt you'll find willing listeners. They're bitter men."

The friar nodded, then entered and knelt beside Nunez and Ortiz. I strained to hear and could detect the substance.

For an hour he spoke softly with them, urging them to join him in prayers of forgiveness and to prepare their souls for death.

The two spoke occasionally, making some small comment, asking a brief question. Ultimately, Nunez agreed.

"Yes, father, I will pray with you. Perhaps Our Lady will hear a sinner and welcome him to paradise."

Anunciacon turned to Ortiz: "And you, my son? Will you join us?"

Ortiz spat. "Damn you all," he muttered. "Life is worth nothing if a dung hill like de Luna is allowed to govern men. The sooner I die the better."

"It will not harm you to join us. After all, your immortal soul. . . ."

"Will probably burn a little hotter. So be it."

The priest produced his rosary and, as I witnessed from the doorway, began a long and fervant prayer in which Nunez joined wholeheartedly. Ortiz turned his back, making occasional obscene noises.

For an hour they stayed so; then the priest rose, blessed the two condemned men, and walked slowly to his own hut of branches and pine straw.

I wrapped myself in my blanket and slept fitfully, remaining half awake through the night to check the security of the watch. I wanted no efforts made to free the prisoners, therefore maintained this extraordinary watch.

At dawn, one of my guards gently shook me from a doze. I splashed water on my face and walked to my uncle's shelter.

He was already up and at his devotions. I entered, prayed a moment with the commander, then repeated details of the scene I had witnessed.

"Nunez prayed for forgiveness and freely forgave you, asking that the Lord not blame you in his death; he admitted his wrong doing."

"He did? But the other did not?"

"No, Ortiz refused."

"Thank you . . . I appreciate the word."

OCHUSE
December 19, 1560

Two hours later the drum began its mournful roll, and the two prisoners were routed out, their hands still bound, and marched in a file of infantry to the gallows tree. Already the company was gathering. A few stood close, but most hung back, unwilling to be too close to the act of violence. The two victims were marched into place; the hangman, a grizzled old soldier who had performed the task many times in his career, had fixed the ropes with their nooses over a limb. Below were two short tubs on which the victims would stand. On signal, the tubs would be kicked away, leaving the victims clawing for air as the ropes stretched their necks.

Nunez and Ortiz were halted. The hangman approached and wound a piece of dark cloth around the eyes of each man. Then, aided by two troopers, he hoisted the men into place; both rocked unsteadily on their new perches.

Then de Luna approached, followed by the two friars.

The priests moved past the other officers and began the prayers offered for the condemned. For a minute they prayed softly; there was hardly a sound from the hundreds who hung back, eyes wide, looks of sadness, disbelief and . . . in some, pure sleeplessness on their faces.

The friars crossed themselves, and stopped speaking.

The hangman looked at de Luna. The commander stepped forward, turned his back upon the men, and addressed his company.

"Last evening, Fray Anunciacon, on his own and with no instruction from me, visited with these men. He spoke to them of salvation and offered his prayers to seek their place with our Lord. One man, Alvar Nunez, after a time accepted our Lord's grace and asked for pardon and the prayers of our priest, freely admitting his error.

"The other man, Juan Ortiz, refused the offices of the church. Therefore, I have determined to pardon Private Soldier Nunez; take him down, hangman."

The surprised official stepped forward, unbound the eye cloth and, using his broadblade knife, cut the wrist bonds. Quickly Nunez leaped down and fell on his knees, grasping Anunciacon around the legs with both arms.

The hangman looked at Don Tristan.

"That is all. Do your duty, sir!" the commander ordered.

The hangman nodded, stepped back and gave the tub supporting Ortiz a lusty kick. It toppled and spun away, leaving the figure supported only by the rope. Legs kicked wildly, and those nearby could hear the rattling gasps in the man's throat. Slowly, his antics grew fewer, and after perhaps two minutes he was still.

Porras, standing well back, muttered to Sanchez: "The poor bastard! His neck never popped; he strangled!"

Sanchez, his face white and the corners of his mouth working, nodded, said nothing, then turned and darted away into the crowd.

De Luna intoned: "May the Lord have mercy on his soul."

The crowd thus dismissed moved slowly away.

Nunez, still weak and unbelieving, was helped away by Fray Salazar.

Ortiz, his body swaying softly in the morning breeze, remained where the rope had left him. His body would hang there for the next fourteen days.

OCHUSE
January 3, 1561

The execution of Juan Ortiz did little to salve the feelings within the camp. The comment by Porras to Major del Sauz that the hanging was an act of barbarism reached the general's ears, though not from the sergeant-major himself.

Day by day, conditions worsened. De Luna regularly assembled the people, announcing new marching dates for the departure for Coosa, only to cancel them when it became apparent that at least half the military command and many of the non-military simply would not go.

In his shelter, de Luna drew more and more apart, seldom speaking to his subordinates save to harrangue them for their laziness and unwillingness to serve as true Spaniards.

Gradually the encampment drifted into two separate physical factions as well as philosophical ones. Those who remained loyal to the commander moved closer to his

. . . the soldier knelt and hugged the friar's knees; his unrepentant friend remained on the scaffold.

presence, their officers ordering them to pick up their shelters and put them where they could protect his presence, if need be.

The remainder, proclaiming their support of Ceron, also moved, putting their stick and canvas lean-tos to the west. Each day the dissenters respected the general less, some even refusing the simple courtesy of the military salute. Few would completely carry out even basic military instructions.

Del Sauz, Xaramillo and I remained the heart of the loyal officer corps. Porras, Sotello and Acuna, along with Alonso de Castilla were most outspoken among the opposition. The remaining officers were divided but not so vocally.

The two friars worked desperately to avoid violence, and to heal the discord.

On January 4th, de Luna ordered del Sauz to call the company. Without counseling with me or his other loyal detachment the commander stood on his mound to speak; perhaps a hundred of the dissenters were present. The remainder refused to appear.

It was a gray day, but warm. Food was fast running out again, and de Luna, desperate for some sign, now made a statement which put him in an almost impossible position.

"I have called you together," he began, "to review our situation. Because of the disloyalty of some officers and men, and because we have not worked as loyal Spaniards are able to do, food supplies are disasterously low. We have, by my conclusions, enough only at half rations and assuming a reasonable harvest from the waters . . . to last us four weeks. Beyond this, we will be without.

"Therefore, I am dispatching our remaining vessel today to Vera Cruz, with a message to the viceroy urging his most urgent assistance, and advising also of the conditions under which I must attempt to lead this expedition. I have listed for his excellency the names and situations of those men and women who have evidenced disloyalty to me, to him, and to our King. I am, by the authority granted me as commander of this expedition, pronouncing that as of this date each of them is a traitor to Spain, subject to death . . . and to the confiscation of all property, here or elsewhere within the empire.

"I am further advising the viceroy, and all those present, that any person who talks with or otherwise communicates with these traitors, without my express permission or leave, shall also be considered as a deserter to our cause, and subject to these same punishments!

"All this I send to the viceroy this day. And . . . as God permits me the means, I shall carry out these commandments and punishments.

"Y dicho . . . I have spoken!"

At four o'clock, on the tide, the small barque slipped from its anchorage and moved towards the mouth of the bay, bound for Vera Cruz. Her captain carried the lengthy account signed by Don Tristan. In it was a full report of the del Sauz mission, the events of the ensuing weeks, and as promised, the names of several hundred he had classified as traitors. It was a fine day for January, and the captain made his exit swiftly. In 17 days he was at anchor in Vera Cruz. A week later his message was delivered to Mexico City.

The effect of the edict of January 4th was exactly opposite of that hoped for by Don Tristan. The remaining soldiery, sensing the growing instability of their commander, talked in small groups, then, one by one, slipped into the camp of Ceron and his dissenters. Of the total military force available for duty, only five officers and fewer than 100 men could be counted on as loyal.

On Sunday, January 29th, de Luna sat at dinner following Mass (held twice to accommodate the situation) with Fray Salazar and Fray Anunciacon. His mood was black.

"I shall have every man of them hanged, drawn and quartered in Mexico's great square," he vowed. "They are scum, traitors, and are destroying the most noble mission ever set forth in the name of the King."

The two friars, who moved back and forth between the two camps, gave soothing replies in both quarters, dispelling rumors, helping spell out the falsities of reported statements made by one group or the other.

Fray Anunciacon spoke in his usual quiet tone.

"Don Tristan, you are a man of wisdom, a man of education. Think of the feelings of these others. They are frightened men; they do not want to die."

"They've betrayed their trust, and I shall stretch every neck in their accursed camp!"

"My friend, think what you're saying. The Christian is a man of peace, not of violence. Forgive them as our Lord forgives your trespasses . . ."

"I shall forgive no one. I shall hang them all, as soon as possible."

Fray Salazar interrupted wryly. "May I remind your excellency that at the moment you have not the power to hang even one of them. In fact, if a show of power were to begin . . ."

Anunciacon cut him off: "Don Tristan, right now our task is survival. Can we not work together in harmony to assure that we all are still alive when spring comes? You said yourself . . . food stocks soon will be gone. If this spirit prevails as planting time nears, I fear for the physical peace of this camp . . ."

"What would you have me do? They revile me! One man threatened to spit on me yesterday. Can I—the general—accept this?"

"You can take a first step by remanding your order, Don Tristan. It is unthinkable to suggest the execution for men who simply have a goal of survival."

"They have committed mutiny, they have disobeyed military orders. I will commute nothing."

"In the spirit of Our Savior, Don Tristan, reconsider. You could perhaps restore the division by such an act."

"As I did by saving the hide of that worthless Nunez?" de Luna replied sharply. "And where is *he* today? With Ceron, where else! Yes . . . I have every right to be forgiving . . ."

That night, in Ceron's camp, Anunciacon tried again. Ceron's response was similar.

“The man has lost his senses; the devil himself has taken command of his logic,” the master-of-the-camp insisted. “Who else would condemn half a company for their wish to remain alive! No, good Father, I can’t ask his forgiveness, or risk the safety of those who dissent from him. We shall keep the peace, *this* I do promise. But at this moment I’m more concerned with safety here on earth than I am in answering a call to salvation through love. Watch him well! I fear that soon you may have to take him in hand and secure him as a man who’s lost his mind.”

The two friars, seated around a tiny fire in their own hut of straw and branches, spoke gravely as the Sabbath came to a close.

“We have God’s ordinance, my friend. He tells us to love one another, to seek peace, to return good for evil.”

“Our role in these difficult days is to be certain that the peace is kept. Be wary; don’t let either group suspect for one moment that we show favoritism. Pray for strength! Perhaps our brothers have met with success and that help will come soon.

“Amen . . . and Amen!”

MEXICO CITY
January 29, 1561

The three friars had been in the city of Mexico approximately four weeks when the messenger arrived announcing the tragic division at Ochuse. It was also the first report they had had of the actions at Coosa.

Fray Pedro de Feria and his associates had worked tirelessly to gather supplies, riding into the countryside on mules to smaller parishes where they encouraged the clergy to work.

On the coast near Vera Cruz, Feria spent three days planning with Angel Villafane, who had painstakingly gathered surpluses and had commitments from the spring and summer harvests.

"It's coming," he allowed, "but slowly. We've pushed the people hard. Mexicans eat what they produce; they seldom save it."

In Vera Cruz Villafane was already outfitting two caravelles which would be ready by mid-February. "Do all you can, my friend," the friar pleaded. "They are hungry, and there are children. Never forget that."

The night of the messenger's arrival, the viceroy summoned the three Dominicans, along with Fray Domingo de Santa Maria, for discussion.

The four, who had spent an hour at the cathedral in a special Mass, arrived for dinner. There had been no prior warning of the messenger's arrival, or of his message. As they joined Velasco, the thick pouch from Ochuse lay on his desk, its contents neatly piled; alongside lay the sheet on which the viceroy had been making notes.

"We're grateful for your always warm hospitality, your excellency," began Fray Santa Maria formally, "but you will think us a nuisance. We've been here so many times recently. . . ."

"Always a pleasure, my friend," Don Luis returned, "but tonight I ask you for more than pleasure and good company."

"Oh?"

"We've had a messenger from Ochuse, from Don Tristan."

All four Dominicans began spewing questions simultaneously, but the viceroy held up both hands, smiling. "Wait, my friends. The message is involved. I suggest that we enjoy a good dinner first, then look to problems we can hardly solve immediately."

Hours later they were still seated in Velasco's study; each man had read and reread the contents of the bulky file. To begin, they were delighted that Anunciacon and Salazar were alive, and that the Coosa party had survived.

But the balance of the report dismayed them. The absence of food they could understand, but the dismal findings at Coosa and the grave divisions and actual mutiny left them stunned.

"What recourse do we have, excellency?"

"First, of course, we must continue to try to relieve their hunger. You are aware of the two vessels now loading?"

"Yes."

"I have asked Capt. Biedma, one of my most trusted lieutenants. . . ."

"I know him," Feria interjected, "a good man. . . ."

"I've asked him to head this shipment and to carry one message from me to Don Tristan, and another to Juan Ceron, who is my close friend. Perhaps this will help."

"There was no direct word to you from Ceron?"

"None!"

"Then . . .?"

"Beyond that, I don't know. It's a matter of opinion whether the party should move to Coosa. Some say yes, the others, no."

"Don Tristan wants the mission to succeed . . . above all else."

"He's a good officer. And Ceron is a good officer. I can't judge between them yet. Meanwhile, we'll do all we can to make certain of their comfort."

"And then?"

"I still await formal orders from the King. He has promised assistance, too, in supplies, at least. A ship is due to sail from Vera Cruz for Havana and Madrid this month. De Luna's report with my notations will be on it. Before we go beyond this moment I want his guidance. After all," and he paused, reflecting, "after all, it was he who nominated Don Tristan. I should not like to take any action that will prejudice that choice."

The priests sat quietly. There, in the silence of the moment, the political overtones came through clearly. There were hundreds of good men and women waiting, perhaps near death . . . but one could not make a move which might discomfort the direct appointment of the King. It might be . . . unpleasant . . . later.

On February 4th, Capt. Biedma sailed with the two caravelles. Nine days later they landed at Ochuse. For the moment, there was food. That same week de Luna's report, forwarded by the viceroy, began its journey to Madrid.

On February 13th, the two caravelles arrived, creating a new area of decision. How would the food be handled? In whose care would it lie? Who would be responsible for care and distribution?

February passed. Then the first week of March. At Ochuse, the uneasy truce continued; people lived as though in two hostile twin cities, those loyal to the general fearing even to speak to Ceron's sympathizers lest they too be branded as traitors.

Only the friars moved with impunity between the camps, seeking to return the leaders to harmony.

A compromise placed a contingent of men under the friars' command, and they were placed in charge. Happily, this worked and opened the way for further serious talks. Salazar, seeking an audience with de Luna, had food prepared, and he, together with Fray Anunciacon and I, joined in a meal together.

When it was over and the fire banked, the four of us stretched back, almost contentedly. Salazar's comments began with praise for his own foresight.

"This Maria, she is a marvel with even the simplest foods, eh?"

There was general assent. The priest continued: "There is nothing like food and wine to make a man forget his troubles . . . or perhaps make him mend them."

De Luna raised his eyes, but he remained silent. The priest continued:

"Would it not be well if we might accept this bounty as a sign that we should end our differences and approach the opportunities here constructively."

De Luna nodded. "I couldn't agree more."

"Then . . . why not begin," the friar urged hopefully.

"Begin? Begin what? Begin how? I have given the orders of the commander. I have told everyone the King's will. They have defied me. They have mutinied, deserted, become traitors! Don't speak to me of 'beginning' old friend. I am ready. It is *they* who must move to action."

Anunciacon and I said nothing, our eyes playing back and forth on the debating pair. Salazar began again, his hands gesturing with feeling as he spoke.

"Don Tristan, no man has followed you with greater loyalty than I, is this not so?"

"It is so."

"No man has worked harder for the cause and suffered more, physically and of the soul, in that Brother Anunciacon and I have failed to bring the savages to Christ. Is this too not so?" De Luna nodded agreement.

"Then, my commander, believe me when I say that I speak from my heart. Like you, I believe that this cause can yet be saved . . . but . . . we will never do it sitting here like so many prisoners, unwilling to speak, unable to move."

De Luna said slowly, "I repeat, good brother, the first step is up to *them*!"

Salazar was persistent: "Like the Christian martyrs, you must be willing to walk the second mile. And you can, with harm to no one. I beg you . . . revoke your edict; remove the threat of death and confiscation. Restore these men to your citizenship."

The general hissed slowly and softly, "Never!"

"Consider, Don Tristan, that a small number only truly took action to provoke you. The others have followed their officers because they act from tradition. They love you, believe me, and were simply torn by emotions. Now . . . their pride is hurt that you have turned against them. Appease them! Grant them pardon, and they will return to you, loyal and your good friends!"

De Luna simply shook his head. Salazar pressed on.

"I have spoken with many of them, including several officers. If you would grant this one change, the others will again sit down with you and confer upon a way to resolve the problems and press on, to make Ochuse a success. Please . . . I literally *beg* you . . . "

De Luna remained silent.

"I have one other point only," Domingo de Salazar concluded. "These men are loyal Spaniards. They wish to side with your authority. They want your protection. They have followed Ceron only because they fear for their lives; they have new assurance that *now* things will be different on the march. The ships from Vera Cruz have given them new hope. *You* can cement all of this. But you must begin by . . . "

"I must begin nowhere!" de Luna broke in, his face dark with anger. "Good friar, don't you *see* what is *happening* here? I am the symbol of the King's justice and honor. I have been charged with a great enterprise of Spain, and for lack of support that enterprise now will fail. If I accept their pitiful, slanderous laziness, it will be I and I alone who shall be held responsible for that failure. *This I will never submit to!"*

"Don Tristan, to err is human, to forgive. . . ."

"To forgive these swine is not divine, it is hypocrisy. Can't you think for a moment what will be said in New Spain . . . and in Madrid . . . if we come limping home with our tails between our legs, weeping and crying because a storm struck us and we faced a season of privation."

"They will understand, excellency, you have 900 witnesses. . . ."

"I have 900 weeping, wailing children," retorted the general. *"No* . . . Don Luis and His Majesty will count the pieces of gold we have squandered; they will look at their maps and study the reports from France and see that we have failed in our mission. They are weak, Father, weak . . . and that I will not be . . . do you understand?" The last words lisped as he clung to the last syllables.

"I repeat, my commander, that a good word, now, could untie this knot, could return people to work, perhaps begin a motivation that would achieve your fond dreams. . . ."

"They have waited until now to urge upon you this mission only because there have been no further orders from Mexico. I know them! Ceron is certain that Fray Feria has convinced his friend Don Luis to order the expedition recalled. Juan Ceron is Don Luis' dear friend, you know. Had he had *his* way, Ceron would have commanded here, not me. No . . . I will make no change. They must come to *me!* I will not go down in the history of my country as a man who bequeathed a bad example."

In this manner, days passed into weeks, and weeks into months. March passed, April came. Our tiny supply of seed corn was planted and fervently cultivated. The two camps lived and worked side by side, with almost no communication. Babies were born, men died. But de Luna and Ceron held firm. The commander would not rescind his indictment; Ceron refused to submit to authority and agree to march to Coosa.

By now, this was a purely academic exercise; food stores were dwindling again. Capt. Biedma had returned to Mexico, carrying small numbers of the sick and injured, promising to report in detail on the sad state of the colony. No further word had been received.

Fray Anunciacon as the senior priest sped between the two camps many times daily; as days passed, he confided to Salazar that he was fearful lest a chance spark fall among the flammable feelings and provoke violence. He prayed fervently for harmony and said Mass twice daily, once in each camp.

It was as he and Fray Salazar prepared for such a Mass that Anunciacon struck upon his plan.

"Domingo," he began, sounding out his colleague, "I would say that basically the general is a man of good will and very much a Christian, would you not?"

"Indeed! He keeps the commandments most completele, is not lustful, is kind and generous . . . if stubborn!"

"Then . . . what would you think of this?" . . . . and the senior friar unfolded his idea to Domingo de Salazar.

"I will pray for it!" Salazar replied. "The Lord looks after His sheep. He is the good Shepherd. I believe it may work."

Palm Sunday was approaching, and as they drew towards the highpoint of the Christian calendar, the two priests appealed to both de Luna and Ceron to permit a common observation. Reluctantly, the general agreed. Ceron, fearing that he might be condemned for failing to heed the pleas of the Dominicans, concurred.

On Sunday morning, Fray Anunciacon confessed himself and prayed to God for peace. Then, he proceeded to the cross which had been raised when the company first landed, and where Mass for the full company had often been said.

The mass began with its familiar chants; the men, many of whom stood alongside friends they had not associated with for months, were subdued and emotionally charged.

The two priests moved back and forth, each performing his function. The company, alternately standing and kneeling, stared ahead.

The moment came when Anunciacon was to consume the blessed sacrament. He held the cup in his hands, then suddenly halted his ritual. Turning slightly, he said: "Don Tristan de Luna, you are called to join me here—at the Lord's Table."

The general's head snapped up; he looked about, suspicious, fearing some surprise. Seeing no signs on the faces of his adversaries, he moved quickly forward. Fray Anunciacon motioned for the general to kneel. Then the priest, taking the consecrated wafer in his hands, intoned in a loud voice that carried to the farthest ranks of the company.

"Do you believe that this blessed sacrament, which I hold in my unworthy hands, is the true body of our Lord Jesus Christ, Son of the Living God, who descended from heaven unto earth to redeem us from the power of sin and of the Devil?"

The general, his face grave but calm, answered crisply: "I do believe it."

Fray Domingo continued. "Do you believe that this same Lord will come again to judge the living and the dead so that He may reward the good and punish the bad?"

Again, de Luna answered unhesitatingly, "I do believe it."

The friar quickly continued: "Then, if as a loyal and true Christian you believe in the Real Presence in this Blessed Sacrament of the Supreme Judge of us all, how, without fear of His judgment, do you permit the existence of the many wrongs and sins which have offended Him and which we have suffered and wept over for these months past? It is your duty as the superior to correct them and to read in your heart whether hatred, disguised as zeal for justice, plays any part in your indignation. The least ray of the Divine Light which you have before you will allow you to distinguish between the two emotions. You witness the innocent perishing along with those you hold guilty, and you wish to combine the punishments of some with the injustice you inflict upon the others. How will you be able to explain yourself on the terrible day of Judgment if to your own detriment you abhor and rob all of us of the peace for which, for the sake of men, God made Himself man? Do you wish to deprive us of this felicity and further the articles of the Devil, the Father of Discord?"

The stately friar, whose dignity seemed to swell as he spoke, then turned and walked to the rough altar below the cross. De Luna remained fixed for a moment, then rose and retreated to the spot he had vacated minutes before. The Mass was resumed and continued to the final chants and prayers pealing upon the fresh morning breeze; the company, kneeling on the pure white sands, was drenched now with the warm spring sunlight; the effect was complete.

The benediction was sung and the Amen, . . . and for a moment the company remained silent. At this moment de Luna stood, walked to the mound, turned and raised his arm.

"If you please . . . remain a moment and hear me," he began.

No one moved.

"My friends," he continued, "from the time I left Mexico I have never intended to offend anyone. I have endeavored only to discharge the obligations under which the King has here placed me to the best of my judgment, which is based upon the wisdom of others wiser than I. However, if in the present dissension I have been at fault, with all my heart I now ask your pardon for the wrong which malice or my own ignorance may have caused, and I pardon any who may have offended me."

He began another sentence, but the words were heard by no one. Immediately, Ceron, Porras and the other dissident officers had leaped forward and threw themselves at the general's feet, begging his pardon.

The two friars, standing back, beamed. "God has worked for us again, my brother," Anunciacon smiled.

The company, watching an act which few would have believed possible, stood and stared at the spectacle. Some crossed themselves. The soldier Sanchez slowly slumped to his knees again. Nunez, the forgiven deserter, stood with tears flowing down his bearded, craggy face.

De Luna, almost speechless at the outburst, begged the men to rise.

"Come, my friends, get up. We are all weak with emotion as well as hunger. Let us make this a day of devotions. Tomorrow we shall meet together to create a new plan. Together we shall yet make our work here a success."

"Amen," murmured Salazar.

MADRID
December 24, 1560

The weather during winter's first weeks had been delightful in Madrid. The seasonal flowers were bright and the bush green. Late on the morning of Christmas Eve, Ximinez sat with three agents whose activities for past weeks had directed the totaling of the relief effort for Ochuse.

Now, with the ships putting on cargo at Cadiz, the task was all but complete. The minister received the final tallies, thanked the civil servants for work well done, wished them the greetings of the season, then ushered them out.

Relaxed, he sat at his table, completing his summary for Philip. He took a light meal, napped for half an hour, then donned a suitable cloak for his meeting with the King.

It was four o'clock when he was ushered into the royal apartment. Philip was bent over a scroll, intent on his study. Valencia de Luna sat cradled in pillows of satin with gold ribbed cloth, her youthful figure now swelled in the mid-term of pregnancy.

Ximinez bowed to her and to the King, who barely acknowledged the minister's presence. Ximinez coughed, then walked briefly back and forth, his eye on Philip. Without raising his eyes the monarch asked, "You have the lists?"

"I have, your majesty."

"And the final totals are satisfactory?"

"They are, your grace, ample food for many weeks. Our people responded well."

Philip read for a moment, then, still without casting his glance upward, put out his hand for the minister's document. "Contreras will join us shortly. Be seated."

The King rolled out the minister's figures and scanned them briefly, nodding his head affirmatively as his lips formed the totals. At length, he pressed the scrolls together and pushed back his chair. At that moment a page entered and announced a third guest.

Don Juan de Contreras was one of the government's most trusted agents. In his mid-forties, he had held several commissions before Philip's reign in both diplomatic and administrative roles; he was honest, forthright, wealthy, pious.

The four toasted the season over mulled spirits, then Philip called the men to business. The celebration at the cathedral would begin early in the evening but could not start until he arrived. He did not want to keep the people waiting.

"We have discussed your mission before, senor," he began, "thus I will be brief. The reports are here correlating the burden for your fleet. I assure you, Ximinez has been most thorough."

He handed the report to Contreras, who slowly scanned the lines of figures, paying note to the totals. "Very good . . . very good indeed!" he replied at length. "This will feed them for half a year and more, allowing also for seeding the fields. Your Highness' loyal people respond well, as always."

Philip coughed slightly and began once more:

"Your mission is to convey the vessels to Vera Cruz and to report to the viceroy. Now . . . please repeat to me the other instructions I have given!"

Don Juan squared his shoulders and spoke, almost like a youth reciting lessons for the school master:

"I shall say to Don Luis that you are appointing Don Angel Villafane as new governor of La Florida. Don Angel is to accompany this fleet to Ochuse, and there shall review conditions as he finds them. It shall be at his option that the expedition may proceed or withdraw, and in the event of the former, all effort must be made to execute settlements as planned, on both seas. The supplies delivered should make this possible. Failing this, settlers are to be withdrawn to safety as rapidly as possible, using these vessels. Food carried shall be placed ashore for the nourishment of those colonists who either remain permanently, or who are last to withdraw. And finally—I shall urge the viceroy to assign additional friars to accompany the caravan to replace those who may have died or been otherwise removed. In all of this we are to act to protect the feelings and authority of present officers and preserve the pious goals originally stated by your majesty's government."

Philip stood listening, perhaps slightly amused at his associate's grand elocution. Then he nodded and replied: "Thank you, my friend. I have given you a difficult and thankless assignment. I know you will execute it well. Present the written dispatch to Don Luis, then be prepared to explain my reasons. And present, too, my warm regards to Don Tristan. I fear fate has played false with him."

Contreras nodded. "Anything else your grace?"

"I urge only speed. These people will be hungry, very hungry. Don't fail them."

Ximinez and the diplomat departed together, moving to the former's apartments. For an hour they reviewed other matters which Contreras would command for his government. They shared a cup of wine. As the conversation became relaxed, the minister quietly approached a final point.

"I will trust to your tact and judgment not to mention—ah—madame's condition to anyone."

"Of course."

"It could help no one . . . and a loose word could complicate matters to no good end."

"I understand. You can trust my discretion."

Half an hour later Don Juan Contreras walked to his home, where family and friends would celebrate the birth of Christ in the traditional manner.

Forty-eight hours later he departed for Cadiz. On February 16th they dropped anchor at Vera Cruz.

MEXICO CITY
February 26, 1561

The arrival of Juan Contreras and his fleet brought a wave of relief to Angel Villafane and to Don Luis Velasco. For a year, the two had struggled to find food to keep the de Luna colonists alive. Now, at last, there was grain and other foodstuffs enough to bridge the gap between life and death, and to extend the life of the colony, if circumstances warranted.

That last point, however, furrowed every brow around the viceroy's table as Contreras presented his report, examined in detail earlier by Velasco, and now studied by Fray Santo Domingo, Fray Feria, and two others whom the viceroy had included in the discussion.

One was a layman, Juan de la Madre de Dios, a civil servant experienced in the internal affairs of Mexico; the second was Fray Gregorio Beteta, en route home to Spain after vacating the bishopric of Cartegena.

The administrator had been chosen by Velasco to accompany Villafane as personal secretary; Fray Beteta, a long-time friend of Villafane, had been invited to the discussions because of his zeal for conversion of the Indians. His record at Cartegena had been significant; now, it was felt, new clerics must be sent to La Florida, to replace those who had returned to Mexico City, and Beteta was interested, despite his long absence from Spain.

The conversation was guarded, for each was anxious to protect the future against any feelings stated against Don Tristan; yet each save Villafane had reasons for rejoicing somewhat at the announcement of the King of a successor as commander of the colony.

They dined well, toasting the arrival of Contreras, who was plied with questions about news of the Spanish court. The new arrival answered easily, casually brushing aside items of gossip, concentrating upon the King's new programs for the navy and his rebuilding of the army.

"His majesty is determined that the New World will remain totally Spanish," he emphasized. "His agents follow every intrigue in Paris and London. That is why he is deeply concerned for the future of this enterprise."

"But—he did not elect to send you to observe for him?" Velasco asked . . . for the benefit of the others, for he had probed this point several times that afternoon.

"No, my mission ends when I place the ships and stores in Don Angel's capable hands."

"And his orders to Don Angel," Feria added, "I still am not clear on them. He is to press for the ultimate success of the mission . . . but where is the dividing line? What is his basis of judgment to be? What should decide him on pressing on . . . or turning back?"

"Don Angel is a soldier of great experience," Contreras replied. "His Majesty relies on that experience. If the people are well, and their morale suitable, and if there appears to be a reasonable chance for success . . . then he will press on. That was exactly as His Majesty phrased it."

Villafane shrugged. "He does me great honor, but no favors. Like Don Tristan, I may be damned either way I turn."

Don Luis spoke deliberately: "Remember—there are still other possibilities to build worth into your venture."

Villafane replied that he'd appreciate the wisdom of the viceroy's years.

"The words of good Father Feria here suggest that your alternatives may rest in many directions, not simply the obvious," he began.

"You mean that we may have manpower only for half of the mission?"

"That's one thought. A well founded position at Ochuse without the march to the sea is better than no result at all."

"Obviously."

"And if you succeed at Ochuse—if you can establish yourself free of major support from me—then perhaps you might also begin to look to the west."

Fray Beteta interrupted, his rather harsh voice rasping out his words. "With such a beginning we might soon safeguard the route back to Mexico by land, following Cabezo de Vaca's example. There are many known Indians en route. . . ."

"It would be an obvious move," Velasco continued. "A colony which could be supplied by land and water . . . with posts en route. Very appealing, no?"

Villafane rubbed fingers through a finely shaped beard. "Again, you are giving me suggestions, but not orders, correct?"

"Of course."

"Then, let's discuss numbers. Suppose, following Father Feria's estimates, that we have 400 good people, still able and willing to pursue the mission . . .?"

"There may be more, or less," Feria shrugged. "If food is plentiful . . . and if they have resolved the differences. . . ."

Fray Santo Domingo, calm and deliberate as usual, turned to Velasco. "What of these differences?" he asked. "The ship captain's story is difficult to believe. Ceron is a man of honor . . . and Don Tristan certainly has always shown compassion. . . ."

"Ceron is my friend as well as a fine officer. At one time I had hoped he might lead this effort."

"Just so! Therefore, how shall Don Angel approach the matter? To relieve Don Tristan without action against those who defied his authority is hardly proper."

"Especially when His Majesty ordered Don Tristan relieved without knowledge of this latest incident. In fact, we know nothing of Philip's reasons for acting against de Luna. . . ."

"I'm sure Don Angel appreciates the problem and will meet it with his customary adroitness," the viceroy said. "I can't give a commander an assignment and then spell out each of his decisions. These things he must work out for himself, as conditions dictate. And as for the King's action . . . well . . . the King giveth and the King taketh away. . . ."

Villafane stood and paced slowly back and forth, his arms clasped behind him. "It's hardly a pleasant prospect. The people are at odds, they are half starved, and who knows what their attitude may be? Don Tristan has been my friend for many years, and I have served with Ceron and the others. Any request I make will provoke new problems. About all one can say for me is that I bring new groceries!"

"That in itself will make you a savior," Contreras observed.

The talk continued in general terms for hours. Beteta and Juan de la Madre were invited to join the relief corps, the one as historian, the other to assume direction of three additional friars whom Fray Domingo was in the process of selecting.

"History tells us that the cross must be raised amidst a storm of difficulties," the priest declared. "God's work is never easy. He has presented a great challenge to me. I rejoice in it!"

February 28, 1561

After two days rest the party departed for Vera Cruz. Don Angel, his orders as clear as they could be in his mind, shook the hand of the viceroy. "I will do my best, what else can I say?"

"Your best is always an example to others, Don Angel. Act with wisdom, promote justice, go with God!" was the reply.

Once at sea, the vessels began what should have been a routine voyage. However, almost at once the fleet was carried by adverse winds and blown far to the east. For thirteen days they fought to regain a proper heading but failed. As Don Angel reported later, they kept all ships within sight only with the greatest difficulty. Then, as suddenly as the winds had come, they stilled. For days the ships wallowed in rolling swells as an almost complete calm held them firm.

In his log, the relief commander later wrote: "What should have been a voyage of less than fourteen days grew into weeks. Fray Beteta was convinced that Satan had us in an evil spell. But then, in the fifth week, winds became favorable and we moved without further difficulty toward Ochuse."

That change occurred on Palm Sunday, at almost the identical hour when Don Tristan de Luna, moved by Fray Anunciacon's prayer, publicly offered forgiveness to Ceron and his confederates.

OCHUSE
April, 1561

The restored concord within the expedition generated cooperation, but it brought no solutions to old problems. Daily, the officers reviewed alternatives, but always the result was the same. Nearly five months of inactivity had reduced food stocks, with only the modest shipments from Mexico to supplement them. All lived on less than half ration status; day by day the list of disabled grew. Shellfish were becoming more difficult to obtain. The average soldier or farmer sank lower and lower in spirits, his dream of owning land and becoming master in a new land abandoned. More and more the men spoke of Mexico; with each day the simple pleasures of the old life assumed a brighter hue. Those with energy to care were homesick. Few would even talk of Coosa or lands to the east.

Only the two priests somehow maintained the air of enthusiasm. Daily they said Mass, somehow extending the tiny supply of sacramental flour left by Fray Feria. In their prayers they spoke of God's mercy and His wisdom in sending them to the new land. The people listened, prayed, then shuffled back to their routine tasks. The officers returned to endless planning sessions which produced nothing.

And then the fleet arrived.

OCHUSE
April 21, 1561

It was the black freedman Nito Gonzalez who first saw them. He had waded into the shallow seeking scallops when he looked up and spied the ships, sails at the half, bearing down the bay from the west.

Gonzalez straightened up, cupped a hand over his eyes to screen out the early evening sun. It was no illusion! First he saw only the one . . . then another . . . and another.

Still clutching a handful of shells, Gonzalez splashed out of the water and up the well-worn path. As he reached the crest of the slope, he saw others lolling on the ground and began to shout.

"Ships—I see ships—there are ships coming down the bay!"

His call was like a signal to arms. Even the weak and bed-ridden staggered to their feet to join the mass of humanity hurrying forward to the water's edge. By the hundreds they stood quietly, each with his or her own thoughts of what those vessels, larger by far than those that had come before, might mean.

De Luna, standing with the others, muttered to me: "They're big, full ships, lying deep in the water. They're from Spain. Mateos did it! And Ximinez. I was right to stand firm. We will complete our plan, despite them!"

I'm afraid I said nothing. My eyes roamed the faces of the people as they followed the deliberate progress of the flotilla. "Poor uncle," I thought. "He dreams on. He just won't see what's in their minds."

Long after darkness had fallen, the crowd stood and watched. De Luna ordered huge bonfires built to guide the seamen, and near midnight the rattle of anchor chains was audible. By then many of the weaker colonists had drifted away to slumber and dream the sweet dreams of warm food and full bellies.

At one o'clock a ship's boat broke onto the sand. The commander, a young naval lieutenant, asked immediately for Don Tristan de Luna.

"I'm here, awaiting your word, lieutenant," he replied. "You are like an angel from our Blessed Virgin. Who is your commander?"

"We are under the command of Don Angel Villafane, excellency, who bids me tell you that he brings a great store of food and supplies, and greetings from both the viceroy and His Majesty. He hopes that you are well and bids me tell you that he urges you to join him on board for the morning meal. Is that convenient?"

De Luna, not usually an emotional man, shook visibly as he spoke. "Tell my old and dear friend that I am grateful that it is he who joins me to plan this company's salvation. Indeed, I shall join him with pleasure."

"I'll have the boat for you at the sixth hour, excellency. And," he added softly, "I suggest that you come alone."

"Of course. And thank you, lieutenant."

The young man saluted smartly, sprang into the stern of the longboat and gave the order to shove off. Moments later the craft disappeared in the darkness, though sounds of its oars were audible for many minutes more.

April 22, 1561

Don Tristan de Luna was piped on board Don Angel Villafane's flagship promptly at six o'clock next morning and saluted by the ship's company with the full military honors deserved by his rank. It was a gorgeous morning, a light wind promoting a gentle lapping of the waves in the bay; the rays of the early sun played upon the blue-green water, and on the shoreline sent long shadows streaking from the trees across the sandy soil.

Don Angel stood back from the rail, and as the salute was completed, rushed to his old friend's side, grasping him in a bearish embrace. Both looked at each other with genuine affection born on the campaign field and continued in mutual trust.

Seamen and officers stood back, watching with interest, saying little, eyeing the fresh green shoreline and anxious to end their weeks aboard ship. The two officers moved into the master cabin and enjoyed a hearty meal, the first truly fine food, as Don Tristan said, that he had enjoyed in months.

The meal over and the utensils cleared, the two sank back into the cushions of the cabin; light streamed through the windows of the forecastle and the fresh breeze cooled the oak paneled quarters.

"Magnificent, absolutely magnificent," beamed de Luna. "My friend, as always, you are the perfect host. And never was a man more welcome than you are. I'm anxious for you to see how desperately we need whatever it is your ships carry."

Villafane nodded sagely, and fingered his stylish beard, a habit he had developed at the university when deep in thought.

"I'm only sorry Providence has kept us so long in the delivery, old friend; seven weeks! Can you believe it? The captain says he's never seen such conditions or even heard of them. It was almost as though an unseen force was purposely holding us back."

"Whatever it was, it made our stomachs shrink the further," the commander responded. Then, seriously, he looked at his old comrade. "Things have been hard here, Angel, very hard. If you had not arrived . . ." and he shook his head, the words left suspended.

"Then the reports have been correct?"

"We sent many . . . and most probably have grown in the telling," de Luna continued, "but some, like those of Feria must have been accurate."

"Feria's a good man; he has spoken well for you. And he has worked like a demon, scouring the countryside for every scrap of corn and every uneaten bean in sight. The parish priests hate to see him coming anymore."

"He has served God well here," de Luna conceded, "as did all the others. The Dominicans are able men."

"Their reports, plus those of the ship captains, have given us a picture, but it's never like being here and seeing first hand . . . or living through it."

"Hardly. And His Majesty? He too has responded well, I gather?"

"Indeed. Most of what you see in these ships came from Spain. Philip and Ximinez have been busy in your behalf."

"Well then, we can get on with it! Now we can press forward!"

"Perhaps . . . but first, old friend, I have other news."

De Luna was about to phrase another question, but Villafane's expression froze the words on his lips. The old colleague's face had a shadow of concern that spelled bad tidings. "Suppose you tell me," he said quietly.

"The fleet arrived in Vera Cruz two months ago, with Don Juan Contreras aboard. You remember him, of course."

"He's been courier for the royal house for a generation. Yes, I know him."

"Philip had received several accountings of your work from the ship captain, three reports from Don Luis, and a long interview with the priest you sent to him."

"These should have given him ample reason to help us. After all, who can predict a storm such as we. . . ."

"The reports, I'm sure, were factual. His Majesty acted with his usual urgency to supply relief."

"It hardly seemed like urgency to us . . . but at last you are here."

"Precisely . . . but . . . there is more."

"So?"

"I think you can best determine it from this," Villafane continued, handing the captain-general a copy of the King's instructions to Don Luis Velasco.

De Luna read the text slowly, his eyes narrowing as he came to the final lines. Then he reread it, finally folding the stiff paper into tiny squares.

"So . . . you are more than a messenger of good will, eh?" he said.

"Unfortunately."

"And where does this leave me? He says nothing about my future role here."

"I have read the paper many times, my friend. Believe me, it is not a pleasant message to bring. But . . . I have my own interpretation of the meaning."

"Tell me, I'd like to know."

"I, Velasco and Contreras debated the meaning time after time. Both agreed that I have authority to use very broad judgment in deciding what's to be done. Your role, if you will, is to remain as second in command, to help form the decisions, and to take such part as you feel you can best serve."

De Luna heaved a great sigh. "My friend, I know this isn't your doing, and that you're trying to soften this for me; but tell me, why . . . WHY? Have I failed so completely? WHY did Philip order this? If he had known of the problems with Ceron and Porras, I could understand. But he didn't. He couldn't. Then . . . why?"and he shook his head in disbelief.

"I can't pretend to know," Villafane said softly, "but I *do* know that together we may still make good the original projections."

"Can we? You haven't seen these people yet."

"Things are bad?"

"We have ended mutiny, but we have not substituted hope."

"Well, first things first. These are the orders . . . now . . . we must work together, establish complete harmony between us, and define your role. Above all, you must not lose face."

"Thank you."

"We agree then?"

De Luna looked at Villafane and smiled wanly. "When a man is faced with banishment or hanging, he usually will choose the former. Of course I will work with you. As you say, we have had many miracles as well as plagues in this place. Perhaps another sign will come from God to restore me."

Villafane put an arm about his old friend's shoulders. "Together, we have triumphed in campaigns before; this is a new challenge, that's all. Now . . . let's talk a bit about how we'll proceed. I think perhaps a good meal for all is indicated first . . . perhaps even a fiesta of sorts, to raise their mood. Then, after two or three days, we'll begin to orient the officers, and finally advise the people. Meanwhile . . . we shall keep the contents of that little paper strictly between us, eh?"

"That would be . . . ah . . . most considerate."

That afternoon unloading procedures began, paced by the seamen and a small military guard brought by Villafane. The new commander stepped ashore with de Luna to inspect storage facilities and made small suggestions for improvement, then moved about with his old friend to greet officers, to talk with the people, to generally observe the tenor of the camp. The evening meal aboard ship included Ceron and del Sauz and I. Meanwhile Fray Beteta, remaining aboard a second vessel, hosted Anunciacon and Salazar, who were ecstatic at the arrival of an old and valued colleague.

That night, in the quiet of his cabin, Angel Villafane began a new chapter in the diary he had begun the night of his appointment to these new responsibilities.

"Today, I breakfasted with Don Tristan, and showed him the orders of the King: he took it well. Then we made brief plans for continuing our work here together. He looks ill, wasted and thin, yet still the determined man I have known so long. Later I inspected the camp and made ready for discharge and storage of supplies. The officers, like de Luna, are badly used. Had I not seen them myself I would hardly have believed their deterioration. The common people have fared even more poorly. Many have died: everywhere there is nakedness and poverty, and the stares of the women and children went straight to my heart. I cannot judge yet whether Don Tristan has failed to perform acts which might have alleviated this, but for the moment we must assume that the causes lie in acts of God which no man may question.

"This evening included del Sauz, Ceron, and Ramirez in our company; all are very weary, and show the effects of their experiences, as does Don Tristan. We spoke candidly of the hostilities here, for which Ceron now shows remorse. Del Sauz also began his account of his adventures at Coosa. There is conflict between the statements, and tomorrow we shall begin questioning at length of both he and his officers and the original clergy, both of whom dined tonight with Fray Beteta.

"Who can say where all of this will end? Ochuse is potentially a beautiful place. The weather today was balmy, but the soil here appears poor and reports say that our people have gleaned all but the tiniest shellfish from the waters.

"There is much to determine, many facts to sort out before we reach decisions. Meanwhile, I make my prayer to our Blessed Virgin, asking for wisdom and patience with those who have suffered much in the name of their country and the holy quest."

He put down his quill, settled back, and stared at the ceiling rafters.

"Poor Don Tristan," he muttered aloud, "but for the grace of God . . . there go I. How can we help save him?"

He shook his head, rose, stretched, and began to pull off the loose shirt he had worn under his light armor. It had been a long day, the first of many he would pursue before his final judgment was made.

OCHUSE
April 24, 1561

For two days the shoreline bustled from dawn to dusk as sailors acted as longshoremen, discharging tons of food and other supplies; each load was placed on horses equipped for cartage, and hauled to shelters improved under Villafane's watchful eyes.

At each meal food was carefully if simply prepared, and each family was given ample supplies. Fray Beteta, who had suffered through a great starving time in Central America, wisely limited the supplies to be certain that the sudden profusion of food did not do more harm than good.

Between their supervisory chores Villafane and de Luna walked slowly back and forth through the encampment, talking casually with soldiers and peasants alike. The new commander was a genial man, and he recognized the need to personally evaluate the temper of the people he had been sent to lead.

At first he was appalled at the reed-thin legs and protruding ribs of the children and at the gaunt faces of the older women. But gradually, as half a dozen full meals filled their stomachs, most greeted him warmly, anxious to talk of their experiences. Men who had marched to Coosa and fought the Napochies were eager to tell of their exploits. The word quickly spread through the camp that the man who had brought the relief supplies was a congenial fellow, and good company. He was willing, too, to spend time telling of the news of home, and this made him even more popular.

On the morning of the third day he summoned all officers and the three friars to a conference on board the flagship. The sixteen men crowded the cabin, but Villafane made space usable by having the junior officers seat themselves in rows on the deck facing him. De Luna stood at Don Angel's right, with Ceron and del Sauz slightly removed. The three friars stood, backs to bulkhead, at Villafane's left.

"I have asked you here because this morning we must begin deliberations to determine the future of this expedition," he began, "but before I state my mission and objectives, Don Tristan has information he wishes to convey . . . personally. . . ."

The captain-general nodded to Don Angel, squared his shoulders, then faced his officers.

"Don Angel, my very good and faithful friend, has brought us more than food and new hope. He also carries instruction from His Majesty. I need not repeat for any of you, save perhaps for good Fray Beteta and Sr. de la Madre, details of what has befallen us here. We began with a noble company of 1500; today with the return of Maj. del Sauz's company, we have just over 900. More than 200 lie sick, some at death's door. Save for exploration, we have not carried out the orders which our King had set forth. There have been problems, of which you are fully aware, some of my making, some of God's will. Causes do not matter. The result is what counts.

"Of these many details His Majesty knows only part, but, based upon his knowledge when Don Juan Contreras sailed with this fleet as King's messenger, King Philip reasoned that a change of leadership might benefit us all. Accordingly, he has commissioned Don Angel to become captain-general and governor here, and all of us, myself included, will work to his good government."

A low murmur broke out as the men, apparently taken totally by surprise at the announcement, made comment to one another. But de Luna had not finished.

"Now," he continued, "there may be some who will say that I will not react well to this order, and that I will feel badly used. Not so. King Philip is my sovereign and liege lord; I have served him at his side, and in many fields of battle. This is one more assignment. Also (and he turned to Don Angel) . . . also, I have served side by side with Don Angel, as many of you know. He is my good friend, and we respect each other. I know that he is an able soldier and a capable administrator.

"My role, as he explains it to me, is to serve as his second in command. This I will do gladly. He shall have my fullest cooperation, my counsel and judgments. I ask only that he have yours also. That is all I have to say."

Bowing slightly, he stepped backward half a pace, gesturing to the new commander to resume his statement.

Don Angel thanked his friend for his generous comment, then turned attention to his charge to the officers.

"I am aware of the unpleasantness which has divided you here and of the happy results brought about by Father Anunciacon.

"Please know that from my point of view, these things never happened. We are beginning afresh, to solve our problems, to make decisions, to go in such direction as good judgments dictate. Am I understood?"

There was a low murmur of assent, and most heads nodded affirmatively. Villafane continued: "I know that your first question will concern the future of this company. At this moment, I have no answer. His Majesty and the viceroy have provided sustenance and ordered that I survey the people, their strength, and the potentials for success both of the original mission or other options. Fray Beteta and his three associates here have come in the hope that the efforts to work for the kingdom of Christ on earth among the savages may be satisfactorily resumed. Here, too, we must examine the facts.

"I am going to meet singly with each of you, in order of rank, to ask your opinions. I ask only frankness. Please do not try to impress me with either your bravery or a sudden desire to go home. All of you, save the padres, are soldiers. You have a duty to perform. The first act is to help me make some decisions.

"Now . . . as to how we shall proceed; at twilight this evening Fray Beteta will join his comrades in the saying of the Mass; it will be called for the full company, and following the holy acts Don Tristan will repeat the message he has given to you this morning. Then, I shall tell the people what I have just told you.

"For the balance of this day I want each of you to spend as much time as possible getting your own thoughts together, on where you've been, and what you have seen, and what you have learned. Tomorrow morning I will begin my questions. I shall want to begin with you, major, and then speak in order with the officers of the horse. Following this I shall meet with the men of foot.

"I may ask that each officer also nominate two soldiers with whom I may wish to talk, although this is not yet certain. Think on it.

"Finally, this word to remember: if we find that we can press on, there is still a very real possibility that we can succeed and perhaps build a great empire here. Each of you could still become men of great means, able to own fine houses and sire great families. We can live in the annals of our country as men who developed a continent for Spain. If we fail, you shall return as members of a force which did not meet its demands. Your records will always reflect this, perhaps destroying for all time opportunities for promotion in the service of your King.

"Bear these thoughts in mind as you prepare for our interviews.

"Are there any questions?"

There were none. Most sat with eyes either riveted on the face of the speaker or cast down at the deck.

"Very well then. Fray Anunciacon, will you dismiss please?"

The friar uttered a short prayer, the assembly broke, and the men were ferried back to the beach in quick trips of the longboat.

All but de Luna. He remained with Villafane, retiring to a cabin with the papers he had painstakingly collected in recent weeks.

On shore, Ceron walked slowly scuffing the sand with his battered boot. Porras walked beside him. At first neither spoke. Porras broke the silence with one word.

"Well?"

"I say we simply lay it all before him. Villafane's a good man. He could have begun with a very different attitude towards us, you know."

"He could . . . but not if he expects to hold this stinking company together. No, old friend, he could not begin with hangings or anything else that would divide the people again."

"I've known Don Angel for a long time. He's hard, but fair, a good officer. And you know what I'll bet?"

"Tell me."

"He'll gather every fact, every crumb of evidence, then turn around and take us all home."

"Why do you say that?"

"Look at his career! Spotless . . . success in everything he's ever touched. If he presses ahead, look at the odds. What are they? At best an even chance for success in any route he goes . . . no, not that much, far from it. No . . . he'll make the tally . . . then start back. That way *he* remains a hero."

"So?"

"We tell our story, Don Tristan tells his. In the long run, who loses?"

"Our careers . . . as Don Angel suggests. . . ."

"Our careers," spat the master of the camp, "are worth a warm moist fart in hell, and you know it. After what's happened we would go no higher, even if we established Paradise on the Atlantic. No . . . I say follow through . . . be a good boy . . . play the game . . . and we may get back to Mexico in one piece."

"You're a wily little bastard, Juan," Porras smiled, "and you know, you usually seem to come out as you say you will. All right . . . I'll pass the word."

"Do that. Full cooperation . . . every indication of help. And I'll bet my full back pay that we'll be on the first boat to Havana . . . or wherever he decides to take us."

"Beautiful!"

OCHUSE
April 25, 1561

On the following morning conferences began. As Villafane talked quietly with the officers, Beteta spent hour after hour with the two original indefatigable friars, tracing over and over again the events of the past 18 months, and especially their half year at Coosa.

Beteta, of medium height and weight, was a bundle of energy; his speech was stacatto, his rasping voice low pitched, his hands always in motion, seeming to direct his words as they flowed forth. He was a man of great drive and optimism; his mind held a firm grasp of the union of the institutional, intellectual and mystical realms of his faith, and he viewed the mission of his order in the New World as a holy grail which he and the others were destined to achieve.

His arrival in Mexico City en route home just as Don Juan brought new direction to the de Luna expedition seemed to Beteta a sign from heaven. "I was meant to help bring the Word to the thousands of red heathen who dwell here," he had told the viceroy. "I will gladly alter my life to assist those of my order who remain there. It may be the great opportunity of my life to truly do the will of my Lord."

During the first hours ashore he had rushed hither and yon, aiding in the hospital, talking with the people, hearing confessions, assisting with the Mass.

There had been scant time for him to relive the moments at Coosa and elsewhere in the interior. But this was his mission. Now . . . with the military interviews begun, he urged the two weary priests to accompany him, and they walked, their habits thrown back, into the morning sun as it rose over the beachline. The sand squeaked gently as they walked, their feet sinking into the moist, almost pure white grains; the imprints quickly filled with water, then sand, and the rippling wavelets wiped the beach clean in moments.

"Well, my comrades," he began, "at last! At last we can talk . . . tell me . . . TELL ME! How have you fared? How many souls have been brought to Christ? In this new land, this Coosa . . . have you trained a chaplain? How many were baptized? When we return there, will there be a church constructed? Have we brought the Light to their heathen lives?"

The other two continued to walk in silence, their eyes on the sky, where gulls swung lazily in lofty arcs, their whiteness accentuated against the severe blue of the morning Gulf sky.

The silence continued for a minute, then two, the only sounds the soft rippling of the water, and squeak, squeak of six feet plodding gently forward.

Beteta broke the spell. "You are very quiet, my brothers. This tells me . . ."

"That there is little to say," interrupted Anunciacon. "And that, I fear, is the truth."

Salazar broke in: "Like you, we had heard tales of Don Hernando's survivors . . . the great city, the mighty nation, the rich fields, the friendly, cultured people. It sent us into the forest with the will of the disciples."

"And . . .?"

"And we found . . . almost nothing."

"Nothing? Impossible!"

"Oh . . . not really nothing in the sense you take it, good brother. No . . . there were people, but no nation. There were villages, but no cities. Fields, but no great granary."

"Then . . .?"

"We found Coosa and with Salazar's gift for tongues we made friends. We helped them, they assisted us. We joined them in battle, they gave us food to send to Don Tristan. But, though we became friends, they are not the base of a great civilization; they are barely able to sustain themselves."

"And their enemies?"

"Worse off still. *They* invade to steal from the Coosans."

"And your success with the people . . .?"

"We baptized one woman . . . that was all."

"One woman! Unbelievable!"

"Very believable, having been there, I assure you."

"You used no force, of course."

"Of course."

"Then in your opinion?"

"Our opinion? Ah . . . there you ask a difficult question. Who knows the ultimate will of these people," and his hand gestured back towards Ochuse.

Salazar added, "I have seen them suffer unto death with the fevers of this place, and seen mothers watch their children waste into death. They are hardy men; but do they have the will to begin all over again? That I don't know. Perhaps you and Don Angel can draw better conclusions. We've lived too close to the trees . . ."

Beteta shook his head. "I can't believe it. Why . . . for twenty years men have said. . . ."

Anunciacon broke in: "Men have said that *here* was another great empire, ready for the making, ready for the Word. Well, we have been there. We have walked the forests, seen the fields, eaten and lived with the people. The whole story was either a hoax to begin with . . . or the years have taken a severe toll, just as they have etched themselves into his face and mine."

Fray Beteta stopped and swung his arm in an arc across the inland area. "And what of *here* . . . of all this? Are there no people close by? Can we not . . ."

"We see a few, mainly fishermen or hunters who come this way to swim in the blue waters. No, Beteta, there is no empire here, and not even tall tales among the red-men, who by the way are very good at spinning stories to deceive us."

A few yards from the tide line a gray limb, long bleached by the sea, lay half buried in the sand. Beteta approached it and sat down.

"My God . . . then . . . it's all been for nothing! All those people . . . their suffering . . . the storm . . . the lost fleet. And . . . nothing has been achieved! And now . . .".

"Now? Who is to say? That's up to Don Angel."

"What would *you* say if he asked *you,* Fray Salazar?" Beteta questioned.

Salazar thought a moment. "I wondered that myself when he spoke to us in his cabin. I've thought of nothing else, frankly. It's not an easy decision, I've prayed to Our Lady . . . and now . . . I think I know."

"And you would say?"

"I would propose that we return to Mexico. I do not believe one can ride a half dead horse into battle, and these people are half dead. Their spirit is gone. Even full bellies and promises will not make them whole again. I would say . . . 'let us go home, Don Angel.' "

Beteta nodded. "And you, Fray Anunciacon? Do you agree?"

The solid, graying friar folded his arms and looked out across the four leagues of water that separated the beach line from the long island across the bay. "I have thought of this a great deal. I love this place, despite its troubles. Yet . . . it's not I who must be considered, I tell myself. I look at the women, the children, the men ravaged by fever, the slaves who will never be anything else, no matter where they go . . . and I ask myself: what is best? And I must agree with Fray Domingo, here. I cast my lot to return. I see no other way."

Beteta, his usual fervor sapped, stared at the sand between his sandled feet; with his great toe he tried to inch away intruding grains.

"Of course," he said, ultimately, "after all, God gives man a human spirit, and the endurance of man only. What can we expect?"

"If you had marched through the swamps, carrying women who faltered at each step, or watched the tiny ones cry until death halted their whimpers . . . you would feel that you too had watched the Master stumbling towards Calvary, good brother. If nothing else, this has made me feel very close to Him . . . for we've shared a similar burden."

Beteta stood, jerked his head erect, and stared at the two.

"So be it! You are my brothers; you've seen more than I will ever see. If you are to tell Don Angel that we should return these people home . . . then I cast my lot with you! But . . . is it not sad . . . sad. . .?"

The three started back, the sun now warm on their heads. Overhead, the gulls were marking the presence of small fish in the water, and within 100 meters of the sand a porpoise played. It all seemed so perfect, so much what they had dreamed of. Yet . . . now . . . it was impossible, too. With no other words, they retraced their steps to the encampment.

There, the settlers were at their work, some struggling to patch clothing with cloth and thread brought on the ships.

Women cooked, the ill sat in clusters and talked.

Beteta gestured towards the fleet.

"Let's go aboard. I've brought a small supply of choice wine. It's a perfect day for such an excess. Join me."

OCHUSE
April 27, 1561

Hour after hour, Villafane conversed with his officers. First to be interviewed was del Sauz. The short, wiry veteran was honest, straightforward, simple in his answers, in character with his usual manner.

Villafane was thorough. "The countryside at Nanicapana. Tell me about it . . ." he urged, and the veteran army field commander gave true, terse answers. The soil was sandy, the river only modestly productive of fish, the fields largely abandoned, the people few in numbers.

Minute after minute Villafane pounded away. "Would proper cultivation make this a good site? And the river? Was it navigable, or had the ill-suited craft employed for women and children made the journey more difficult?"

After a time, the questions shifted to Coosa, the long march overland, the lands under cultivation, and the people themselves.

Here del Sauz brightened—slightly. "They were good people, the most likable Indians I've ever seen," he began, and then recounted events there, with special praise for Fray Salazar's mastery of the language, and the work of the two friars in encouraging intercourse between the two races.

"You do believe, then, that these were the same people described by de Soto's survivors?"

"Absolutely! They described the men who remained behind and the events when Don Hernando was there."

"Do you believe that de Soto's survivors merely exaggerated their size and wealth . . . or were the tribes truly decimated in these two decades?"

"Ah . . . there I cannot say for sure. Our communication became adequate, but such points are hard to explain when the thought barrier is present. Remember, their pride screened some things from us."

"If the . . . ah . . . the difficulty had *not* arisen in de Luna's camp, would *you* have felt comfortable in returning . . . to begin a city at Coosa?"

Del Sauz hesitated, and this time spoke very deliberately.

"I . . . think I would have. You see, we remained behind for several weeks after our advance guard returned to Nanicapana and then to Ochuse. We had settled in well. Our shelters were adequate, and there was food. I think . . . if it were my decision now, I would send a force of not more than 300 there . . . and begin. Our whole force, of course, would overburden the people. They would be overwhelmed. But with 300 . . . I believe we would succeed."

"Is it true that their chief and his leaders accompanied you for three days on your return?"

"Yes."

"And you would call them, then, your . . . ah . . . friends?" Villafane pounded away, repeating and reinforcing his key points.

"I would."

"And what of the work for the Lord? I have had reports from Salazar and Anunciacon; they were not optimistic, even with all of their abilities."

"Perhaps they expected too much, too soon. As I said, the Coosans were simple people of good heart. Given time, perhaps. . . ."

Villafane nodded, then continued. "When you returned here, what did you find? How would you describe the state of affairs in the camp?"

"I can only say, commandante, that the people, or rather the soldiers, were divided. The common people were more . . . well . . . confused. Some favored Ceron, others remained loyal to Don Tristan."

"All of this began *before* your return?"

"Yes, excellency."

"How did you side, major?"

"I was always loyal to my general, excellency."

"And when the schism was healed . . . what did you do?"

"I attempted, as he ordered me, to assist with a new plan, and to bring the forces back together, through simple work and drill."

"Which was only modestly successful. . . ."

"They were starving, excellency, we all were. We survived only because of your arrival."

Villafane stopped his questioning, rose and paced back and forth slowly. He stopped, looked pointedly at the major: "Tell me, honestly, what is your opinion of Don Tristan's leadership? *Was* much of this trouble due to—shall we say—ineptitude?"

"Is that a fair question excellency? After all. . . ."

"You have my solemn word that no one will ever extract your statement or any other from what I ultimately say or do. I swear it."

Del Sauz shook his head slowly, pursed his lips, bowed his head slightly and spoke, his eyes resting on the ground.

"I have served my King for a lifetime, excellency. I have followed good commanders and bad, strong men and weak, honest men and scoundrels with nothing as their goals save personal gain. To me, Tristan de Luna is one of the finest human beings I have ever met."

"I see."

"He is honest, strong, courageous. He has never asked a simple soldier to perform any labor he would not first assume himself. He has shared his load with us all, asking no privilege. I have seen him, with my own eyes, carry his ration and divide it with the sick.

"As to his judgment, who can say? Any act after the storm would have been a guess. He took advantage of opportunities to communicate with the viceroy, and he used us as best he could to keep people busy and thus away from personal sorrowing."

"Would you say he fulfilled the King's order?"

"He tried, excellency. He alone demanded that the company proceed back to Coosa. He believed we were capable, and that the country would sustain us. He never lost sight of that, even after my company returned with its report, which I confess was short of optimistic."

"Then, major, what of Ceron? You know him too."

"I know him well, your excellency. We have been together in one mission or another for 20 years."

"What of his role? *Why* did he side with Porras and the others? And . . . major . . . why were those members of *your* command the ones to begin the agitation? What caused it? Was there evidence of this before they left you and started for Nanicapana?"

"None, excellency. Sanchez is a good soldier. In fact, he had it very good in Coosa, living with a pretty Indian maid, even encouraged in this by the maid's father. No . . . I saw nothing . . . he spoke often of home, but then, we all did."

"Why did Porras join him? Why was he influenced? After all, he has a fine record also."

"I can't say, excellency. I only know what I saw when I returned. After we arrived, Don Tristan ordered us to have no fraternization with the dissidents. I obeyed him."

Villafane ceased pacing and dropped down, resting against the sand, propping himself on one hand. "Then what of Ceron? Why him?"

Del Sauz shrugged. "Who knows? I can only guess. All of us knew that the viceroy had all but promised him the mission, and he ended as camp master. It was a blow to his pride. Perhaps he felt that by opposing the commander he would finally take command. But . . . that's a poor answer. I don't know. He's never said a word to me."

The questioning continued for another hour, the commander repeating and rephrasing points on which he sought specifics, points dealing with de Luna's acts towards his officers and the actual physical state of the people at prescribed times. On some del Sauz could be specific, on others he could judge only by comparison with certain events, as in the case of Fray Anunciacon's confrontation with the commander during the Mass.

At length the two walked slowly back to the group, where the new captain-general summoned a second officer, then a third.

Most testimony followed the same vein. On basic points there was little disagreement; all praised the commander's actions and enthusiasm following the storm and his efforts to gain relief supplies. Only when they spoke of the long treks into the wilderness was there a question. With Porras, Villafane was curt, incisive.

"You have a fine military record, captain, one any young man may view with pride."

"Thank you, sir."

"Your role in the march through the wilderness to Coosa was viewed with pride by your commanding officer. That is why he chose you to lead the relief mission back to the main body."

"I'm glad I pleased him."

"Yet, en route back, something changed your opinions . . . at least, I must assume this."

"I . . . yes . . . I did alter some of my values."

"Was it something that had happened to you at Coosa . . . some *thing* or some person?"

"No . . . not really; I had a good life there, and enjoyed the people. But . . . it was obvious to me that bringing the remainder of the company there would spark a tragedy."

"The food was inadequate?"

"That, and the difficulty of the march. If we had brought them there, we would have had to begin a city in the wilderness with no tools, no supplies, no medicines. Coosa is over 350 leagues from Ochuse, excellency. Do you know what it's like to consider such a quest with nothing but bare hands and broken spirited men?"

"I think I can imagine."

"And . . . well . . . that was it. I didn't want the blood of women and children on my hands."

"Did you come to this conclusion alone?"

"Yes . . . no . . . no . . . all of us in the squad reached the conclusion . . . if not simultaneously, then as we marched along, recounting what we had seen, and reviewing our orders."

"So . . . even though you had pack horses loaded with grain and had left a happy company at Coosa, you developed a phobia, is that right?"

"I do not understand the word, excellency."

"You developed a fear of this place, this Coosa?"

"I liked Coosa; I feared for the welfare of the people if they went there."

"And so as you returned, you took exception to Don Tristan's plan, is that correct?"

"I told him that I felt it was an unwise scheme."

"And Ceron backed you?"

"He did."

"You had spoken to him about this before the public gathering?"

"He had heard me discuss this with Don Tristan in an officers' meeting; and we had spoken privately, yes excellency."

"Were you confident that he would support you?"

"I . . . think it would be better if you asked him that question."

"Why?"

"We had no agreement. I don't know what or when he decided to do as he did."

The questioning continued, but without further value for Villafane. Porras was not a complicated man; he did not feel a sense of guilt, but rather he was convinced that his act had indeed saved the lives of many of the colonists.

"Do you feel Don Tristan was a worthy commander, then?"

"Yes, excellency, we were all pleased to return to his counsel after he agreed to cancel the ban upon us."

"But you *did* disagree with his one major decision?"

"Yes, excellency."

"This is the conduct of a soldier, captain? A Spanish soldier?"

"Not ordinarily, major, but there are certain situations. . . ."

"To a military man, discipline and order are all important. Your action must be regarded as a severe breach of conduct, whether or not the end result may have saved lives . . . and you will note that I said *may.*"

"I understand, excellency."

Villafane's interview with Ceron was cordial, two old friends and comrades in arms fencing verbally over points which both understood well. It was a matter of ethics . . . and perhaps personalities now, and Villafane understood this.

"I suppose, Juan, that when we return to Mexico you will want to make a full statement in your own words to the viceroy," the captain-general began.

"I think it would be appropriate."

"Even though you were forgiven by Don Tristan, there are still military questions to be considered."

"Certainly."

"What I must do now is to look beyond those acts, and determine if now . . . today . . . we should turn this whole affair around and sail home, or whether there is still sufficient fire in the bowels of these people to push ahead and do the job."

"I understand the problem. Are you asking for my vote?"

"Indirectly. But first I want to know why you agreed so readily with the plan to oppose Don Tristan, and why you allowed your authority to be used to send a squad back to Coosa and deceive del Sauz into coming back when you knew . . . ."

"Don Angel . . . you were not here then. When you arrived our people were badly off; the skin tight on their bones, their bellies swollen, the hospital filled. But that was nothing compared to conditions when Don Tristan wanted to march us into the wilderness. Then we had a dozen horse loads of food . . . and little more. Since then we have had small shiploads . . . small, I add . . . but at least enough to sustain life. I tell you (and he stood chin to chin with his superior) . . . I tell you that Spanish bones would now line the path between here and Coosa if we had marched out as he wanted. We used methods that I deplored, but I say to you that at that time Don Tristan had taken leave of his sense of values. He could only see his orders, his reputation, his honor. He told us as much. I say that in such a situation good judgment must take precedence over military law and discipline. Today, these people are alive, thus I'm proud we acted as we did."

"And now . . . what about now? What about their will to push ahead?"

Ceron spoke slowly, deliberately. "Don Angel, I was a party to this expedition from its inception. I sat with Fray Domingo de Santa Maria and Don Luis when reports of French explorers were received. Together we laid plans, made maps, built a force, dreamed dreams. Don Tristan was a late comer, chosen to lead us for reasons I have never understood. I was to have been the leader, then all that changed. But I tell you there is no man who wished success more than I . . . and now I say we cannot push these people further. You've seen them! Most are burned out, incapable of work, perhaps ever again. They are no longer the stuff new colonies are made of."

"Then, you believe Don Tristan a good commander?"

"I do . . . but like us all, subject to error. He made a bad decision, we opposed it. There was nothing more. I may be punished for my part here, but my conscience is clear."

OCHUSE
April 28, 1561

As the interviews continued, my uncle tried to keep busy, out of sight of the company. He took most of his meals alone, or with Villafane, who sometimes joined him. In the evening he pored over his records, trying to update his own accounts of what had happened. Frequently, we spent those hours together, for he counted on me as his scribe, despite the inadequacies of my notes.

It's difficult now to think of Don Tristan without a twinge of remorse. There he sat, the man who months before seemed to sit at the very threshold of new frontiers. Now, now he sat quietly as sentence by sentence his former subordinates wrote his finish.

As we worked, we would go over various chapters in our adventures, trying to reconstruct the exact chronology, or the very language which had been used by key men and women. As we talked and wrote, Don Tristan would often halt, his eyes registered on some event far away, and he'd ask a question that hardly seemed relevant.

One evening, the interruption began this way:

"Cristobal, what do you think del Sauz said?"

"To Don Angel, you mean?"

"Of course."

"He told the truth as he sees it, no more no less. He's that kind of man."

"But what *is* the truth as he sees it? After these weeks, does he still believe in me?

Has he changed his mind about his doubts, I mean? If the chance to begin again tomorrow were to occur . . . would he go?"

I shrugged. "I don't know. Del Sauz is a soldier, not a glory hunter. He's past the age when he expects to be a grandee. Oh . . . he might go if the price were right. Otherwise? I just can't say."

"At Coosa . . . did he have a woman?"

"Perhaps several, but no one special."

"Others did though, eh?"

"Men like Ortiz did, certainly. They found comely wenches the first week or so. They needed no interpreters."

"Many did this?"

I nodded.

"Did you?"

"I enjoyed the affections of Wechumka's younger sister, no less," I replied.

My uncle nodded gravely. "Then no one was immune to this . . . this license."

"I won't say no one uncle; I suspect Salazar and Anunciacon's confessional was busy enough."

My uncle pressed on. "These men, yourself included, would the women attract them back to Coosa?"

"Who can say? Not me, certainly, though I'd go if the opportunities and orders were proper, if that's what you're getting at."

"I don't really know what I'm getting at, as you put it. I'm trying to look back and ahead at the same time. Do you think this point of view's being given to Villafane?"

"Enough to let him draw his own conclusions. After all, he's been in America for years. He knows what happens when Spaniards and Indians mix."

My uncle lapsed into silence again, then glanced up once more. "What do you think Villafane will decide? Has he indicated to you . . .?"

I'm afraid I parroted an answer that I'd heard others give. "Looking at the whole picture, uncle, I'd guess he'll order the command abandoned. After all, in his place, would *you* risk *your* career?"

"I've thought of that, of course, but Angel is a man of great courage and dedication. He's never been a self-server. That's why I have hope."

"Uncle," I broke in, "suppose you had the opportunity to stay yourself. What would you do . . . even as second in command?"

Don Tristan leaned back and folded his arms across his chest. Cristobal, you were one of the first I spoke with after King Philip made his appointment. I told you then that I believe Spain *now* has a great opportunity to master this continent . . . perhaps forever. We can grow strong on the wealth taken from Mexico and Peru; we have every chance to crush our rivals and to re-establish the only Holy Church universal. I also believe in the story every cavalryman knows . . . the one about the missing nail in the horse's shoe. To me, failure here could be like that nail. If we give up and go back it will not be simply one small venture with a record of defeat. There are enough of these in our journals, the Lord knows. But . . . we were something different, something very special. You realize of course that in all the annals of our history there has never been a venture so large, so well planned, so perfectly outfitted as this? What then if we fail? When will another king risk so much? When will there be time to plan so thoroughly, or an opportunity to gather so many worthy people? No . . . my nephew, if we turn about now, someday, perhaps many years from now, all of Spain's great aims may fail because we did not have the courage to walk our second mile. There . . . that's a long speech . . . but that is why I am so concerned . . . why I would risk anything to succeed."

When I left him that night, my thoughts returned repeatedly to Don Tristan's monologue. 'What does he think he is, a prophet?' I thought at first. Yet . . . the thread of what he had said wouldn't leave me. It disturbed my sleep, and bothered me for days. Even now, after so many years, I awake sometimes in the night and wonder . . . could he have been correct?

OCHUSE
May 1, 1561

The reports which continued to Villafane were by now repetitive. The two friars spoke with fervor of the heroism displayed by officer and commoner alike. Salazar's account of the storm was classical in its interpretation, and his praise for Ceron and de Luna in the aftermath was full and complete. Anunciacon spoke at length of the commander's desire to push the quest for the creation of the Lord's kingdom among the savages, and he recited the instructions given as they left Nanicapana for Coosa.

"We have all been victimized by fate," he added, "and perhaps by dreams painted with too broad a brush by those who returned from an expedition which in most respects was a failure and required a silver lining to save face. Those dreams . . . perhaps more than anything . . . led us astray."

"You've spoken with Fray Beteta of your feelings?"

"Fully, your excellency. He concurs with our thinking."

"Which is?"

"That within 400 leagues there is no opportunity to carry out the full mission for the Holy Church. We are not responsible for military tactics or decisions; but for our part, we see no reason to remain here now. We do not believe that we can do more now than sustain the spiritual nourishment of these people until they can be safely removed."

"And this is what you recommend?"

"Regrettably, it is."

On the seventh day Villafane asked Don Tristan to accompany him in a longboat on a brief expedition up the great river. "I need to see more of this country for myself," he said.

For half a day boatmen moved them against the current, through the salt marshes, and up the slow moving stream whose bluffs looked cool and inviting below their canopy of pine and oak. At noon, they pulled ashore and built a small fire on the sand, making a light meal. Don Angel dismissed the sailors, suggesting that they rest or swim. The two officers, alone, began the discussion which brought Don Angel's decision to its conclusions. He began with his observations.

"I've spoken, now, with the officers and friars, and with ten of their company."

"I'm impressed with your energy."

"It's better to say that I'm trying to reach a decision before we all find new troubles."

"The men were open with you?"

"For the most part, I think so."

"My nephew told you what you needed to know?"

"He was most helpful. In fact, I plan a citation for him for his excellent work."

"Rameriz is a good boy, a credit to his father. I hope he did not damn me too severely."

"Hardly; he can say only good things about you."

"There are small blessings, then."

"In fact, my friend, there is no condemnation of you. These people look upon you as—well—a saint operating under a cloud. In all the discussions I did not hear a single man say that he would or could have done things better than you did. Only on the point of the march to Coosa was your judgment faulted."

"And if we had marched then, by now we would have carried out at least half of the King's mission. *This* is where there is a difference of opinion.ı.

"The question is, what to do now . . . to push on . . . build here . . . begin posts en route to Mexico . . . or retire the colony."

"You have my opinion, good friend. I would begin at once and march inland with 400, build, resupply . . . and a year from now move eastward. The others . . . well . . . some might be sent home, the others could plant and build here, and next year outposts might be started to the west. But give up? Never! We have just begun to succeed. With what you brought us, success is in sight. If we turn back, history will never forgive us. In fact . . . the whole of civilization and our country might be altered."

Villafane chuckled. "You've a magnificent flair for the dramatic, Don Tristan. No, I hardly think that our rag-tag army will influence anything beyond its own survival."

"When will you make your decision?"

"I have already made it."

"Then . . .?"

"I am going to begin embarking the sick by week's end; the rest we shall arrange to return as soon as bottoms can be obtained. There is plenty of food to care for those who cannot go at once. . . ."

"But you *can't*!" de Luna shouted. "You *can't*! Not when we're within sight of success! We have food, we have a chance now to do. . . ."

Villafane placed a calming hand on his friend's wildly gesturing arm. "I have not finished."

De Luna, suddenly calm, responded: "I'm sorry, please forgive me."

"I said that I shall move people out as quickly as possible. Some may not wish to go. Some may wish to remain here, with you, to develop this first city. That I will permit. However, those who would remain must do so voluntarily . . . no other way."

"You mean . . . I may stay with a cadre . . . *if* I can find a few willing souls . . . or something like that?"

"Now . . . don't let your imagination run away. I'll assign twenty men from the force I brought with me, and we will seek out another 30 from the remainder. Suppose we try to get fifteen farmers and woodsmen, and the rest soldiers . . . that will form the making of an outpost, permit you to maintain the settlement here until the viceroy has time to review the situation."

De Luna was silent for a moment, angrily twisting his hands behind his back. His glance circled the view . . . the water . . . the white sands . . . the tall pines and oaks he had come to admire. Ultimately he turned back to his old friend: "What can I say? If I refuse, it's all over. If I agree, I'm left as post commander in charge of Nowhere. It may take even Don Luis a decade to reform and renew the effort."

Don Angel shook his head sympathetically. "It is your reputation I consider, Tristan," he began, "for if the expedition is abandoned, they will always refer to you as a man who failed with the greatest colonial force Spain has ever mounted. Can you face that? This way at least offers some hope."

"Very slight . . . and another separation of who knows how long from my family . . . not to consider the investment that is lost forever. My friend, you are looking at a ruined man. My lands will be sold, perhaps even my home . . . everything."

The discussion ended without the former commandant making a decision. Later that day they returned to the company, drifting lazily down the sparkling river, for the moment forgetting the trials which plagued them.

For a few hours they were like young men again, exploring a wilderness in which they were the rulers, seeking out new adventures under a cloudless blue canopy.

Next morning, as he joined Villafane for breakfast, Don Tristan announced his agreement to the former's proposal. "If we can get thirty volunteers we shall continue," he said. Then, the two called for a council with del Sauz, Ceron, Captains Juan Siguenza and Jorge Miranda, who had come with Villafane, the three Dominicans and myself.

Slowly, Villafane explained the findings as he interpreted them after a week of probing.

"It is with greatest reluctance that I am compelled to order the bulk of the expedition returned to Mexico, moving in stages as vessels are available," he said. "We shall maintain the stores here and depart with the women, children, ill and injured as soon as this is practical.

"However, it is possible that we shall maintain a position here, with Don Tristan in command. He wishes to try, and I uphold him in this. Now . . . no . . . wait . . . let him give you the details."

Briefly, de Luna outlined the agreement reached between the two commanders.

"I can only hold out the hope that once reports have reached the King of the potential of this place, he will outfit another force to supplement us. We will have the privilege of laying out a city, planting the fields, and beginning a fortified land route to the south and west. I can promise those who stay very little. But I will promise my honor and support, and to share with any who will remain the hopes for an act worthy of Spaniards. Don Angel has said that he will assign 20 of his newly arrived men . . . *if* 30 others will remain. That is the plan. We shall announce it to the people tomorrow. But first . . . I must ask: will any of you remain? Are there any here that I may count on?"

The group sat silently. Seconds ticked by as each searched his private thoughts and conscience. I was first to break the silence. "I will remain, uncle . . . and proudly," I said.

"I, too, will remain," del Sauz said softly.

"And . . . if Fray Anunciacon approves, I would be part of your company," Salazar offered.

De Luna smiled. "Well, then . . . it is settled! We have the nucleus, now let's see if there are stout-hearted fellows enough to make our cadre. Thank you . . . thank you and God bless you!"

Next morning Fray Beteta presided at Mass, after which Don Angel and Don Tristan addressed the company, the former detailing his plan for vacating the place, and de Luna making his appeal for men at arms and farmers to remain with him. At the conclusion he said that he asked no immediate response, but urged all to think—and pray—over the matter.

"Then, we shall set noon tomorrow as our deadline," he concluded. "If by then we have not made our complement, we shall abandon the plan."

He did not have that long to wait, however; by nightfall more than 50 had volunteered, including four married couples and the widows of two men who had died recently. "We believe in this place," they told him, "and we believe in you."

OCHUSE
May 15, 1561

In the days that followed plans were completed for removal of the survivors. The vessels, large, broad beamed merchant ships, were provisioned and watered, each capable of carrying over 150 passengers and crew. Even so, it would require more than the single voyage to carry off the total company. Villafane worked in his own methodical manner, listing each colonist by name and rank, with his condition and even the pitiful personal possessions to be returned. Those in best health would remain with de Luna until the vessels should complete a single run to Havana, where the sick would be disembarked for medical care; then, two vessels would return to Ochuse to board the remainder, leaving Don Tristan and his force until such time as Don Luis Velasco should send further reinforcement or counter orders.

The preparations had consumed fourteen days. As Villafane went about the business of completing his findings and notes, de Luna divided his hours between assignment of new duties to those who would remain, including the temporary residents, and the writing of a personal accounting to the viceroy, to be certain that his views would be properly represented.

With good food and a new sense of purpose in the camp, spirits rose; some who were to remain began preparation of farm plots and turned over the soil. Others began work on more substantial buildings, made of felled pine logs, with roofs of pine straw and clay plaited over thin oak limbs. The floors were of packed sand, and each building was given several windows, with a center hole in the roof through which the smoke of the cooking fire might exit. De Luna's private quarters were slightly larger, but of the same materials. As before, there were no efforts at fortification.

The day of departure was a mixture of joy and sadness. Those who were to go on board were up before the first streaks of dawn, shouting, singing, almost unable to believe that for them the ordeal was almost over. There was sadness, too, at leaving comrades with whom they had shared much.

As they shared a final meal, the three Dominicans prayed together, Anunciacon torn with emotion at leaving his brother. "But we shall be together soon, I feel it . . . here!" he said, pounding his solid chest.

Salazar grinned. "Of course, and remember, I am younger than you are. I was made for this life . . . more than you graybeards!"

Beteta simply shrugged. "It was an experience . . . and a disappointment. Who knows if we shall have another such challenge?"

Ceron avoided de Luna. So did Porras. Others, even among the one-time defectors, sought him out, wrung his hand, and thanked him for his kindnesses to them. "You have done your best for God," they said.

The common people sought him out also, to mumble a goodbye, to shed a tear of sadness, to wish him well.

As he stood watching the longboats ply between ship and shore, each loaded deep on the outward trip, de Luna thought how different this was from the day when they had first disembarked, when the great adventure had just begun.

At three in the afternoon, the last boardings were complete. De Luna and Villafane, with the Dominicans and the other senior officers, took the noon meal on board Villafane's flagship, toasting success to the voyage and to those who remained.

"I ask only that you forward my report directly to the viceroy, with your own, and my letter to my wife," de Luna urged. "Meanwhile, we'll fight the good fight, eh?"

Villafane gripped his old friend by the arm: "I hate this . . . more than you'll ever know," he said in a low, even tone. "No man deserves a better fate than you do. But . . . I'm ordered to do what is best for these people . . . the rest you know," and his voice trailed off.

At dusk, those who remained stood on the shore and watched the small fleet tack down the bay, moving towards the sunset, into the west, to the mouth of the bay.

Del Sauz and Salazar flanked their commander. They said little. Minute by minute the sails became smaller, at length disappearing altogether as day ended.

"They will just make the passage before dark," del Sauz noted.

"But it is a red sunset . . . a sailor's delight," the friar added.

"What does it mean for us?" their leader questioned. "Now we can only work . . . pray . . . and hope those in authority believe in what we've done."

"We'll try," Salazar agreed.

The trio turned without further word and walked back to the settlement. There, a few men and two women were singing a peasant song, their uneven voices floating on the sultry air. Now we could only work . . . and hope. Everyone knew this.

MEXICO CITY
June 16, 1561

Don Angel Villafane's fleet made a rapid passage to Havana, sped by favorable winds and cloudless weather. In the Cuban city, the sick were hurried to religious hospitals for medical aid and good food; those able to continue were placed aboard two ships and continued on to Vera Cruz with the commander. The remaining two vessels returned to Ochuse to board the balance of the returning force. They would sail directly to Mexico and join Villafane's command there. No one could be certain what their next assignments would be. Few thought that far ahead.

Villafane himself, with Ceron, Anunciacon, Beteta and Mateo de la Madre de Dios, who had carefully recorded the activities during Villafane's stay in Ochuse, hurried to the uplands and Mexico City. Their coming was greeted with mild fanfare. After one day of rest, they made their presentations to Viceroy Velasco.

The meeting, which included leaders of church and state, began with a light supper and good wines, a tradition from which Don Luis seldom departed. The pleasantries over, he sat back behind his heavy table and turned to Villafane.

"Now, senor, we await your report. You are here, the bulk of the people are apparently safe and well. That we know. For the rest . . . we await your words."

Don Luis, his usually serene face now grave, glanced at the bulky notes held by Villafane. His eyes scanned the expressions of the others, then he drummed his knuckles nervously on the solid surface.

"You have obviously recorded many details, Don Angel," he observed. Villafane nodded once.

"How would you suggest we begin? Do you want to read all of that to me, or comment, or both? I would prefer a general discussion, but I suspect that you have prepared in your usual orderly fashion."

Villafane leaned forward slightly, his eyes narrowed. "I have written a full report which includes statements as well as observations, Don Luis. They are for the record and may be read at your pleasure. Also (and he held a smaller missile) I have a memorandum written by Don Tristan which is for your eyes and the King's. However, I think we should begin this evening with oral reports from those who were present, and those whom you sent as your messengers."

"Gentlemen?" Velasco asked, scanning the group.

"I concur with Don Angel," said Fray Anunciacon.

"Agreed," added Ceron, whom some suspected might already have made his statement in private to the viceroy.

For hours the men of Ochuse spoke, often seconded by Villafane, who supplied information from the individual interviews without disclosing identities where officers had requested anonymity.

Don Luis and Fray Domingo both sat with writing materials in hand, making notes, occasionally breaking in with a question.

The account of the great storm they passed over quickly since there had been prior reports. But Velasco probed repeatedly at his commander's reactions in the aftermath. Fray Anunciacon summarized the point best.

"Like all of us, he was stunned for the moment, both by the loss of life and the gravity of our situation. In fact, the first night Sr. Ceron had to assume charge of affairs.

"But by next day Don Tristan was bright and enthusiastic, setting an example as a true Christian leader should."

This satisfied the viceroy, who passed on to other factors.

"To the officers, I would then say, do you feel Don Tristan acted wisely in attempting to move the company to Nanicapana? Would it have been more practical to proceed towards Coosa, whose direction he suspected?"

Ceron spoke first. "It appeared that we might find food there, excellency, and the distance was more certain. We had only estimates of Coosa's whereabouts. And we were becoming sorely pressed for stores."

"I would concur, excellency," Fray Anunciacon added.

Velasco was thorough as an inquisitor. Each detail, each judgment was pursued. Had each segment of the company received equal treatment? Had ample attention been given to the sick? Had all local resources been exhausted in gathering food? And so on and so on.

When the accounts of life at Coosa were related, the viceroy was incisive with his inquiries, seeking numbers, conditions and prospects among the Coosans. Here Villafane tapped his volume of notes.

"I have here statements from all officers as well as the friars, excellency, and perhaps best qualified of all to speak is Fray Anunciacon. He was there. He saw it all . . . the good and the bad."

The viceroy gestured to the friar. Anunciacon, intense and deliberate to avoid misphrasing, spoke slowly.

"I have repeated my feelings many times, to many questioners. By now I am confident of my feelings because retelling reinforces them.

"Of Coosa itself I can only say that it was a blessing in that its largess stayed the hand of death from us. But it was far from the civilization and land of plenty we had been led to expect. Survivors of Don Hernando's party had painted a picture of a people much like those Cortes found here. That was false—completely false. Their tribe was of a few hundred, and their enemy when we fought perhaps a like number. Both were very poor.

"What would have happened had Major del Sauz's party *not* been recalled, and had the full company marched there? I don't know, but I fear we would have the death of many innocents on our consciences by now, with little to show for it.

"Coosa was an experience I shall never forget. As a priest I have always believed that given time I could win any man to Christ. At Coosa, I failed, as did Fray Salazar. Would we have succeeded by our example of love had we remained? Again, who can say?

"In all things, God works for good, and for His kingdom. Hopefully, He made Capt. Porras and others the messengers of His will, and the world will profit. I can say no more than that."

The discussion of the mutiny, the division of the camp and the friar's role in these were discussed also; as the evening wore on Don Angel filled details more and more from his voluminous notes, climaxing with the specifics of the decision to retire from Ochusc with the bulk of the company.

"You are satisfied, then," the viceroy continued, "that it was not in the best interests of Spain to pursue any of the original goals set forth in His Majesty's charge?"

Villafane rose and stretched. They had been closeted now for over four hours, and his limbs and bottom were numb. Pacing deliberately back and forth, arms clasped behind him, he spoke. "There is a point, Don Luis, beyond which it is unwise to drive a human being. This lesson is well learned in a military campaign and was the key to my observation. Most of these people were in fact soldiers. Those who had made the march to Coosa most of all had been disciplined and fed. Their reserves were high.

"The rest? When we arrived the stink of death was hovering over the place. Skin was pulled tight on the people's skulls. For some, hair was falling out, and teeth. They were palsied and frail. Even after we fed them, they lingered in a sort of stupor.

"Some . . . I suspect . . . would in time have become sturdy again. But their zeal was gone. They no longer saw great visions of a new city, or of the new life they had come to build. They were sick and they were tired and they wanted above all to return to Mexico alive . . . for whatever that was worth.

"That is what I saw, excellency, good, simple people who had endured much. I did not believe my orders gave me the right to force them further. I am certain that had I tried we would have suffered further disaster."

The meeting adjourned shortly after Villafane's emotional statement. Next morning the viceroy isolated himself and began a painstaking review of his messenger's written materials. These required hours to digest, but he made notes regularly as he found new points of emphasis.

He saved Don Tristan's message for last. It was late afternoon when he opened it, and he was surprised at its brevity. It said:

"I have poured forth my soul to my good friend Don Angel, baring my most secret and intimate thoughts concerning what has befallen my company at Ochuse and elsewhere. His reports and documents will, I am convinced, motivate you to permit me to continue the work we have lately begun here. I have prayed to our God each day for strength and guidance. Why we have failed thus far is concealed in His own mysteries, for we have pursued our goals in the spirit and letter of our charge.

"The others are with you now, safely I pray. Fifty good men and women remain with me, well provisioned and in good health, able now to concentrate upon that which we must do. I cannot, of course, accomplish all that was proposed with such a force. But I can begin! Therefore, I urge your permission to continue here, with the understanding that a new force of similar size may be raised shortly, to come here to my command. By then we shall have constructed a suitable base, and with good fortune we shall quickly create the defenses sought by His Majesty!

"This I pray you to consider, and to urge upon noble Philip, who hopefully may see all reports and judge me guiltless.

"Again, I thank you for all that you have done in behalf of my enterprise, and I remain your servant in Christ. . . ."

MEXICO CITY
June 23, 1561

In the days that followed, Don Luis, aided by Villafane, took steps to assimilate the veterans of Ochuse into the life of Mexico. Soldiers were given furloughs, then assigned to garrisons where their careers might be resumed.

Those who had come off the land were returned to it with such consideration as in the times seemed reasonable.

At intervals, the two leaders conferred further on the fate of the fifty who still remained in La Florida. As he pondered, the viceroy also deferred his report to his King.

MEXICO CITY
July 1, 1561

Finally, a decision was made. As he penned his orders to de Luna, the viceroy was kind, thoughtful, objective. After suitable phrases praising the one-time commander's character and willingness to continue, he said:

"It is now apparent that no suitable supplementary force can be raised and supplied from Mexico in the foreseeable future. We, too, face problems which will require our forces here, and I dare not draw again upon the resources of those who have just returned.

"I shall, of course, forward your letter along with Don Angel's full account to His Majesty, and it may be that shortly he may wish to begin anew, perhaps drawing upon your experience to again direct such an enterprise.

"For now, however, I see no merit in sustaining so small a force in your position. Consequently, I order that you shall embark your forces upon the ship which bears this message; it shall in turn carry you to Havana where you are to stay in residence until orders are received from Madrid.

"I salute your noble effort and your strength of purpose, but I feel that there is little to be gained for you or your subordinates in further sacrifice."

Within two weeks that order was aboard ship bound for Ochuse. Copies of the order, de Luna's report and the summaries of Don Angel Villafane were placed aboard the flagship of the annual silver flotilla for Cadiz. Letters from de Luna addressed to the King and to his wife also were carried. Good weather prevailed and both vessels reached their destinations promptly.

OCHUSE
August 20, 1561

The departure of the main party and Villafane's fleet created a new work environment for those of us who remained. Don Tristan set the example, dividing us into four work groups. Three entered into the long delayed task of beginning something that resembled permanent housing. Villafane's fleet had brought an abundance of tools, and while few of us were journeymen, we fell to with a will, cutting trees and assembling huts in which a family or four men might live comfortably. Our efforts were hardly professional, but del Sauz, whose experience had developed talents of many sorts, provided able guidance.

The others turned their efforts to the fields, clearing trees, burning stumps and brush, and plowing (though our cavalry mounts were most uncooperative in their roles of stump removal and plow pulling).

By day our hours were long, but for the first time in two years we did not want, and we hardened our bodies and mellowed our spirits as the accomplishments rose or grew before our eyes.

It was a month after the fleet had returned for the remains of the company and had departed again. It was the afternoon of the Sabbath, and as usual Fray Salazar had performed the Mass out of doors, before the cross. Now, with a good meal under their belts, more took their ease, though a few chose to walk about or wade in the shallows.

Del Sauz and I left the campsite and walked to the west. It was a gorgeous afternoon, with the sky a deep blue and the huge pines swaying in time with a fresh breeze that kept the day from seeming hot. The beach sands were freshly worked to a virgin smoothness by the recent tide, and from time to time a sand crab would scramble away from us, to dive and disappear into the whiteness a moment later.

In the shallows. countless gray-green fingerlings scurried about in schools, and overhead half a dozen gulls played in easy arcs, with one occasionally plunging into the wavelets to claim a prize. Altogether, it was like a stroll through an unspoiled Eden, and for a time the major and I simply shifted our feet approvingly through the damp sands, drinking in the sea air and rejoicing in a feeling of well being.

I broke the silence. "Things have changed."

Though del Sauz is not engraved in my memory as a brilliant conversationalist, this time he surprised me.

"Absolutely perfect!" he began. "Just as it was the day we arrived. It's as though

God made a perfect model for us, unspoiled, as comforting to a man's senses as any place can be. Isn't it strange though . . . I have not thought of it this way in almost two years."

I nodded. The feeling was inescapable. Now, with the tragedy and trauma behind us, everything was as it had been . . . serene, peaceful, quiet . . . a place where a man might truly be one with God.

Del Sauz began anew. "It's amazing how the human mind and body can recuperate. When we came back from Coosa, I was convinced that there were not fifty men who had the will to start all over . . . yet . . . look at them!

"Fatigue makes cowards of us all, my friend. Someone told me that once when I was a young adjutant, slugging along the mud tracks of France, league after league. And it's true! Let a man miss a few meals and a few hours' sleep and his will begins to ebb away.

"Only here the problems were compounded many times over."

Del Sauz gazed across the water again. We were approaching the small bayou to the west of our camp now, and we sought out a hillock with a blanket of seagrass to sit on. Stretched out, looking straight upward, I got the wonderful feeling of aloneness that separation from others promotes. We lay there for many minutes. I may even have dozed into a nap, I can't be certain. But at length I raised my head, propped my chin on one hand, and asked: "Mateo, thinking back on it all now . . . and knowing what you know and feeling as you feel, do you still think the right choice was made? Given the chance, and perhaps new leadership, wouldn't the people have succeeded?"

Del Sauz did not reply quickly. When finally he spoke, he studied his words with great care.

"Believe me, I've relived those days many times, for no man's opinion was more involved. Today? I would have to answer you this way—and you're a good judge for you saw at Coosa everything I saw.

"When we followed Porras back and saw the great division, no one was sure Villafane or anyone else would come to help us. And I am still convinced that marching the whole company to Coosa would have promoted desertion. *But* . . . we might have returned there with our 200 and perhaps a hundred more in good health, and begun a camp. We *might* have succeeded there."

"And left the remainder where they were . . . hoping?"

"What else? That's what we ended up doing anyway."

"Any other thoughts?"

"Some . . . but only one of real importance."

"About Villafane's decision?"

Del Sauz shook his shaggy head affirmatively. "I think," he said slowly, "I think he made a mistake by quitting. I wasn't sure then myself, so I don't fault him. But . . . *then* we could have surely put 200 at Coosa . . . and another 200 here. Santa Elena might have had to wait, and I'm no strategist, but half a house would have been better than none."

"Well," I began, "he *did* do that in part. We *are* here, and. . . ."

"And we are temporarily salving the pride of a fine man who will not return to Mexico marching in second command of a mission that failed. No, Cristobal, my friend, don't deceive yourself on that score. We are enjoying a brief vacation here, nothing more. On this I would wager the back pay I'm due and much more. Spain's history tells us this."

I lay back down, sobered by my friend's prediction. Working in the shadow of my enthused uncle, I had accepted his spirit of belief that *now* we were really beginning, that all that had gone before was just an unfortunate prelude.

"How long?" I asked.

"Who can say?" he replied. "Probably the word will come from the King. Philip is not a man who forgives anything easily, especially failure. We'll lie here a time . . . long enough to buoy our hopes. Then we'll be called back."

I couldn't sleep that night. Not that I cared that much for myself. Often, I reminded myself of the great experience I'd enjoyed here; I had little invested save time. But my uncle? This was his life! What would he do? How would history treat him?

ABOARD SHIP EN ROUTE TO HAVANA
October 21, 1561

This was my third sea voyage, and under other circumstances it might have been enjoyable. The warm October days made lolling about on the deck of the fast frigate like a great holiday.

But for those being recalled from Ochuse, it was a saddening thing.

My uncle had accepted the orders with the dignity of the professional soldier. With me beside him he had read and reread the brief letter from Don Luis, forming the words in his lips and struggling to find some rays of hope hidden in the text. The ship captain who delivered the message was of no help. He had not seen the viceroy but had simply been given the diplomatic pouch along with his own orders. The rest had been routine, just another assignment to him, except that the visit to Ochuse was still another experience in the life of a sailor.

It did not take long to abandon the site. We had just harvested our first grain, and the tiny settlement had achieved a feeling of home for us, but there was little else to board save the tools, arms, surviving horses and the tiny company. In three days the job was done, the vessel watered, and the return voyage begun.

We left the settlement intact. Salazar had insisted on a final Mass before the weathered cross, and Don Tristan had spent a final hour walking by himself, shuffling among grain fields which had eluded him so long.

Now, we were two days at sea, and a euphoria had descended upon many of us. That second evening my uncle and I sat on the deck, watching the moon play on the waters, listening to the gentle creaking of the rigging.

"Well, uncle," I said, breaking our silence.

The captain-general turned and looked at me. "Well, indeed! Here we are . . . going back as we came."

"Almost like writing the final chapter of a great book, with no inner ones."

"Almost," he agreed wryly, "but there's still hope. We learned much from our errors. And when fate deals a bitter blow, one must be philosophical. What else can one do?"

"You'll seek an immediate audience with the King?"

"As quickly as Don Luis can arrange it."

"You think there's still a chance to begin again?"

"To begin? Of course . . . but now, as I think on it, the less I'm inclined to be part of it."

"But . . .?"

"No . . . hear me out. When Don Angel was with us, I was convinced that I could regroup our people and achieve our goals. And in these last weeks you and Salazar and del Sauz and the others have helped prove me right. We *could* have begun again.

"But . . . now I try to look at it all from the eyes of the others. Who am I? A sick, fumbling man who made mistakes and sowed enmity among the people. I did my best. I did what I felt was right, what a good soldier should. But I didn't succeed. With such a record . . . well . . . what can I expect, honestly?"

"You've been an inspiration to many, uncle, and all will say so!"

"Of course, and I appreciate your loyalty. But a King has many heroes and each is eager for a great command. I'm sure they are already lining up to succeed me, should Philip elect to begin again."

"But if you will not try again. . . ."

"I will recommend that the plan be re-enacted, but I shall not actively seek its leadership. I will ask a fair hearing, some adjustments of my resources, and then . . . well . . . perhaps this time I will be wise enough to enjoy the life of a gentleman and the company of a beautiful wife."

We talked on for many hours that night, recalling incidents, conversations, decisions. It was amazing to me to see how much my uncle had mellowed in the past week. His disappointment was well concealed, and his judgments of others were calm and reflective.

Porras he forgave as being simply a man of weakness.

Ceron he reviewed as an opportunist but through it all a man who did what he believed was right.

Salazar and Anunciacon he praised to the skies.

"Who knows what would have befallen us had they not been the men they were!" he said.

Finally, I told him of del Sauz's prediction that day on the sands by the bayou. "Does that surprise you, I mean, that he calculated it all so well?"

Don Tristan shook his head sadly. "No, not really. Mateo's an old soldier and a wise one. I suspect he reasoned that any other than Villafane might have treated me with considerably less favor and that this outcome was inevitable. And he was right! Don Angel is my friend, and he had his own career to consider. All in all, it is not hard to analyze. Del Sauz was good to stay with us. He has been a good friend. I hope fate treats him well."

When we arrived in Havana I was given the duty of preparing the transfer of troopers and colonists to other assignments. As a captain of horse I was billeted at the city's military headquarters and not with Don Tristan in the governor's palace.

We saw each other, of course, but not regularly. And when each left the island, we traveled different routes. Many times in the years to come I was called upon to write testimony in his behalf; yet we never again had opportunity to serve in a common cause. That was my loss.

MADRID
August 21, 1561

"Well, what do you make of them?"

The question, posed by Philip to Ximinez, referred to the pile of documents which both had now examined in detail. The minister still held the copy of the viceroy's orders to Don Tristan. Ximinez raised his large gray, hairy eyebrows, cocked his head slightly . . . then shrugged. "Who can say? I suppose he was right."

"Of course! It'll be months before we can even consider another fleet . . . and this time I'm afraid poor de Luna would hardly be the man to lead it. He's plagued, should we say, by ill fortune," and the King pursed his thin lips.

"A gross understatement, I would say."

"Make a suitable summary for the Council and draft a reply to Don Luis praising his usual energy and judgment."

"What about Senora Valencia? Shall we tell her . . .?"

Philip broke in: "I shall write a note myself and enclose his letter."

"By the way, where is she? I haven't seen her for weeks."

"In the country. The loss of the child has depressed her."

"I can imagine."

"She has style, Valencia. A pity that life is so short . . . and there are so many worlds to conquer."

"A pity. You say she's in the country . . .?"

"At the house of a friend. I'm afraid this will depress her further. His Mexican property will be forfeited now, of course. Perhaps we should send some substance . . . to show our compassion."

"I'll see to it."

"I knew you would. Oh . . . and will you write the note also? I'm not good at that sort of thing, as you know."

"What about de Luna? Should we respond to his letter also?"

Philip thought a moment. "No . . ." he said slowly, "do not, but ask Don Luis to recall him to Mexico City. Find some task there to occupy the man whom I suspect will soon begin to petition for a new command of sorts and for consideration of his investment."

"I would imagine. And . . . you don't care to have him return to Spain?"

"Not for awhile. What would it accomplish? After all, he's a pauper now . . . and his wife can hardly welcome him . . . or he her, eh?"

"I am sure of your highness' wisdom."

Ximinez worked swiftly. By nightfall a messenger was en route to Valencia de Luna. He carried the letter which Don Tristan had painfully penned weeks before, along with the other documents the king had suggested, including a brief note of salutation . . . and a purse containing five gold coins.

To Velasco went a cleverly written order requesting that the former captain-general and governor of La Florida be ordered to Mexico City and there given " . . . such duties as will make him useful and reasonably occupied. . . ."

To the King's Council went a scaled down but precise accounting of the Villafane report, with the viceroy's comments, and a notation that the result would be a subject of discussion at the next Council meeting.

Then, a hard day behind him, the minister walked to his favorite tavern where he ordered a light meal and two bottles of his favorite wine on which he became blissfully drunk.

PARIS
September 20, 1561

The arrival of the monthly pouch from Madrid caused Catherine's ministers to rejoice. Included was a summary of Ximinez's statement on the de Luna expedition as sent to the Council members.

Catherine's response was predictable.

"Summon the heretic Admiral. Tell him to hurry the provisioning of the ship of his Jean Ribault. We now have an open sea to this land they call La Florida. Move on with it. This may be the perfect place to settle these renegades who cause so much ill will. And who knows? History might record that we gain France a new world as we rid it of a plague."

Jean Ribault sailed as ordered.

Queen Catherine and her son, successor to the stricken King Henry of France.

HAVANA
December 20, 1561

Tristan de Luna was alone in his pleasant suite in the palace of Cuba's governor when Velasco's second order reached him.

He had enjoyed a pleasant reception there, had written extensively as he developed second thoughts to both the viceroy and the King, recognizing that his legacy to Spain's history might be incomplete without a full accounting of the adventures in his own name. Between writings he visited his former charges in the mission hospitals and prayed long hours each day in the chapel. Otherwise, the commander visited the island's points of interest and waited.

Orders from the viceroy reached de Luna one morning as he was seated enjoying the spectacle of flowers in the gardens of the governor's palace. The governor himself delivered it, carefully sealed in wax with the ornate sign of the viceroy's office.

The soldier's fingers trembled slightly as he tried to undo the seal. His host tactfully stepped away, leaving de Luna alone.

The letter was brief, friendly, but painfully clear. Don Luis had followed the King's instructions with his usual care.

"The documents related to Ochuse have been reviewed by His Majesty and the royal council, and it is their belief that it will not be possible in the near future to re-institute proceedings to establish the colony in accordance with your original design. Therefore, it is suggested that you rejoin me in Mexico City so that I may have benefit of your counsel in planning such other settlements as Spain may soon require in the New World. I have asked the governor of Cuba to arrange transportation as soon as practical. . . ."

Don Tristan gazed at the bold strokes on the page. He also read clearly what had not been said. Slowly his head fell, and his eyes fixed on the ground at his feet. So! His disgrace was confirmed. He was denied the opportunity to recoup his reputation. Ochuse was over. The King's interest had shifted elsewhere. He re-read the letter, carefully folded it and placed it inside his shirt; then he rose and walked towards the house. His shoulders stooped forward, and for the first time, the commander who had stood firm during the disasters of La Florida gave the appearance of an old man.

POSTLOGUE

I am an old man now, weary with this world. For many years now, friends have urged me to re-tell the story of my adventures in La Florida and of my uncle.

We parted in Havana in the early winter of 1562, he answering orders to report to the viceroy in Mexico City, I to return to Spain. For a time, he remained there, fruitlessly seeking to gain favor with Philip, who by then had become obsessed with many other things. First it was to protect La Florida from the French interlopers. When word of their colony reached Mexico, Don Tristan was certain he would be called again to action. But this role fell to Don Menendez de Aviles and with it the glory of combat and the success of founding a permanent city. Later, the King became obsessed with England's transgressions and began his great folly, the Armada.

When at length he returned to Spain, Don Tristan sought to recover his Mexican estates and his reputation. Countless pages of testimony were taken, with accounts from many principals being forwarded to the King.

At length, my uncle accepted the loss of the mortgaged Mexican properties and turned instead to claims for his salaries and fees as governor of La Florida. These claims the King avoided by a succession of strategems.

Don Tristan returned to Barobia where his brother Pedro had died. By now, the children by his first marriage were well grown, and he drew pleasure from their eventual marriages and his succession of grandchildren.

Valencia he never saw again. For a time she was maintained in genteel obscurity by the King. Then, before Don Tristan's return, she entered a nunnery and died there, a wasted and penitent woman, of a plague which decimated the order.

I do not know to this day how much Don Tristan knew of her liaison with Philip and its sad aftermath, even at the day of his death. The affair was well cloaked, and he seldom spoke of her in his later years. Sometimes I believe he knew it all; at others, I wonder if perhaps he believed she had fled to her cloister because of shame over his failure. I don't know. In any event, her death so saddened him that there was never another woman in his life. When he died, he still held obstinately to his goal of clearing his name, and the proper recording of the events which so altered his life. I have long meant to make this record. Now I, too, can meet my maker with a clear conscience.

The others in the story of the First City? I'm sorry, but I can provide few details. Don Luis Velasco lived out his life in the successful splendor of his appointment. The backwash of Ochuse damaged him not at all.

Don Angel Villafane continued to serve his country as a journeyman soldier of fortune, always performing with credit. However, he never received the assignment for which he hoped, one which would have engraved his name brightly in history's hall.

Ceron, Porras, del Sauz, Castilla and the rest? I can't say. All returned to Mexico and resumed military careers. I suppose that if one were to search diligently enough he might find records of their deaths in some remote outposts . . . or in a few cases, in Mexico City's cathedral itself.

The gallant friars? Again . . . I don't know. I heard little of them again, except for the documents which they filed with the King's court to answer inquiries on our ordeal. They were truly men of God. I cannot speak well enough of them.

Admiral Coligny? He, of course, carried through Catherine's proposal. Capt. Jean Ribault's ship landed on the east Atlantic coastline in 1562 and made plans for the first colony of the Huguenots, which arrived two years later. Their settlement, named Fort Caroline, was destroyed a year later by our own Menendez de Aviles. All of the French heretics were destroyed!

Ochuse . . . ah . . . as nature it is still there! Perhaps there are even a few of our primitive huts standing. Other matters have occupied our King's mind, as del Sauz predicted. There were no further efforts at settlement there. Perhaps a wayward vessel or two has called there by chance, but none by design, that I know of.

It is sad for an old man to write thus, to see the one great event in his life end in failure. But—that is how it was. Yet . . . sometimes I awake in the night's dark hours and wonder: What would life have been like for me—or for an entire continent, for that matter—if the great storm had not struck us? We should have all gone to our rewards with a different conscience . . . and with a secure empire for Holy Church and country.

Truth, however, is stranger than fiction. And this was the truth.